The Ashram

The Ashram

*A woman's emancipation
from her oppressive culture and fear of men;
a physician's overcoming of his inability
to cope with death and learning to love.
An inspiring tale of two souls' journey
halfway around the world toward
spiritual enlightenment.*

A Novel

By

Sattar Memon

Copyright © 2006 Sattar Memon

All rights reserved.

ISBN 1-4196-3776-2

To order additional copies, please contact us.
BookSurge, LLC
www.booksurge.com
1-866-308-6235
orders@booksurge.com

DEDICATED TO:

MARJORIE

Writer's Digest Editors' Testimonials

"... Few novels manage to both tell a rousing, dramatic story and convey a deeply spiritual outlook on life. *The Ashram* is one of these few.

The Ashram shows how holiness can be lived in the real, human world, yet it never condescends, preaches or stints on the frailties of its thoroughly human heroes and three-dimensional saints. Dr. Kingsley's spiritual growth is an organic part of his fight to save the woman he loves—a fight that includes plot twists and adventures to fill a summer blockbuster. In short, *The Ashram* will both enthrall readers and leave them feeling richer for the reading.

                        -David King, Co-Author: *Self-Editing For Fiction Writers*
                        Contributing Editor, Writer's Digest

"... This author bests James Redfield as a creator of action/adventure. *The Ashram* is a rare combination—it explores the ancient and enduring questions, at the same time involving the reader in an exciting page-turner.

The Ashram immerses the reader in the sensory bath that is India; as an American doctor, Jonathan Kingsley, searches for solace after the death of his wife. Jonathan finds more than he consciously sought: more about life's only certainty, death; and more about life's joy and its deeper meaning. Sattar Memon's forte is that he shares the secrets of this ancient civilization so that readers come to the same realizations Jonathan discovers in his quest.

-Robert Gover, Editor, Writer's Digest School
Author of: *One Hundred Dollar Misunderstanding, Here Goes Kitten, The JC Kitten Trilogy, And The Voodoo Contra,* and many other books.

"... this is an outstanding piece of writing and an incredible beginning. As someone who does not know a great deal about the culture of India, I find the information set forth in the story to be thought provoking and emotional. The writer's voice is unique, flowing, and textured with a vibrancy that adds depth and character to both scene and setting. The characters are living, breathing beings with whom we share pain and suffering.

-**Annette Blair,**
Author of: *Thee, I love, Lady Faith, Lady Patients, The Rogues Club*

acknowledgements

I am profoundly indebted to a great many people responsible for creating *The Ashram.*

My wife, Marjorie, deserves the first credit for her everlasting encouragement, her candid Western perspective and her saintly forbearance at my long absences when I remained holed up in the study to write this book. I am also grateful to our fine sons—Javed and Adam—without whose help in typing, re-typing, and proofing the manuscript, and letting me see India through their eyes, this book would have been nothing but a stranded concept on the computer!

Many thanks to a lot of friends for providing unconditional critiquing and emotional support. These good folks are: Salman Wasti, Rick Varieur, Roxanne Dunkelberger, Patti Traynor, Bhartiben Patel, Ila and Ulka Amin, Ronika Patel, Marcie O'Brien, Bhadresh Patel, Pammi Suri, Amrut Patel, Vijay and Meenu Malhotra, and Nishat and Naeem Siddiqi.

Writer's Digest provided three invaluable editors: Mr. Robert Gover who saw *The Ashram* not just as an enduring mystery but also as an essence capturing the spirituality of life and death; Mr. David King who shook up all plot turns and twists until they all dovetailed into a beautiful story with an enlighteningly surprise ending; and Elizabeth Ridley who treated this "Indian story" with much creative tenderness.

I will always gratefully remember the constructive criticism of my work by my fellow writers from RWA of Rhode Island: Gail Eastwood, Karen Frisch, Mary Kruger and Annette Blair. And my special thanks to Mahendar and Santosh Paul for pouring so much love into creating the tellingly true cover art.

Although innate, certain places—the childhood mosque in Khedbrahma where I prayed with my late father; Ghoom monastery in Nepal; Brahmakumari University in Mt. Abu; India; and Unitarian Church of Providence—have silently spawned the equinox of Oneness in my heart. Finally, my utmost thanks to one man who has had so much guiding and creative impact on many critical curves of my life and career: my dear brother, Dr. G. N. Memon. Much love to all.

Sattar Memon

PART ONE

chapter one

"A young woman vows to burn to death voluntarily," the announcer for All India Radio reported.

Dr. Jonathan Kinglsey sat forward in the rear of the car, straining to hear the evening news over the pounding rain and whistling wind.

"Speaking from the vigil at her husband's deathbed," resumed the announcer, "Seeta, a 22-year-old schoolteacher from the village of Baramedi, has announced that, upon his death, she will join him atop a blazing pyre, hold his head in her lap, and travel together with her beloved to heaven. She is to become the first suttee India has seen in a half decade. More on this in a moment."

Jonathan was aghast. Had he come halfway around the world only to encounter it again? "Did you hear that?" he demanded. "That can't be true! A suttee? In 1967?"

The driver glanced at him in the rearview mirror. "Sir, what can I say? Baramedi is the same village in which the last suttee happened many years ago. Anything can happen there. Bride-burning, dowry-death, suttee—you name it, sir."

The driver, Mohan—a slim, thirtyish fellow with a trim-mustache and a pleasant, polite face—wearing khaki uniform and a chauffeur's cap, had been assigned to transport Jonathan from New Delhi to his destination at the Ashram, a spiritual hermitage, in the mountains.

"Sir, are you all right?" Mohan asked.

Jonathan's head was bowed, his mind in a fiery reverie. He had tried to push away the vision, but the sight of the coffin and the beautiful body inside all ablaze, blasted through his defenses.

"Sir," Mohan repeated, his good-natured countenance furrowed in apprehension. "Perhaps it is only a story. Do not let it get you that way!"

"Yes, yes, I'm all right," Jonathan said, the memory drifting away, but his heart still pounding. "Mohan how far are we from New Delhi? How far is the Ashram from here?"

"These hills are . . . halfway, so we have a few more hours to go. That's all, sir."

Jonathan nodded.

Lightning streaked across the windshield and a clap of thunder rattled the windows.

"You will like Ashram's peacefulness," Mohan continued. "A busy American doctor like you will doubtless find it a welcome change."

Just what Jonathan needed after the maelstrom of professional and personal tragedies back home. Peacefullness. Jonathan had quit his busy medical practice and responded to the advertisement in the Boston Globe. The government of Himpal was looking for a volunteer physician to accept a six-month position serving the poor mountain community at an Ashram—a Himalayan-based spiritual hermitage, whose mission was to shelter, educate and rehabilitate young women abused by incest, rape, prostitution or attempted female infanticide. He looked forward to his arrival at the Ashram and the chance to use his medical skills to help people in an exotic location—a welcome change from the drudgery of his depressing, purposeless life in Portland, Maine.

"I look forward to the change," he answered, opening a small case. From it he extracted a Nikon camera and began to attach a wide-angle lens.

Mohan glanced into his mirror. "Oh, I see you take photographs!" he said smiling.

"Yes. It's a long-time hobby," Jonathan answered, struggling with the lens, his hands shaking. "Mohan, how does a young woman volunteer to burn alive? I just can't . . . buy it. She has to be drugged or psychologically imbalanced to want to do such a thing. Isn't it possible that the whole thing is not even her idea?"

"Yes, that is possible. But sir, don't worry," said Mohan. "This could be just a rumor. Sometimes, politicians make up things. They create a crisis to make money . . . win elections, you know."

"But supposing it's not a rumor?"

"I don't know, sir. Baramedi is a rough border town; half in India, half in Himpal. And Himpal is an independent country. India being the world's largest democracy, I don't see how we can trespass on such a little kingdom."

"Yes," said Jonathan. "Tell me, how far away is Baramedi?"

"Fifty to sixty miles from here, near the base of the mountain on which your Ashram is located, sir."

"So it's on the way. Could we stop there?"

Mohan cringed. "You mean Baramedi, sir? Oh no! Judge Sahb would kill me. He ordered me not to mention one word to you about the suttee. Please sir, don't tell him I discussed it with you. I'll lose my job."

"Of course not. Don't worry, Mohan." Jonathan reassured Mohan, but began to wonder as to what the Supreme-Court Judge was hiding from him—and why?

"Is Judge Sahb running for an election?"

"He could be India's next Minister of Law!" said Mohan and paused. "But sir, if you ask him about the suttee, he may tell you everything. He loves to explain to foreigners. Only problem is . . . the way he talks—it comes out like he is a big boss. Blunt and lecturing. Other than that sir, he is a good-hearted man. Very fatherly." Mohan bobbed his head. "Really."

Judge Sahb, Jonathan's host and the uncle of a partner and dear friend back home in Maine named Suresh, had meant to shelter him. He knew more about me than he had let on, thought Jonathan. Suresh must have filled him in on some of my troubles. "But what about dowry death—and female infanticide. What's that all about?"

"That I can tell you," said Mohan. "Hold on a minute, sir." The car struggled through a large puddle, fanning wings of water up to the car's windows. "In these types of villages," Mohan continued, "if a wife does not give birth to a son, it is all her fault. Sons are treasures; girls are burdens. As our Prime Minister Mrs. Indira Gandhi says, 'these villagers treat sons as credits and daughters as debits.'"

"Is that because of the farming?"

"Yes, that and herding, construction—everything involving the use of physical strength. So the girls are often killed off in infancy. Or they can be dumped onto another family in marriage by providing the groom's family with a lump sum gift called a dowry."

Jonathan shook his head in disgust.

"Yes sir," Mohan continued. "Worse yet, some grooms marry and then kill their wives so they can remarry and get more dowry. That's why they call it dowry death."

"These are god-damn cri—mi—nals." Jonathan's words came out staccato as the car rocked over a pothole around the bend in the road. Reflexively Jonathan leaned away from the window facing the valley of unfathomable depth.

When the car stabilized, Jonathan looked out the window. Suddenly, a blanket of mist had billowed up from the valley and seized the car into a blindingly thick fog. It was turning dark.

Around the bend, a bolt of lightning lit up another hill nearby. Jonathan was pretty sure he saw a dark castle-like premise atop that hill, its tower-like dome lit.

"What's that building, Mohan?" Jonathan asked, moving closer to the window to his right and wiping the mist off the glass with his palm. "The weather is getting worse, maybe we should stop there overnight. What do you think?"

Mohan hesitated. "Um . . . this rain is unexpected, sir. Down the plains, the land is all parched from terrible heat. This storm can disappear—as quickly as it came."

"Why, is there some problem with the place?" Jonathan peered at the building when another bolt of lightning shone over it.

"Well . . . I don't know sir, but some people who stayed there say they hear—in the middle of the night—voices, like women screaming . . . children crying . . ."

Jonathan looked out the window. A clap of thunder shook the whole car.

"But sir, I'm not afraid of anything. I'm more afraid of the forest brigands and dacoits on the road. People . . . if they stop, these armed robbers jump out of the bushes. They loot the travelers and throw them and their vehicles in the valley . . . down there. You never see them again."

"I see," said Jonathan while experiencing a quickening sensation in his chest. He castigated himself for his stupid insistence on traveling to the Ashram on such a dark, dangerous night.

"Mohan, is it possible to—," he couldn't finish. His body got pushed against the back of the seat, as the car abruptly stopped.

Then suddenly an object struck the car so hard that it began to rock precariously. Petrified, Jonathan clutched at the door handle.

"Oh no!" whined Mohan.

"What is it Mohan?" Jonathan sat up on the edge of the backseat and asked. "Why did you stop the car?"

"A tree has fallen in the way. But it looks like a small tree. I can remove it. I'll be right back. You stay in, sir. Please."

Quickly the dangers on the road flashed by in Jonathan's mind. "Wait! Mohan, wait!" he shouted.

But Mohan had already opened his door and exited the car. A dank, chilly splash of rain slapped Jonathan in the face. Wiping his face he shouted again; but it was too late.

As Mohan closed the door behind him, Jonathan could not hear the noise of the motor. Now Mohan was out of sight. Jonathan's words merely hit the glass panes. They turned foggier.

chapter two

Seeta repositioned her dear Moti's head in her lap and dripped some water into his dry mouth. She looked at his body and sighed. The fever from tuberculosis had melted his body like snow in the hot sun.

The water trickled out of his mouth into her lap.

Oh, God no! Was he gone? Her best friend, her partner, her ally. No, God, please, it was too soon. The sun was going down. Seeta lit an earthern diya placed amid flowers under Lord Krishna's picture on the shelf next to her.

He slowly opened his eyes. "I . . . I . . . just dreamed. I saw a tall white angel holding your hand. He told me not to worry. He said he . . . he will protect you."

Seeta's tears began to flow freely. She covered her mouth with the end of her torn sari, a single-piece dress worn by native Indian women, and said to him, "Please don't say such things. You are my angel. You are not going anywhere—not without me."

His pale hand fumbled to find hers. He held her hand

gently. "I'm so lucky to have you as my wife. I . . . I love you very much and . . . and . . ." He couldn't finish. He was too short of breath.

The flame of the earthern diya began flickering.

How had she found such a man in Baramedi, where every girl, by the age of fifteen, had been raped by a landlord, a merchant or a policeman? Routinely one heard cries emerging from the roots of shaking corn stalks, muffled shrieks from behind closed bedroom doors, while the jewelry-laden wives obliviously chewed betel nut downstairs. And if some unfortunate soul resisted or spoke up, invariably she disappeared without a trace. The police reports routinely chalked up the mysterious disappearance as either a kidnapping, having been washed away with the floods, or having run away to a whorehouse in the city for higher wages.

If only the wells, rivers and cliffs had lips. But even if they spoke up who would pursue the truth behind the bodies they harbored? The victims were poor. They were ignorant. And, worse, they were girls.

Where would Seeta go? What would she do?

She looked at her husband's shriveled body; death seemed to be burrowing into the hollows of his cheeks, ribs and emaciated belly, methodically, ruthlessly.

"Oye Kishanchacha!" Somebody outside the hut was yelling for her father-in-law.

Startled, Seeta looked up. It was a voice that made her break out into a sweat and sent ice cold shivers through her; the voice of a man whose presence—or even an inkling of his presence—made one shake like a leaf in broad daylight. All the villagers, properly averting their eyes, simply addressed him as *Sarkar*. The government, the ultimate ruler. The Boss.

Seeta, in her mind, had dubbed him *Khunkhar—a* bloodthirsty beast.

Briefly, a scene from her childhood chilled her heart and soul. She had been only seven then. She and her friend, Savita, whose looks were slightly more developed, lay their bellies over an outcropping at the edge of a pond in the woods. They were playing the game of rocks, dropping rocks suspended by a string tied around their fingers to see whose rock made a bigger splash and circle in the water.

All of a sudden, Seeta noticed a grown man standing behind them. Blithely unaware of the danger, Savita carried on with the game, giggling. The undulating waters reflected a man wearing a hood, bending forward to grasp Savita. Seeta turned around and shrieked.

The hooded stranger kicked her into the water, grabbed Savita, crushed her into the crook of his arm and disappeared into a thicket.

Seeta, not a very good swimmer, gulped water and splashed, but finally managed to paddle ashore. Coughing up water and short of breath, she heard the terrified cries of her friend. Shivering and frightened, covering her mouth with her hand to hold back her screams, she tiptoed in the direction of Savita's cries.

When she spotted something through the tall scraggy bush, she froze. There crouched a naked man with a hairy back, thrusting himself between the flailing legs of Savita, who was pinned mercilessly down on a rock.

"No! No! Please let me go!" cried Savita.

Seeta, with a shaking hand over her mouth and tears rolling down her face, watched in horror at the unforgettably heinous transgression: Savita crying for mercy, the man slapping her and shouting at her to shut up, frightened monkeys shrieking and jumping up the trees and birds noisily flapping away into the blood-red sunset.

Finally, Seeta ran back home as fast as she could, and amid the sobs told her mother what she had seen.

"Quiet!" her mother cried.

As if the treetops had eyes and the walls had ears, her mother looked around and whispered into Seeta's ears, "That man, that Satan, is Sarkar. Keep quiet and don't repeat what you saw—anywhere. Promise me." Then she embraced Seeta tightly and broke down. "I just don't want to see your body floating in the lake. Please Seeta . . . if you meet a man, any man, do not look into his eyes. Please!"

Seeta dutifully promised, but her promise was not what had sealed her lips. On the third day, the villagers found Savita's putrefying body floating in that pond. The rock tied around her waist had been unable to hold down the bloated corpse. Her privates were lacerated beyond recognition, and her nipples bitten off.

From that time on, Seeta stopped going to the river to fetch water, and never to the woods to gather firewood. Still she heard about many young girls regularly disappearing.

"You'll be caught too and shipped to the whorehouses in Delhi and Calcutta," her mother had warned her. "Always look over your shoulder and keep your nose out of Sarkar's way."

"But how, mother, I don't even know who he is!"

"Never mind!" her mother had said. "Just stay out of every man's way. Every man is a Satan, though perhaps Sarkar is worse in some ways. Besides, a woman of good character never looks into any man's eyes. Do you hear me?"

Yet, in time, Seeta had come to match the evil man's voice with his face.

"Oye Kishanchacha," Sarkar hollered again, snapping her out of her reverie. "Come out here, you lout. I want to talk to you."

Reluctantly, she looked out the small window in the hut.

"Come out, you coward," he hollered. "I know you're hiding behind your pretty daughter-in-law's sari. I want my farm rent."

Bapuji, Seeta's father-in-law, napping in the distant corner of the hut after sitting up with his son all night, sprang up. He looked at Seeta and his son's still body.

"Bapuji, he sounds drunk," she said. "Please don't let him in."

Bapuji motioned her to keep quiet, and wrapping his turban haphazardly, went out into the yard.

"*Jay-Ramjiki Sarkar Sahb*," he said. "Please have a seat. Right here on the bench in the shade. *Arrey, beta Seeta.* Please make a cup of tea for our honorable guest."

"*Jee*, Bapuji." Seeta rested Moti's head on the pillow and rose to light the primus.

Sarkar lit a biri and blew the smoke at Bapuji. Then squinting sarcastically he said, "Don't con me, you old fool. Where's my money?"

"You know the season has been bad for the last three years," Bapuji said. "I promise you, by next season—"

"Don't lie to me. I've heard your son is ready to die and his lovely bride is pregnant. Isn't that true?"

"Well . . . my son has been ill for a long time. He could die at any time, but I don't know about her being—"

"I said, stop lying or—"

"On Kalimata's oath, Sarkar Sahb; I am not lying. How could my son impregnate her? He is nothing but skin and bones. He is so weak, his own breathing leaves him breathless."

Suddenly Sarkar turned quiet. He stared at Bapuji for a moment. Then he smiled, and putting his comforting hand on Bapuji's shoulder, he said, "Well, listen . . . relax and pray. Your son is still alive and may even survive the illness. You never know."

Bapuji folded his hands, pleading with the visitor. "But, Maalik, what if he—"

"If he dies, something has to be done. Abortion by a barber, send her away to another state, sell her to a brothel in Old Delhi. Or push her down a well. We'll do something. Now go to bed." Sarkar ground the butt of the biri into the dirt. "I'll take care of it."

The flame of the earthern diya began flickering restlessly.

"Wait a minute." Seeta heard Sarkar snap his fingers. "I have a better idea. If your son dies, we've got to provide poor kid a proper cremation! I think we can do that. And . . . and get rid of this girl too. She is nothing but a blemish on your family—and our whole village."

"Maalik, I . . . I don't understand. What—."

"You don't understand, old man? We can announce that Seeta wants to hold her husband's head in her lap on a blazing pyre, and become a suttee! Whole Hindustan will come to know right away and they'll rush here to worship her. And you? You would be the proud father-in-law—of goddess suttee!"

chapter three

For the next 24 hours Moti lapsed in and out of unconsciousness. At times he breathed heavily, at times Seeta eerily watched his bellows freeze.

Seeta wiped his forehead and heard the playful sounds of little children outside the hut. If only she had had children. Just one baby would have filled her life. Just one little one. But Moti, dear Moti, had encouraged her to continue her education instead. Though he was illiterate, he was very proud of her hunger for learning. He had roamed from hut to hut bragging about her the day she'd been hired to teach at the local school.

He was the only one who had encouraged her.

Seeta was the eldest of nine children. She had grown up helping her mother with the house chores and playing the mother to her siblings when her parents went to work as farm hands. There was no money or time for Seeta to go to school. Besides, education was not for her caste. Her aunt had once told her mother that girls are supposed to stay home and raise the family. Education makes them shameless and disrespectful, she had said. But Seeta had managed to get some education from the schoolteacher who had eventually employed Seeta's mother as a maid. Of course, even then Seeta had had to fake illiteracy.

And then, at age fifteen, Seeta had married Moti and had truly begun to live. His relatives weren't happy about the measly dowry that had accompanied her, and she had once heard some town folks encouraging him to have her killed so that he could remarry and get a bigger dowry.

"Go to hell," he had told the men. "I love my wife and she is worth her every ounce in gold."

Seeta was street smart too. The predators called her the "slippery salamander" because she had always stayed one step ahead of them, always looking over her shoulder. So she had survived until her marriage. But now her only true protector was about to say good-bye.

Where would she go? What would she do?

Late in the evening, she heard Sarkar and three other men approach the hut. Frightened, Seeta looked at Bapuji who quickly exited to greet the rogues outside.

Seeta felt stunned once again by how much Sarkar looked like a normal, regular man. He had an ordinary, day-to-day face and build, so normal that if she met him somewhere else she would never have perceived the monster that he truly was.

Seeta saw through the hole in the wall as Sarkar greeted Bapuji with a triumphant smile and a hug. "Kishanchacha, the plan is all set."

"Sahb, please forgive me," Bapuji pleaded with folded hands. "If I can't come up with the money you can seize my cattle, my belongings, everything."

"Everything, huh." Sarkar laughed. "Sure. Everything! You have been lying to me for two years."

Sarkar's three companions nodded.

"But I swear I am not—"

"Enough begging. Stop your stupid wailing. Is your son dead yet?"

Seeta shuddered as she looked at her husband, gasping for breath.

"God forbid, Bhaiya," Bapuji said. "Please don't say that."

"Listen to me you ignorant, old man." Sarkar wagged his finger. "You know the farmhands at my field? She's been sleeping with them for months. Your daughter-in-law is nothing but a *chheenal*—a whore."

Seeta peeked out the window at that. Bapuji looked stunned.

"And not only that," Sarkar continued, "she's two months pregnant. Now when are you going to listen to me? I'm trying to help you, old man. Listen to me."

"Maalik, this can't be true. I'm an old man, a poor man, but I have my *Izzat*—my honor."

"Exactly. I know you're an honorable man. Why do you think I'm trying to help you? Now, what are we going to do? If the whole town knows about—"

"Oh, no, Maalik. Please. Don't do that. Please, give me a few seconds. Let me first ask Seeta if she is pregnant or not. I'll be right back."

Bapuji came inside and knelt by her ear. "You heard?"

She nodded. "You believe him?"

"Of course not. Keep quiet and play along. We will find out what he is up to."

As Bapuji returned to Sarkar and his men, Seeta peeked through the window.

"You think I am lying to you," Sarkar said. "Not me. I'll never do that to you, Kishanchacha. What did she say?"

Bapuji sat down in the dirt, his fist covering his eyebrows in mock despair and shame.

"You see?" Sarkar said. "Nothing but a whore. Shameless *Chheenal*."

"Now what am I going to do?" Bapuji asked meekly.

Sarkar smiled. "Don't worry." Then he lit up two biris in his mouth and gave one to Bapuji. "The plan is all set."

Seeta knew that if anyone could take a swift decisive measure to curb the rumor from spreading, it was that Satan. Notoriously well connected, Sarkar could do anything—start a riot, break someone's leg, scare away a witness, even have somebody die accidentally, as long as there was something in it for him. Politicians counted on him for successfully undertaking covert actions that the law couldn't see or contain. In fact, they promoted his flesh pedaling. Sarkar shrewdly considered Bapuji but he didn't gloat. He didn't need to gloat. The lion doesn't gloat over a wounded animal.

"Chacha," Sarkar resumed. "The proclamation is all done. All we have to do is wait for your son to die."

Seeta slapped her ears shut and looked at her husband's listless body, hoping he didn't hear their conversation; that he was still dreaming of angels.

Then she heard a slight noise behind her. The diyas flame suddenly went off. She rushed to her husband's side. But it was too late. Her sole protector was dead.

She let out a big scream and threw her head over his chest. Shocked, Bapuji looked at the smiling faces of the four visitors and came running in.

Women from nearby huts came running and began comforting crying Bapuji and Seeta. She was crying loudly and pulling her hair out.

Later, as Seeta washed Moti's body, Bapuji came out with tears in his eyes. He said to the village leaders, "I don't know what am I going to do? I don't even have enough money to buy ghee and wood to cremate my son."

"Don't worry, chacha," Sarkar put his hand over Bapuji's shoulder and said tenderly. "It's all taken care of. Flowers, ghee and . . . sandlewood logs. I assure you, before sunset tomorrow your son will get a proper Hindu cremation. And that pregnant blemish will turn into a holy suttee. Don't worry. I swear."

"Oh no, I couldn't," Bapuji pleaded with folded hands. "No, no! I'd rather die. God forbid, I can't take two lives. I'm sorry."

"Listen to me, you ignorant peasant," said Sarkar, wagging his finger. "Yesterday, you were up against the wall. Now suddenly you fear hell and God. Let me tell you something. Soon the news of your shame will spread like a pestilence. You are going to lose your house, your animals, your honor—everything. And the town council is going to throw you two out of here. Yes. We don't want some sinister old man here who uses his daughter-in-law as a whore for his own livelihood. Shame!"

"Now you listen to us," one of the others said. "So far we've kept all your dirty little secrets. Either you go along and become a millionaire, or we blow the whistle and kick you out of here."

"Maalik, you are the town father, and I am an old man, but—"

"Yes, we're the town fathers," Sarkar said. "And we are doing something that's right for everyone. You don't have to do anything. We'll do the job. In fact, it's already half done. We've been spreading the word," Sarkar said. "The crowds are already starting to arrive. It's going to be magnificent."

"My God . . ." Bapuji looked skyward. "I wish I were dead. I can't take this."

Seeta collapsed against the wall beneath the window. It was so well planned, she should have seen it coming. If she became suttee, not only would the only educated woman in town—the nail in everybody's shoe—be gone, but it would also bring a lot of honor and money from everywhere. She was vaguely aware of the men talking over their plans while Bapuji wept. The loot was to be divided evenly among all, and a temple was to be constructed at the suttee site. Bapuji was ordered to stay behind the scene, to mourn and wail as expected by the society. To play the good father-in-law.

"You fools!" said the man with the scar. "You can lock this old man up or even finish him, but how are you going to have the girl sit on the pyre? She is no dummy."

"She's grief stricken," said another. "We'll get one of our wives to comfort her with a drink. After all, we may need some privacy to bathe her husband's corpse and hollify it properly for cremation. Get it?"

"All right. Who will get her dressed and decorated once she is drugged?"

"I will," offered one of the men. "My wife is an expert at decoration."

Seeta began trembling. Either the devils thought she didn't hear them talk or they didn't care. She was only a woman, after all.

The gang put their plan into action. Before long, concerned friends urged Seeta to be consoled by spending some time with one of the villains' wives, where she was offered a glass of plain milk. Intending to allay any potential suspicion, Seeta's hostess also poured herself a glass of plain milk. Seeta politely requested some sugar.

When her hostess left for the kitchen, Seeta switched the glasses. A few minutes after consuming the drink, Seeta faked grogginess. "Oh, Lord, Krishna," she said. "I could fall asleep right now."

"So sleep," said the obese hostess. "This is real milk, no watery white stuff here." Then she yawned, too. "Let's rest. We both are so tired."

Each fixed a pillow under their heads and lay on the clean mat on the floor. Seeta pretended to be asleep until she heard her hostess snoring. Then she sat up and secured her sari around her waist. Moments later, she heard a vehicle approaching. Brakes squeaked. Two men disembarked, talking.

"You know, Chief, I think you got the best candidate for suttee this time around."

"*Barkhurdar*! She'll make good ashes. She's certainly too smart to hang around here."

"But Guru, we must do a clean, quick job. That way the law can't chase us."

"Law? What law? *I* am the law here. Besides, I work with big shot judges, all the way into New Delhi. Now let's just get the girl; she is a slippery *Chhipakli*."

Quickly Seeta lay down beside the hostess and covered her face. She trembled, and her knees felt as if they had turned into marshy quicksand.

chapter four

The early morning breeze, carrying the scent of jasmine, blew in the filmy curtains of the window overlooking the garden. The tall Victorian tower in Mahatma Gandhi Square banged out five out-of-tune strokes against the rusty old metal. A couple of stray dogs began to bark near Joshi's home. Then came the rattle and clop of what sounded like a horse and buggy outside on the cobblestone driveway.

In Jonathan's semi-conscious mind, the horse and buggy was bringing Becka to him. It was after midnight, she'd finished her shift at the hospital. A prematurely cold autumn night frosted the windowpanes of his colonial brick building, whitening the thick gray smoke sprouting from the hospital chimney. On nights like this, she had to use the buggy. It made perfect sense. He rolled out of bed and watched her getting off the buggy, the neighing horses' breath rendered visible by the cold air. He reached for her hand to help her down.

"*Dudhwalla!*"

The shout was followed by the sound of metal pails banging together. Jonathan came fully awake to the sounds, scents and heat of India. He rose and looked out the window. Below him was the donkey-drawn cart of the local milkman.

Not Becka's horse and buggy.

Looking down, he noticed a scattering of lightly scented rose petals on the windowsill. Presently he heard Joshi's voice from the hall, where it sounded as if he were ringing a little silver bell and singing incantations. Evidently, he reasoned, even Reformed Hindus performed early morning pujah, or praise of Lord Shiva. The sound calmed Jonathan.

Despite roosters crowing in anticipation of a new dawn, Jonathan was so tired, he soon fell back to sleep. When he awoke again, it was already past 10:00 am. He quickly headed for the shower. He had a lot of questions for his host.

The aroma of the omelet's ingredients—roasted onions, chopped green chili, and cilantro leaves—roasting in a pan of spattering butter greeted him at the breakfast smorgasbord: fried black-pepper pappadum, chopped fresh fruits sprinkled with blood-red pomegranate, and green garlic parathas, served with guava juice and a steaming ceramic kettle of tea cooked with milk, sugar, ginger, and cardamom.

Joshi, his teacup in one hand, and *The Times of India* in the other, rolled his smiling eyes above the rim of his spectacles. "Good morning, Dr. Kingsley."

"Good morning, Judge Sahb. Please, call me Jonathan."

Judge Joshi rose from his chair and shook Jonathan's hand. "I was terribly concerned about your safety. I'm so glad you decided to turn around. That tree—Mohan told me—was too big for both of you to remove from your path. And then of course, that flying debris. Someone could have been hurt. Anyway, please join me. Mohan . . . serve some hot tea to Doctor Sahb."

As Mohan poured the tea, Jonathan gave Mohan a smile of gratitude. His nerves had been jumpy the night before.

Mohan lowered his eyes as he poured the tea, a small smile on his lips.

Joshi resumed the conversation. "Look at this newspaper," he said. "The suttee hasn't even taken place, and the bloody tabloid is filled with sensational fodder."

Jonathan forced himself to concentrate on Judge Joshi's semi-British English. His words were delivered firmly but with a smile supplanted occasionally with dramatic facial expressions and the indispensable gesticulations.

"I assume that Mohan has explained what we heard reported on the radio?" said Jonathan. "Is this sutteeism... Judge Sahb, like... like a ritual suicide?"

The judge smiled. "Sutteeism is more than a ritual suicide. It's the epitome of a woman's loyalty to her husband, or so it is said. Much more than self-immolation as a protest over some noble cause, as exemplified by those Buddhist monks in Saigon last month."

Jonathan felt his toes curling, recalling the hideous report of monks burning to death in protest of the war.

"Mohan!" Joshi called the servant. "*Cigarka dibba lao. Aur do paani.*"

Mohan dashed into the room and bowed: "*Jee Huzoor,* Yes, sir," he said, and rushed out in a moment and was back with an ornately carved sandalwood cigar-box and two glasses of water.

Jonathan gulped the cold water down his dry throat. During his medical practice, he had witnessed natural and unnatural deaths, including the struggling exits of patients clinging to the bed sheets, unwilling to let go. But the idea of a healthy young woman dying in flames was overwhelming. He tilted back his head slightly and closed his eyes. The words "self-immolation" echoed in his mind.

A flame popped up in front of his face.

"Cigar, Dr. Kingsley?" Judge Joshi held an expensive crystal lighter monogrammed *J.J.* in one hand and a cigar in the other. He lit Jonathan's cigar.

"Thank you Judge Sahb," Jonathan said. "About the suttee I wonder... how does one muster up the willpower to jump into the flames?"

"The East views death differently," Joshi said. "Indeed, sutteeism is a total antithesis of the Western perception of death."

"Antithesis of the Western perception of death?" The Oxford-educated judge, Jonathan had been told, was a diehard Anglophile. It would be intriguing to hear what the man thought of the West.

"In the West," Joshi said, "most suicides are an escape from pain. The serene ending of a life made unbearable by a variety of causes, can be peacefully terminated by an overdose of Valium or asphyxiation in the comfort of one's favorite car. Such suicides are almost humdrum in this mad world."

Jonathan nodded. "And suttee?"

Judge Joshi set his glasses on the marble table, relit his cigar, and inhaled the smoke. His hair—sparse in the middle and densely curled on the sides—lapped over unusually hairy ears. His eyes, set between bushy brows and the ubiquitous dark under-eye shadows, were imposing. But when he smiled, a prominent gap between his upper incisors radiated a sense of credibility and verisimilitude.

"Dr. Kingsley," he said when his cigar was drawing, "are you sure you want to explore this matter at a deeper level? I must caution you, the subject is rather barbaric."

"I'm sure," Jonathan said.

The judge sat back and puffed on his cigar. "Life, humans are not sacred here. Cows are. There are so many people here that if one drops dead, it is no great event. They keep on moving, like a pack of rats chasing a few scarce crumbs of bread. Life moves on."

Jonathan cringed. It was not news to him, but the judge's matter-of-fact assessment did strike him as barbaric.

"You see," Joshi went on, "the illiterate rung of Indian society finds sutteeism quite... venerable. They even canonize the poor victim. On the other hand, the middle class deplores the nonsense, but has no time or resources to have it expunged." Joshi chuckled. "The upper class couldn't give a rusty penny to get involved."

"Actually, that could be said of the West as well."

"It is the human condition." Judge Joshi took a puff. "Sutteeism does provide a tremendous spiritual uplift to the oppressed masses. Simultaneously, the so-called guardians of society get to amass a great deal of money exploiting the angelic miracle. Converting the scorched flesh into a deity."

Jonathan shuddered and fought off the return of raw memories. "That's awful."

"These are cruel old traditions," Judge Joshi said. His dark eyebrows drew together in a genuine display of compassion. "These poor chaps still suffer the consequences of illiteracy, poverty, superstition—you name it . . . Mohan!"

"Excuse me." Jonathan rose and placed his cup on the table.

Joshi's keen eyes studied the guest from the U.S. In his half-sleeve, oxford cotton shirt, khakis and leather sandals, he looked comfortable. His polite and reserved demeanor reflected intellect, decency, and substance. Joshi liked him very much.

The phone rang, and K.C., Joshi's secretary, summoned the Judge. "I should take this call," he said. "Would you like to stretch your legs a bit?"

"I would love to see your garden."

"Of course." Mohan brought the phone and Judge Joshi took it. "Mohan, show our guest the gardens."

In the foyer, Jonathan passed a large photograph of a saintly old man with long white hair, a flowing beard, and large engaging eyes. It made Jonathan pause. His was a mystical face. Even in the black and white photo, the spiritual aura was so intense that as Jonathan began to move away, he felt as though the saint's eyes were following him.

"Whose photograph is that, Mohan?" Jonathan asked.

"Swamiji. He is the swami of the Ashram where you are going."

"Have you met him?"

"Oh, no, I get goose bumps just looking at him. He has a blessed smile, but those eyes! They follow you everywhere. Like they are watching you all the time. I have heard he's a miracle man."

"I see..."

Mohan led Jonathan outdoors to a padded wicker chair under the gazebo.

"Have a seat," he said. "I'll bring you some cool water and the Times of India."

When he returned, Jonathan asked, "Mohan, may I ask you a question?"

"Please."

"I have noticed a distinct absence of women in the house."

"Ah, Mrs. Joshi, sir," Mohan said. "Died ten years ago. Big heart attack. She was a beautiful lady. Judge Sahb misses her so much. We all do."

Jonathan felt a sudden stab of compassion. He thought of his own beautiful lady. His heart. His Becka. He still remembered their first kiss, and their beachside wedding. He remembered the reflected ocean in the tears on her beautiful face when he first kissed his new bride. Then the picture darkened as he remembered listening, waiting, wanting to hear the crying but not hearing it when Sarah was born. He sharply interrupted his own thoughts. "That's very sad," he said to Mohan.

"Oh, but she is still with us," Mohan said.

"Pardon me? I thought you said—"

"She is gone out of her body, but her spirit is with us. Always. I see her sometimes at night. I hear her footsteps, the rustle of her sari. Some dark nights, the chair squeaks, you know. And Mrs. Joshi loved walking in the garden."

Jonathan nodded. This was certainly a different world.

"So many nights I hear her in the bedroom." Mohan turned and pointed at the open window on the second floor. "That bedroom where you slept last night was her private room."

Jonathan looked at the window. He recalled getting up early in the morning, and finding the rose petals strewn over the windowsill. Despite the heat, he felt a chill.

He shrugged it off. "Mohan, show me your garden, please? How do I say 'thank you' in Hindi?"

"*Shukriya*, and there's more," said Mohan, glowing with the pride of a teacher, "*Baba, Bapu*, and *Babu* are endearing Hindi words for the Holy Father, father, and dear sir. The suffix 'ji' is added to impart respect and love. Let's walk through the garden."

A half-moon shaped garden was contoured with a semicircular driveway. Three life-sized cement baby elephants sent forth water jets from their trunks into a tall basin where the water bathed the feet of Mahatma Gandhi's statue. The waterfall from the basin emptied into a step-down circular pool where lilies and lotus flowers blossomed. It was breathtakingly beautiful, both visually and aromatically.

After a while, Mohan left Jonathan to read the newspaper in peace. Quickly, he went over the political news: Mrs. Indira Gandhi was at the forefront of the fourth general election, and Harold Wilson in England was facing strikes from the Labour Party. The next page showed a photograph of President Lyndon Johnson holding his dog in the air by its ears while his aides stood by in gleeful plaudit. God, talk about tacky. A caption above the picture said, "General William Westmoreland urges the President, 'We can win the Vietnam War; give me two-hundred thousand more troops.'"

"Sure," Jonathan mumbled. "Two hundred thousand more body bags, you mean. Poor kids."

Jonathan found that the more he wanted to avoid reading the details in the suttee story, the more he felt compelled to. He began reading the dreadful story of a previous suttee case. As he took in the details—the huge crowds cheering the young woman as she burned, the carnival atmosphere—his breath came faster and faster until he slammed the paper down with force.

Mohan promptly fetched a stool to rest Jonathan's feet. He begrudgingly accepted a shoulder massage at Mohan's unwavering insistence, feeling very awkward. And although Mohan relaxed his shoulders, his stomach remained in knots.

Then Mohan brought the afternoon tea, complete with biscuits, petit fours, and cucumber-mint chutney sandwiches. The teapot was insulated by a black-on-gold embroidered cozy that resembled a bishop's miter. Jonathan felt intoxicated with the sweet scent of the white and pink blossoms of the Firangipani tree and the gentle breeze creating waves in the delicate mauve flush of Jacaranda and the scarlet flora of Gulmohar and he began to relax. His fatigue insurmountable, he dozed off.

Jonathan slowly became aware of a scratching sound nearby. He looked at his watch. Two zebra doves pecked querulously at the crumbs on the sandwich plate. He closed his eyes and drifted off again.

He awoke to a familiar voice.

"Ah-ha!" Smiling, Joshi approached, his hands folded behind his back. "There you are. How do you feel? Refreshed, I hope?"

"Absolutely. Mohan has taken good care of me. Please, join me."

"Thank you, Jonathan." Judge Joshi sat. "I have had another phone call. I just learned that I'll be required to visit Baramedi tomorrow—this bloody suttee business. Some humanitarian groups are up in arms, the press is hounding, and so the capital is hard-pressed to place all the checks and balances in place."

"I don't blame them."

"As the government's emissary, I'm afraid I'll have to leave early in the morning on a fact-finding mission. We've got to take the initiative on this one."

"Of course," Jonathan answered. "Actually, I was wondering, Judge Sahb. Would it be all right with you . . . if I went along?"

"To the suttee site? Baramedi?"

"Yes."

"Hmmm..." Joshi moved his palms over the handle of his chair. "That should be all right, I suppose." He peered into the sky and then at Jonathan. "The trip could be treacherous, and what you might see, you might find quite repugnant. You mustn't grieve your soul."

Grieve his soul? His soul was already grieving, would always grieve, he believed. Why had he not been able to prevent his dear Becka's death?

"Frankly, Judge Sahb, my soul would be more grieved if I did not explore this matter further."

Judge Joshi studied Jonathan's face a moment, tapping his foot. "Well, in that case come along. I know I will welcome your company... and of course the Western perspective. Splendid."

"Thank you," said Jonathan with a smile. Reflexively he reached into his pants pocket and retrieved the wedding rings. He had found that following Becka's death, he had been unable to bring himself to either wear or part with them.

As he squeezed the wedding rings, one shot out from between his sweaty fingers, fell to the cement floor with a metallic ping, orbited in concentric circles, and came to a wobbly end at Jonathan's feet. "I'm sorry," Jonathan said, scooping up the ring. "I'm very clumsy today."

There was a moment of awkward silence as Jonathan replaced the rings in his pocket.

Joshi broke the ice. "I've heard wonderful things about this Ashram—you are headed to. There's no better place for a spiritual quest."

"Well... at the risk of sounding arrogant, I'm not going there for a spiritual quest. A lot of abused women and children are there. They need a volunteer physician for a few months."

"Forgive my presumption. A lot of people, especially Westerners, do visit for enriched spirituality. Hindus too, go to the Himalayas for religious purposes. What is your religion, by

the way? Not that it matters. Just for the sake of conversation."
Joshi smiled to cover his curiosity. "I'm a Hindu—a reformed one. A convenient subdivision of Hinduism."

"Ahh . . ." Jonathan crossed his legs. "I'm not much into any religion. My mother is a staunch Catholic. And my father was a proud Unitarian. I was only a little boy when I asked him, 'Dad, what is Unitarian?' Oh, he laughed. He wouldn't stop."

"What was his answer?"

Jonathan grinned broadly. "He said, 'My dear boy, a Unitarian is a fellow who's religiously agnostic about his atheism.'"

"Good Lord!" Joshi laughed hard. "That's some definition."

"My dad was a World War One veteran. He'd seen so much blood and gore. When he returned to Maine, he met a sweet little pet groomer—my mother. They both believed in peace and humanity. Dad became a forest ranger and Mom worked at an animal shelter. But he died when I was eight years old."

"Yes, young or old, it is always hard losing one's parents. I, too, lost my father at an early age." Joshi sighed. "Death is a horrible thing."

Jonathan had no response. "Horrible" hardly seemed the word for the sneaky, relentless, haunting evil that plagued his life. First his father, then Sarah, then Becka—dear Becka. And there were the deaths of so many special patients, friends, relatives. And then here, this suttee. The faster he ran from death, it seemed, the more he ran into it. He almost wished he could share Mohan's comforting belief in ghosts.

"How is your mother?" Joshi asked. "My nephew, Suresh, has told me over the phone that she was quite ill."

"Yeah . . ." Jonathan sighed. "Not too well, I'm afraid. In fact, she's very sick. Like a lily-pad walker. I didn't want to leave her, but she insisted that I come here and try to do some good. She said that's what my father would have wanted, and I agreed. I had to."

"Yes, of course."

But as soon as he had said it, Jonathan wondered if he hadn't come because he simply couldn't stand to see another loved one die. "What is death?" he said suddenly. And then, as though he needed to conceal the blatant cry of his own soul, he improvised. "I mean, how does Hinduism, your scriptures, regard death?"

"Hmm..." Joshi said. "That depends upon how one wants to look at them. According to my English law professor, death is an axiom whose prompt arrival enlightens the soul. We Hindus regard it as a transformation, inevitable and often welcome. The soul transcends the barriers of the flesh—the Maya—and approaches the goal of Moksha—the ultimate freedom. The Ashram in which you plan to serve could really change your ideology on life and death. The Swamiji at the Ashram is the master of such spiritual, deep matters. Soul's ascension after body's cremation..."

Jonathan peered into the sky contemplatively and asked, "Have you ever witnessed cremation?"

"Oh, yes, yes... many times. The first was my father's funeral when I was six years old." He paused a moment. "I lit the fires."

"You... pardon me?"

"In the Hindu religion, the eldest child initiates the rites of cremation. I had to follow that custom when my father died."

"When you were six?"

Joshi gesticulated, but his words were not coming out and his eyes glistened. After a few seconds he regained his composure.

"Actually, I protested, cried a lot, even threw a tantrum. But I had no choice. My mother and my uncle gently and persuasively convinced me. 'Beta,' they said, 'you have the honor and the privilege, being the eldest son, to liberate Papa's soul to heaven. Don't be afraid. You won't be hurting Papa by starting the fire. Papa and God will be pleased that you performed your duty.'"

"Judge Sahb, forgive me, I didn't—"

"No, no." With his fist, he wiped his moist eyes and gave a nervous laugh. "The shared pain may draw us closer. Anyway, here is this six-year-old child who has nothing but fond memories of the father who has brought him up, played games with him, and bought him precious gifts and clothes. And now he is being asked—rather forced under coercion of emotions in a way—to bury those tender feelings and set his own beloved father afire. You see, that's cruel to a little boy who does not know or care about holy customs or scriptures."

"Yes," said Jonathan, deeply moved. "It must have been horrible for you."

"Quite so. Terrifying, actually. I was absolutely petrified at the whole bloody tableau. I still recall vividly the men pouring ghee—the clarified butter—and setting off squibs from swift flames engulfing the kindling. As my father's body caught fire, I clung to my uncle's legs, hesitantly looking at the pyre, but I kept my eyes to the ground, crying and shuddering with fear. The crumbling sandalwood logs emitted redolent smoke. The meaty smell of burning flesh, and . . . my little face, burning with sweat." Joshi sighed deeply. "I tell you, it was too much. I screamed and ran away."

Becka's cremation—that painful memory again rose unbidden. And simultaneously, the would-be suttee—shrieking, writhing in pain, trying to escape the blazing pyre—flashed in his mind. A cold tremor bolted down his spine. He shuddered and shook his head.

"Are you all right?" Joshi asked him.

"Who, me? Oh, I'm fine. Are you all right, Judge Sahb?"

"Yes, but look at you. You are shivering."

"Yes, I am. I'm sweating and feeling chilled."

The chill refused to leave, although it was ninety-nine degrees in New Delhi.

chapter five

Shortly after breakfast the next day, Joshi and Jonathan began their journey in an old Indian-made jalopy with the ostentatious title of *Ambassador*. The one hundred and fifty miles took nearly six hours to travel over old dirt roads, an endless maze of ruts and rocks that made the car creak and groan the whole distance.

When they approached Baramedi, "traffic"—meaning trucks, bullock carts, bicycles, or simply people on foot—turned heavy. The morbidly curious were converging on Baramedi, a river of humanity whose diversity lit up under the bright sun. Despite the sad theme, Jonathan was appalled that people looked and behaved as though attending a festival. They wore bright colors and jovial, celebratory demeanors.

Ahead of them, a bullock cart had toppled into a ditch, its pair of emaciated oxen parked placidly beside the scattered cargo. Equally placid were the ejected villagers, who were smoking biris and joking beside the cart. As Joshi's vehicle passed the accident site, the villagers respectfully stood up with folded hands. Nothing appeared to faze them. Slowly, arduously, somehow life managed to move on—always forward.

"What is this? Some kind of a party? Don't they know a woman is going to burn alive for no reason?" he demanded.

"Ignorance," Judge Joshi answered more calmly than Jonathan expected. "And remember, there is a reason. It is just not a good one."

"How did this fanaticism ever get started?"

"It dates from the dawn of civilization, during Vedic times," said Joshi. "In Hindu mythology, suttee Seeta, who was Lord Rama's wife, burnt herself only to be reincarnated as Uma, the next lovely wife of Shiva. Mythology aside, sutteeism was considered a royal custom around 316 BC, when the widow had to either marry her husband's brother or a near royal relative, or be humiliated with his concubines. Often, the suttee was a preferable alternative. Of course, in those years, Indians revered women who died on their husbands' funeral pyres. They considered it a divine blessing for a widow to follow her husband into eternity."

"Why does the government let this go on? Why don't they ban it?"

"Ah, but we have. That is why we are here."

"*Jay-Ramjiki*, Judge Sahb," the villagers greeted Joshi as they passed.

Joshi echoed the gesture: "Praise Lord Rama," he said warmly. Then he turned to Jonathan. "What irks me the most," Joshi continued, "is that the local politicians—as we learned from the last suttee case—had a field day collecting revenues from the visitors. At five rupees per person, ten thousand visitors a day, that is fifty thousand rupees per day. Multiply that by 365."

Jonathan nodded and tried to figure the equivalents in dollars. It hardly mattered. He felt nauseated.

As they approached the town of Baramedi, Jonathan spotted rows of buses, tractor trailers and other modern means of conveyance mingled among the horse-drawn tongas and carts, camel and donkey carts. A river flowed heavily at the foot of the hill.

Mohan carefully negotiated the car over a rickety, narrow bridge. Joshi held his breath throughout the squeaking passage, sighing with relief at the end.

"Can you imagine if the bloody bridge collapsed? Look at that river!"

"It does sound like it's ready to go, and traffic is heavy," Jonathan said.

The car strained up a long slope onto a crowded plateau. There was not an inch of land unencumbered by people. They were jammed shoulder to shoulder.

"Here we are," Mohan said. He tried to pave the way for the two, but they still had to elbow and push their way through the thick wall of humanity.

Jonathan had become curious, despite his disgust. If the suttee were set for sunset, why all the smoke now? And . . . and that odious fleshy smell? He noticed that Joshi's face wore an identical confusion. Suddenly he felt afraid. Was he too late?

Joshi got hold of a police officer trying to manage the crowd from the periphery and introduced himself. The policeman saluted immediately.

"What is going on here? The suttee isn't planned until this evening. What is all the smoke and smell about?" Joshi demanded officiously.

"Ma . . . ma . . . Maalik," the policeman stammered. "Maalik, I regret—the fact is, the suttee has already—"

"What!" Joshi shouted. "Oh, please, dear God! She has *already* burnt to death?"

"Yes, yes, Maalik. Early this morning."

Jonathan felt sick to his stomach. The ground beneath him began to feel unsteady. Through a heavy fog of despair, he could hear Joshi screaming at the policeman, but of course, to no avail.

Joshi turned to Jonathan. "I am sorry, my friend. It seems we are too late. The policeman says she announced this morning that she wanted to join her husband's soul as soon as possible." He patted Jonathan's shoulder. "I know how you feel. Nobody is getting away with this. I'll take them to task. I promise you."

"Thank you," Jonathan said. "I'm sorry to be so intense about this." He smiled weakly. "You must find it difficult to figure why I am so involved in this, emotionally, I mean."

"Perhaps," said Joshi ambiguously. "I myself could cry right now. But there is no time for that. Come, let's get to work."

A cadre of policemen had gathered around Joshi. They escorted the three to a kind of altar where a smoldering mass of ashes surrounded a large pyre the size of a family car. Half-burnt logs, piles of coconuts, and garlands of orange marigolds formed the circumference. The police weren't allowing people any closer than five feet from the spectacle and repeatedly pushed back the frenzied, crying, chanting men and women with the force of their sticks. But that didn't prevent the devotees from tossing coconuts, garlands and money at the pyre.

Jonathan observed the scene as if outside of it, wondering if he'd made a terrible mistake in going there. Yet, his instinct seemed to be telling him to stay with it. His chest tight, he persevered along behind Judge Joshi. Powdery-red metallic dye called sindoor, rice grains and silver coins littered the area. The vast amount of smoke at the central mound obscured the details of the scene. Jonathan drifted, seeking a view of the pyre's center, but with no luck. He had a thought. Joshi was out of sight but Mohan remained in tow like a loyal guard.

"Mohan," he said. "What do you see in the center of the pyre?"

Mohan gestured with his hands. "Fire. All day, all night."

"No, no, not fire. Pyre. Look in the middle. Do you see anything there?"

Mohan peered at the smoke-shrouded center. "Nothing, sir. All ashes."

Briefly all heads turned as several policemen escorted a string of rotund bronze-skinned priests with thick white paste over their foreheads and glistening scalps to the site. They chanted unintelligible mantras. As they circled the pyre, their cacophony grew louder, and after a few times around they stood still, bowing at the suttee with folded hands. When they were escorted out, their shaved heads and bare torsos poured streams of sweat.

Then there was more noise on the opposite side as a few men picked up the body of an elderly woman.

"Looks like some old woman suddenly passed away," Mohan said.

"Passed *away? Just now?*"

"Yes. Yes, sir. Like fainting." Mohan imitated unconsciousness.

Jonathan smiled. "Ah, passed out. Where are they taking her, Mohan?"

"I think I saw a tent behind that big banyan tree. It's for government officers, police and priests—for resting. I think they'll take her there."

"Where is Judge Sahb, Mohan?"

"I think under the tent, too. Talking to villagers."

It seemed to Jonathan that the people around them were all tuned to different frequencies, and that he and Mohan were the only sane observers in the area. Even the police seemed outside reality, staring at them, as if they were spies.

It was then that he realized he had his camera with him. That explains the suspicious looks from the cops, he thought. He circled the pyre. He had seen all sorts of injuries come through the ER, but he had never seen any sight that had affected him the way this one did. He had seen suicides before, yes. His heart stopped for a moment.

The present, he told himself. I must think in the present. Maybe there is still something I can offer. Let the past rest for now. He strode slowly around. He raised his camera to his eye, but found his view suddenly darkened.

"No pictures allowed, sir," a big fellow declared in a booming voice, his spade-like hand covering the lens.

"But I'm with—"

"No pictures."

An obese priest wearing white threads across his bare chest walked in front of them carrying a brass plate of ashes. Jonathan watched several visitors pinch a bit of ashes, rub it on their foreheads and, bowing in obedience, leave coins or rupee notes on the plate. Then they each looked at the pyre with an expression of reverence and awe.

When the offering came to Jonathan he politely declined. "*Nahin. Shukriya.*"

The priest said something to Mohan, who rubbed the ashes on his own forehead and left a one-rupee bill in the plate.

As the priest moved on, Jonathan asked Mohan, "What did he say?"

"He said that rubbing these ashes of sutteemata can fulfill any wishes."

Jonathan cursed under his breath. "Is nothing sacred?" he said too quietly for Mohan to hear.

"Are you all right, Sahb?" Mohan said.

"Mohan," Jonathan said quietly, "how would you like to burn to death and have your ashes sold for pennies?"

"Oh. Oh, Sahb, I see. They are probably not even her ashes, probably just from a cooking fire. I am sure of it, I mean . . ." Mohan looked away, pretending to seek Joshi.

"It's all right, Mohan. I'm sorry."

"No, sir, it is entirely my fault. Sir, I overheard some villagers saying that Seeta was very young and beautiful."

"How did they know? Were they from this village?"

"No, sir. But see that Neem tree? Under that tree, they have her picture."

"I would like to see her picture, Mohan."

"Of course, sir. Most definitely."

Photos of the victim—or the saint, depending on one's point of view—were set up on rickety chairs. The husband's face was not visible because of the customary flower curtain that hung over his portrait. He was beside his wife, who was not well revealed because dust and glare on the photo marred the rest of the details. The garland around her neck was made of roses. Beside her photo, a vase of native pink, Indian roses emitted an exquisitely sweet redolence as the hot breezes blew.

As he looked at the photos, Jonathan heard music—a harsh but rhythmic sodality of flute and fife and a single-stringed dulcimer. The drummer held a barrel-like percussion instrument under the crook of his knee. He beat the drum with the verve of a soldier while the blind singer roused the emotions with his raspy-voiced crescendo. His blind eyes blinked blankly at the blazing sky.

"He is singing a Bhajan, sir—a devotional song," Mohan said. Then he smiled sarcastically, "Sir, he is a Surdaas, meaning a blind man, but he can tell whether you throw at him a quarter, half rupee or a whole rupee. Really, sir."

"He looks blind to me."

"Watch this, sir."

Mohan threw a coin, which bounced off the singer's bowl. Automatically, the blind man snatched it neatly out of the air. Mohan grabbed his wrist and scolded him for his shameless trick. The blind man wailed and prostrated himself at Mohan's feet, speaking Hindi faster than Jonathan thought possible.

"What is he saying, Mohan?"

"You won't believe, sir. He says to me, 'You are right, my lord, I'm not blind. But please forgive me because I'm filling in for the *real* blind guy who is out on a bathroom break.'"

Even in the midst of all of the trauma, Jonathan could not withhold his laughter.

Mohan then escorted Jonathan into the shade, where a snake charmer unleashed a mongoose on a de-fanged cobra. Pierced by the mongoose's sharp teeth, the snake collapsed into a lump of flesh. The next show featured a suicidal scorpion that struggled to cross a circle of flames. When he could not, he stung himself to death.

Monkeys boldly grabbed peanuts and bananas out of people's hands and shrieked violently if someone resisted. Jonathan saw a stray cow make a meal out of a blind beggar's lunch. According to Mohan, cows were sacred animals and one dare not punish them. "The loser should feel lucky that she chose to accept the food from him. That means God is satisfied with him."

"It's like a carnival here," Jonathan said. "I see no regret or tears and even the priests seem false in their displays of emotion. Again, he felt an urge to take pictures, but Joshi had warned him that he could be arrested if he did.

Further from the pyre, Jonathan saw rows of beggars with mutilated limbs. Some were obviously genuine lepers, but some, Mohan explained, were deliberately disfigured by organized gangs who used them to incite sympathy from the almsgivers. And all around them, vendors hawked toys, saris, and glossy photographs of women sitting on top of funeral pyres. Several sari-clad women protested by holding placards with anti-suttee slogans. Colorful posters of Lord Rama and his wife Seeta bobbed above the crowd.

Eventually, Jonathan and Mohan joined up with Joshi, who was talking to the man who had prevented Jonathan's intended photography. He was a big hulky man with a pockmarked face. Joshi introduced the man as Buttasingh, the councilman, or representative, of Baramedi. When Buttasingh removed his sunglasses, a pox-eaten gray bulge of corneal opacity was revealed, under which he bore a triangular scar so deep that it prevented complete closure of his left eyelid. The damaged eye roved around. He smiled at Jonathan.

"I am sorry for my sharpness earlier," he said. "I thought you were the press."

Jonathan said lightly, "Don't worry about it."

He noticed that Joshi was wheezing slightly. "May I suggest that we find the house of the dead woman's relatives before the crowd kills us?" Joshi asked.

"My dear sir, I have handled these crazy cases before," Buttasingh offered. "Wife beating, child exploitation, dowry death—everything. Allow me to be your servant. It's not easy dealing with stubborn villagers and their stupid customs."

Joshi carefully looked him over. "Very well. Thank you."

"But, please, before dealing with these people, you must make a brief lunch and siesta stop at my humble abode," Buttasingh said. "You must be exhausted after all this."

"We are also pressed for time," answered Joshi flatly. "We must decline."

"But surely the foreign gentleman must be tired," Buttasingh insisted.

Judge Joshi looked at Jonathan, who tried to smile, but without much success.

"Very well," Joshi said. "*Accha chalo.* Let's go."

At Buttasingh's house, a woman with a sari-covered face quickly kneaded the corn dough. Then on an earthen skillet she made flat cornbread that she served with daal, a paste made from lentil, salty lassi made from yogurt, cumin seeds and salt.

After the simple but sumptuous lunch, the councilman ushered his special guests to the second floor of his brick home, where two jute-woven cots covered with soft, white, cotton-filled mattresses stood. The ceiling fan, whirling at the highest speed, sounded like a low-flying bomber but did little to nullify the hot air that blew in through the cracks in the glass window. Jonathan unsuccessfully struck his last matchstick to light his Winston, but a blast of hot air blew the flame out.

As the judge began snoring, the palm-leaf fan he'd been holding fell to the floor. Jonathan picked up the fan and used it to swat the flies. Then he covered his face from a searing shaft of sunlight that strayed through a hole in the slate roof. But how could Jonathan sleep? The heat, the noise, the horror, and the simple overpowering strangeness . . . the strangeness that . . . that.

Jonathan fell into thought about the young Seeta. Had she had a happy marriage? Had she ever had a child? He recalled her wedding photo, the rose garland around her neck, the roses in the jar.

Becka had loved roses; growing roses was her passion. Her magnificent smile was what he would never forget, despite all the hard times when he had rarely seen it. She had first come to him as a surgical nurse, shapely and beautiful, and with a devotion and wit that energized the entire team.

"I'm Rebecca Hall, Dr. Kingsley," she had said. "Where do you want me?"

That had been an opener! Jonathan smiled in spite of his misery.

"Good to meet you, Rebecca," he had answered. "Please, right there will be fine." Concealed by his mask, his smile was broad and approving. And she had gotten to him. Already.

"Thank you, sir," she said. Jonathan had noted a slight drawl.

"I'm guessing you're from a little south of here—maybe even south of Virginia?"

"Yes sir," she said, stepping into her place, "Atlanta."

"So I guess you don't mind the New England winters."

"Ask me again in February."

It had been so natural from the start. And when it turned cold, Rebecca had found she didn't mind New England winters at all. Together they had walked along the snow—covered sidewalks of Portland, stopping for steamed clams and ale in the afternoons. After late shifts, they snuggled into a cozy inn for coffee and thick slices of rum cake.

It was shameless fun at the hospital, stealing glances at each other and laughing at the most trivial events. Back then, everything had seemed so funny, so joyful. They walked in the thick winter snow as if they floated on the cushion of an efflorescent spring. And saying good night at the end of an evening had seemed equally unnatural. Both had struggled with the barrenness of turning out the lights alone.

On her twenty-sixth birthday, Jonathan arrived with a bouquet of pink roses.

"How on earth did you know?" she squealed, delighted at both the flowers themselves, and that Jonathan had chosen them.

"I thought, what is most like Becka? Beautiful, charming, and sweet, but also gentle and strong. It was an easy choice!"

"Oh, Jonathan, thank you! I love them!"

As they embraced, he became suddenly and keenly aware that he had arrived earlier than planned. Rebecca still wore her bathrobe. He could remember the softness of the satin, how it was scented with the perfume she wore, and most of all, how it clung alluringly to her magnificent body.

He became self-conscious. "I guess I came early—I got here early, earlier than . . ." he stammered.

Rebecca had burst out laughing her sweet melodic and never mocking laughter. "Dr. Kingsley," she drawled, "Are you backing away from the practice of making house calls?"

"Uh, no . . ." he said smiling uncertainly.

"Come on in, cowboy," she said mischieviously, "and wish me a proper Happy Birthday."

And there began the soiree of senses: Her hungry breath against his ear, tensing his body, sending ripples of electricity through him. He could not get enough of her, wanting to taste and caress every ounce of her being; the intensity of that night climaxed by the snapping of rosebuds, the petals spiraling down to the floor, and releasing the rousing sweet redolence. Oh!

"Oh, Becka! I miss you so much," he whispered.

After a few seconds, he opened his eyes. There was a vase of roses on an end table. He hadn't noticed them earlier.

From nowhere a butterfly came in the room and settled on a rose. Then it left the rose and fearlessly settled on his forehead. When it flew away, Jonathan smiled and pulled the rose out of the vase. He stroked the rose against his rough face. A few petals came undone over his lips and neck.

chapter six

Every time the wind blew, the dry limbs of the Neem tree hooding the two-story brick home of the councilman squeaked and its limp leaves snapped into ripples of hot breeze that poured through the cracks in the windowpane. Outside, clothes—drying on the line tied between the trunks of the two trees—flapped unrhythmically over two stray dogs that panted and dug deeper for a cooler spot where the woman in Buttasingh's house had washed pots and pans earlier. When they curled up comfortably, their slowly blinking eyes oozed the languor of the early summer afternoon of a village in India.

Jonathan got up and walked out to the balcony. He sat down on a paillase cushion, lit a Winston and blew the smoke in the direction of two geckos and a housefly on the wall. The geckos' strategic lunges to swallow the fly remained unsuccessful; the fly kept taking off with equal cunning and swiftness.

"Good afternoon, sir..." Mohan greeted Jonathan as he descended the cement stairway. "Sir, Judge Sahb will not get up for another hour. Would you care for some tea?"

"Tea?" Jonathan glanced at the sun.

"Heat kills heat," the councilman said.

"*Accha*," Jonathan said. It was supposed to mean 'very well," but his pronunciation must have left something to be desired, he thought, since the other two laughed. Glad that the icebreaker had worked, Jonathan said, "Thanks, well, maybe no tea for me, but I wouldn't mind some cold water." He took a seat and lit a cigarette. "Who is that?" he asked, noticing a small female covered by a worn out white sari. She lay on a jute-string cot under the cool shade of the larger tree, her body still, curled up in fetal position, seemingly lifeless.

"Gopal's mother," Buttasingh replied.

"Is she ill?"

Buttasingh shouted something in Hindi, and a depressed and docile looking man appeared. He replied in a soft, withdrawn voice.

"He says she is very old, sir," Mohan said. "She has diabetes, a bad heart and her kidneys are failing."

"How old is she?" Jonathan's question was relayed.

"Pretty old, sir," Mohan said. "Sixty-five."

"That's old?"

"Yes, sir. People live very stressful lives here. They get old fast. The stress of heat, livelihood, hygiene . . . you know. My father died at age fifty-nine."

"I'm truly sorry to hear that."

For a few seconds, Jonathan simply stared at the silhouette of the emaciated and motionless body. This is such a strange country, he thought, and I am a stranger here. But I am also a doctor. He went to her and touched her forehead. She had a fever.

"Mohan, water, please."

He soaked a piece of cloth with water and lay it across her burning forehead.

"Once a doctor, always a doctor," declared Joshi coming down the stairs and toward him. "I think we should find the suttee's father-in-law and talk to him. What do you think?"

"Yes, we should," Jonathan said, as he continued to tend to the sick woman.

"I will tell Gopal to take his mother to the missionary hospital and arrange for some intravenous injection of fluids," Joshi said. "Shall we leave now?" He was refreshed from his nap and ready to get back to work.

"Feel this," Jonathan said, holding out the frail woman's forearm.

Joshi, perplexed but curious, took her arm. Then his eyes widened.

"Good grief," Joshi said. "Her entire body is pulsating."

"She has Water-Hammer Pulse," Jonathan said. "The sign of a floppy, leaky outlet valve of the heart that is not able to pump effectively. Look at her neck and her feet. They're swollen from a backlog of blood. It's called congestive heart failure."

"Can anything be done?"

"Actually, yes." Jonathan wrote on a slip of paper: Diagnosis: congestive heart failure, secondary to Aortic Valve Regurgitation. Treatment: Digoxin, Furosemide and adequate anticoagulation. "Take this with you to the missionary hospital," he instructed Gopal. "These are pretty old and inexpensive medications. I'm sure they have them there."

Joshi translated.

"Let's go, Judge Sahb. Now I'm ready."

"This is absolutely wonderful," Joshi said. "The poor lady is going to bless you as long as she lives."

Buttasingh and Mohan opened two large white umbrellas over the heads of the two dignitaries as the four of them took a footpath across the oven-hot fields. Jonathan noticed the sparse weeds along the path, quivering hopelessly like strands of dull hair on a senescent skull in the impossible heat. A scaly lizard darted across in front of him and into a crackling pile of dried up leaves. He kept moving his toes to avoid singeing them on the melting upper soles of his rubber sandals.

After a mile or so, a lush mango tree appeared. Under its

shade was an old lady with a shaven head wearing a plain gray sari, seated beside a large earthen pot. Joshi signaled a brief halt. The aroma of the ripening mangos, the cuckoo heralding the monsoon, breezes ruffling the thick green mango leaves, and a cow lying in a puddle of the spilled water, ruminating contentedly with her eyes half closed, collectively felt like paradise.

"Are you thirsty?" Joshi asked.

Am I thirsty? I could drink a lake. "Yes."

Joshi gave the woman a coin. She scooped water out of the pot with a shiny brass *Lota*, or small jar, and poured it into Joshi's cupped palms. When she nodded to Jonathan, he was too thirsty to think about hygiene. He sat knee-to-chin, cupped his palms, and watched as she poured them full. The water was cool, sweet and delicious.

"How far is the bloody place, anyway?" Joshi asked. "It's hot as hell."

"Beyond this hill, sir." Buttasingh said. "On the river bank."

Joshi took another drink and then poured some water over his head as they started off again. "Ah! I surely hope and pray it rains soon. We do not need another disaster so soon."

"You had a bad year recently?" Jonathan asked.

"A decade or so ago," Joshi said. "That the season had failed was evident from the long line at the pawn shop. Poor farmers stood there swallowing their pride, selling their wives' gold ornaments and other valuables in order to feed their families and the dying cattle. Rivers turned into slim tracks of sand, and those lush mountains looked like ghostly gray monuments."

"You visited the area then?"

"I was district judge for this county. Surprisingly, I recall the incidence of malaria went down dramatically. No rains, no puddles." Joshi craned into the distance and smiled. "Well here we go. I see a cluster of huts behind those trees."

Jonathan strained to see dirty brown huts blended in with the dry soil and barren trees. "How hot does it get here?"

"Very hot," Buttasingh said. "One hundred fifteen to one

hundred twenty degrees Fahrenheit. Some summers we see birds dropping dead from the treetops. On the land, the dogs are first to go. They just pant to death." Buttasingh pointed to a hut. "The one on the left, sir, with the lamb on the leash."

It was a mud-covered, thatched hut reeking of cow dung. But the yard in front was of nicely leveled dirt, a wavelike pattern brushed into it. Two large wooden poles marked the entrance and simultaneously supported the roof. A four-foot-long bristle-broom rested in the corner outside a door that was constructed of tightly woven thatch around several half-split bamboo sticks and reinforced with thick jute string. Beside that door there was a small hole in the wall that served as a window.

As the men arrived, the drowsy chickens stood up and squawked half-heartedly. The tiny lamb sniffed and bleated.

Buttasingh politely announced their arrival, calling out to whomever was inside. Slowly the door opened. Jonathan peered in. Soon, a doddering old man came into view. At first, the old man appeared confused and apprehensive, but when he recognized the councilman, he rushed forward to greet him and the rest. He wore a curious smile.

"This is the suttee's father-in-law," stated Buttasingh as if pointing out an animal at the zoo. "His name is Kishanchacha, but they call him *Bapuji*—vernacular for beloved father."

Bapuji was a frail man with a hollow, bony face. His hands and feet were leathery and covered with calluses from years of toiling under the hard sun and soil.

"*Jay-Ramjiki*." the old man hesitantly mumbled, with folded hands covering his face. He appeared overwhelmed and intended to touch their feet, expressing the ultimate respect for them. But when he got to Jonathan, Jonathan restrained him at the shoulders and gave him a gentle hug. His generous action brought tears to the old man's dark and shriveled eyes.

"How are you?" Jonathan asked Bapuji. "*Aaap kaise hain?*"

At first, the old man, as well as the others, appeared baffled. But after a moment, they all laughed. Bapuji's toothless mouth drew an ear-to-ear smile. He replied, slowly, "*Bahot khub, bahot khub, shukriah.*"

Mohan translated, "Very very good. Thank you."

The old man ducked into the hut and emerged dragging a sturdy cot toward the shade tree. Mohan rushed to assist him. Together they covered the cot with a thick cotton mattress upon which Joshi and Jonathan sat, while Bapuji sat on the ground in front of them with downcast eyes and a reverential mien. When he removed his turban, a circular scar with a cross inside, reminiscent of a cattle brand, stood out on top of his scalp. He wore a cotton shirt and a sarong-like lower wrap called a dhoti. Engorged vessels in the temple area pulsated, and sweat beads formed over his forehead.

Joshi, with Mohan providing Jonathan with a running translation, immediately said to the man, "We're here to find out what happened after your son died. Tell us about your daughter-in-law. What drove her to this act?"

Bapuji looked frightened and did not answer directly. After a long pause he pulled out a biri from his pocket, lit it, took a deep drag and carefully exhaled away from Jonathan so as not to offend him. Jonathan watched his face as the biri smoke floated away. Finally he shrugged.

"Old habits die hard at this age, sir. Forgive me. Anyway, after my son's sudden death, she completely lost interest in the world." He paused to rub his eyes. "She kept crying, sat there beside my son's body, wouldn't eat and, despite all our pleas, wouldn't listen to anyone. In the middle of the night, when my son's body was prepared for cremation, she told us that she wanted to be cremated with her husband. This was an arranged marriage, and she had not even seen my son before they were married. It was really shocking for all of us, and . . . and—" He had a coughing spell that left him short of breath.

When he had recovered, he continued. "We tried our best to change her mind, but she was determined. She said to me, 'Bapuji, my mind is made up. There is nothing left for me in this world. If you try to stop me, I will run away and kill myself, so please give me your blessings.' She begged me not to intervene. What could I say or do? I'm a helpless, old man."

"Helpless?" Joshi yelled. "You were helpless in front of this young girl? You, with all your wisdom and age, stood by and watched the life snuffed out of your son's little bride? This makes you a participant in this outrage! Do you understand?"

Joshi's anger shocked the old man. His lips started to quiver. Tears rolled down his face and fell to the parched dirt floor that absorbed them like ink on a blotter. With the end of his turban, he wiped the tears and held his hands in a submissive gesture.

"Chacha," Buttasingh said, "don't worry. We're not here to punish you. We just want to gather some information, so we can prevent such cruel happenings in the future."

The old man looked at Buttasingh and nodded. "Maalik . . . I begged her to give up her outlandish plan. I volunteered to take her place on the funeral pyre as a substitute human sacrifice." He looked at Buttasingh. "We called Buttababu and Bholanathji, our temple priest. They both told her to respect her own life, but she refused to listen to anybody. If there were anything I could have done to prevent my poor little daughter-in-law from doing this, I would have done it. Today she is nothing but ashes!" Another series of cascading tears rolled down his face and disappeared into the thirsty earth.

The sorry scenario evaporated Jonathan's anger at the suttee, leaving behind only a deep sense of sympathy and remorse. At odds with Joshi's harshness, Jonathan smiled and offered, "I am sure you did all you could to prevent this unfortunate incident."

Touched, the old man offered Jonathan a biri, which Jonathan put in his pocket.

"I'll smoke it later," Jonathan said, "when it cools down."

While Joshi continued to question the old man less severely, Buttasingh disappeared into a nearby hut. Fifteen minutes later, he emerged with an aluminum kettle of cooked tea and a few earthen cups of red clay.

Surprisingly to Jonathan, the tea was refreshing and invigorating. The atmosphere grew cordial. Jonathan took some photos. Before long, three men approached and greeted Joshi and Jonathan.

"Judge Sahb, this is Bholanath," Buttasingh indicated a rotund man with discolored teeth and breath that reeked of tobacco. "He is our temple priest."

The priest folded his hands at the judge. "*Jay Shri Krishna.*"

"And this is Murli, our barber," Buttasingh said.

The barber was a lanky fellow with Coke-bottle glasses and dirty white clothes. He removed his white Gandhi-cap and bowed to the judge.

"And this is Jalim Singh, our police chief."

Buttasingh indicated a red-cheeked, mustachioed hulk in a khaki police uniform. As the law-keeper struck his heels and delivered a crisp army-styled salute to the judge, his baton vibrated over his hip.

"Bholanath, Murli, Jalim Singh—gentlemen. I'm glad you came," Joshi said. "I would like to ask you a question. Please, sit down."

Murli the barber, and Bholanath, the priest, promptly sat down on the ground. But Jalim Singh, the police chief, opted to stand stiffly on guard.

Jonathan studied the three. Buttasingh's introduction of them seemed to indicate that they were friends, rather than casual villagers who had just stopped by. Buttasingh's face was tense.

Jonathan pulled out a Winston and struck a match, but the wind blew it out. Then Bapuji was at his elbow, signaling him toward the shelter of a large tree. There, Jonathan extracted his lighter. Bapuji sheltered it in his hand and he lit his cigarette in one strike. Jonathan then lit one for Bapuji. Bapuji looked at him with a strange intensity and said softly, "Mary, Betty, Cindy."

"I'm . . . sorry, what?"

"Mary, Betty, Cindy."

Jonathan thought back to his earlier experiment in Hindi. Bapuji must be returning the complement with the only English he knew. Jonathan smiled. "*Aaap kaise hain*—how are you?"

Bapuji slowly but intensely shook his head. "Mary, Betty, Cindy."

"I'm sorry, I don't understand—"

"Bapuji!" Jalim Singh, the police chief, called. Bapuji pasted a smile on his face and scurried over. Jonathan followed, shaking his head. What was Bapuji trying to say?

"Give me your description of the suttee," Joshi was asking the three newcomers. "You did witness her immolation, did you not?"

"Maalik, what happened, happened." The priest Bholanath pointed at the sky. "God's will. You are a scholar, so you know. Not a leaf shakes without His command."

Joshi shook his head in disgust. "What do you have to say? What's your name? Murli?" he demanded of the barber.

The barber folded his hands over his mouth. "Judge Sahb," he said softly, "how I wish she were my daughter. She was the glory of our village. We are nothing without her. She is our pride."

"Blithering idiots," Joshi shouted. "Gentlemen, hear me carefully. I am asking a simple question. How did she look? How did she behave when the fire started?" He looked at the police chief. "You. Answer me."

"With your permission, Judge Sahb." Buttasingh appealed to the three. "Brothers, please. Why are you all wasting Judge Sahb's precious time? He is not here to arrest you. He is just answering his duty. Just tell the truth—that's all. Just the truth."

"Thank you, Councilman," Joshi said.

"It is nothing, Maalik," Buttasingh said. "No need to thank me. In a small way—if I may say so—I'm a lawman, too. It is my honor to serve you."

"Your honor," began Jalim Singh, the police chief, in an emotionless voice, "the suspect surrendered to the fire without resistance."

Before Joshi could scream, the holy man said, "Maalik, when I saw her sitting on top of that funeral pyre with her dead husband's head on her lap, she looked like a goddess from heaven. There was a smile on her face. She wore her red bridal sari trimmed with brocade. Her voice was lifted with hymns, inviting the gods to bring chariots with white horses to deliver them to eternity."

"Stop the *Baqwaas*! Just give Judge Sahb the true story."

Jonathan raised his eyebrows at Mohan, who had been translating for him.

"It was incredible to witness the fire," the priest continued. "She did not feel any pain. She was entranced, not even a sigh, let alone a scream. And she made no attempt to escape from the deadly inferno. In just a few moments, the flames took over and nothing was left but ashes. The crowd broke out into a chorus, 'Sutteemata Amar Raho,' Mother suttee, be immortal."

Suddenly the lamb in the yard began to bleat urgently. Jonathan was alarmed to see that the twist of thin rope around its neck had somehow slipped and was cutting into its flesh. Immediately he rushed to remove the noose, but as he tried to free it, the animal thrashed and convulsed, and the thin cord burrowed further in its fur.

A voice from behind startled him. "I'll take care of it." The police chief pulled out a large army knife and cast open its long, shiny blade. The sun's reflection on the blade lit up his face. Expertly, he laid the blade opposite the crying lamb's throat and nicked off the rope with the subtlest movement. The blade was as sharp as a scalpel.

"Remarkable," Jonathan said.

"It was nothing," the police chief responded arrogantly as they returned to Judge Joshi and the others. "Rampuri knife. You should have seen my work with this when I was on the frontier, fighting the Pakistanis. It can slice a liver in two in a split second."

"I don't doubt that. It's very impressive."

Judge Joshi had begun to cough and wheeze.

"Are you all right, Judge Sahb?" Jonathan asked out of earshot of the others.

"It's the dryness, I can tell. My lungs stiffen."

"Perhaps you should rest." Jonathan said. "How far are you with your inquiry?"

Joshi stood up and put his hand over Jonathan's shoulder. "I'm not sure I'm getting anywhere," he whispered. "But I smell a rat."

Jonathan kept a poker face. The four town fathers were studying him.

"Do you have any questions for any of these chaps?" Joshi asked aloud.

"Um . . . Maybe later," Jonathan murmured. "I'd like to confer with you first. Privately."

"Fair enough. " Joshi stood up and shook the dust from his clothes. "Mohan, let's go. It's about five-thirty."

The three townsmen bid them a humble good-bye.

On their way back Buttasingh urged Joshi to take a different route. He said his soul felt terribly disturbed with the suttee matter and he wanted to say a quick prayer at the Sarasvati temple.

The temple turned out to be a small, neat building made of carved ledge columns. As they entered the cool stone proscenium, Joshi signaled Jonathan to park themselves on the ledge benches outside the iron-barred doors while Mohan and Buttasingh removed their shoes and entered the inner sanctum. Soon Jonathan heard them ring two bells, which gradually crescendoed, only to be followed by an eerie silence. Before Jonathan could fathom what was going on, he heard a loud bang and a phrase shouted twice in the councilman's voice.

"For heaven's sake!" Joshi looked at the sanctum scornfully. "Buttasingh just cracked open a coconut on the altar stone— like this." Joshi imitated the act with a cupped hand. "He is urging the goddess, Sarasvati—the deity of knowledge and the enlightenment—to grant him strength. Moral strength, presumably." Then the Judge said, "Buttasingh is very religious. Whatever . . . his help came godsent."

Jonathan watched the two worshippers emerging from within, their hands folded in somber submission, their foreheads bearing the vermilion and the rice grain.

They had just arrived at the councilman's house when from nowhere came the Police Chief, running. "Judge Sahb," he said, "I must beg your forgiveness for this terrible news, but—"

"What is it, Jalim Singh?"

"Judge Sahb, I just received a message. The bridge over the river is completely destroyed."

"From what?"

"Overloaded truck, Sahb. There must have been a hundred villagers on it. When the truck came upon the bridge, it just collapsed." Then he turned to Jonathan . . . "Dishonest contractors, sir. They bid low, but mix lime and sand—no cement."

"Good grief." Joshi said, disgusted.

"Judge Sahb," Jonathan said, "do you mind if Mohan and I take a ride? I would like to see it, the bridge, maybe take some pictures."

"Well . . . be careful. And Jalim Singh, you stay here. I want to talk to you."

Twenty minutes later, Jonathan and Mohan stood on the riverbank, watching the sunset light up the shallow waters of the Vasundhara River. A cloud of parrots had taken over an entire banyan tree. Below them was the rubble of the recently collapsed bridge. The truck's nose was buried in the mud and its rear slanted upward. A haze of dust kicked up by the homebound herds was held hostage in the chilling evening air.

"May I ask, sir," Mohan said, "what you are looking for?"

"I don't really know," Jonathan said. "I just have a bad feeling about this."

Mohan nodded. "Yes, yes, it is all very bad. But we should be safe at the councilman's house."

After Jonathan had taken several shots of the disaster, satisfied that there was nothing that could be done that day, the two returned to the councilman's house. No one was pleased about having to stay overnight, but there was no alternative.

After supper, Joshi, aggravated but exhausted and still wheezing heavily, went to bed. Jonathan paced. There was so much about the whole situation that put him on edge. Why had the town fathers been so fixed on convincing them that the suttee had been peaceful? Even Bapuji was not entirely credible—and what of the Mary, Betty, Cindy remark? And then there was the collapse of that bridge—the only way back. It was suspicious, or at the very least, too coincidental.

Yet, he told himself, I am a stranger to this culture. People react differently to authority here. And of course, as much as he hated to admit it, the darkness and the senseless loss of human life had brought back his own loss—of Becka.

Joshi had said it was a rough town. But they wouldn't dare hurt a distinguished American visitor, would they? Just for exploring the sights in the cool of night?

Downstairs, he found his host, Buttasingh, talking to Murli, the barber. When he saw Jonathan, the councilman stood up. "Sir, *aap*? May I help you?"

"No, thanks." Jonathan answered amiably. "Where's Mohan?"

"He is staying at the police chief's house. There's not enough room here for all."

"I see. Would you mind showing me where he is? I'd like to go for a walk." Jonathan stretched his arms in the air. "I can't sleep without a little bit of exercise."

Buttasingh hesitated. "Are you sure, sir? It may not be entirely . . . safe."

"Oh, I'm sure I'll be all right."

"Very well, I'll send for him."

Five minutes later, when Mohan arrived, Buttasingh offered Jonathan a flashlight. "Just in case . . . Doctor Sahb."

"Sir," Mohan said as soon as they were outside, "Buttasingh is right, I think. Little bit dangerous, no?"

"Little bit dangerous, maybe, but worth the risk."

Mohan fiddled with the flashlight. "I don't know how well it works. It may need new batteries."

Jonathan glanced back at the house. "No light, Mohan. I don't want them to figure out the direction of our mission."

"Mission?" Mohan asked, his voice cracking. Then he cleared his throat and whispered, "Mission?"

"Shhh—yes. Mohan, I want you to take me to the suttee site."

"No, no, no! Please, sir." Mohan stopped. "This is really dangerous. Let's go back. Please, sir."

"Have a little courage, Mohan. Are you afraid?"

"Who me? No, I'm not scared of anything—except Judge Sahb. He'll kill me."

"But that's tomorrow. If you don't help me, I'll kill you *now*."

Mohan stiffened. Once again, Jonathan realized he needed to adjust to the culture. He laughed and patted Mohan on the back. "I'm only kidding! You don't have to come if you don't want to."

Mohan smiled self-consciously. "Very well, then. Let's go."

The night surrounding them was dark but not quiet. The blackness seemed to accentuate the chirping of crickets and howling of wild animals. Mohan, however, was unusually silent. They headed across a field and through a thick hedge, carefully watching their footing. Then suddenly, Mohan froze.

"Mohan, what is it?" Jonathan asked quickly.

"The hut," Mohan whispered. "Do you see? On the left side."

"What about it, Mohan?"

"See the light inside, going on and off? It is the house of *Chudail.*"

"*Chudail?* Who's he?"

"No. Chudail is *she*. Female. Bad, bad—evil female. Bitch."

"Bitch? What do you mean? In what way?"

"You know," Mohan whispered stiffly. "She makes spells, murder by mantra."

"Oh!" Jonathan suppressed his amusement. "You mean a *witch.*"

"Yes, Yes, dangerous bitch—I mean *vitch*. Listen. Hear her laughing?"

"Mohan, that's probably some hyena crying for food or something."

On the other hand, Jonathan knew that what he was hearing from his right side was not his imagination. Something was definitely moving along, brushing against the dry vegetation. He held his left arm in front of Mohan to stop him. Suddenly the movement to his right ceased.

"Mohan?"

"Yes sir."

"Give me the flashlight."

Mohan trembled, moving closer to Jonathan. "Why sir?" he whispered

"Give me the damn light!"

"Here it is."

"Mohan, it's not working. What's the matter . . ."

Suddenly, a dazzling light burst into their faces from the darkness, blinding them.

"Who are you? What do you want?" Jonathan demanded awkwardly. Mohan hid behind him.

"Empty your pockets," said the voice in English. "Now!"

"Hey, okay, okay," Jonathan said, faking nervousness. He pulled out his wallet with a shaking hand, then dropped it. When he bent over, he pretended to retrieve it, but then grabbed a fist full of sand and threw it just above the stark rays of the offending light. At the same time, he switched on their own flashlight to briefly reveal the covered faces of two men. Shocked and blinded, the men ran into the bush.

Jonathan went after them, but a rock caught his leg. He hit the ground with force.

Mohan was at his side in an instant. "Sir, are you hurt?"

Jonathan carefully flexed his leg and ankle. It was not broken—nothing that needed immediate attention. "I'll live," he said, frustrated. "Did you see anything?"

"No, sir, I'm sorry. It was too dark."

With less confidence, they continued toward town. After only a few minutes, they reached the town center, where the suttee site slowly smoldered. Jonathan could make out the locations of the guards, who were seated in a cluster on the opposite side of the site. Some were smoking, other were dozing on mats. Jonathan studied Mohan. "Can you keep them busy?"

"Busy, how?"

"Here." Jonathan gave him a few ten rupee notes. "Tell them I'm from America. I'm so touched by the suttee, I'd like to take their pictures. They'll be in newspapers in America. Famous, overnight."

"Okay, okay. But, sir, please hurry up. Whatever you want to do, do it fast!"

"Thanks buddy."

While Mohan distracted the watchmen, Jonathan closely studied the pyre. The smoke, the dust, the people and the searing heat, all were gone. He found a branch and poked the pyre. It was surrounded by coconuts—husked, unhusked, burnt, semi-burnt. As he stirred the embers, one coconut exploded right at his knee. Marigolds were still there, most lying benignly on the central mound of ash. Rice grains had also been tossed in and blended with the dust and ash. But, he noted, the money was gone—no bills, no coins. He pulled out a small pocket camera from his jacket pocket and pretended to take pictures of the guards standing and sitting in front of the pyre, but he actually focused on certain parts of the pyre.

Before long, Mohan returned to Jonathan. "Let's go, sir, please. These guys are butchers."

"Just a couple more minutes, Mohan. Almost done."

Mohan peered over his shoulder. "I'm curious, sir. What are you looking for?"

"Look there, Mohan. On the burnt end of that big log there. What do you see?"

"Nothing, sir."

"Nothing?" Jonathan probed with the fire poker.

"Oh, that. That's a coconut, sir."

"That big?" Jonathan knocked off the ash with the fire poker. The round object came tumbling down to his feet. Mohan drew in his breath. The object was clearly a skull. It grinned up at them. Mohan shrieked. Jonathan bent down quickly to examine it more closely, but Mohan's shriek had alerted the guards and they were quickly approaching, yelling at them. Jonathan heard the click of a rifle bolt being thrown.

Mohan regained control of himself enough to advance toward the guards, a nervous smile displayed and speaking in a sheepish tone. "No problem, brother. No problem." Mohan bobbed his head. "Really. I grabbed a pinch of ash to sanctify my forehead. But there was an ember inside. Stupid me!"

The guards snickered, easily convinced. One of them chastised Mohan. *Salley Phattoo!*: "Coward jerk!"

Jonathan hastily took advantage of the opportunity to examine the skull for signs of violence. He noted missing upper incisors and a fracture on the vault. The wound was serious enough to have rendered the person unconscious—possibly enough to kill. The skull could not be that of the husband. He had died a natural death. Jonathan photographed the remains.

He moved to the left, found a thighbone and took another picture. There was enough left of the bodies for a forensics examination. He had to tell Joshi. He called to his companion. "Mohan, let's go. I'm all set."

They thanked the guards, with whom Mohan seemed to have become fast friends, and took an alternate route back to Buttasingh's home. Just before arriving there, Mohan said, "Sir, I have something for you."

"What's that, Mohan?"

Mohan pulled something from his pocket and showed it to Jonathan. It was a jackknife with a mirror-bright polished blade.

"Rampuri knife." Mohan looked proud.

"Doesn't that belong to the police chief?" Jonathan said, puzzled.

Mohan smiled wryly. "I think it might. How did it come to me?"

"Let me guess. He was so pleased with you, he said: 'Mohan, here—.'"

Mohan laughed. "Remember the boulder that tripped you? It was lying right beside it."

Jonathan paused to think, feeling grateful toward his new friend. "You were right," he said. "This mission was dangerous. In fact, my friend, I believe someone in this village is a killer."

"If there were only one, sir," Mohan said, "I would be very surprised. Truly."

"Hmm, how tall, do you think, was Seeta?"

"I don't know sir, but all Indian women are short—like five-two, five-three. Why?"

"And her husband?"

"Same. Maybe two inches taller. Maybe."

"How tall are you?"

"Me? Five-foot-six. Why?"

"I know that poor girl was burnt; I saw a lot of small bones. I saw a femur there—I mean a thighbone."

"No surprise, sir," said bemused Mohan. You should have seen four thighbones. Two people. Remember, sir. Two people burnt."

"Yeah . . ." Jonathan was lost in thoughts. "Except . . ."

"Except?"

"Except it was too long to belong to a short woman—or a short man."

chapter seven

Jonathan awoke at five-thirty in the morning and peeped through the window. The peacocks crowed, cows mooed and the shepherds' calls urged on the slow moving buffalo. Before long, the muezzin's chant of *Allahu-Akbar* . . . *Allahu-Akbar,* calling Muslims for early morning prayer, blended with the jangle of the temple bells.

Women with their heads and mouths covered by gray saris and men in turbans went about their daily business. The early morning haze thickened with the dust from the street sweeper's bristled broom and the hammering hooves of passing cattle. Then, with the first ray of sunrise, the peacocks calmed, the herd disappeared and the fog burnt away. And hope rose in Jonathan's heart.

After a quick morning tea, Joshi, Mohan and Jonathan headed for the post office.

"Hello!" Joshi roared into the phone at his secretary. "Hello, K.C.? Are you awake? . . . K.C., listen. It has been one hell of a trip. Say a prayer for us, will you?" Joshi related the unexpected collapse of the bridge and hinted of some mysterious findings, but declined to elaborate in front of the postmaster. "We must talk in person. We are taking a detour via the upper bridge of the Vasundhara. I hope to be home by noon. Have Mishraji keep lunch ready."

When he stepped out of the office, Jonathan was unhappily surprised to see a jeep parked behind his car. The original color of the jeep was hard to discern because of peeling paint, rust and dents.

One of the occupants disembarked.

Joshi cringed. "Bholanath? What are you doing here?"

"Maalik, all of us were worried sick," the priest said with folded hands. "The road to the upper bridge is terrible. We thought in case you run into—"

"Bholanath," Joshi said. "I do appreciate your concern, but let me assure you, we will be taken care of in case of an accident or anything of that sort. I just spoke to New Delhi."

"Oh . . . Still, Maalik, please allow us to escort you—only up to the bridge. We will return after that. Even our scriptures say, *Atithee Devo Bhava*: Guests are angels. We must protect you from any harm. Please, Judge Sahb."

Joshi glared at the pujaree. "You are a stubborn man, Bholanath. Suit yourself."

Joshi started toward the car, then stopped and wagged a finger. "Only up to the bridge. Is that clear?"

As Mohan turned the ignition on, his and Jonathan's eyes met in the rear view mirror. It was time to tell Joshi just how dangerous these people could be. When the car picked up momentum, Joshi turned toward Jonathan. "Interesting trip, isn't it?"

Jonathan looked back through the rear window. "What are they up to now?"

"Silly rural customs. First the welcome goes on forever. Then the good-bye never ends. Obstinate people."

Jonathan raised his eyebrows. "Just obstinate?"

"I know what you mean. Let's talk about it. What is your take here, Jonathan?"

"Well . . . I think you, Judge Sahb, have made some observation as to—"

"Yes, I have, I have. Let me first hear from you. I shouldn't bias you with my findings." He smiled at Jonathan. "Occupational hazard, you might say."

"Well . . ." Jonathan exhaled hard. "First and foremost, I'm not certain which it was, but I fear one of the people on that pyre was not a volunteer."

"Of course, the husband was—what did you find?"

Jonathan then told Joshi about their discovery of the large, fractured skull with missing upper incisors.

"Good lord!" Joshi's eyes widened. "Are you sure? And what on earth were you doing there in the dark of night? Mohan!"

Mohan cowered but offered nothing in his defense.

"Listen, Judge Joshi," Jonathan continued. "I have pictures. Mohan distracted the guards to allow me the opportunity to do so."

"That is splendid!" Joshi said, trying to contain his enthusiasm. "Both of you deserve tremendous credit—but it was nevertheless a foolish thing to do."

The other two were silent.

"All right," Joshi said, "let me have that camera. Important evidence. I know you have a lot to say about the four men."

"You mean the filthy four?"

"Yes, very apt."

"They set up the whole thing just to sucker the poor villagers and make money."

"And the old man?" asked Joshi.

"Bapuji? Him I'm not sure of. He looked sincere, but nervous. Yet he told us the suttee decided to kill herself after her husband died."

"Yes, and rumors were circulating long before then. Do you think he is in on it?"

"I think he's a half-hearted player. Perhaps forced to play."

"I see. And who do you think is the leader? If there was a victim, who do you think ordered the murder?"

"I don't know. It's confusing. First I thought it was that councilman."

"Anything is possible, but to me, he seemed more like a family man. That sort."

"Can't rule out the police chief. You see, there's this . . ." Jonathan pulled out the knife from his pants pocket. Jonathan recounted the altercation with the bandits of the previous night.

Joshi examined the weapon. "I would bet that this belongs to the police chief."

"Yes, I think he used it to free the struggling lamb at Bapuji's hut."

"It's an army issue," Joshi said, "not available to civilians."

"Jalim Singh claimed that he fought in Pakistan," Jonathan said.

"But this looks newer than that. Perhaps he has his own access to governmental weapons?"

Jonathan nodded. "Or maybe it's just a new knife, or maybe it's his and he keeps all his weapons squeaky clean."

"What did you think of the barber?" Joshi continued.

"I thought he was the sneakiest, most slippery of them all. He may not have social status, but he's brainy. That could serve him well." Jonathan answered, thrilled with the role of detective. "And leaders need to plot and plan."

Joshi sighed, then laughed. "This is getting complex, isn't it? The same could be said of the pujaree, Bholanath."

"I know."

"And that's not the end of it," Joshi said. "There could be a fifth person! Someone we'd never suspect."

"So what do you do?"

"The first step is to secure the pyre, prevent tampering of evidence. Second, witnesses. We need to contact those who have seen something and are afraid to talk. We need to interview ordinary villagers, especially women. Women always know other women's business. Now, from the medical point of view, wouldn't the bones be charred from the intense heat by now?"

"That depends on the intensity of the heat and the length of the exposure. If you noticed, Judge Sahb, the fire burned mostly around the periphery, while the central ash-mound just smoldered with smoke. From what I could see last night, most of the bones have survived."

"I see . . . I see." Joshi nodded. "It sounds plausible."

"What we must do immediately is seek help from forensic medicine. What do you call the crime-solving branch of the government?"

"CBI—Central Bureau of Investigation."

"We should have the CBI analyze the bones for age, gender, and any indications of trauma or violence."

After a while, the Vasundhara Bridge appeared. "Mohan," Joshi said, "toot the horn. Let's say good-bye . . . this time for good!"

Mohan tooted, and the jeep turned around.

"Thank heavens," sighed Joshi. "It is an uncomfortable feeling being followed toward the only route of exit by people whom you suspect of serious crimes."

"I was half expecting them to run us down," Jonathan said. "It's a good thing you mentioned that you had spoken with your office."

"Yes. It left them guessing as to how much we knew and how much we'd reported. Not even knowing what you found out, I thought the precaution was justified."

"They wouldn't go back and talk to that postmaster, would they?"

"Perhaps. But we should be long gone by then. I hope. You have not been seeing my country at its best, I'm afraid."

"Well, perhaps when I get to the Ashram—"

"Not likely. Remember, you will be dealing with a clinic for abused women. Some of it . . . may not be pretty."

They drove in silence for a while, enjoying the scenery. But before long, Mohan said, "Judge Sahb, we have a problem."

The Ambassador dipped into the slope down toward a shallow dry creek bed and then emerged on the other side. There, in front of them, the road was strewn with boulders.

"Roadblock," Mohan said.

"Yes, and behind us is a fast approaching vehicle," Jonathan said, turning.

"They must have spoken to the postmaster," Joshi said, stiffening in his seat. "Jonathan, I am so sorry for having gotten you into this."

"Look, the other car is still pretty far back. Let's move some of these boulders. We can do it. Come on, Mohan." Before Joshi could object, they had cleared the smaller boulders in the center. They'd still need to move one of the extremely heavy ones to make enough room for the car to pass. But hard as they struggled, they couldn't get it out of the way. The car following them was not close enough to identify, but its outline was that of some type of a jeep.

Certain that the driver had more than conversation on his mind, Jonathan desperately tried to think of a way to move the boulder. On the shoulder, he spotted some dry limbs. But as he reached for them, a movement caught his eye. There it was—standing, hood up and ready to strike, the deadly poisonous King Cobra!

"Easy . . . easy," he whispered, not sure to whom.

The snake swayed his hooded head, the white-ribbed trachea distended, his forked tongue tasting the air with rapid fire. Jonathan stopped blinking. Any abrupt move could be a lethal mistake. He could hear the vehicle in the distance, struggling steadily along the rough road.

Then he thought of his father. His words echoed in Jonathan's ears, *Son, most animals are afraid of us. As long as we do not mean to harm them, we have nothing to fear from them.*

His eyes burned from staring unblinkingly and he could hold out no longer. When he opened his eyes, the cobra was gone.

"Thank God . . ." he exhaled, feeling oddly close to his father. He lowered his head.

"Doc Sahb!"

The voice, coming from behind, was familiar and hearty. He turned. There, beside their vehicle stood the silhouette of a man with his arms wide open, and three other burly figures standing beside him. Who could they be?

"Who are you?" Jonathan asked.

The stranger walked down the slope, smiling. "Doc Sahb." He patted his chest. "Gopal."

Of course! Gopal, Buttasingh's neighbor, with the dying mother! They'd been journeying on foot.

"Oh yes . . . yes." Jonathan said, a surge of relief passing through him. Gopal and his men quickly hauled the tree limbs up the bank, shoved them under the boulder and rolled it off the road.

Once again at the wheel, Mohan turned the key. "It won't start!" he yelped. "Looks like it's overheated."

Jonathan looked back. The beat-up Jeep was just entering the dry streambed behind them. Eyes squinting, Gopal followed Jonathan's gaze and mumbled something.

"He says, 'bad trouble.'" Mohan said. "Sir, sometimes if we roll the car . . ."

"Right."

Jonathan grabbed the back window frame and tried to push the car forward. In no time again, Gopal and his men rushed to his aid and rolled the car forward as if it were a toy. Mohan popped the clutch. The car sputtered. Then the motor fired and the car caught speed.

"Thank you, Gopal! Take care of your mother!" Jonathan shouted to the men still running alongside their vehicle.

"Godspeed, Doc Sahb," Gopal shouted back, his hands folded together in the air.

Through a thin cloud of dust behind them, Jonathan and Joshi could see Gopal and his men standing in the middle of the road and forcing the oncoming vehicle to halt.

"Thank God for Gopal," said Jonathan as they sped away.

"He got the medicines, you know," said Joshi. "His mother awoke this morning a new woman. He'll be indebted to you forever."

They kept their eyes glued on the road behind them for several miles and soon were greatly relieved to see the narrow road merge with the finished two-way road to New Delhi.

But then on the outskirts of New Delhi, the Ambassador stalled again. Permanently. From a nearby gas station, Joshi notified his office about the location of the abandoned vehicle and ordered an air-conditioned taxi. They headed for home.

K.C. met them at the door in his crisp cotton kurta and dhoti. Joshi greeted him and then introduced Jonathan. Mishraji came running with the rest of his entourage and followed them into the living room. They stood there, smiling at the trio who had returned safely.

"Mishraji," Joshi told the overwhelmed chef, "didn't you have enough of our ghostly faces?" He shook the dust from his hair and shoulders. "Get K.C. Sahb some tea. We must bathe first. I feel like a filthy rag."

Mishraji nodded and scurried toward the kitchen.

"K.C., most important," Joshi said, "get on the phone and get hold of our guy at CBI. Ask him to dispatch enough men—armed and equipped photographers, forensic chaps, the whole team—right away. Tell them to move fast before the thugs fix or destroy the evidence."

"Right away, your honor." K.C. rose to trigger the wave of action.

The judge rose too. "One more thing. Apprehend the four men I described—on sight."

In half an hour, even after rejoicing in the cold, leisurely shower, Jonathan was too preoccupied to sit down for lunch. Instead, under the shade of a trellis, he opened his journal.

My dear Rebecca,

How can I describe the immense satisfaction of this journey? Thank you so much for inspiring me to proceed with all of this work. Some would contend I have no business being here, but I feel I have a valuable purpose here. I have a chance to combat the ill effects of those who prey on women, the sick and the young ones. Yes, I can foresee the risk, and yet I find the risk empowers me. I was feeling tired every which way, but since my arrival, I have not had a single dull moment. India is special. Its people are special, chock full of heroes, villains and victims, but nobody gives up. They move only in one direction—forward! I am so fortunate to have met Joshi and Mohan.

Becka, honey, I am thinking of you. I think of you all the time—"

Jonathan paused as he saw Joshi approaching. "Well, we made it," he said. "Doesn't that feel good?"

Jonathan rose with a wide smile. "You bet."

"Calls for a celebration. What do you say, Jonathan?"

"Absolutely!"

"What would you like to have?" Joshi gleamed with joy.

"Some tea would be nice."

"Nonsense! That's no celebration." Joshi yelled at the gardener, "Ramdev, have Mohan bring two glasses of Chivas. And some roasted cashews."

"How is your breathing now?" Jonathan asked.

"Fine." Joshi sat down and sighed a relief. "Oh, that nap was invigorating."

The phone rang inside the house. Jonathan looked back, wistfully, unready to hear any bad news about his mother's health.

It was for Joshi, Mohan said. Joshi excused himself and went in. Within five minutes he returned, looking smug.

"That was a lady from the Ashram. Archaic, audacious and blissful." Joshi laughed. "I trust you are aware that there are no phones, radios, electricity, none of the necessary evils we call civilization at the Ashram. Poor lady was calling from the foothill post office an hour and ten kilometers away."

"What did she say, Judge Sahb?"

"An English woman, Kate Brown. She had a message from the spiritual head of the hermitage, Swamiji. The long and the short of the whole saga: heavy rain in the foothills damaged the track to the Ashram, and it will take a few days to be rebuilt. In the interim, Swamiji advises you to explore India—to understand the plight of the poor and to study the extremes. India is a living school of life and death. That was his message."

"India? What part of India?"

"I know. Your question is quite valid. 'India is a living school of life and death.' How apt, and yet he is only suggesting what I said earlier. Yet, of course, he is absolutely one hundred percent correct."

Jonathan looked at Joshi, perplexed.

"You see," Joshi said, "life and death are two opposite sides of the same coin. One so nurturing, the other so destructive. And yet the coin keeps rolling."

"I know what you mean," Jonathan said.

"And I think that's what Swamiji meant. You have seen the poverty, death and suttee. Now see the opulence and grandeur. My dear friend, India is so vast, so poor, so diverse, so disorderly and yet so humbling. When you study India, you will be convinced there is a God, because only God can run India."

"You know, it is ironic. Here I am, in India. And I'm supposed to see a bit more of it soon. I had never planned such a trip for myself, but Becka—I had always promised to take her. I wish I had kept that promise."

"Regrets are painful," said Joshi sympathetically. But in a moment he brightened. "But this is a time for celebration. Mohan!"

When Mohan arrived, Joshi said, "Jonathan, you must forgive me for not going with you on the tour, but I have to meet with the CBI and Mrs. Gandhi's secretary about the suttee."

"Of course."

Joshi instructed Mohan to take Jonathan to historic old Delhi to see "drama in real life."

Jonathan soon tuned out the tour itinerary. He had no real interest in sightseeing. He was feeling too agitated and sad thinking about the suttee. And Becka. And Becka so badly wanted to see India. Jonathan had promised to show her India. He never kept his promise.

Becka had always fought for life, even if she'd lost that fight in the end.

Suddenly, he remembered the cat and smiled gently. It had somehow found its way to their backdoor. As it sat, mostly bones, barely audible in the winter wind, Becka had heard it. It had taken a while for them to locate the little fellow, but once she had her hands on him, Baggy, as he came to be known, would never again want for food or comfort. His right front paw had been mangled somehow, and although it hadn't appeared that he had been in a fight or hit by a car, he had some deep cuts up and down two legs. Her nursing training and natural ability had been the cat's physical salvation; Becka's heart had been his rebirth. Within two weeks, one couldn't even tell that the little animal had ever been wounded. And like a puppy, it never left Becka's side. Baggy cried when she went to work, and greeted her at the door when she returned. More than once, he presented her with gifts of the highest levels from the feline world: freshly killed field mice in the winter, and moths in the summer.

Jonathan chuckled softly remembering Becka's discovery of the first "gift."

"Well . . ." she'd said, tempering her voice as if speaking to an adult human, "what a . . . thoughtful gift!"

"I don't think you'll hurt his feelings if you say you'd rather he kept them outside," Jonathan had teased her.

"I wouldn't be so sure," she said, laughing, and stroking the little cat. "I think when he was sick, he must have spent his time studying English."

As Jonathan sat there, resting in the Indian afternoon, he thought of Becka in winter on their worn, comfortable couch; Baggy in her lap, a cup of coffee in her hand, and a smile for him.

That was life.

He realized Joshi had asked him a question. "Pardon me?"

"I asked what you thought of the plan."

Jonathan stood up. "I think you're right. I'll see you when we return."

When Joshi left, Jonathan began thinking about his strange involvement in the suttee case. It had developed from conversation, to curiosity, to concern and now a mission. To what, he wondered, would it lead him?

"Gutergoo . . . gutergoo . . ." He saw two doves busy building a nest in the brick wall above Swamiji's portrait. Soon the doves flew away. Jonathan replaced a straw that had fallen from the nest. He stood there, blissful, staring at the saint. The sage's big eyes and the smile seemed to radiate mystical sensations.

chapter eight

The next morning, Mohan appeared after breakfast in a matching pair of what appeared to be home-pressed gray cotton bush shirt and pants. His open-toe sandals were polished, and his feet were clean. His 5'6" frame carried a heavy shoulder bag with a camera and other tourist paraphernalia, which he neatly tucked away in the trunk of their rental car—a more respectable looking British Morris.

Their first stop was an impressively expansive monument resembling the Taj Mahal.

"Sir, this is Humayunka Makbara—meaning King Humayun's tomb or mausoleum. His wife built it when he died. And this is her tomb." Mohan pointed at a second monument made of red and white sandstone and black and yellow marble.

"Wonderful monuments," Jonathan said. "What beautiful, immortal memorials of a wife and a husband." Then, as though he wanted to record the moment for Becka, he took a picture. How, he wondered, could this be the same culture that produced suttee?

On their way to Red Fort, they stopped for lunch at Chandni Chowlk. The square was densely packed with shoppers and sellers. Aromas of the fried onions and garlic drew them to a snack shop. After enjoying some freshly fried Mughlai Samosas and steaming tea, they drove toward Red Fort, a massive, walled fort made, aptly, of red sandstone.

"Sir, this elegant fort was built in 1648," Mohan said. "This barbican, sir, was added by King Aurangzeb against the will of his imprisoned father, who told him, 'Why did you throw a veil over the face of a palace and make a bride out of it?'"

"Make a bride out of it. An interesting comparison," said Jonathan.

"Yes," Mohan continued. "And the centerpiece was a magnificent peacock throne made of solid gold with peacocks behind it. The beautiful colors resulted from countless inlaid precious stones. The figure of a parrot is the center, carved from a single emerald.

It was carted off to Iran by Nadirshah, in 1739, where it was broken up and taken to Tehran, where it was rebuilt and displayed."

At the intersection, Mohan rolled up the windows, as the professionally maimed beggars and pesky street vendors surrounded their car. Jonathan looked at them sympathetically and thought of the extremes of India. On one side, the massive fort that once represented the grandeur and glory of the Mughal Kingdom, broken in many places, but still standing tall; across from it, the great Jama Masjid. And between them, men and boys begging for pennies.

A boy, who looked no older than ten, hawked newspapers. He flashed the front page of the *Capital Times* at Jonathan. "Bride-burning in Baramedi."

Jonathan quickly rolled the window down and looked at the front page, which bore Joshi's picture. He fished out a five-rupee bill from his pants pocket and purchased the newspaper. The article confirmed that a young village woman had become suttee. However, it also raised the question of whether it had been genuine, or possibly brought about by a gang's murderous greed and intent to defraud ignorant villagers into parting with their pittances in exchange for salvation. The newspaper had credited the success of the above revelation to the Supreme Court Judge—the Honorable Jayaprakash Joshi.

Mohan glanced quickly at the paper at traffic lights. "Did they print your picture, sir? Or . . . mine?"

"No, Mohan, I'm sorry. I know you worked very hard. They should have printed your picture."

"We both worked hard, sir. Mainly you."

Jonathan smiled warmly. "Are you married, Mohan?" asked Jonathan.

"Yes sir. Actually, my wife is pregnant."

"Wonderful! Congratulations. When did you meet your wife, Mohan?"

"At my wedding, sir."

"What?"

"When the Barat—the crowd of groom's people—goes to the bride's house after a marriage ceremony, they bring the bride to the groom's house the next day. I had never seen her before."

"Oh, I see. An arranged marriage."

Mohan shrugged. "That's the way in India. You get married first, then you fall in love."

Jonathan laughed.

"I know foreign people feel it's crazy," Mohan said. "But when you know there is no way out, nothing called divorce, you work it out. You become dependent on each other. Call it love. Whatever."

"You're right, Mohan. Human nature is very finicky. Given many choices, it hops around like a butterfly. Given one choice, it adapts. Mohan, getting back to the suttee, what about the education? I'm sure that would help—."

"Are you joking, sir?" Mohan interrupted. "If the girl is educated, even a little bit, in that caste, she is even more of a burden."

"How's that?"

"Because now the old, uneducated farmer says, 'Oh, now she is going to tell us what to do. Talk back to us. Disrespect us. Now she will say no to milking the cows, making dung patties for fuel, cook, clean . . . make babies—she'll be useless."

"And with regard to dowry-death, how does the society look the other way? And how are police so easily bribed? Is it possible that Seeta was killed because of her meager dowry?"

"In that class, anything is possible, sir. In poor villages, even the scripture favors boys. In older days, when they spoke Sanskrit, if someone wanted to bless a woman, they would say, '*Shatputra bhava.*' That means 'May you bear hundred sons.' Not daughters—sons."

Jonathan shook his head.

"I think the words of one villager put it in clear terms: 'Bringing up a girl is like watering someone else's plant. When the plant grows up, it belongs to someone else's family, not yours. It's a stupid waste of investment.'"

"Will this be your first child?"

"No sir, fifth. Four girls, so far. We pray this one is a son."

"I also wish for you and your wife that it's a boy. What if it's a girl?"

"Lord's will, sir. We will love her equally the same, sir."

"That is a wonderful attitude, Mohan. You and your wife are wonderful people." Jonathan sighed and stared at the clouds.

Mohan asked, "Are you all right sir?"

"Yeah . . . I'm okay." He looked at Mohan. "I just can't stop thinking about that poor . . . suttee. Something . . . strange. Suspicious."

chapter nine

The next day, they drove to Rajasthan—the land of Rajahs and Maharajahs, of kings and castles, of palaces and striking penury, but most importantly of all, the land of sutteeism.

"Yes," Mohan said, "this is where most of the suttee cases occurred."

"What made it so common here, particularly?" Jonathan asked as they enjoyed their elaborate breakfast at the Rambaugh Palace Hotel.

"Because the Rajputs, the fierce warriors, were very proud people. But the Rajputs were disorganized, outnumbered and poorly equipped. So when the warrior husbands died or were defeated by moguls, the wives jumped into burning flames to save honor. They preferred death to being a mogul's slave or a concubine."

A waiter interrupted with a call for Jonathan from Judge Joshi.

"New developments in the suttee case," Joshi said. "I am afraid the thugs may be a step ahead of us. It seems Councilman

Buttasingh was questioned, and has divulged that perhaps Murli, the barber is guilty of our suspicions."

"So fast! That's excellent news. So how are they a step ahead?"

"The barber has disappeared."

"I see. What about the pujaree, Bholanath and the police chief?"

"Buttasingh says they had nothing to do with it, but he did help us arrest them."

"Really?"

"Yes, but before his arrest, Bholanath informed us that, per the suttee's wishes, at the hundredth hour of cremation all the contents of the pyre—bones, logs, ashes, and all—were dispersed into the waters of Vasundhara, which merges with the holy Ganges down the plains."

"The evidence is gone?"

"Except for your photos, which, I'm afraid, aren't enough. I made a mistake—an egregious mistake—in not securing that site myself."

"So what's next, Judge Sahb—if I may ask?"

"Of course. We are not done yet. CBI's men are canvassing the farms and villages, looking for witnesses. The people are terrified, but there is always a chance that someone will be angry or scared enough to talk. So how do you like Rajasthan so far?"

"It is a very dry and somewhat inhospitable state, but people still have that romantic sense of pride and honor."

"Rajasthanis are the most colorful people. Don't forget to photograph them. You'll see men with pastel-colored turbans and soup-strainer mustaches, and women wearing chunky silver ornaments and dresses of vivid colors. Cameras love them. *Life Magazine*'s staples."

"My camera is ready, Judge Sahb."

"Good. Now tell Mohan to take you to the Thar Desert. It's called the oasis of magic and romance. If you have time and energy left, see Jaisalmer. The place is a fantasy right out of *A Thousand and One Nights*." Joshi paused for a moment, then said softly, "and Jonathan . . . please be careful. We may not be able to convict them, but we've robbed the Baramedi gang of their profits, and most likely of the suttee temple. No one builds temples to murder victims. So the income they planned on will not materialize."

"You think they may come after me?"

"One can never be too careful with evil villains like these. They make powerful enemies."

"Don't worry, I'll be careful, Judge Sahb. Thank you."

The evening passed uneventfully. However, the next morning, when they drove into the parking lot of Akbar the Great's palace in Sikri, Jonathan spotted a beat-up jeep that looked familiar.

Jonathan studied the vehicle without alerting Mohan who was, to Jonathan's relief, greeted by a former classmate turned guide. His classmate was seated in the next jeep, awaiting the return of his customers.

As Jonathan studied the jeep from a distance, he was at a loss. It was ridiculous. How could it be the same one? And how would they even know that he was there? Did they have an insider? A mole?

"Mohan, you go ahead and visit with your friend. I'm going to stroll around on my own."

"Oh, no, sir, I will accompany you."

"I'm okay, really," Jonathan insisted. "I won't be long."

Mohan's friend was delighted and Jonathan wandered inside quickly, preferring a little time to think time on his own.

The mosque, for some reason, was roped off. When Jonathan drew a stern look from the big, burly guard, he realized that instead of studying the stunning architecture, he was studying the people. The guard must have suspected that he was a pickpocket. He shook his head, smiled at the guard and continued on.

The hallway leading to the outside was long and dark, with the bright sunlight glaring through the tunnel-like passage. Jonathan brought his camera from his shoulder bag. When he looked up, what he saw at the exit made him freeze.

It was the outline of a man in uniform - a familiar uniform; the police hat, the gun holster and the loops on the shoulders. Jonathan felt his heart racing, remembering his friend's warning only a day before. His breathing turned shallow. He had nothing to defend himself with, and there was only the long passageway between the two of them.

Suddenly, Jonathan remembered that he did have a weapon of sorts. With lightning speed, he raised the eyepiece to his camera and looked through the viewfinder. But he needed to get closer. He raced forward.

Jonathan made his way out of the exit, struggling to adjust to the light. He could see no movement on either side or ahead of him. But then he caught it! The edge of a boot, a steel boot glinting in the sunlight. As he started toward his target, it rose and darted from behind a bush and sprinted around a corner. Not sure what he'd do if he caught up with him, Jonathan began to give chase as best he could under the circumstances.

Just then, he heard a shrill, piercing scream. He looked straight ahead to see a little girl hurtling through the air, still clutching the disengaged rope swing on which she had been joyfully swinging a moment before. Instinctively, Jonathan headed toward the girl as her little companion ran for their parents.

Fortunately, she had landed in a thick myrtle hedge. Her nose bled and her shoulder was badly bruised but there would be no lasting injury. Jonathan gently picked up the girl and gently held his handkerchief to her little nose.

"So, are you doing a little flying today," he asked smiling, knowing that she couldn't understand English.

Her parents arrived and he handed over the injured girl, explaining as best he could that she would be all right. They thanked him repeatedly as he backed away nodding and heading for the parking lot.

When they reached Agra, Jonathan looked at his watch. It was already a little after six. The plan was to see the Taj Mahal at night, under the moonlight. The Taj looked its best then, according to everyone he had talked to.

Everyone was right. When he went through the high-arched entrance, Jonathan stood frozen. Under the moonlight, the Taj looked so pure, so white, so magnificent. Slowly, Jonathan walked closer to the great edifice. He saw couples hand in hand, some hugging, some kissing. They were all quiet, some just cried. A man said to his lady, "I love you my darling. Don't ever leave me again. I'll die without you."

Jonathan ascended the stairs and went behind the Taj. Yamuna's dark waters shimmered under the moon. He put the wedding band on his index finger and made sure when he took the picture that the ring touched the shutter.

Becka. And all the immortal, sweet memories. He looked at a couple and they became he and Becka. He held her hand, embracing and kissing her. Becka's hearty laughter echoed over the Yamuna Valley, her smile made more luminous by the moon. But soon, she seemed to be walking towards the edge of the cliff, smiling, waving at him.

Jonathan ran to her, screaming. "No! Becka, no! Turn around. Come back...please."

"Are you all right sir," the man asked.

Bewildered, Jonathan stared at the couple, now themselves again.

"Yes, I'm...I'm fine. Thank you," he said.

The man patted Jonathan's back and said, "take care." Then the couple walked away.

Jonathan turned around to leave, but still shaken up, turned the wrong way, stumbled down a few steps and landed on a flat corner of the Taj. Promptly, he rose but the excruciating pain along his shinbone made him sit down.

"Here, hold this staff."

Jonathan looked up to see a sadhu seated in the corner. But...it wasn't just a sadhu. It was that familiar saintly face, flowing white beard, large watchful eyes and mystical but blissful smile.

"Swamiji?"

"Take the support of this staff my son and climb the steps. It's all right. We all need a little support sometimes."

Jonathan wanted to ask him who he was and if they had ever met before. But the pain in his leg was so unbearable; he just grabbed the staff and went up four steps. Then he extended the staff back to the sadhu and thanked him.

"My son, don't thank me." The sadhu pointed skyward. "Thank God. He is the one."

The next morning, Mohan drove them back to New Delhi. They arrived at Joshi's residence in the late evening. Jonathan took a good long shower and quickly made a journal entry before joining Joshi for dinner.

My dearest Becka,

"I saw India's glorious past. Relics and regalia of that great era that saw their masters' lust for grandeur, power and fame. Now all that's left is the destitute, living on a day-to-day basis—breathing polluted air, pulling rickshaws, carrying fellow humans on the cluttered streets of old renaissance cities. There are makeshift shanties right along massive walls of the Red Fort. Oh, how I wish you were here. You'd have absolutely loved the whole spectacle.

On the other hand, I know you were with me. You're always with me in spirit. And those royal lovers, the kings and queens of India, I hope they are with each other too, smiling at their immortal edifices—the tokens of their love, their devotion for each other.

chapter ten

It was Jonathan's last night at Joshi's. He was filled with mixed emotions. New Delhi was supposed to have been only a brief stopover on his way to the Ashram. In the beginning, he had not known how to take Joshi. But by his last day, he had come to feel not only welcome and at home there, but almost more of a partner than a guest. He knew, even when he settled down at the Ashram, that he would not forget New Delhi, Joshi and Mohan. And most importantly, he would never forget the suttee case—solved or not. He knew that the young woman was only one victim in a society that regularly victimized women, but somehow the callousness of her particular murder, and the carnival that had surrounded it, had made an indelible impression on his heart.

When he descended for dinner, Jonathan saw Joshi standing in front of his wife's portrait, a drink in his hand. Joshi greeted Jonathan and settled down into his impressive, overstuffed Victorian chair.

"That is a beautiful chair," Jonathan said, taking a seat across from Joshi.

"Thank you very much." Joshi rubbed his palms over the silk padding of the arms. "It was a gift from my wife . . . on my fiftieth birthday." He stood and walked toward his wife's portrait, pulled a handkerchief from his pocket and dusted the frame's upper rim. For a few seconds, he just stood there, looking at the portrait, his hands tightly clasped behind him, his knuckles pale.

Jonathan spoke. "My wife loves antique furniture. Loved it, I should say."

"Yes, it's hard to remember they're gone sometimes, isn't it?" Joshi slowly turned to Jonathan and sat down. "Actually, the chair is a mélange of several different cultures. The frame is made of ebonized wood, as in your Philadelphia rockers. The seat is overstuffed, Turkish style. Its high, padded backrest is upholstered like the popular Empire Gondole chair, and I'm told it resembles French Bergère."

Animated and childlike, Joshi got up and pointed to the legs of the chair. "See," he said. "It has cabriole fashioned front legs. Now look at the back legs. Their curves are reversed to prevent tipping over. That is a Victorian feature, allowing comfort to supersede elegance. Clever, isn't it?"

Jonathan approached for a closer view. "Absolutely. And what is this scene embroidered on the back?"

"It's Lord Krishna dancing with the milk maidens from Gokul—his birth place. Indian mythology. And, oh, I forgot. The entire fabric is Kashmiri silk. The rug it is resting upon is made of Persian wool."

"Sir . . . I'm sorry." Mohan said from the doorway. "Khana is ready."

"Shall we do some justice to dinner?"

"Let me guess." Jonathan sniffed. "Biriyani . . . beef biriyani."

"Good gracious!' said Joshi. "You are a *Chhupa Rustom*—one who knows a lot but always keeps quiet."

"It's your nephew, Suresh's fault. Every time Becka and I visited him, beef biriyani and raita was our standing request. And when it came to spices, Becka always outdid me. I mostly sniffed and sweated."

"Well, we'll see how you do tonight," Joshi said. "I'm very sorry to disappoint you though—no cow meat here." He paused for a moment. "Candidly speaking, I had my share of beef, pork, frog legs—you name it—during my law school days in England. But since my wife passed away, I haven't touched beef. She did not appreciate my gluttonous consumption of it."

The dinner was an elaborate, aromatic feast. The first course consisted of Kachoris, stuffed with green Toor-lentils, and Indian-style tomato soup served with baked cumin-papperdum.

"Delicious," Jonathan said.

"Are you sure it is not too spicy for you?"

Within seconds Jonathan began to sweat.

Joshi ordered one of the servants to shut off the ceiling fan. Then he turned to Jonathan. "It's a big bloody rotor. Makes a monster of a noise and all it does is swirl the hot air in circles. You'll enjoy the Khas-tatti punkha—the manual fan, I mean."

Jonathan looked up. Hung from the ceiling was a two-by-six foot screen of matted root tendrils of a Khas plant that a servant was spraying with water from a bottle.

The servant then kneeled on the alabaster floor and pulled the rope to and fro.

Within a few seconds Jonathan experienced an exhilarating coolness and his profuse sweating ceased. That drew a big proud smile from the punkha operator.

"Remarkable," Jonathan said. "I like your help. They all look so happy."

"Thank you. I know having servants in the house is not interpreted very kindly in the west—promotes servitude and renders their minds servile and so forth. But you see over here, the societal dynamics are quite different. Unemployment is rampant, and a college education means nothing. Mohan has a B. A. This . . ."

He pointed at the servants. "This could be viewed as perfect social symbiosis. They get employment and the employer gets cheap labor. It's far better than bloody begging, purse-snatching, or pilfering."

Fortunately Jonathan didn't have to respond to Judge Joshi's contention, because he called Mohan and the other servants and introduced them to Jonathan. The servants dropped their tasks and rushed to their master, hurriedly arranging their turbans, stretching their coats, and stroking lint off themselves.

Jonathan observed that the servants while bringing dishes from the kitchen mumbled to each other in Hindi and wore smiles that ranged anywhere from nervousness to levity. It was a comfortable, peaceful, well-run household.

Joshi raised his head when the biriyani arrived. "Can you smell it? Mishraji's flagship dish—layers of sautéed onions, lamb cooked in special garam-masala, yogurt and basmati rice." Then he pointed at a bowl. "And your raita: yogurt, shredded cucumber, red pomegranate seeds, lemon juice and salt. It cools the biriyani's fire. And if that's not enough . . ." He grabbed a tall brown bottle of Taj Mahal beer. "This will do it. There is nothing like cold beer with Indian food."

Jonathan chugged down half a glass of beer. "It hits the spot."

Both laughed as Joshi poured more beer for Jonathan.

In the middle of the meal, wiping his runny nose, his face red and perspiring, Jonathan said, "Nice, spicy food."

"I'm pleased you like it. The chef will be most pleased to learn of your satisfaction. Oh, don't forget the cauliflower dish with parathas. Here."

Jonathan broke a piece of the flat bread. "What's the green on the paratha?"

"Mishraji loves to pound fresh mint, cilantro and basil onto his bread. Try it."

It was refreshingly wholesome.

In the end, when it came to carrot halva and shahi kheer, Jonathan said, "Judge Sahb, I'm stuffed. No room for dessert."

"Hmm . . . me too. Let's take a stroll. We'll have dessert and tea later."

Swiftly the servants removed their plates. In the living room, Joshi turned on a radio. Unexpectedly, and perhaps accidentally, the judge belched.

"Oops! I'm so sorry. It's a terrible habit—though okay by Indian gustatory norms. Belching after a good meal here is a complement to the host or the chef. You seem a bit pensive," Joshi went on. "Too many spices?"

"I'm sorry, I'm still thinking about that poor woman's tragedy. What about her family, her dreams? Did she have any children?"

"Sad, isn't it? I have the same questions. I'm most anxious to find answers."

"I sincerely hope you can. It seems that everything ends with cremation."

"Yes," Joshi said. "That is the whole point. You see, in Indian mythology, fire, especially the act of cremation, bears special significance. When you cremate the body, the soul is purified by the fire and leaves for the Swarga, or heaven. The mortal body, which essentially is nothing but a vehicle, must therefore blend away with the elements of nature. As you say, 'Ashes to ashes.'"

"Yes."

"We have a minority here in India. They are called Parsis or Zoroastrians, holdovers of an old Persian religion. Anyway, when one of these Parsis die, they don't believe in cremation or sepulcher. Instead they expose the entire body on the top of a tall tower so that the vultures can readily devour it."

Just then, Mohan walked in with a huge platter of carrot halva, shahi kheer and tea.

Joshi was startled. "I apologize for the unsavory juxtaposition of arrival of the dessert and my tale of vultures devouring a dead body," he said smiling slightly.

Mohan stopped, then headed back to the kitchen, mumbling apologies.

"Mohan, please come back," Jonathan said. "When I was in medical school, we used to dissect a cadaver and then go out to lunch. That's life."

Joshi laughed. "A case of occupational hazard, I suppose. All right, if you don't mind. Mohan, set up the dessert."

Hospitality in India, Jonathan observed, was a never-ending process.

"What you said about Parsis is interesting," Jonathan said. "Some Native American Indians, Apache and Cheyenne, follow the same death ritual."

Joshi said. "I was surprised to read somewhere that only ten percent of dead folks are cremated in the United States, versus twenty percent in Canada and as many as sixty percent in the United Kingdom."

Joshi laughed loudly and slurped down the rest of the tea. "There are two good things the British have learned from India: tea and cremation."

"Maalik," Mohan said. "The mechanic is on the phone. He says our car needs a new carburetor. He is awaiting your permission."

"What permission? Tell him to go ahead. Replace whatever needs to be replaced." Then he turned to Jonathan. "What a bloody clunker. Bet you have never seen such a metal monster in the States."

Jonathan laughed. "You'd be surprised. We have a bunch of them. My mother drives a real land yacht called an Edsel. A 1958 model. Judge Sahb, do you know the story about the Titanic and the Hindenburg?"

"No, I don't."

"Well, someone said God once complained to mankind, 'I gave you full and unconditional control over air, sea, and the land. And see what you did with them: Titanic, Hindenburg, and Edsel.'"

Joshi roared with laughter. "Oh, my, I haven't laughed like this in ages. When you're gone I am going to miss you."

"Sahb . . .," Mohan stood there holding a tray. "Drinks."

"All right, here we go. A toast to you." Joshi raised his glass.
"Toast to us." Jonathan raised his glass and looked at Mohan. "To the three of us."

chapter eleven

The judge personally went to the railway station to bid Jonathan goodbye.

"Look at them," he said, indicating the rushing passengers slowed down only by the weight of their possessions. "Traveling light is just not the Indian way. Like refugees, they are carrying everything but the kitchen sink."

As the 234-ton, Beyer-Garrat locomotive pulled up into the broad-gauge shade, the station broke into a frenzy. Red-turbaned coolies leapt onto the sides of the slowing coaches and rolled in through the windows to toss their dirty white marker clothes onto the seats to be sold to someone at a hefty price. Before the departing passengers could get off the train, embarking passengers charged aboard. Sellers of magazines, snacks, flowers and fruits emerged in droves, as if an army of worms had arisen through the ground. Most noticeable was the baritone tea and snack vendor. With his mouth twisted aside and his red bulging eyes seeking needy faces, he yelled, "*Chaiwalla . . . Chaiwalla, Garram . . . Garram . . . Chaiwalla; Chat . . . Kachori . . . Bhajiwalla. Garram . . . Garram Chaiwalla.*"

After ten minutes, the hullabaloo quieted down. The train conductor looked at the giant round clock suspended by long pipes from the network of the rods and the brackets under the iron ceiling. Although years of smoke, soot and steam had rendered the time within the clock a closely-guarded secret, somehow the conductor discerned something and adjusted his wristwatch accordingly.

Jonathan looked at Joshi and Mohan, both looking somber. Then he raised his camera.

"Smile," Jonathan said. He took a picture of them waving a mock good-bye.

Soon the conductor cross-waved the signal flags over his head and blew a long departure whistle. The locomotive answered with a sky-piercing whistle that shuddered the hearts of those unaccustomed to the pangs of good-byes. Joshi just didn't know how to initiate the parting words. Nor did Jonathan, but someone had to say something.

"This is great," Jonathan said. "I'd heard so much about the experience of traveling the Indian Railways."

"Yes, that's true. Trains in India are called the great unifier of the masses. It's the longest rail system and the largest employer in the world."

"That's amazing. A kind of lifeline of the nation, right?"

"Yes, indeed."

Jonathan turned to a somber Joshi and shook his hand. "Judge Sahb, thank you very much for everything."

"Not at all. Thank you. I enjoyed your company, Dr. Kingsley."

"I enjoyed your hospitality, and it was very instructive to see rural India in your special company. I really don't even know where to begin."

"Nonsense! No more thanks. Just give a tiny promise to this old man."

"Anything."

"May I have your word that on your way back to the US, you will grant me the good fortune of being your host again?"

"Of course. I'm no fool!" They continued shaking hands. "Besides, who else would want to put up with some moody American, anyway?"

Joshi put his hand on Jonathan's shoulder and looked into his eyes. "On the contrary, my friend, you are a very special person. Who else would have gone out on a limb to look into what really happened to a poor little village woman?"

Suddenly, Rebecca's face flashed in Jonathan's mind. He looked at the judge, but couldn't maintain the gaze. He looked away and swallowed.

"I would be most obliged, Judge Sahb," Jonathan said in a soft tone, "if you will kindly share with me the results of your investigations. I feel terrible. I wish I could explain to you how."

Further words would have been drowned out by the locomotive's ear-piercing whistle.

"I will, and that's a promise. Now, let's get you seated. The train is about to move."

"Yes, you are right. I'd better get going." Jonathan hastily walked toward his coach, then stopped, turned around and said, "So long. Thank you and take care of yourself."

Then, impulsively he returned to give Joshi a hug. At first Joshi was stiff, but soon he began patting Jonathan's back, and his embrace got tighter.

"You take care of yourself too," Joshi mumbled. "God speed, Jonathan."

Jonathan turned to Mohan, shook his hand good-bye and then boarded the train. The metal monster lurched forward, the brakes squeaked, the coaches hesitantly click-clacked sideways as tearful people waved at each other. Jonathan stood in the doorway, waving at Joshi, who looked frozen, his hands clasped behind him and his telling eyes now covered by his sunglasses.

"May you find peace, love and happiness at the Ashram. Jonathan, my friend, I'm going to miss you. Good-bye! Good luck!"

He remained motionless as the distant horizon began to swallow up the train and the cloud of smoke that sadly broke down over a converging stretch of two shiny tracks.

The train lumbered through and clattered past the tin-roofed shanties, where children frolicked in the puddles and restless clusters of mud-covered pigs rummaged through the garbage.

Soon it gained speed. Meadows, grazing cattle, creeks and geometrical harmonies of the farms scampered by. Jonathan settled into his seat, his head gently rocking with the rhythm of the train, his mind pondering the next stage of his journey.

PART TWO

chapter twelve

"Paani?"

The sympathetic sherpa offered him some water, but Jonathan was panting too hard to drink. It had been a mistake to let go of the Land Rover and try to travel the ten kilometers from Himpal's capital, Shivner to the Ashram-hill on foot. Even though the sherpa carried most of the luggage, Jonathan found even the camera and his backpack overwhelming.

"No, thank you," he said in his halting Hindi.

When he'd caught his breath, he nodded at the sherpa, who smiled and resumed the uphill trek, his head pitched perfectly for balance. Jonathan stood up and followed, concerned that he not get separated from his guide.

Sure enough, when Jonathan rounded a bend fifteen minutes later, the little man was nowhere in sight. Then he heard a songbird and paused to listen. He looked up and saw two birds sitting atop a stupendous deodar tree, its sprawling boughs festooned with a mesh of lichen and moss. At his feet a brook bubbled from under a shelf of melting snow. A black

Himalayan pheasant with puffed-up plumage squawked past him. He put down his camera bag and spread out his arms, inhaling deeply. Rudyard Kipling's words came to his mind. " . . . the smell of Himalayas, composed of rotting pinecones, damp wood-smoke, and the dripping undergrowth . . ." He knelt for a quick drink at the water's edge and struck off on the path again, marveling at the freedom he felt, so far from civilization.

"Ashram, near, soon," the sherpa said as Jonathan caught up.

After walking a few more kilometers, the sherpa stopped and looked back at the struggling Jonathan. "Look, Ashram!"

Jonathan stood on the edge of the plateau, panting but smiling, and took in his home for the next few months. It looked like a dream. The sickle-shaped Ashram compound faced the Himalayas like an ant-mound at the foot of a giant oak tree. The snow-clad cascades of the distant summits, with Kanchenjunga at its apogee and Mount Everest close behind, overlooked the Ashram like guardian archangels. The Himalayas overlooked the Ashram with the poise of a stupendous sentinel guarding his querulous brood with mystical stillness but parental promptness.

Jonathan experienced a strange feeling—an awe; a pleasant fright. He felt he was acquiescing to something supernatural, involuntarily but with elation.

The sherpa smiled brightly and pointed at the peaks crowned by the clouds. "God's place."

Slowly, both men walked across the Ashram's central courtyard. He noticed two women bearing garlands in their hands, standing in the doorway of the central hall.

The smiling sherpa indicated that Jonathan should continue toward the welcoming team. Both women wore saris, but clearly one was Indian and the other Western.

"Welcome, Doctor Kingsley," said the Western woman. She came forward, lopping a garland around his neck. She had deep violet eyes, high cheekbones, red hair and a Raquel-Welch-like smile. Her strong English accent had a singing quality. All the layers of her sari failed to conceal her striking curves. In fact, they accentuated them.

Jonathan smiled back at her. "Thank you, ma'am, thank you very much."

"I'm Kate." She extended her hand. "Kate Brown. I'm Swamiji's assistant."

"I'm Jonathan." Her hand felt warm and moist. "Nice to meet you."

A drop of sweat formed on his forehead and fell on her wrist. Noticing, she burst into laughter, swaying forward so that her sari revealed lush cleavage. She adjusted it halfheartedly. "I'm sorry, Dr. Kingsley, but you seem to be—" She began to laugh again.

He realized he was still holding her hand and let it go quickly. "I'm sorry, I guess I'm . . . I mean, I didn't . . ."

She looked at him and then at the sweat drop that seemed to have been absorbed into her skin. "No, I beg your pardon. I didn't mean to laugh at you Dr. Kingsley, but—"

"I know, I know." Jonathan smiled and said, with some relief, "You can tell I'm a little nervous. It's all so overwhelming, your welcome, this beautiful place."

Meanwhile, the Indian woman stood demurely in the background, her eyes to the ground. But a faint smile played on her lips.

Kate said, "This is Geeta, Dr. Kingsley."

"Please, call me Jonathan," he said to Kate, but his eyes focused on the young Indian woman, bronze-skinned and strikingly attractive. Very slowly, she lifted her big black eyes and looked at Jonathan. When she came forward with the garland, Jonathan tried to put her at ease by extending his head and gently guiding her hands and the garland over his neck.

Her hands felt so soft and her wrists so lissome that Jonathan felt as though someone had stroked his neck with white Asian lilies.

"*Namaste*, Babuji," she murmured almost inaudibly. "*Om Shanti*"

"*Namaste*," Jonathan said. "*Bahot, Bahot Shukriya*, Geeta."

His unexpected Hindi words painted a captivating smile on her face. Her pearl white teeth shone brightly and confidently.

"Please come in, Dr. Kingsley," Kate said. "Would you care for a cup of tea?"

"Tea? Sure. Thank you."

"Great. It will make you feel wonderful."

Kate led him into a reception area—a large, open structure with a slightly raised platform at one end and comfortable furniture scattered around. Bookshelves lined one wall, and an old upright piano, piled high with music, stood in a corner.

Kate pointed toward a wooden love seat. "Please make yourself comfortable. Geeta will inform Swamiji that you're here."

Jonathan took a seat, and Kate sat next to him. Within minutes, Geeta brought in a tray of tea and sliced fruits. When she placed the tray in front of him, he could not help but notice how gracefully she moved, keeping her gaze fixed to her feet like a rosebud bent to a bed of lush grass by the morning breeze. While he poured, she helped the sherpa unload and settle Jonathan's luggage.

A tall young man, broad-shouldered and bearded, wearing an Afghani topi, flowing salwar-kameez and a black vest walked in, carrying a wicked-looking billy club with iron bands spread along its length. He raised his right hand to his lips, smiling. "*Salaam alikum*, Doc Sahb."

Jonathan sat up and copied the gesture. "*Salaam.*"

"Rasoolmian, our guard," Kate said, then spoke to the guard in Hindi. He tucked his billy under his arm, picked up Jonathan's luggage and walked out.

"He's as devout a Muslim as one can get," she said when he was gone. "Prays five times a day, gives to the poor, fasts the whole month of Ramadan. But with that iron-ringed lathi of his, he won't hesitate to break anything or anyone in two. And yet he has Swamiji's trust and love."

An Ashram founded on the Hindu tenets of nonviolence, with its own guardian thug? Jonathan sighed and settled back into his seat, sipping his tea. A cool breeze drifted in, bringing the scent of pines and making him glad of his warm tea. Kate announced that she had administrative duties and left him alone. He put his teacup down and closed his eyes.

The inactivity was a pleasant change from the hectic time he had since arriving in India, and from the stressful times he had at home before he came. The silence of the mountains was immense. It prevailed even beyond the vastness of the Maine wilderness.

He thought of Geeta's greeting: *Om Shanti!* Thanks to Mohan, he knew the meaning—I, the soul, exist in a state of peace. Soon his own mind seemed to echo the chant: *Om Shanti! Om Shanti! Om Shanti! Om Shanti!*

Slowly he became aware that the chant wasn't entirely in his mind. He listened carefully, his head tilted and his eyes closed. No, someone else was chanting the greeting, his voice low and resonant.

When Jonathan opened his eyes, he saw two people: Kate, and a tall, gray-haired man hunched over a well-worn staff. The man's shoulder-length hair, eyebrows and overgrown mustache were all silvery white. Jonathan discerned a peaceful smile hidden among the wrinkles. Jonathan recognized that blissful, mystical face from the photograph in Joshi's home.

"Dr. Jonathan Kingsley," Kate said. "Meet Swamiji."

For a moment, Jonathan didn't move. Before him, he saw a frail old man wearing layers of plain white clothes and a full length, off-white robe. No paraphernalia of asceticism. Only a peaceful, slightly amused and totally disarming smile.

Instinctively, Jonathan reached for the frail man's hand, but then he caught himself and put his hands together. "Thank you for your kind welcome, sir."

The old man put his large hand on Jonathan's shoulder and said in a shaky voice, "I've been waiting for you, J.K."

Jonathan was shocked. The last person who'd addressed him that way was his father, who'd been killed when Jonathan was only eight.

Jonathan smiled at him. "I'm glad I'm here. This is a very nice place."

"This is your home," said Swamiji, smiling a joyous smile.

It was then that Jonathan noticed some Parkinsonian tremors in Swamiji's hand, and the slightly slurred speech. Johnathan had to concentrate to read Swamiji's face, as it took a long time for his expressions to manifest themselves. How ill was Swamiji? Even in this spiritual retreat, on his first day, was Jonathan being exposed to the threat of death?

"It's not as bad as you think," Swamiji said. "I know you've been worried about her, but I have good news."

Her? He looked at Kate. She looked equally blank.

"Your mother," Swamiji said, as he sat down in a wicker chair.

"Oh, of course. What about her?"

Swamiji gently put his staff down and folded his hands in his lap as if he were about to slip into meditation. "I do hope you'll forgive me for meddling, but I was inspired. And the news is good. She is feeling much better."

"Well, thank you, sir. You're right. Ever since I left the States, I have been worried about her. I haven't had much luck with phones here so far."

As soon as he said it, Jonathan remembered that Judge Joshi had said there were no phones at the Ashram. So how had Swamiji heard about his mother?

"No," Swamiji said. "We don't have phones. We are underprivileged in that sense."

Jonathan stared at the old man's staff, trying to get his bearings. It was as if Swamiji was carrying on a conversation with his brain rather than his voice. He looked at Kate, whose eyes were grounded to the floor.

"I'm sorry, sir," Jonathan said. "I don't mean to be rude, but how did you know I was . . ." He hesitated. Did he want to question this power of clairvoyance or—whatever it was? Would he offend his host? And what kind of answer would he get? It had to be coincidence, or lucky guessing, or perhaps Kate had relayed a message she'd picked up in town?

"Divinity," Swamiji said. "I'm a tool of the divinity. I'm not sure if it's a blessing or a burden, but I am glad. I'm glad this old body is of some use to the Almighty."

"A tool? That . . . sounds like a wonderful . . . burden, Swamiji. I wish I could say the same."

"But you can."

"Pardon me?"

"We all are tools of divinity. Most of us just don't know it. Fortunately, we don't have to."

"We are? Forgive me, Swamiji, I don't understand."

Swamiji smiled simply and stroked his beard. "Say . . . a healer sees a frail old woman in a remote Indian village, for instance. He makes a correct diagnosis and saves her life. The healer didn't have a premonition. Did he have to?"

"You mean Gopal's mother?" Had Judge Joshi told Kate about that?

"*Gopal, Gowardhan, Krishna Kanaiyah.* He is the one."

"He is the one," Jonathan said carefully, his head spinning.

A sound of ringing bells permeated the Ashram, high-pitched and sweet. Swamiji slowly leaned closer to Jonathan and put his hand on his head. "At any rate, welcome! First rest. Lord has granted us enough time to talk."

Swamiji struggled to his feet. Kate assisted him and Jonathan promptly stood up and helped him with his staff.

Damn, that staff looked familiar.

Swamiji smiled at Jonathan and thanked him. Kate took his hand and helped him out of the reception hall while Jonathan simply stood there quietly looking at the back of the fatherly figure in white who shuffled along like a slow-moving bundle of clouds.

Jonathan felt odd. He'd never felt comfortable with the professionally holy, even while working with chaplains at the hospital—and they were part of his own culture. He had always sensed something mildly dishonest about their certainty—how could anyone be that certain? He'd hidden his doubts, though, and gone along with them for his patients' sake. Then, when he'd seen Bholanath praising a young girl as a saint for burning herself to death and watched Buttasingh cracking coconuts for strength, he began to have serious doubts about working for someone at the height of Hindu religious culture.

But strangely, he didn't feel uncomfortable with Swamiji, and that fact made him feel odd. He hadn't been compelled to pretend, or to disguise anything to either Swamiji or himself. He wasn't even sure that he could have. He felt that the gentle old man knew just who he was and accepted him as such. That feeling was stimulating—awakening, even.

Kate stood at the door, talking with Swamiji. Geeta scurried around, preparing an elaborate welcome dinner for their special guest. The Ashram was in direct contrast to Baramedi. While the Ashram offered joy, hope, and life, Baramedi offered only sorrow, despair, and death.

"Hello?" Kate was waving her hand in front of his face to draw his attention. "I think you need some oxygen, Mr. Healer."

Jonathan smiled. "Thank you for introducing me to Swamiji."

"Oh, don't worry about it. He thinks you're a special soul. And don't underestimate him. This sweet, innocuous old man, in his own mysterious ways, is steering a lot of people's destiny. I used to feel condescending toward him, but now—"

"What was it he said as he left? I couldn't quite catch it."

"Oh, to me? That was a blessing. It means, 'May you live long, my daughter.'"

"Oh. It sounded familiar to me. I'm getting used to the language, I think."

"Yes, and Swamiji is quite a linguist himself. Fourteen different ones, last count."

"Really?" Jonathan said, astounded. "So have you been here long, Kate?"

"Actually, this is my third time," Kate said. "I think I'm going to settle down here. Third time's the charm, after all."

"You like it here that much?"

"I do. This year's is the most interesting group since I've been here. We have somebody from Germany, Holland, France, the United Kingdom, India, and the States, including you. It's definitely an interesting mix."

"India. You mean Geeta?"

"You like her, don't you?" Kate sounded curious.

"She seems nice. She doesn't say much, though." He paused. "I like you too, Kate."

Kate's expression revealed nothing. "How charming."

"Me? Charming? There's a good joke!" Jonathan answered, laughing. "What can you tell me about Swamiji, this Ashram—and you, of course?"

"How many hours do you have?" Kate smiled and took a seat. "Swamiji is one you must experience yourself, I'm afraid. I'll tell you one thing, though. He has X-ray vision. You think a thing, and he knows what it is."

"I noticed. One feels almost naked in front of him. I've never seen anyone so astute."

"There's more going on than just astuteness. Last year, a young Muslim woman was brought here. Datura poisoning, they said. You know Datura?"

"Yes, don't the seeds contain poison? An Atropine-like substance that dilates the pupils. The person turns red, hot, sweaty, and the heart pounds terribly. How did she come to eat Datura seeds?"

"She wanted to kill herself," Kate said.

Jonathan felt the poison of Baramedi, the poison he ran from back home, that he had seen packaged away when he arrived at the Ashram, tear and begin to leak into the placid life at the top of this mountain.

"But she couldn't," Kate went on. "She'd tried everything under the sun: threw herself in the river, tried to hang herself, doused herself with kerosene. But every time, someone came to her rescue—"

"Why was she suicidal?"

"Her six-year-old adopted son had died mysteriously in his sleep, and the poor woman was known to be infertile. That makes for real hopelessness around here. She blamed God for killing her son. She ranted and pulled her hair out in front of Swamiji. It was a bloody mess."

"So what did Swamiji do for her?" Jonathan asked.

"He just said, 'Beta, no need to kill yourself. That was not your son who died. It was an angel—sent to you by God to fulfill your life. Now he has been recalled by the Holy Father. Go back to that little angel's grave and you will find a seed that has sprouted into a little plant. Bring that sapling home and nurture it. As the plant thrives, a life of your own will flicker in your womb. By God's will, next Maha Shivratri; a child will fill up your lap.'"

"What happened?"

"A daughter happened—full term. She brought the baby here. When Swamiji picked up the baby, she spit up all over his face, grunted and pulled his beard so hard, Swamiji said, 'Who invited you here, you little tigress!'"

Jonathan sighed heavily, feeling the old ache, the old regrets. "How? How does he know what to say? How to help?"

"That's another long discussion, and I'm not so sure I understand that part myself." Kate paused and gave him a careful look. "And as I said before, I don't know much about Geeta. She's only recently arrived. There are so many. As for the rest, how about if we talk as I show you the place?"

"Great. I'd love to see it."

"And by the way, there is going to be a get-to-know-each other session tonight. It's going to be fun. You'll like it."

Kate led Jonathan through the Ashram's striking property. From its cool, darkened library, they visited the 4,000-square-foot central hall, used as a reception site for large assemblages at meditations and festivities. A life-sized statue of Lord Buddha and a rather incongruous grandfather clock graced the wall behind the seating assembly. The left arm of the main hall connected with the women's residential area. To the left of the women's quarters were the men's living quarters. Beyond that was the guard shack, where Rasoolmian spent most of his day.

To its right, the main hall connected with the library and stockroom, beyond which was the large kitchen. It passed through to the Kanya Khand and Kumar Khand—the girls' and boys' halls. Although their educational halls were marked separately, the boys and girls studied in a coed environment.

A separate building, which included the maid's quarters, housed the dispensary where Jonathan would work.

On both sides of the dispensary were the footpaths down the hill to the rest of the world. All vehicle transportation ceased at the base of the mountain, leaving the footpaths as the only established entry and exit.

At the end of his tour, Jonathan gazed at the peaceful, apparently productive, estate. "I can see why you like this place so much," he said. "It's very soothing. What part of England are you from?"

"Liverpool."

"Ah, I should have recognized the accent. Fab Four country, right?"

Kate laughed. "I knew them back when they were the Quarrymen and only knew 'Love, Love Me Do.' Anyway, I'd best be going. Swamiji will be looking for me."

"What exactly do you do?"

"Well, I'm his organizer, secretary, librarian—sort of a general dogsbody."

A sweet-sounding bell rang. Jonathan raised his eyebrows.

"Four o'clock p.m. Tea break for the adults. Playtime for the school."

"Everything seems to be pretty regimented here. What's the daily schedule like?"

Kate grinned as they continued their walk. "Hope you're an early riser!"

Jonathan looked at his watch. He heard the cheerful sound of young Himpali boys and girls exiting the school and running into the vast central hallway for sports and games.

"Dr. Kingsley," Kate said, "I'm supposed to help Geeta in the kitchen before reporting to Swamiji. Let me show you your room. Perhaps you'd want to stretch out a bit. You must be knackered."

"Not really. I'd rather check out the dispensary. And, please, call me Jonathan."

"Lovely. Will you stop by for a cup of tea? The kitchen is right there."

"Yes indeed. I'll catch up with you later. Thanks so much, Kate." He extended his hand gratefully. She took it warmly.

The dispensary was very clean but distressingly bare. There was a wooden cot, and a cupboard containing Mercurochrome, tincture of iodine, bandages, gauze, a camp stove with an aluminum pot for sterilizing metal needles, real-glass syringes and a few forceps.

Behind the door hung a stethoscope and an old German sphygmomanometer. He tried on the stethoscope and one earpiece fell out. He pressed it back in and held the warped plastic diaphragm against his chest. Apparently his heart still beat. There was some good news. The sphygmomanometer had a leak in its rubber tubing. He cut the leaky end of the tube and put the whole ends together, managing to get what he assessed to be a fairly accurate reading of his blood pressure.

Well, he'd expected things to be crude, and they were. But they would do.

Jonathan stepped out of the dispensary, pausing to gaze again at the Himalayan Hills forming a pious and peaceful shelter for the compound. He lit up a cigarette and inhaled deeply.

In the kitchen, he saw Geeta and Kate working side by side. Kate was busy with a wooden mortar and pestle, pounding ginger and garlic, as Geeta washed rice. He didn't want to startle them, nor did he want to get caught watching them and their beautiful bodies at work. He cleared his throat.

Geeta was startled, but he thought he caught a subdued smile on her face. Somehow, she was not quite the retiring flower that most Indian women were. Her expression was somewhere between pleasure, uncertainty and fear.

Jonathan smiled, putting her at ease. She smiled back, then nudged Kate, who stopped pounding and turned around.

"*Om Shanti*, ladies," Jonathan said.

"Oh, hello, Jonathan," Kate said.

Geeta looked flustered and stepped away into the stockroom.

"It smells good, whatever it is. I did declare my arrival, but you were pounding away like you were settling someone's hash. Is this a new therapy? Primal pound?"

Kate smiled. "So tell me, how did you find your dispensary?"

"It needs some work. Could use some new equipment and supplies—basic stuff. Is there a budget?"

"To an extent. Give me a list of the supplies and I'll take it up with Swamiji. By the way, you'll be seeing patients starting tomorrow. Some house calls, too."

"House calls? How?"

"See that pony under the tree?" Her effortless laughter rolled out of her. "She moves like a Rolls and doesn't need petrol." Kate wiped her hands and they sat down next to each other.

"So," he said, "we've got a minute. Did you always like India so much?"

"No way! I remember when I first came through Bombay's Sahar Airport and experienced eau de India. It hit me like a strong surf. I was drowning in the air!"

"But you survived."

"You get used to it, though like I say, I had to run from it twice before I did. And each time I returned, I saw this burgeoning mass of people—on the streets, in the train, on the beach hawking their wares. It seemed there were more of them each time."

"And yet you came back. Why?"

She looked out the window toward the Himalayas. "I don't know how to describe it, but there's a sense of ancient wisdom, a spirituality, that permeates through India's soul. It ... draws me here year after year."

Jonathan looked at the peaks and then the garden. Then he turned to Kate. "Maybe it's the serenity of this place, the wisdom of Swamiji? I'm an unbeliever and I find him intriguing. How old is he?"

"Who knows? I suspect he's in his nineties."

"Nineties?" Jonathan would have guessed eighty at the most.

"Astonishing, isn't it, especially since he eats hardly anything. No meat, no spices; just fruits, nuts, milk and vegetables. Small breakfast, no lunch and a light, early supper. Nothing after sunset. He's in bed by 10:00 p.m. and up by 4:00 a.m." Kate looked at her watch. "Oops, it's half past four. Let's join the rest of the gang for high tea. There's lots of goodies, gossip and giggles. You coming?"

Jonathan looked back at the clinic. "Actually, if I'm to start work tomorrow, I should get you that list of supplies. Won't take a minute."

Jonathan hurried to the clinic. He was well into his list when he noticed that the stethoscope that he'd left on its hook was now on the floor. Then he spotted a drawer pulled open. He knew he had not left it open.

He looked out the open window to the trail down the hill, but saw nobody. Going through the drawer, he found that nothing was missing. But who would sneak into his infirmary, and why? It gave him the uncomfortable feeling of being watched.

Maybe it was the maid, opening the window to air the place out—yet why would she rummage through a drawer? He was in a spiritual compound halfway up the Himalayas, with an armed guard. Petty theft was probably not a problem. He returned to making out his list.

Suddenly he heard the crunch of twigs outside. He rushed to the window to see a human form stumbling down the trail. He could not fully recognize the person in the failing light but the man's long, lanky back looked familiar. Very familiar.

chapter thirteen

People were gathered in the main hall after dinner to meet each other. Several others had arrived recently and Kate had arranged a special social to welcome everyone. Jonathan sat quietly, still uneasy. He had gone straight to Rasoolmian's quarters as soon as he had spotted the suspicious figure rushing away, but the guard had been unable to find anyone. Although there was limited access to the Ashram, apparently it was not difficult to be elusive on foot, especially during the prayer hour when most were occupied in meditation. The next day, on his house call journey, he would visit the post office and discuss it with Judge Joshi by phone.

Here in this haven of peace, with its tall trees and graceful mountains, already he'd been invaded. Possibly it had been a villager seeking sellable items to steal. But with my luck, Jonathan thought, the break-in is related to the ugly business at Baramedi. Yet how was that possible? Surely only Joshi, Mohan and he knew of his location. A household servant, perhaps? But they were all so loyal to Joshi. Of course, anyone could be bought.

The after dinner get-to-know-everyone meeting—Satsang, according to Swamiji—was about to start. Swamiji sat on two layers of thick mattress parked at the entrance to the library. Geeta and Kate sat on either side of him.

Two Buddhist monks played a flute and a string instrument called a Santoor. Another monk stroked a singing bowl to evoke peace and piety. Kate soon joined in and accompanied them on the piano. Her piano music sounded like the Christmas carol: "What child is this, who, laid to rest on Mary's lap, is sleeping?" The Buddhist monk played in unison the same tune on his flute. The audience consisted of a few newcomers and several saffron-robed monks from the nearby Ghoom monastery, all of whom sat quietly in lotus positions with their eyes closed. So did Swamiji, looking oblivious and enjoying the enrapturing music.

Jonathan found himself looking at Geeta. She kept her eyes on the floor at her feet but didn't seem relaxed by the music. Instead she seemed . . . sad or lonely. He realized she had looked that way since he had met her, but he had taken it for simple deference. Now he felt there was more to it. Who knew what women had experienced?

She glanced up at him. As soon as their eyes met, a faint, almost imperceptible, smile surfaced on her face. Jonathan smiled briefly and nodded. She immediately lowered her head.

Kate looked up at the wall clock and stopped playing. When the music stopped, Swamiji opened his eyes and smiled blissfully.

"*Om Shanti!*" Swamiji said softly. "Peace be with you, *Assalamo-Alaikum, Shalom, Sat-Shri-Akal,* God bless you. Oh, beautiful children of God, how shall I greet you?"

Swamiji's gaze scanned everyone's eyes. To Jonathan, it seemed to go on for a long time. At last he spoke. "Let us speak in English tonight as we get to know each other. Please tell us your name, where you come from, your occupation, why you're here, whether or not you feel comfortable, whatever you feel we need to know."

There was another silence. Apparently no one was willing to go first. "You may not find anything interesting in this old man's story," Swamiji said, "but allow me to introduce myself first. I'm Bikramchandra Bibhuticharan Chattopadhyaya. You can see why they call me Swami. If they called me by my real name, I'd never get to dinner on time."

Everybody laughed gently, including Jonathan.

"I was born in Calcutta many decades ago," Swamiji said. "Do you know how old I am? Don't worry. I don't know, either. At my age, I have enough trouble remembering my name." More laughter. "Occupation? I have none, and yet they don't call me unemployed. I'm a lucky man; I get free dinners."

Again everyone laughed. Jonathan began to relax.

"Now, I could go rambling on forever and my used-up brain wouldn't even know when to stop me. So raise your hand if you are willing to share with us something more enlightening."

A fellow in an olive silk swathe stood and faced the group. "My name is Guillaume LeClerc. I am from Languedoc. I am an artist. I make stained glass windows. I am fifty-one years old, but I feel very young inside me."

He paused, seeming to absorb the group's receptiveness.

"Five years ago, my whole family died in a restaurant because of a terrorist bomb. My mother, father, wife and my children, all gone. I was outside in my car looking for my wallet. Since then, I have been very depressed. Now I have come here, and we shall see. I cry less, even now. I still miss them, though." LeClerc's lips quivered and he seemed self-conscious. He sat down quickly and covered his face.

"Let us all pray for brother Guillaume and his family," said Swamiji.

Everyone closed their eyes and remained still for a few minutes.

Jonathan looked at LeClerc. Then he looked at Swamiji and the rest of the group consoling the grieving Frenchman. As a requirement for a psych class in med school, he'd had to attend a group therapy session. It had felt very similar; everybody spilling their guts and crying and hugging and loving one another. Was this the advanced spirituality Swamiji was selling?

A few moments later, a tall blond man stood up. "My name is Claus Schroder," he said. "I am from West Berlin. I am fifty-eight. In my twenties, I saw Germany humiliated by the Allies and devastated by the Depression. My father had fought in the first war and seen . . . horrors. We were very poor and survived on cabbage, crow, and potatoes. Then came Hitler with a message of hope, and it seemed as if Germany was turning around. My father considered him the savior of the country that he loved and had fought for. And soon, so did I."

His voice was quiet and flat, almost mechanical.

"I was the eldest child. I found a job in Hitler's army as an S.S. officer. I was sent to a small labor camp in Poland where I . . . I did . . . I became a full-time Jew-killer. I stuck it out for nearly two years, but soon I grew so heartsick I deserted and returned to Berlin. I was sure my father would turn me in for abandoning the army when Germany needed me most, but I no longer cared. Yet when I got home, I found that he had been shipped to the Russian front. He never returned. Eventually an allied bomb killed my mother.

"When the Russians came, I escaped to the allied section of Berlin. I still don't know where my brothers and sisters are. But I was glad I didn't have to kill innocent Jewish men anymore. Today, I'm an engineer. I never married. I've never told anyone my past. I feel very guilty and lonely. I'm lost."

Jonathan's skin felt prickly. If this were true, why would he relate it now, so openly? And if it were, couldn't he still be the same—maybe he was the mole! Jonathan studied a gaping scar on Claus's left cheek. The man had inflicted genuine tragedy, yet, if his admission were honest, possibly he was worse off than his victims—maybe even worse off than Jonathan? And if his story was true, Claus must still believe in healing.

"My son," Swamiji said, "you need not feel guilty for Hitler's karma. All the deaths he caused should have propelled him to seek peace with himself, as the deaths you caused have propelled you. He paid for his karma and left the world unnaturally. His tormented soul was lost. Your honest and sensitive soul is well on its way to being found."

Guillaume stood up and hugged Claus. That broke the dam. Claus started to cry. Kate came forward and hugged and comforted him, too. Jonathan refrained. It all seemed too superficial, too scripted. Soon Claus regained his composure.

When calm prevailed once again, another tall man stood up.

"I'm Stephan Hahn," he said. "I'm from Amsterdam, Holland, where drugs and sex are almost free. I am an editor. Well, I was. I did lots of drugs and women, which ended my first marriage. I married three more times, and they all ended for the same reasons. When my son from my first marriage grew up, he did drugs and became a prostitute to support his habit. He went to jail many times, and I helped to get him out. One day he slashed his wrist and almost died. When I turned to comfort him, he started to cry and told me, 'Dad, you weren't there when I was growing up. I feel scared and very sad inside.' Then, one day, he shot himself in the mouth."

Hahn paused, breathing heavily. "My whole life has been wasted. I don't have anybody to call my own. I feel I'm useless and I have used everybody. I'm here because I am too much a coward to kill myself."

"No, my son," said Swamiji promptly. "He who does kill himself is a coward."

Jonathan, shamed, felt his face flush red. Becky killed herself but she was no coward. He refused to think of his beloved wife that way.

"Brave are those who withstand the pain and comfort others," Swamiji continued. "You have so much to offer; you speak many languages and you are good with letters. Share your God-given talents with the deprived children of God. Give them the love and the care you did not give to your son."

Before he realized what he was doing, Jonathan had patted Stephan's back. With teary eyes but with his composure intact, Stephan placed his own hand over Jonathan's.

Jonathan feared his turn was coming up. He felt awkward. He had come to help heal abused women—not to find enlightenment.

Kate seemed to note his struggle. She stood. "My name is Kate Brown. I'm thirty-three. I was brought up in Liverpool, England. Ever since I can remember I wanted to be a performer—a singer or an actress."

Jonathan smiled at her. She returned the smile.

"I really thought I could find a niche somewhere in the entertainment business. Hope you don't think I'm patting my own back, but I was voted Miss Teen in the final year of school. To abbreviate my story, I didn't become an actress, but I applied for a job modeling for bug-spray and I got it. I went on to model for a mouthwash, then a perfume, diamonds, and so on. My lifelong dream seemed to be coming true. One evening, during a hobnobbing all-night party where actors, singers and celebrities show off, I met a very handsome guy named Kevin. Kevin Wilson. He was prop master for the ad company I worked for.

"Well, Kevin and I got married. I couldn't have been happier. My modeling career continued to soar and I began to move onto stage. I did Shakespeare with a touring rep company. Soon I received offers to do movies.

"It was too good to last. After three years, I began to feel fatigued and threw up at the sight or thought of any food. I was diagnosed with hepatitis. I knew it had been a gift from Kevin, but he wouldn't admit it. On the contrary, he accused me of sleeping around with other men. So I had him followed, and that's when I discovered he was bisexual.

"Well, it didn't end there. I was hospitalized because of jaundice and a failing liver. My mother got scared and thought I was dying, so she confided in me that I was adopted. The story was pure Dickens. My father was a sexton at a country church and found me abandoned on the doorstep.

"As you can see, I lived, but by then, my hair had fallen out, I had lost lots of weight, and my skin was badly wrinkled. That sort of thing tends to put off ad clients. Then, just when I was feeling most abandoned by everyone I knew, my mother—stepmother—had a fatal stroke. In the end, I rented a hotel room and started to drink with a whole bottle of sleeping pills at my bedside.

"Then a miracle happened. When I turned on the telly, I heard the London Vedanta Society talking about this miraculous sage from the Himalayas being in town, and that he was willing to listen to and steer any hopeless person in the right direction. I assumed I qualified as hopeless, so I went downstairs and purchased a newspaper, where I saw Swamiji's blessed face, which instantly built hope in my heart. I had read testimony of several lost souls who had successfully found the path of hope and happiness. Immediately I flushed the pills down the toilet and headed to meet Swamiji.

"When I found Swamiji at the Vedanta Society, he told me he would like to talk to me alone. I was scared but curious. When I met him privately, he put his hand on my head and said, 'My child, you are not only very beautiful, you are also very lucky.' Lucky? I thought it was a sick joke. But he said I was very lucky because I was loved by not one parent, but three—my adoptive parents and my real mother.

"Now remember, I hadn't said a word about my past at that point. I tried to tell him, but he stopped me and told me he had come to take me to my destiny, where my brothers and sisters would give me their love and be loved by me. He said he had a job for me and that it would be the last job I would ever need." Kate looked at Swamiji and smiled. "Of course, he didn't say the position was unpaid."

People stood and applauded, and Jonathan joined them gladly. Kate laughed and cried at the same time. After a brief moment, all settled down.

It was Jonathan's turn. But did he want to spill his troubles to these people? He had nothing against them, and they had opened up to him. But he still wasn't sure they would find healing—he'd heard of so many cases of people going on spiritual retreats for a high and then having it fade after only a few weeks with no real gain. To him, it was not only a waste of time, it was also a risk. If he began to believe in healing and then found it wasn't there, it might well kill him.

"You know, my children," Swamiji said, "skepticism is not always healthy. We all think we are individuals, protecting ourselves against attacks from outside. But in this vast universe, we are nothing but tiny clusters of microcosms. Our problems are not unique. What has happened to you has happened to mankind countless times. If you hang on to your unique pain, you are wearing self-applied shackles. The future, my children, is nothing but the past."

Jonathan listened to Swamiji's words carefully. Was he saying that Jonathan's urge to protect himself was superfluous? But Jonathan had opened himself up to Becky and he hadn't learned—he'd been hammered! He simply did not believe in the inherent goodness of the universe.

"Dear friends," Kate said, "thank you very much for your love and support. I could go on forever—once a performer always a performer! But time is running out and we still have one very important person among us to hear from. This selfless person has given up his lucrative medical practice in the United States to function as a volunteer doctor at our Ashram. Ladies and gentlemen, Dr. Jonathan Kingsley."

Jonathan faced Swamiji, Kate, Geeta, and the rest. All of them waited, eager to hear what he was going to say.

Well, so was he.

He looked at Swamiji, who was gazing at him with a faint smile and haunting eyes. Whether he could heal these people or not, Swamiji was a good, honest man. He deserved honesty from Jonathan, at the very least.

"Swamiji, ladies and gentlemen, good evening," he began. "I urge you not to believe a word Kate said. That introduction sounded as if it had been provided to her by my mother."

That drew some chuckles from the audience.

"Folks," he said, "I'm . . . I'm really sorry. I'm afraid there's nothing exciting in what I have to say. I know, you're going to think I'm an uptight Yankee; and you might be right. But, we doctors have never been accused of being exciting." People laughed. "First let me take this opportunity to introduce myself. My name is Jonathan Kingsley. I'm forty years old. I was born in Allagash, Maine, way up in the northeast. Nice country with mountains and rivers, bordering Quebec, Canada."

Jonathan paused. How could he say this without offending these people?

"Seeking God is . . . not the main reason I'm here. Understand, I don't think there's anything wrong with spiritual seeking, but I'm here to help heal people's bodies. I'm grateful for the opportunity to do that." Jonathan nodded at Swamiji, who was still smiling. "This is a different part of the world . . . a different culture. It's an experience for me—a good experience. It's clear that everybody here is warm, appreciative, and above all, very loving."

Some of those listening to him appeared confused. Guillaume seemed put out. Swamiji, however, continued to smile gently.

"It's getting late," Jonathan continued. "I expect we are all thinking of a restful night. But before I sit down, I just want to share with you something very . . . how should I put it, something very sad? While I was in Delhi, I came across a suttee case."

Geeta studied him with greater intensity than he'd seen before. Was he offending her by referring to the ugly side of her culture?

"I imagine you are familiar with sutteeism, so I won't elaborate," he said. "But what struck me was that element of humanity that we don't see here. The young woman who burned—maybe was forced to burn—was only twenty-two years old. That's all, twenty-two. It was outright oppression, outright cruelty. And this woman was murdered because she belonged to an untouchable class, because she was defenseless. Society didn't care for her; society didn't bother to protect her. But above all, she lost her life because, I think, because she was a woman. This injustice, this cruelty, this barbarianism . . . I just haven't been able to get past it."

Jonathan stopped. Those around him were stunned silent.

"I'm sorry. I didn't mean to preach. But think of this poor woman. Did she have a good marriage? Did she have dreams of a home, a family, being a loving mother, a loving wife? I guess it doesn't matter now." Then looking at Kate and Swamiji, he said, "I think I'm going to stop here. Thank you folks, for listening to me. Thanks."

At first it was silent, but then, following Kate and Swamiji's lead, everyone clapped enthusiastically. Geeta, however, immediately left the hall. Stephan and Claus hugged him and praised Jonathan, followed by Kate.

"What a speech!" she said in his ear. "Who says doctors are not exciting?" She winked at Jonathan. To the others, she said, "Watch out guys, a messiah is born." Swamiji looked as if he wished to speak, but Guillaume raised his hand. Swamiji signaled him to proceed.

"Doctor Kingsley," Guillaume demanded, "are you saying you don't believe in God?"

All eyes returned to Jonathan.

"What I'm saying," said Jonathan, "is, if I can be of some assistance to my fellow human beings without the expectation of any kind of reward, that's good enough for me."

"You're not answering my question," Guillaume insisted. "Doctors deal with life and death every day. That makes them think they are omnipotent and invincible. What will you do when you get sick? Who will you call?"

Jonathan felt annoyed, as if he were being punished for feeling different.

"If I get sick in France," he said, "I'll see the first English doctor I can find."

The crowd roared with laughter. Annoyed, Guillaume began to holler at Jonathan—half in English, half in French. Stephan and Claus tried to calm him.

When the din subsided, Swamiji said, "I like this. This is a very honest and spiritual intercourse. Though might I suggest, perhaps from tomorrow onward we can deal with touchy issues with a little more compassion and patience. You were all wonderful—so honest and brave. In so many beautiful words you shed light on many sensitive issues. A beautiful baby is abandoned on the steps of a church. A son's heart yearns for his father's love. An overly ambitious ruler perverts love of country and family into a horror for all involved. A man is appalled by the loss of an innocent woman. What you have talked about is life.

"We ask ourselves, 'What is life?' My own Gurudev used to say, 'Each and every letter in that small word has meaning: LIFE.' "L" stands for Learning and Loving. The soul had to pay for its karma by entering a body. It must use the vehicle of life to complete the journey so that it can be born and mature. The second letter, "I", stands for Introspection and Invocation. One should continuously scrutinize oneself. "F" stands for Forgetting and Forgiving. That's not always easy, but if you do it you will feel better, bigger and happier. And when you have learned how to forget and forgive, learned to throw yourself and your ego at God's mercy and pray, then you have arrived at the final letter of life, the letter "E". "E" stands for your Existence to attain the Enlightenment. That is the utmost goal of our existence—enlightenment.

"And what is death? Death is an inevitable link between two lives, two incarnations. You graduate from your secondary school. Do you call that death? No! You are heading for a higher body of knowledge, your college or university. Then you strive for your doctorate and you attain enlightenment. When you are enlightened, you teach others; share your wealth of knowledge with those who do not have it and need it.

"Death is not ominous. Someone dies somewhere, a baby is born somewhere else. Someone aptly said that winter is the mother of spring. When winter comes, we all see that gray snow of doom that covers everything around us. It all looks frozen, still and dead. But wait. There comes the sun of spring and the snow starts to melt. A seed sprouts. A sapling lifts its head. Flowers blossom. Fruits ripen. The seasons roll on. And so it is with life. Birth, the soul's maturation during life, the arrival of death, the soul wearing the cloak of another life—they are integral parts of one and the same cycle."

Swamiji stopped. The wall clock rang nine times. Jonathan rose and prepared to leave. It was all very well to talk about death as a natural part of the cycle, he thought, but it still felt like a powerful force, chasing and surrounding him all the time. Dad's death, Becky's death, baby Sarah's death, Seeta's, as well as the countless deaths of other patients and friends. Yet he found himself thinking of facing that pain; confronting the evil forces that had pursued him so relentlessly. Perhaps if he found they were stronger than he, at least he would have the peace of knowing that.

Suddenly, Rasoolmian entered the hall and approached Jonathan. "I'm sorry, Doc Sahb. A woman has just arrived from down the hill. I have sent her to the hospital. She could use treatment. A thousand pardons, sir, I know you just arrived and . . ."

"No, no, that's what I'm here for!" Jonathan answered. "Let's go."

chapter fourteen

At the dispensary, two sherpas were helping a young woman, battered and bruised, out of a palanquin. When the woman put her feet on the ground, she winced.

Kate and Geeta had followed and quickly assisted, helping the young woman inside.

How do I approach her, Jonathan wondered. She's apparently been abused or assaulted. How will she react to a male—and a foreigner at that—attempting to examine her?

To everybody's surprise the woman answered in English, "Thank you, Ma'am Sahb."

"Oh! You speak English," Kate said.

"*Thoda . . . Thoda*," she said, her voice very soft.

"She says 'very little,'" Kate explained.

"Great! That will come in handy. Now tell us where it hurts, which foot?"

The woman leaned forward and, pulling up her sari and petticoat a bit, pointed at both her feet. But Jonathan's attention was drawn to her wrists, lower legs, neck, and forearms. They all bore signs of healing scratch marks, bruises, and minor lacerations. Her left big toe was blackened from a blood clot under her nail and her right wrist was swollen.

"May I see?" Jonathan examined her ankles and feet. She winced when he touched her ankle. It appeared to be badly sprained.

Geeta departed. Her face wore a mix of anger and resignation.

"What do you think, Doc?" Kate said softly.

"It's not so bad," Jonathan responded, smiling broadly at the woman. "The ankle is the worst of it and I think it is sprained, but not broken." Immediately she looked down. Geeta returned with a glass of water for the woman. She drank it down without taking a breath.

"It looks as though you may be dehydrated as well," Jonathan said. "Where are you from?"

"Bu . . . Bulundi."

He looked at Geeta, then at Kate. "Where is that?"

"I think it is one of those foothill villages on the border. There are quite a few of them: Bulundi, Buxgunj, and your suttee site, Baramedi," answered Kate.

Jonathan began to wrap her ankle. "What does she do there? Is she married?"

"*Aapaka Dhandha?*" Kate asked.

The woman shook her head.

"Not quite ready to open up," Kate said.

"No surprise there." Jonathan studied her face and felt a tinge of sorrow. The woman had remarkable eyes. He found himself wishing to see her look at him instead of the floor so that he could see them better. Something about her felt comfortable. It was a refreshing change.

"*Namaste,*" he said. His halting Hindi had been an icebreaker in the past.

The woman looked up reluctantly. "*Namaste, Babuji.*" The softness in her voice was soothing. Her voice bathed his senses like the gentle tune of a lyre.

"Please stand up. Let's see if it hurts when you bear weight."

She tried to stand up, but winced in pain. Kate and Jonathan supported her. Slowly she lifted her downcast head and her eyes, deep, rich, and absorbing, locked on Jonathan's again. She blinked twice before she looked down. They walked her toward the main building.

Jonathan looked at her dark silky hair, parted perfectly in the middle and pulled back cleanly into a large bun. A dime-sized red bindi adorned her forehead. Her graceful neck was uncluttered with ornaments, and a yellow-gray sari covered her shapely body.

Jonathan heard familiar, uneven footsteps. Geeta escorted Swamiji towards him and Kate. Swamiji's eyes were focused intently on the new arrival. When he approached, the woman promptly stood up with folded hands.

"This is our latest patient, Baba," Kate said. "She is from Bulundi."

"Yes," Swamiji said, "I know her. Her name is Gauri."

When Swamiji sat, Gauri promptly prostrated herself at Swamiji's feet and began to cry. Jonathan looked at Kate, who was equally mystified.

To Jonathan's surprise, Swamiji let her cry. How strange, he thought, that this modest old fellow should tolerate that kind of worship.

After a few moments, Swamiji began speaking in quiet Hindi, which Kate translated for Jonathan.

"Rise my child," he said. "I know you have a role to play. You have been sent here with a purpose. It is going to be a difficult task. But the Almighty will grant you courage."

"Which means?" Jonathan whispered to Kate.

"Welcome to the Ashram, I think."

After a moment, Gauri sat up and wiped her tears, but still did not stand. Her eyes remained riveted to the floor but her gaze looked different now, more guarded than deferential.

Swamiji began talking to Gauri in rapid Hindi, which even Kate didn't seem to grasp. Jonathan left them alone and went to study the Buddha's statue at the far end of the hall. Eventually he heard a chair creak and turned to see Kate helping Swamiji rise. Jonathan was glad. It had been a very long day, and Swamiji was more than ready for some rest.

Swamiji laid a hand on Gauri's head and, to Jonathan's heart-stopping surprise, said 'Mary, Betty, Cindy Raho."

Jonathan rushed over. "Forgive me Swamiji, but . . . what did you just say?"

Swamiji simply smiled his inscrutable smile.

"Oh, I told you earlier," Kate said. "It's just a blessing. It means, 'May you live long, my daughter.'"

"No, the actual words. Mary, Betty—"

"*Meri beti zinda raho,*" Swamiji said softly. Jonathan could hear the differences now. Differences that had been there when Seeta's old father-in-law in Baramedi had repeated those words behind the Neem tree.

"And, if you were to say only the first three words?" Jonathan paused to get the pronunciation right. "*Meri beti zinda?*"

"Well," Swamiji said, "in the right context, it might mean, oh, 'My daughter is alive.'"

chapter fifteen

Jonathan stood at the phone in Himpal Post Office and listened to the burr in his ear. Finally there was a click and a familiar voice said, "Hullo! Kaun?"

"Mohan! Is that you?"

"Doc Sahb! It's me, Mohan. So nice to hear your voice again, sir."

"Same here, my friend. How are you? How's your family?"

"Very good, sir. My wife had the baby."

"Great! It's a boy?"

"No, sir. It's a girl!"

"Congratulations to you and your wife."

"Thank you, sir."

"Is there any word on the suttee case, Mohan?"

"Well, sir, the Sutteewala case is generating a lot of sensational press. The ministers are trying to decide how to handle the delicate situation. The suspects have either disappeared or have strong alibis. The pyre is, of course, cleared out. Throughout India there is uproar, unrest and rallies, you know. So now the prime minister, Mrs. Gandhi, has ordered all politicians to come up with answers."

In the background, Jonathan could hear Joshi giving curt orders to the servants. He sensed Mohan becoming distracted. "Sir, Judge Sahb is here. Would you like to speak with him about this?"

"Yes, please, Mohan."

After a moment, Jonathan heard the sound of someone clearing his throat.

"Well, well, well," Joshi roared into the phone. "I remembered you in my prayers this morning and here you are! How are you, dear friend?"

"I'm fine, Judge Sahb, and thank you for your prayers. I think I could use them. How are you?"

"Not bad for an old man with one foot in the grave. Oh, before I forget, I have some news for you from home. Yesterday I heard from your Aunt Edna. What a lovely lady. She wanted me to convey to you that your mother is feeling quite well. She said you must send them a detailed letter and photos of India soon. She said she is also mailing you a detailed letter."

Jonathan felt a chill, remembering Swamiji's earlier words about his mother.

"I wrote them a long letter a few days ago," Jonathan said. "Please forgive me for rushing, but Mohan said there was some more news about the suttee case. Can you fill me in?"

"It's heating up to the wire. Meetings early in the morning, late at night and so forth."

"Yes, that's what Mohan began to say. I'm glad they're pressing for the answers and not sweeping it under the rug."

"Oh no, there is no question of backing off here. This has struck the popular imagination somehow. A poor woman murdered for financial gain, quite sensational. The politicians can't ignore it."

"Great! Judge Sahb, I . . . This may sound strange, but I think I may have some news on the case."

"From the middle of nowhere? How could you hear about the case?"

"Well, actually it's something Bapuji said to me in Baramedi. I'm sorry I didn't tell you earlier, but I didn't realize its significance until last night." Jonathan presented Joshi with Bapuji's remarks.

"So the old man was trying to say his daughter was still alive?"

"I have to guess that, yes. What else could he have meant?"

"Well, I don't mean to dash your hopes, but it may only be that Bapuji was wistfully musing 'my daughter is alive up there in heaven,' or 'my daughter's spirit lives still,' or something of the sort."

"But he repeatedly whispered, in secret, and he seemed very intense at the time. And remember those photos I took? She would have to have been quite a large woman!"

Jonathan and Joshi laughed in spite of the seriousness.

"You have a point there," Joshi said. "The CBI is scouring every nook and cranny, looking for bones. Being that their value as relics may outweigh the risk of discovery, they may have hidden them. The holy man, Bholanath, has gone ahead with his plans to dedicate a temple to the suttee. Apparently the locals still believe that she was a willing victim."

"I see," said Jonathan. "Perhaps they need to believe that."

"You have been doing some thinking, my friend!" Joshi said enthusiastically. "Can we chalk any of this up to your new environment?"

Jonathan chuckled. "You decide! So are you in touch with Bapuji?"

"Unfortunately, the news is not good. The day after you left New Delhi, the old man disappeared. He may have been kidnapped, maybe not. Either way, it is not good."

"Oh damn!" Jonathan said. "The best witness is gone. If only I'd understood his message sooner—or reported it to you!"

"No sense in berating yourself, my friend. We can't all be perfect."

Jonathan missed his new friend more than he'd expected.

"Murli, the barber, also appears to have moved on, by the way. And one more thing," Joshi went on. "Gopal, who was too fearful to talk to us earlier, has now decided to assist the investigators. He told us as far as he could gather the thugs in that jeep, who clearly worked for our villain, escaped into the mountains."

"Mountains?"

"Yes. I'm afraid a bandit could disappear into those border villages permanently."

"I see," said Jonathan, thoughtful again.

"So we have dispatched hoards of incognito CBI agents everywhere."

"Good. What is Buttasingh up to?"

"He is helping us, he says. But no doubt he is holding back. Someone beat him up at his farm last night, apparently, and he's walking around with his arm in a sling. In fact he informed the CBI that if this intimidation continues, he might consider resigning his position and leave the village for good. Unfortunately, we have nothing to hold him on."

"Well, your CBI in the villages may come in handy," Jonathan said. "Last night someone broke into the dispensary up here and went through all of my cabinets."

"Good heavens! And you think it is related?"

"I don't know. I saw a figure running away in the darkness. He must have taken one of the footpaths or run parallel to it. There is a guard here, but was unable to find any sign of him. Perhaps it was only a hungry villager."

"Himpali guards can be bribed and the criminals are rich. Do not leave the Ashram unguarded. Promise me, please."

"This guard seems quite loyal," Jonathan said. "But I will comply with your request as much as possible. Actually, I'm on house calls now, and I've got the Ashram guard and a couple of his men with me."

"Good. One more thing, and I hope this turns out to be a good lead. We may have an informer."

"Informer? Regarding the suttee?"

"Yes. A young woman, in fact. She contacted CBI from near Baramedi—at that post office."

Jonathan's mood darkened. "Do you remember what happened to us following your conversation with K.C. from that post office?"

"Yes. I have instructed the official who took the call this morning not to waste time and bring her in immediately. This could be the break we are looking for."

Jonathan's pony rocked its way back up the hill to the Ashram, with Rasoolmian ahead and another turbaned guard behind. His rounds had been relatively trauma-free, and he was glad of the leisurely pace of his pony. The pony wasn't quite the Rolls that Kate had described, but still he provided a pleasant way to travel.

"Good thing you and I have got protection going up this mountain," he said gently to the pony. "If they'll beat up one of their own, there's no telling what they'd do to us!"

As if to say, 'Forget about it,' the little pony stopped to nibble some grass. Jonathan dismounted and walked to the edge of the trail. The drop to the river below was nearly one hundred feet. Jonathan inhaled sharply, taking it in. The only missing component of the perfect moment was the presence of Becky. She would have been urging him, "Get your camera! Get a shot of this, Jonathan!" And once he'd got it in position, she'd be sure to stick her face in the lens, making a ridiculous face, just to make him laugh. And he always did.

Where was she? She would have loved all of this, he thought. This trip was exactly what she had always wanted to do. But now I am doing it all, thought Jonathan, without her. He returned to his pony and began again, fighting the lump in his throat and the pounding pain in his chest.

It was nearly noon when they arrived on the outskirts of the Ashram. There at the river's edge, he spotted Geeta and Gauri fetching water. Gauri seemed to be moving less painfully. He felt an unexpected happiness to see her feeling better.

As he observed their movements, though, he noticed that Geeta was walking pointedly ahead of Gauri, as if she did not wish to be associated with the other girl. Jonathan sadly shook his head. He had thought Geeta would be glad for the company. He was finding the personalities at the Ashram to be much more complex than he'd expected.

His thoughts turned to Kate. She was good company, he thought. Intelligent, beautiful too, but a little haughty. Yet, she had her share of compassion. She had certainly shown that the night before when Gauri had appeared.

Geeta and Gauri were out of sight by the time he dismounted and returned to the clinic. He sorted things out in the dispensary, happy to see that some of the supplies he had requested had already arrived. Kate was something!

"Oh, I've left that ridiculous stethoscope in the saddlebag," he said under his breath. "I'd better get it before I need it."

Out by the trees, the pony grazed, still saddled. Jonathan enjoyed the walk on his own, listening to the mid-day breezes through the trees. When he reached the pony, he heard the clop of a horse's hooves on the packed trail. He rode ahead to a corner and found the trail chained off with a painted 4 x 4-foot signboard that said, in four languages including English, DANGER! FORBIDDEN ZONE. NO ENTRY PERMITTED BEYOND THIS LIMIT.

He was about to turn when he again heard the slow canter of a horse ahead of him on the trail. After a moment, he saw movement and was able to make out a horse and rider through the vegetation: someone in a khaki uniform, gun belt at the waist, and tall dark boots on a big black horse. The rider dismounted under a tree on the trail. Jonathan held his breath. He could hear him pacing and slapping his boot with the riding crop.

Then the pacing stopped and Jonathan heard a quiet conversation. And the other conversant was a woman.

The language sounded like Hindi or Himpali. The man seemed to be upset—he kept waving his crop and began raising his voice. And the woman, she spoke softly, but every once in a while a word or two would carry clearly enough that he almost recognized the voice. It was one of the women from the Ashram. Geeta or Gauri!

What was going on here?

Jonathan tried to ease his pony closer to the mouth of the trail near the danger sign, but the pony fluttered its lips to fend off an insect. The conversation stopped, and seconds later he heard a horse galloping away.

Lovers? He thought to himself. What else could it be? Men and women did not conspire in India. It simply wasn't done. Unless perhaps they were actually two male voices and he had simply misinterpreted the higher one for a female? But that was unlikely. Maybe it was a patient who had gotten cold feet at the last minute. That would certainly seem in line with this culture.

At lunch, he singled out Kate. "A funny thing happened just now," he began.

"Get used to it," she said with a twinkle.

"Actually, Kate, I'm quite serious," he said smiling politely. "I thought I'd get your opinion on it."

"I'm sorry," Kate said, taking a seat. "Go ahead."

After he described his observation, Kate wore a funny expression on her face. "Could you tell whose voice it might have been?" she asked.

"No, as I said, I'm not even entirely sure it was a woman and a man. But that is my best guess."

"Well," she said thoughtfully. "I guess we can't do anything for the time being. But I'll keep an eye out—maybe there is a tryst in the making." She gleamed.

"I thought perhaps it might be connected to the break-in of the dispensary last night—oh, I didn't mention it since nothing was taken, but there was someone there who had been through my things and apparently exited through the window."

Kate sat up straight. "Did you report it to Rasoolmian?" she said.

"Oh, yes, of course. Immediately. But he had seen no one and as I said, nothing was taken."

"Do you suspect a thief?"

"It's possible," Jonathan said, carefully. "It really could have been anything. But let's keep our eyes open. After all, I'd hate to lose that lovely 20-year-old saucepan."

Kate burst out laughing. "Point well taken. Did you notice the new inventory, by the way?"

"Yes, and I thank you."

"No problem," she said. "It was all in storage. I hope it does the trick!"

chapter sixteen

The next morning as the glorious sun rose from behind the white peaks of the Himalayas, Jonathan felt uplifted. He had decided to join the morning prayer, called *Prarthana*. Kate had explained that there would be no idol, no ochre, no flames and no prostration or offering of delicacies to gods or deities. Instead, Swamiji insisted that there be no temple, no building, no walls of any sort—just open ground, facing the sun and the mountains—and rose bushes.

Prarthana had started with a fifteen-minute-long meditation before dawn. Jonathan had tried closing his eyes with the others, but he could not shut his mind off. He thought of Joshi, Mohan, the pyre in Baramedi, and the murderer. He inhaled deeply, holding his breath for a comfortable length of time, mentally reciting *Om Shanti* and then exhaling slowly. But halfway through the meditation, he heard the birds chirping, and felt the sunlight bathing his face. He wasn't getting this.

With the first ray of the sun, Swamiji blew the great conch shell, sounding it for over a minute in segmented, short bursts, obviously exerting himself in the effort. Then there were three minute-long soundings of two large brass bells. Everybody then stood up and began to sing the prayer:

> "*The fire in the radiant sun is you; the cool in the glowing moon is you,*
> *And like the twinkling little stars in big blue sky, so are we.*
> *You put birds in the trees, blossom flowers for the bees.*
> *You send the typhoons, tornadoes, raging rivers and roaring vast seas.*
> *Pregnant with love, you sculpted us tenderly, then awakened us with a spark of life.*
> *You sent us to earth: to live, to learn and to love each other as husband and wife.*
> *You made the wind, you formed the clouds and filled them with tiny drops of rain.*
> *You let it fall gently on tender grass, so the fields of the earth may burst with grain.*
> *You succor the weak, empower the infirm and forgive man's guile.*
> *When I enter my quietus, you'll be there with your divine smile.*
> *The fire in the radiant sun is you; the cool in the glowing moon is you,*
> *And like the twinkling little stars in big blue sky, so are we.*"

Swamiji smiled and greeted everyone, and Kate proceeded with the day's announcements. Then, the residents chatted among themselves informally until breakfast.

Breakfast that morning was chopped fresh fruits, homemade hot cereal mix, whole wheat, barley, oats cooked with bits of almond, raisins and dates, and nuggets of jaggery. Slices of locally-cooked whole wheat bread were served with fruit jams, honey and goat cheese. There were no eggs, ghee, or cream. But there was milk, juice and fresh Himpal tea. No coffee.

As Jonathan went through the buffet, one of the monks began playing sitar music in the corner.

"Don't eat too much, Doc," Kate said. "This music will mesmerize you so much that you won't hear the cries from your overstuffed stomach."

"Good morning, Miss England. How are you today?" Jonathan made some room for her at his bench.

Guillaume looked at them and grimaced.

"Come on, Stephan, Claus, guys, join us," Kate called.

Stephan and Claus sat down, but Guillaume played deaf, sitting beyond them.

"What's with him?" Jonathan said.

"He's a big baby," said Kate matter-of-factly.

"Yeah, I wonder too," Stephan said. "He acts like a nice guy, but then he gets—"

"Weird?" Claus said.

"Watch it, you lot," Kate said. "He's very powerful and filthy rich. He donates lots of money to the Ashram. He talks about being an artist as if he were starving, but I heard he's well enough off to own vineyards in Beaujolais Country."

"Yeah?" said Jonathan. "So why can't he own a toothbrush?"

"Hey guys, cool off now," Stephan said, "or I'll complain to the boss."

"Who? Swamiji?" Claus said. "He'll only say, 'My children, have some anger! Anger is good. Anger is divine. It will send you to God faster.'"

All laughed at that and watched Guillaume glare at them.

"Speaking of Swamiji," Kate looked at Jonathan seriously. "Didn't he look like he was short of breath?"

"When?" asked Stephan and Claus, almost in unison.

"This morning," Kate replied. "After he blew the conch."

"Kate," Jonathan said incredulously, "if I blew that thing for a full minute, I'd be *dead!*"

Kate laughed in spite of herself. "Well yes, but every day I notice his conch blowing gets shorter and shorter. Do you think he's all right?"

"I don't know," Jonathan said. "He is in his nineties, you said. Can't he assign someone else to blow the conch?"

"Are you kidding? He won't let anyone touch that conch. It was a gift from his Gurudev, who told him thirty years ago: 'When you are ready to accept the Swamihood, roam the Himalayas and let me hear the sound of this conch from the Gurushikhar.'"

"What is that . . . Gurushikhar?" Claus asked.

Kate turned her head and pointed. "See that peak with the least snow on top? Years ago, Swamiji went exploring in the Himalayas on foot and remained in meditation in a cave somewhere up there. And when he was ready to renunciate—accept the Swamihood—he blew the conch from there. When he returned to the Ashram, his Gurudev blessed him and took off to undergo a Mahasamadhi somewhere in the distant caves."

Claus looked at Kate. "Mahasamadhi?"

"It's an extreme meditation technique whereby one invokes death on one's own terms. The body is pushed into a deeper and longer trance until the soul simply lets go."

Jonathan went white.

"Jonathan?" Kate said.

"I'm sorry, Kate," he mumbled. "You're speaking of this as some sort of an honor—it's hard to imagine one could regard suicide in that light."

"Well, it's not simply sui—"

"Yes, it's simply suicide," Jonathan said, rising. "I may not know meditation, and I may not speak fluent Hindi, but I know what it means to bring about one's own death."

"But it is more spiritual dan dat," said Stephan.

Jonathan leaned forward. "Frankly, I think this serenity and sweetness business about death is all hogwash. Yes, I have seen death—time and time again, and it is nothing but frightening, destructive and horrifying. There is nothing redeeming about death, nothing, whether one dies in England, India or America."

Claus looked stunned. "But if you feel that way—"

Jonathan raised his hand to interrupt. "Last night, I told you about an innocent woman, a suttee, whom you all thought was a poor victim of her culture. Now Kate's told you about a man who did the same thing and you think he's a saint."

"Death is different when you're ready for it," Kate said.

"You're never ready for it! At best you can delude yourself because you live in a culture where death is glorified. Worshipped. The villagers I saw having their carnival around that funeral pyre didn't talk about how needless, how preventable that suttee's death was—they were eager to pay good money for the murdered woman's ashes!"

"There it is, then," said Claus. "She was murdered, but Kate's describing—"

"Suicide! Yes! In whatever form, death is the end of life—it is a frightening, horrible event. It is not time for a party. I've to make my livelihood preventing death!"

"Are you saying Swamiji is evil?" Kate asked pointedly.

"No," Jonathan said quickly, "definitely not. I can see that he is a loving, caring man, and wise in most ways. But I think he has accepted a part of his culture that I believe to be unbalanced—out of touch with reality."

Claus and Stephan were silent, probably less convinced than simply bored.

But Kate carried on. "I see your point," Kate said. "But maybe your perception of the culture's perception is blurred. If Indian culture worships death, ours runs from it."

"Okay, fair enough," Jonathan said. "But tell me why Swamiji, if he is so pro-death, supports all this life? Why the clinic? Why am I here?"

Kate smiled. "See? You're arguing against yourself. He wants to save lives because he loves life. Not because he loathes death, as you do."

Jonathan shook his head. "I'm sorry Kate, that's a distinction without a difference. If you love life, how can you not loathe death? Death is as terrifying as the darkness of the night, as incisive as a butcher's knife, as charring as raging fire. I simply refuse to . . . saffronize it." He rose and returned his dish to the kitchen. When he returned, he looked into three glum faces. "Um . . . sorry guys. Maybe I got carried away."

They all smiled at him, but said nothing.

He sighed, calmer then. Are all the people in this country really nuts? He wondered. Was he perhaps a little irrational about death? His brutal losses had been so close together and so punishingly . . . But, no. There were a lot of things appealing about the Ashram and the life it taught, but he couldn't let himself be taken in. He'd heard too many stories of people getting sucked in, ultimately believing all sorts of nonsense.

Through the window, he spotted Gauri heading for the garden. Her limp had become even less marked. She approached the flowers and gently touched the tops of each, carefully choosing those that would grace the tables and vases of the Ashram. Her youth seemed ill-fitted to her poise. She bore a kind of gentle maturity that brought tenderness to the surface.

"You like Indian women, don't you?"

Jonathan jumped. The others had gone, but Kate remained. "I don't know," he said. "It may be that they seem so much like helpless victims."

Kate smiled but said nothing.

"Well, I've got to get to work," he said. "I'll see you at lunch?"

"Good luck," Kate said. "Call me if you need my help."

Had Jonathan experienced a milder orientation to Indian culture, he might not have survived the first week at the Ashram. Nearly every patient he attended bore evidence of vicious abuse and malnutrition, with disfiguring disease following a close second.

Treating the illnesses though, would never cure the source. It appeared that every family indulged in the flesh trade: a father selling his daughter, a brother cashing in his little sister, and even worse, a husband making money from his wife's prostitution. Along with treating the physical illness, Jonathan began passing out educational literature and arranging on-site skits to drive across the point that there was a way out of all this. As far as he could, he saw to it that the abuse of defenseless young women stopped.

Soon the word about Jonathan's kind medical ministering spread; folks from neighboring villages brought patients with difficult and often incurable diseases of all kinds. At first, Jonathan hesitated, being improperly supplied. But he found that Kate, Geeta, and Gauri were all willing to help, and with Swamiji's moral encouragement, he took on every case he was presented. To his surprise, the results were gratifying.

Aside from its cultural variation, Jonathan found freedom in his new job with the absence of mercenary zeal or any threat of lawsuit. His patients paid him with fruits, vegetables, and locally made shoes, hats and other items of clothing.

The patient load however, seemed to be increasing. From the few cases that had arrived on day one, the numbers increased over the week to nine. As much as he hated to consider it, Jonathan suspected that there was something sinister developing in the village below. Time to call Joshi.

chapter seventeen

"What makes you say that?" Joshi asked.

"I can't put my finger on it. It's just a feeling. And of course the increase in cases doesn't help," Jonathan explained.

"Tell me again about the voices," Joshi said. "That's got me curious."

"It was the day I called you. I still think it was a male and a female."

"And there haven't been any new romances about?"

"No. It didn't sound romantic anyway," Jonathan answered impatiently. "I think it's suspicious, but I don't know how. What is happening there?"

"There have been problems . . ." Joshi slowed. "The informer . . ."

"She was murdered."

"No, but she probably wishes that she had been. The police found her unconscious on the bank of Vasundhara. She was blinded, her eardrums were perforated, and . . . her nipples and genitals were torn away. They found a pair of pliers, right next to the body."

"God." Jonathan's breath was sucked out of his body. He felt limp, leaning against the base of the ancient telephone box. He restrained himself from kicking down the door. "This guy—whoever he is—is a misogynist. He hates women—period. He must have some childhood problems . . . traumatic past. Something."

"Yes," said Joshi. "It is the evidence of a madman."

"How did that happen? You had arranged to have her protected . . ."

"The very same day. I have taken the postmaster into custody. It is clear that he informed whoever is responsible. But because he has several sons whose lives are at stake, he will not talk." Joshi paused. "I'm sorry. This must all seem terribly barbaric to you."

"It does. Yet, there have been cases only this week here that are similarly brutal."

"Yes? And how?" Joshi sounded exceedingly curious.

"With respect to the mutilation," Jonathan answered flatly.

"Well, then you won't be surprised to hear that there were several other cases reported in border villages. This devil is on some kind of rampage. And I suppose your patients won't speak?"

"No. It's hardly even worth asking anymore. The reaction is always the same—complete withdrawal."

"I almost wish I could interview them. But I am very familiar with the reaction. And now, with this poor woman . . . it is clear only a very fearless or very stupid woman would identify this creature."

Jonathan paused. "Well, I hate to know, but is there any news on Bapuji?"

"None so far. The CBI is keeping an eye out for him. Or his body."

"Poor man."

"Yes. But I have good news, too. Remember how the thugs had cleared the pyre, and dispersed the bones and ashes into the river before disappearing into the mountains?"

"Yes, yes?"

"Well, here is the best part of this horrible story. And it essentially proves the correctness of your hunch about Bapuji's *Meri beti zinda* message."

"You found them, didn't you?"

"CBI found a sack full of bones and some charred female ornaments neatly hidden under the haystack at a landlord's farm. Evidently, as I had hoped, they didn't want to throw away the relics for their cash value; after that, the CBI was all over them."

"What did forensics say?"

"My friend, you are beginning to sound like a cop!" Joshi laughed. "They examined and reexamined them. We even had an expert flown here from England."

Jonathan held his breath.

"Lo and behold, the English expert concurred with the local forensic chaps. The consensus report declared the bones belonged to two males—one tall and middle-aged, and the other short and younger, presumably Seeta's husband."

"And the fractured skull?"

"The fractured skull belonged to the older male."

"No female bones?"

"None whatsoever. Bapuji was right. His daughter lives."

Jonathan said good-bye to his friend and hung up the phone with his mind still reeling. Seeta—alive? Could it be?

The next day before tea, Jonathan heard the children move into the garden outside the clinic window for tutoring. Between patients, he listened to the teacher's voice leading chanted English. At first he thought it was Gauri, but when he moved to the window, he found it was Geeta.

"Mother," she said. "M-O-T-H-E-R."

"Mother: M-O-T-H-E-R," the children said.

Jonathan leaned out his window. He was behind Geeta and to the right, but he could watch the children's faces.

"Father: F-A-T-H-E-R."

"Father: F-A-T-H-E-R."

The children began to pay more attention to him than to their teacher. Finally Geeta turned around.

"Babuji," she said.

"Hi, Geeta," he said in his slow Hindi—he'd been practicing for weeks. "Please, do not let me stop you. I'm just taking a little rest."

Geeta smiled and resumed the lesson but was again interrupted when Rasoolmian came with a message for her.

"You must excuse me," she said to the children, "but I am wanted." Then she turned toward Jonathan. "Perhaps, though, the doctor Sahb would help you with your lesson?"

"Um . . . sure," he said. How hard could it be?

Jonathan came outside and took his place in front of the children. There were twenty-seven eager faces looking up at him.

"Okay," he said. "Say Brother: B-R-O-T-H-E-R."

The children repeated it after him.

"Good! Now say—" What was another familiar noun? Or maybe a verb? Memories of his high school Latin—*amo, amas, amat*—floated into his mind.

"Love," he said. "L-O-V-E."

The kids hesitated, but followed in a softer tone. "Love: L-O-V-E."

"Very good, excellent! Now let's use these words in a sentence. Let's start with you—this boy with the cap. Jonathan picked out a tall, slim boy with large, mournful eyes. "Make a short sentence using the word, 'father.'"

The boy stood up. After a moment, he said, "Father is smoking."

All the kids laughed and so did Jonathan. Instinctively, Jonathan grabbed the child and gave him a hug, his hands searching out the frail bones in the boy's narrow back.

"Excellent. But you know, smoking is bad." He placed his hand over his pants pocket where his Winston box used to be. "Say: Father, please do not smoke."

The class repeated after him in a very serious tone.

"Okay, now your turn." Jonathan pointed at a young girl with long black braids in the front row. She hesitated.

"*Gabharao Nahin, Beta,*" he said slowly, one of his most commonly-used Hindi phrases. "Don't be afraid, my child. Come here. I'll help you." He put his arm around her and sat down. "Make a sentence using the word, 'mother.'"

The girl waited, then ventured, "Mother . . . is . . . *cooking.*"

The kids laughed and so did the girl.

"Wonderful! See, you can do it. Now, do you want to make another sentence?" The student nodded. "All right, make a sentence using the word *love.*"

The student hesitated, then smiled sheepishly.

"Okay, let me help you," he said. "Father says to Mother, 'I . . . love . . . you.' Say 'I . . . love . . . you.'"

The girl repeated almost inaudibly, "I . . . love . . . . you."

The children began to point at her, laughing and shouting, "I love you. I love you." The young girl covered her eyes with her fists.

Jonathan stood up. "That's enough!"

The class quieted.

"Don't be embarrassed, Beta," Jonathan said. "Do you know what that sentence means?"

The girl shook her head.

"No problem. I'll help you, and maybe you can all help me with my Hindi. I love you is *Hum aapse* . . . ." And suddenly Jonathan couldn't recall the Hindi word for *love.* He had heard at least three different words of translation, and all of them were gone. "*Hum aapse* . . . ., *Hum aapse* . . . ."

"*Hum aapse pyar karte hain,*" said a soft voice behind him.

Jonathan turned around. A few yards away, Gauri was bent down, clipping roses, her eyes to the ground. But she was smiling.

A thrill ran through Jonathan. He caught his breath, remembering instantaneously his first kiss at age fifteen. Although sure-footed in general, he found himself stumbling a little as he reached for the railing.

The children giggled.

"Thank you, Gauridevi," he managed to say. And then he repeated, "*Hum aapse . . . pyar . . . karte . . . hain.*" He turned back to face the class, but suddenly, the world around him had a purpose. No matter that he could not identify it. And in that simple exchange, he had gained something he had lost, he thought forever. Hope. "Okay kids, all together. I love you. *Hum aapse pyar karte hain.*"

While the kids repeated this, Jonathan glanced back at the rose bush. It waved back and forth in the wind, two butterflies hovering overhead. Gauri was gone.

Presently the bell rang and both Jonathan and the kids were let out of school. He headed over to the prayer spot to enjoy the view before tea and ran into Kate. He joined her on a bench under a pine tree.

"Kate, do you know anything about suttee?" he asked after a little while.

"Well, only what I've picked up from my reading. Is that still plaguing your mind?"

"Well, we've been seeing a lot of abuse cases. A generation of men has been raised to believe women are meant to be used, so they use them. It's lust, it's power. It's hideously ugly, but at least it seems human to me. But suttee . . . how do you persuade a woman to destroy herself?"

"Well, that I really don't know. I suppose some women, if they've lost the only man who ever loved them, might prefer to die rather than sink to the level of being used again. And, as you say, that kind of using still goes on. Perhaps that case down in Baramedi was—"

"Oh, no, I was actually thinking of suttee in general. That case was different. The woman was actually murdered . . . we think."

"You're not sure?"

"We're sure she didn't go voluntarily, but . . . I suppose Judge Joshi wouldn't mind my telling you. He didn't tell me to keep it a secret. There is some slight reason to believe the woman—Seeta, her name was—is still alive."

"What? And if she's still alive, where—"

There was a crash nearby. Jonathan jumped up to find that Gauri had stumbled right in the middle of the walkway and dropped the brass plate full of flowers.

Jonathan was instantly by her side. "Are you all right? Have you hurt yourself? Is it your foot, still?"

"Gauri!" Kate said, dropping to her knees to help. She and Gauri gathered the flowers back onto the brass plate.

Jonathan glanced up in time to spot Geeta backing away. Her expression was furious.

Gauri stood and prepared to leave, but Kate beckoned her to stay and gestured to Geeta. "Ladies, join us for a moment, please."

Jonathan stood up and offered them seats.

"If you want to learn about suttee," Kate said with a smile, "here are the experts. They know all about the Indian culture."

Jonathan hesitated and looked at Gauri, then at Geeta. Both were clearly unhappy to be there, neither making eye contact.

"It's all right," he said. "I know you are both very busy just now. Go on, we can talk another time."

Geeta immediately departed, as Gauri rose slowly to her feet.

"Let me help you with this plate," Jonathan offered. "It looks a little heavy."

Just then Gauri screamed, lunged at Jonathan and knocked him off his seat.

"Gauri—!"

But then Kate began to scream, pointing at the bench where he sat.

And that's when he saw the snake.

"Good Lord!" he exclaimed.

It was a monstrous-looking thing, moving very sluggishly as if it just had swallowed a rat.

Rasoolmian appeared immediately, carrying a long stick with a noose at the end.

"Don't worry, Sahb," he said. "These snakes are a stupid nuisance. I already killed one yesterday. Stand back."

He took aim and swung the stick at the flaccid snake, but Jonathan caught the stick in the air. Rasoolmian stepped back, baffled.

"Hang on," Jonathan said. "Why kill it? Can't you tell it's pregnant? Here. Give the snare to me."

Utterly confused, Rasoolmian handed the snare-stick to Jonathan. The docile snake was easy to trap.

"It's a gardener snake," Jonathan said. "It's harmless. It's probably looking for a safe place to deliver the babies. Let's go, Rasoolmian, we'll release it somewhere near the lake."

Jonathan and Rasoolmian walked off, leaving the women twittering anxiously among themselves. "India," Jonathan said to himself and smiled. "It's a new adventure every day."

chapter eighteen

The following Saturday, like every Saturday, was a fast day. So instead of attending dinner, Jonathan lay in his bed, thinking.

Kate was an interesting woman, he decided. Pain in the neck, but a good heart, and she knew what she was doing. No one could pull the wool over her eyes. And Geeta. She was a confusing one.

Then he thought of Gauri. He thought of the roses she had clipped and her velvety soft voice as she instructed him how to say, 'I love you.' But her voice could carry strength as well—that blood-curdling scream when she had seen the snake. It wasn't fear that had made her scream—at least not fear for herself. It was fear for *him*. For his safety.

He smiled. Dream on! She's half your age, he thought. Probably thought of you as a respected elder about to be eaten. He chuckled softly to himself. And sighed. But maybe not.

Outside, the bells rang, the signal for the weekly Maha-Satsung, the great discourse. The meeting drew a mélange of people: monks, pujarees, politicians, foreigners and villagers.

According to Kate, it was a haven for shy skeptics. Without identifying oneself, one could jot down a comment or a question and drop it into the large glass bowl beside Swamiji, who sat in front of the audience in a padded chair, not on the usual small wooden platform. Jonathan rose and got ready, finding that he was looking forward to the meeting.

The lingering brilliance of the evening sun lit up the large stained glass window in the back wall of Swamiji's cell, whose wide doors were kept open. Like the sun's ray, multicolored glass strips radiated from the center, magically lighting up the attendees' faces. The vibrant hum of two tanpuras with large sound boxes, and the incense wafting over the dark silhouettes of the attendees created a venerable ambiance.

The Buddhist monks began taking their seats in the back. Today, instead of the six monks familiar to Jonathan, there was a seventh one, who looked a bit unusual: plump torso, his head covered with saffron cloth, his movements hesitant. A new recruit?

"Ohmm," uttered Swamiji in his low-pitched voice and closed his eyes, a signal to all to do the same and begin the meditation.

After a few minutes, Swamiji ended the meditation with his holy greeting: "Om Shanti."

The crowd returned the greeting.

Swamiji reached into the glass bowl and randomly picked a rolled-up piece of paper. He unfolded it, read it and smiled at the audience.

"Someone wants to know, do we need religion and God? This is a very relevant question, and in order to answer it, we need to ask another question. What is God? How did God come into existence?

"Our prehistoric, primitive forefathers didn't practice religion. They didn't know what it was. They were simply scared little souls, frightened by a bolt of lightning, roaring thunderstorms, flash floods, fires and earthquakes. They knew these wondrous and dazzling forces were not the doing of human beings. They were aware, God bless their souls, of their limitations. They figured all these fearful wonders came from something or somebody else." He raised his finger upward. "Someone up there.

"Whatever it was, it was invisible, inscrutable, but powerful—very powerful, they thought. They called that mighty force, God. Our frightened little ancestors identified God and introduced the almighty to their children.

"Today times have changed. We humans are knowledgeable and powerful. Science and technology have shown us what causes lightning, thunder, rain and earthquakes. We even know how to split up the smallest particle of matter and generate inexhaustible amounts of energy. We could even conquer the moon and Mars. We have no fears. So why do we need God? Do we still have to believe in that almighty—that imaginary force?

"Well, yes. Perhaps we have answered the questions that puzzled our ancestors, but we have also raised new ones. How was life created? And even if we answer that, why was life created? Why was this universe created? Why do we suffer from the pains of rape, incest, famines, wars, disease and death? Is there heaven or hell? Why does the soul wear the cloak of this avatar? Is there a soul? What is soul? So we looked for someone to answer all these important questions. Someone who knows everything, someone exceptionally brilliant. And we found him—God!

"There is one more question that led us to find God and give him that title of 'Almighty.' Whose fault is it that some godly people die in a plane crash or a gruesome car accident? Why does a child die prematurely? Whose fault is it that a ruthless ruler sets this earth ablaze and explodes bombs to annihilate innocent souls? Is it the fault of the pilot, the doctor, the king? No, it is simply an act of God. It's God's fault. And we are happy we found him. We needed someone to wear the blame around his neck and be responsible for all our follies and sins. And we found him. God!"

He smiled. "But God says, 'My children, that is all right. I'll take the blame; you take the credit. I'm very proud of you, my children. But pay attention,' He says. 'You are my children; I am your father. I want you to fear me. Be God-fearing.' God fearing? Yes, because a God-fearing fellow will not hurt a child, steal from the elderly or infirm or molest a woman. A God-fearing person will not do all these because he is a decent fellow—he is God-fearing. People like that God-fearing person. They talk to him, associate with him, do business with him. He is trustworthy and dependable.

"You see what happened? Merely by mating the word God with such a disliked word as 'fear' created a new, nurturing meaning: God-fearing. God is now providing society with a glue of trust, understanding, respect, lawfulness and love. He said, 'Love thy neighbor, protect the unprotected, feed the hungry, work honestly and industriously to provide for your family.' And so we have a smooth, orderly, protecting, loving philosophy that discourages deceit and destruction. It's a philosophy that nurtures the good elements of birth, growth and love. What is this philosophy? My friends, we call that philosophy 'religion.' We call it Dharma.

There is no need to read scriptures or offer flowers and food to lifeless idols. There is no need to spin out rituals as long as you are decent in your personal and professional deeds. To me, religion is a way of living, not a doctrine etched in stone, or a dogma filled with purposeless procedures that instills fear and instability among its believers. So, do you need God? Yes. Do you need to practice religion? No."

Swamiji paused. People clapped. He pulled out another slip of paper.

"Oh, another good one. 'Who am I? What is the purpose of my life and where am I going to go after death?'" He took a sip of water. "You are nothing but a flesh covering for the divine energy that resides inside you—the soul. Your soul decided to be born in a family, into a country, as a gender of its choice. The physical body that covers that soul can be black, white, brown, yellow. It could be tall, short, male or female. These are inconsequential aspects of your existence. What is important is that the body dies but the soul does not. The soul is immortal. Bhagvat Gita says it beautifully: '*Na jayate mriyate va kadachin. Nayam Bhutva bhavita va na bhuyah. Ajo nityah sasvato yam purano. Na hanyate hanyamane sarire.*' This beautiful Sanskrit verse means: There is no birth and death for the soul. Nor, having once been, does he ever cease to be. He is unborn, eternal, inexorable, imperishable and primeval. He is not slain when the body is slain."

Jonathan instantaneously thought of Becky and their dead child. But this time he felt more calm and peaceful. He sat still with his eyes closed.

"That is who you are," Swamiji said. "So why are you here? There are many individual reasons, of course, but in general life is a labyrinth of learning. A soul must pass through that labyrinth. The lesson? Learning to forgive and to love. Learning that earthly pleasure is Maya—an illusion. Fight the illusion of temptation—a desire to eat tasty food, a craving for chemicals not necessary to sustain life, the lure of extramarital sex, a blinding ambition to acquire quick wealth, to own the biggest house, the sportiest car, and the most eye-dazzling diamond. These are captivating illusions—Maya. Maya dulls men's senses like ash smothers an ember, like dust fogs a mirror, like dark clouds cover the glow of the luminous moon.

"Finally, where are you going to go after you die? Heaven or hell?" Swamiji shrugged. "Sorry, I can't help you. I don't know. I haven't been there yet."

Swamiji laughed and the crowd joined his laughter.

"But I do know this," he said, his face serious. "Don't fear death. Death is not an end; it is a transition—a bridge that opens a door to another birth. Death helps the soul toward the ultimate goal of enlightenment. Our souls descend to this brief respite of life, this hermitage, this Ashram. They go through the most wonderful experience of loving someone and being loved by someone. They live and learn. Then, one day they say good-bye to this Ashram and move on.

"*Mrityu aur Manavta*: love and death. Both are the ultimate awakeners. If your love does not move someone, the sight of death—its mere inkling—will move him. He will awaken enlightened, anew, ready to embrace the eternal power of life and rectitude. I wish we all could have a glimpse of death. We all will come out like a butterfly breaking open a cocoon. Death is such a liberator!

"So what do you do about your next life now? Well, it's all right if you don't become a scholar of philosophy or religion or don't write books of wisdom. But you must be the master of your own deeds on this earth—your karma. Don't worry about your past and the avatars to follow. No need to die; try life first. Worrying about death is like paying up the taxes before you even start the job! Live a good life and a good death will follow. Mind your current karma well. Why do the Buddhists not care for hereafter? Heaven or hell? Because our heaven or hell is here, today, in your deed, right on this earth."

Jonathan thought about his father's Unitarian philosophy. He found his dad's and Swamiji's ideas and interpretations of God and religion strikingly similar, and he liked that. He still didn't agree with Swamiji's thoughts on death—they still seemed to ignore the true horror of it. But he could see how they fit into his religious philosophy, and he listened to him attentively.

Swamiji pulled out another slip of paper. "Which religion is the best religion to follow?" He laughed. "Finally, one with a short answer. There is no such thing as a best religion or worst religion. It is the way we practice our religion that makes it good or bad. Dharma, or religion, in Sanskrit is defined as dutifulness, righteousness, and you don't have to hide in a cave to practice it. And the same is true whatever your religion is: Christianity, Judaism, Islam, Hinduism. Practice your religion among people. Don't race to become a yogi who hides in seclusion. Be a karma yogi. If while you are living in society and earning your bread, it is perfectly all right to cite the Bible, chant Gayatri or recite Daroodsharif. Now you are a true yogi.

"Yoga means union with God or yourself—your soul. Gautama Buddha, Mahatma Gandhi, Mohammed, Christ—they were the real yogis. These good souls reconciled with their inner core and ultimately with God. You can wander from Dwarka to Himpal, from Kashi to Kanyakumari, Nasik to Nalanda or roam from the Alps to the Andes. But my friends, as long as you don't wander inside yourself, as long as you don't reconcile with your soul, you will not find peace. You will not find God."

As Swamiji stretched his hand into the bowl to fetch the next question, one of the attendees, who looked like a Hindu priest, raised his hand.

"Yes Vyasji?" Swamiji said.

"Maharaj," the priest said, "what is your impression of Islam? People say it makes practicing Muslims fanatics, like the Palestinians killing the Jews. Some say it encourages cruelty towards women. Some Muslims drink, gamble and womanize, and their women, they say, are suppressed and kept behind chadors. What is your learned opinion?"

Swamiji looked at the floor for a second, then he looked up. "Vyasji, nowhere in the holy Quran does it say that by suppressing women or enslaving them, a Muslim gets closer to Allah.

"About the women, the Quran says: 'You people! Fear your lord, who created you both from a single soul. From that soul he created your spouses and through them bestrewed the earth with countless men and women. Fear Allah and honor the mother who bore you. Give women their dowry as a free gift. Men are the protectors and maintainers of women because God has given them more strength.'"

Then he looked at the Pujaree. "As for the veil covering Muslim women's faces, again, Quran indicates: 'O wives of the prophet! You are not like ordinary women. If you fear Allah, don't be so casual in your speech, lest someone with an unsteadfast heart should be moved with desire.'

"These verses from the holy book are saying that men and women are made from the same one source and they are equal. Women are to be honored and protected by the men. Holy Quran cautions women about man's lusty eyes and to avoid flaring up their sexual desires, so women should be careful in what they say, how they dress and avoid even incidental displays of their bodies."

"But this is not the practice of Muslim countries," the man insisted.

"My friend, if some society or country wants to exploit women for pleasure or thinks women should just mind the business of cooking, cleaning, bearing and rearing babies, they will make their own convenient interpretations of these holy directives. But did you know that prophet Mohammed married a widow much older than himself? His wife was not only his business partner but a soul mate too. She was a very good businesswoman and the prophet appreciated her and respected her by marrying her and making her his life partner. Now that's respect."

The Hindu priest kept playing with the Rudraksh beads around his neck, clearly unhappy with this praise of Islam. Jonathan smiled. If you don't think you'll like the answer, don't ask the question.

"Maharaj," the priest said, "you are a holy man and a scholar. I'm impressed with your knowledge of Islam, but don't you have any good things to say about Hinduism? After all, you are a Hindu yourself, aren't you?"

"Of course, my brother," Swamiji said. "I was born in a Hindu family. But I am a Muslim too. And a Jew, and a Christian, and a Sikh—I'm all of them. Like Judaism, Hinduism is the mother of many religions, an ocean of wisdom and knowledge. Look at Bhagvat Gita. It shows the man a way to live his life. But what if man misinterprets the message? If a Muslim believes killing a Jew is going to lead him to Shahadat or martyrdom and a place in the heaven, a Hindu is equally likely to misinterpret what is written in the Gita."

"So you do feel there is no good in Hinduism," the priest said.

"Oh, no. Look at the wealth of knowledge Hinduism has given to humanity. It gave the philosophy of Ahimsa—nonviolence—that Mahatma Gandhi used to liberate India. Like Christianity it has a holy trinity: Brahma, Vishnu and Mahesh. Brahma gives birth, Vishnu gives sustenance and Mahesh or Lord Shiva destroys. But Hinduism is not the only voice with which God speaks. Call him Bhagwan or Parmatma, Allah or Yahweh, Zeus or Odin, it's the same divinity with different identities!"

Leclerc raised his hand. Swamiji motioned him to proceed.

"What about hypocrisy," LeClerc said. "The religions follow double standards throughout the world. Muslims can't eat pork but they can relish lamb biriyani or chicken curry. A Catholic can eat meat six days a week but must eat only fish on Friday. A Jew can not touch dairy food and meat at the same time." He gestured to the priest. "I am sure this nice Hindu man here wouldn't even think about eating cow meat, but some Hindus eat eggs. A fish-eating Bengali Hindu calls fish Jaltori—a waterplant!

"Pigs harbor flat worms, yes," Guillaume said, "but these parasites are destroyed if the meat is well cooked. And what about lamb, sheep and chicken? They harbor parasites too. So how is pork different from other animals? On a broader perspective, do we know if plants experience pain? We even—"

"Stop right there," the Pujaree said. "You are totally wrong. This man is trying to make us all sacrilegious. A grain of wheat is a grain. A bean is a bean. They don't have souls, they don't have sense—"

"Sir, there are fly-trapping plants?" Stephan asked. "Have you heard how their sharp-edged shells clamp down quickly on an insect? Would you call this plant senseless?"

Suddenly, everybody had an opinion, an explanation, a comment or a criticism. All began voicing their responses simultaneously. For a moment it sounded like a fish market on a Saturday morning. Tempers flared, voices were raised and chaos prevailed.

Strangely, Jonathan felt happy. He certainly didn't want to become a rabble-rouser but was happy to see questions and even open and angry doubts were being aired rather than buried. Swamiji's answers to the earlier questions were moving and appealing, mostly, but he was still far from convinced. But one of the best tests of the sincerity of the religion is how it handles sincere questions. Now he could see how Swamiji stood up to the test. Jonathan looked around and smiled. Kate shook her head, glanced at Jonathan, then stood up and began to tap the glass bowl with a metal ballpoint pen. "Gentlemen . . . Gentlemen, please. This is a discourse, not a donnybrook."

Slowly the room quieted down and people began to resume their seats.

"If you want to speak," she said, "stand up and do it nicely and softly. I promise you'll get heard. Let me start from the left of the front row. Right here. Do you have a comment, sir? No? How about you? No comment. Okay. How about you?"

Slowly she worked through everybody, but by this time nobody had anything to say.

"Well," she said, looking at her watch. "If we're all done, I'd urge Baba to say some concluding words. We are running short on time."

Swamiji smiled broadly and looked at everyone. "We should have this Maha-Satsung more often. What excitement! It's been far too quiet here lately."

A soft wave of laughter rose and subsided.

"You all made good points, and it is very hard not to be emotional when talking about our personal religions. I am not religiously irreligious"—He nodded at Jonathan—"but I respect any religion that respects all religions. All religions have something good to offer.

"The Talmud tells a story of a man who wanted to accept Judaism. He goes to a Rabbi and insists the Rabbi teach him the entire Torah. The Rabbi agreed, but only if the proselyte stood on one leg while he did. The man balked, but he wanted to learn, so eventually he agreed. As soon as he was standing on one leg, the learned Rabbi says, 'That which is hateful unto thee, do not do unto thy neighbor. This is the essence of Torah; the rest is commentary.' This is the universal distillation of the essence of all religions. Love your neighbor; be good to all souls. But I would be afraid to call such a universalistic philosophy a religion, because the moment you utter the word, 'religion,' someone wants to tag it with indoctrinations and rituals.

"Mr. Lekhraj, who founded the Brahmakumari philosophy to protect and nurture women and the underprivileged, refused to accept the respect of folded hands or flowers while he was alive. 'I'm a mortal person,' he said to his devotees, 'just like any other person. Please keep your hands in your pockets and offer these flowers to the higher being, not me.' What a humble saint. He discouraged worshipping any human being.

Always watch your belief with skepticism, because belief has a way of transforming into a faith and then into conviction. And before you know, that firm, inflexible conviction freezes into an impenetrable dogma, into futile and fatal fanaticism.

"Now, to the problem of eating meat or vegetables. It is nature's rule that stronger eats weaker. A man kills a chicken for his meal; a chicken eats worms for its survival; a worm swallows microbe-rich soil for its sustenance. The chain goes on. This is the order of nature designed for the survival of the individual species. I am not recommending you eat meat; that is up to you. I personally do not believe in the necessity of killing an animal for my survival because I am a living proof that God has left enough nourishment in fruits, vegetables and grains. Gandhiji was a strict vegetarian. He died at age 79, and not from malnourishment. I am also afraid to make my own soul suffer because of the negative vibrations from something I ate— something that was hurting or crying when it was sacrificed for my selfish survival. What he eats or does not eat is his karma. He will have to reconcile it with his soul."

Someone tapped on Jonathan's shoulder. Jonathan looked back. It was Rasoolmian. He handed Jonathan a note:
> My dear Jonathan,
>
> Important developments have taken place relative to the suttee. I must have a word with you. Please telephone me tomorrow morning—prior to 10 a.m. Looking forward to hearing from you.
>
> Yours sincerely,
> Jaya Prakash Joshi

chapter nineteen

Kate was on her way out to the garden when Jonathan caught up with her.

"Kate," he said, "I've been meaning to talk with you."

"Well, there's a switch. You've not had much to say at all lately!" she teased.

"If you mean at the meeting, I guess it was one of those rare occasions where I did more thinking than talking."

Kate sat down next to him. Gauri and Geeta were busy picking greens from the garden.

"What is it?" Kate said, tilting her head conspiratorially.

"It's about the suttee," Jonathan began.

Kate sighed, and rolled her eyes. "That again."

Jonathan was taken aback.

"I'm sorry," Kate said. "I know it's important to you. But now that you know she didn't die, I was hoping you might get some relief from the whole thing."

"I had no idea I'd become such a bore," he said, half-sarcastic, half-sincere.

"I apologize, Jonathan. Don't mind me. It must be my impatient nature."

"No, I'm sorry. I truly must be running this thing into the ground," he said. "I am grateful though that law enforcement hasn't lost interest."

"Well, what happened to her?" Kate said. She seemed to be interested, in spite of herself. "Did she really get away from them?"

"Well, you can bet she was gone by the morning of the suttee," he said. "Otherwise her body would have been on the pyre."

"They could have sold her into prostitution," Kate said.

"And take the risk that she'd show up again and spoil their temple plans? No, she was alive and free as of suttee morning. I have to believe it. The only question is, where is she now?"

"Jonathan," Kate said, "I don't mean to disappoint you, but if she is alive—and I certainly hope she is—it's going to be very difficult to find her."

"Why?"

"Why? Her abductors can't afford to have people believe Seeta is alive. Surely they're looking for her now and she's just as certain to be aware of this herself. So to remain alive, she must play dead. Do you see my point?"

Of course that was true. Jonathan had not thought of it with all of the other details of the case on his mind.

"It sounds as though finding her is very important to you," said Kate.

"It is, it's a kind of purpose—no that's not the word. It's necessary in a way I can't explain," he said. "Something inside me says it's important; that it's what I need to do." Jonathan put his hands in his lap and looked down. "And I have to listen," he said quietly.

"I think I understand," Kate said.

"You've been so good to me," Jonathan said. "So accommodating. I wish I could be more clear, more open . . ."

"Forget that. What you need to do is accomplish your goal.

There's probably only one way you could actually locate this woman."

"And what is that?" said Jonathan, intrigued.

"You could try looking for her." Kate laughed. "Really. Have you thought of going to the town and giving it a good honest try?"

"I think you could be right," Jonathan said, his heart beginning to soar.

"It might not be a bad idea to take someone with you, though."

"Well, probably. But I think the Ashram needs Rasoolmian more than I."

"I meant for purposes of a guide, an interpreter."

"Kate! Would you?"

"Certainly not!" Kate said sarcastically. "Actually, our fearless leader would be lost without me. I have come to believe, anyway. How about Geeta, or Gauri?"

Jonathan thought he saw her eyes narrow in challenge, or was it curiosity?

"Are you kidding, Kate? They'd never agree to that."

"How do you know? You could always ask."

With the fate of so many village women and then the story of the informer fresh in his mind, Jonathan quickly declined.

"You don't want to ask, I will," said Kate, taking off like a shot. When she returned, she had brought both Geeta and Gauri with her. She'd placed one on either side of her as if the three of them were contestants on the Dating Game.

Jonathan had to smile, despite his dislike of the situation.

"Both have agreed," Kate announced a little too cheerfully. "So whom do you choose?"

Jonathan cleared his throat, and turned uncomfortably. "Have you explained that it's Baramedi I'm visiting?" he asked.

"What difference does it make?" Kate asked defiantly.

"Baramedi?" Geeta said, standing up abruptly. "No, not to Baramedi. No way!"

Kate appeared taken aback, but before she could inquire further, Geeta disappeared into the kitchen.

"What was all that about?" Jonathan asked.

Kate explained: "She equates Baramedi with fire and raging rivers. She can't even swim, poor thing. How about you, Gauri? Would you go to Baramedi with Dr. Sahb?"

Gauri rose slowly. She stood still, looking down and clicking her nails. Then she smiled and said softly, "I will accompany you . . . Dr. Sahb."

"Thank you . . . Gauri," he said, strangely peaceful inside. And surprisingly excited.

She looked at him for a split second. Then she was gone.

Jonathan stared after her, expressionless, almost in a trance. Before he could express his gratitude and awe, Kate burst forth.

"Whoa! Down, boy! You think the old body can take it?" she laughed, almost harshly.

Jonathan felt his face reddening. Suddenly the peace he'd felt within had become turmoil.

"You like her, don't you?" Kate said.

"Yes, but—"

"Just as a friend? Come on, Jonathan!" she said.

"No, I wasn't going to say that."

"So I was right?" she demanded.

"I don't know. I was just going to say that—oh, it doesn't matter. It's too hard to explain. And for the record, I like all three of you lovely ladies I've met here."

"Oh, I bet you do," Kate chuckled. "I didn't know Unitarians had harems."

Jonathan smiled at Kate. "Why not? And we're accepting applications, if you're interested."

"Men! They're all the same—everywhere!" She stood and raised her voice. "Well, I'm not—"

"Oh, come on, Kate! I was only kidding. And besides, it was your joke!"

"I'm not sure just how much of a joke it actually was, come to think of it. It never fails. Men can't stand women who stand up for themselves."

"Kate—"

"Jonathan, the fact is, no man would ever have the audacity

to admit it, but it's true. You all love servile women. Even supposedly enlightened men like you."

Jonathan sat up. His inner peace had been dashed to the ground, broken in pieces and trampled by a hundred buffalo. "Kate, I don't know whether or not men go for subservient women, but one thing I know for sure: not many men fall for the ball-busters."

"Christ!" Kate yelled. "Go ahead, swear. Be cocky. Get it off your chest!" Kate paused. "Since we're being open and honest, tell me something. If Gauri and Geeta—who are neither servile nor ball-busters—both asked you to marry them, which would you choose?"

Jonathan shook his head. "See, Kate, that's the whole problem with you. You get rolling and never see someone else's point. And—"

"So what's your point?" she demanded.

"This is my point. As much as you seem to have convinced yourself that it is so, my mission here is not choosing a woman—someone whom I would like to marry. I am human. I can certainly see that there are three lovely women here—three, Kate. But I'm serious about no one. And the problem is not my inability to make a 'choice' as you say. It's my inability to—"

"Love anyone?"

Jonathan stopped and stared at Kate. "No. The truth is, I still love someone else. Her name was Rebecca."

Both were silent for a moment. Finally, Jonathan rose.

"Excuse me," he said softly as he walked away.

chapter twenty

By the next day, things had lightened up.
At lunch, Kate had apologized for her harshness.
"You weren't harsh, really," Jonathan had responded. "Maybe just a little intense."

"Intense?" she had laughed. "Isn't that the pot calling the kettle black?"

It was true. For nearly a year, Jonathan had been nothing if not intense.

But by 3:30 p.m. that day, he was more like a child in school waiting for the bell to ring. It had all been arranged. Rasoolmian would accompany him into Baramedi, and Gauri would accompany him as an interpreter. Although for her protection, she would be disguised as a male companion. Jonathan wanted no one associated with him in any way, other than the robust Rasoolmian, who could take on anyone who challenged. The risk was too much, the consequences too great.

By 3:45 p.m., the whole picture had changed. In those fifteen minutes, Jonathan witnessed again the results of the hideous disfiguring of a young woman's private parts described so simply days before by Judge Joshi. As a detached physician, Jonathan was able to stitch the tender skin into some semblance of order, and soothe the victim with pain killing medications. But he knew she would never mend. And he would not under any circumstances expose the peaceful Gauri to the ills of the village which he most definitely would be investigating that evening.

"Are you certain you still wish to go?" Rasoolmian asked.

"More certain than ever," Jonathan answered.

Jonathan phoned Judge Joshi and left a message, informing him of his plan to visit Baramedi. In a way, he was relieved not to find his friend at home. He was determined to go, yet quite sure Joshi would not approve.

The Shivner postmaster, who had become quite friendly, insisted Jonathan carry a rifle with him, particularly if he planned to go to the temple in Baramedi.

"Sir," he said, "I'm telling you this for your own protection. I don't mean to scare you, but at such new temples, these crazy villagers offer human sacrifices to Devimaata. They see a white stranger, oh, they think, 'Chop him down. This is a *pukka* sacrifice. Mother deity will be pleased.' Please, Doc Sahb, take this rifle."

Jonathan glanced at Rasoolmian. He nodded, earnestly.

"Okay." Jonathan let him carry the rifle—just in case. He left the pony with the postmaster and climbed into their rented Land Rover.

By the time he arrived at Baramedi, the sun had already painted Vasundhara's waters red. The damaged bridge had been repaired but looked no more stable than it had on Jonathan's last trip across it. A cloud of parrots took over the banyan tree. He smiled nostalgically in spite of his situation.

"Rasoolmian," he said, as they began to approach the little village. "Let me out here. I will go on foot. You stay with the car and come looking for me if I don't turn up by 9:00 p.m."

"Sir?" he answered. "The rifle?"

"No, you hang on to it. I think I might look more conspicuous carrying it." Jonathan showed him a hunter's knife hidden beneath two thin layers of clothing. "I'll be fine with this."

Jonathan was dressed in typical villager's attire. But he scoffed at his own expression of self-confidence. He had little idea how to use a knife as a weapon. Now, he thought, if I were planning to take out an appendix, that would be a different story. He thought as he walked along that, gruesome as it sounded, it would probably be a very effective approach in the event that he were threatened by any knife-wielding marauders.

As he ascended the slope and approached the plateau of the village square, the pealing of the temple bell grew louder. Where Bholanath had decreed that a temple be constructed in honor of their "suttee," token construction had begun and a bell tower hastily thrown together. Kerosene lanterns gave the scene a soft, yellow light.

As he approached, the framework for the temple became clearer. It's amazing, he thought, how quickly one can accomplish something when properly motivated! The temple apparently was to be modest—a plan that did not surprise Jonathan—with a small sanctum where once the bodies had roasted along with coconuts and marigolds. Disguised as a farmer returning home from the fields, Jonathan covered his head and shoulders with a Himpali blanket and ambled around the temple-to-be with other worshippers, smoking a biri.

Villagers milled about in long lines, holding food or coconuts, chanting, some crying and prostrating themselves, others taking in the beatific flames from the earthen diyas placed on the floor. A young pujaree, his forehead splattered with sandalwood paste, head shaven down to a long ponytail, stood by the doorway, mumbling incomprehensible blessings and rubbing vermilion and rice onto the bowing foreheads of the souls seeking salvation—for a fee.

There was a stir outside over a cow and her calf tied in front of the temple. As Jonathan got closer, he realized that the star attraction was the calf—not surprising, since it had two heads. The freak show mentality brought back the anger he'd felt before at what he had come to term the Suttee Carnival. Well good, he thought. It will provide a distraction so I can move a little more freely. But then he spotted the guards.

Dressed in homespun cotton uniforms, they strolled around, bearing lathis in their hands, eyeing the crowds with an odd mix of glee and paranoia. Jonathan kept subtly out of their way until darkness was complete, after which he eased into line to get a closer look at the pujaree doing the blessing.

Concealed behind an obese businessman-like devotee, Jonathan noticed the pots of silver coins and few bundles of paper rupees parked beside the pujaree. The line moved very slowly, so it was hard to get a look at the pujaree directly. Then as the space briefly widened between worshippers, Jonathan noticed something. As the worshipper being blessed by the pujaree bowed, the pujaree swiftly passed a bundle of notes to someone behind him, concealed in a separate room. All Jonathan saw was a hand with a thick metal band around the wrist, but he was certain he recognized it.

Jonathan's heart began to pound. He covered the lower half of his face and began mock-coughing. Soon he left the queue as if searching for a glass of water or relief of some sort, and walked way behind the end of the line.

Once he was well away from the light of the kerosene lamps, he made his way around back. There was a small door. Barely breathing, he waited behind the bush, his eyes fixed on that door. For a while, nothing happened. The distant murmuring of the devotees, the periodic ringing bells, and the howling of the wild animals created a sense of eerie anxiety.

Suddenly, the door opened. A man wearing a white Gandhian cap emerged. He held a cloth bag in one hand and a kerosene lantern in the other. He raised the lantern to his face to secure his path on the steps. There was a hideous disfigurement of his eye—and no sling on his arm.

Jonathan's breath was hard and sharp. Anger choked away his fear as he stood beholding Buttasingh, the councilman of Baramedi.

He felt the hunting knife under his clothing, and his own wretched fury blackly urging him to simply slash the man's throat. Common sense prevailed however, as he pulled together the facts. The cloth bag held cash. The cash was doubtless for Buttasingh and Bholanath to enjoy, but who else? He could see no alternative but to follow.

As Buttasingh walked ahead, his lantern cast hideous nocturnal shadows of his legs and the cloth bag on the opposite side of the road. Jonathan walked very softly, a few yards behind him, well covered under the veil of darkness. The cries of predators in the nearby woods intensified.

Suddenly, Buttasingh stopped. Jonathan slipped back. It appeared that an animal had crossed the councilman's path. He resumed his journey. Jonathan waited a moment, then continued on himself.

Suddenly, Jonathan stumbled over a dry branch.

"Who is that?" Buttasingh demanded, his voice hard, his lantern held high. Jonathan held his breath.

Buttasingh extracted something shiny from his pocket and headed straight for Jonathan.

Jonathan took advantage of the darkness and followed the direction of the dim temple lights.

"Who are you? Stop!" Buttasingh yelled. He ran furiously after his mysterious pursuer.

Jonathan, younger and in better shape, was able to stay ahead of Buttasingh. But was he headed in the right direction? What would happen when the temple guards spotted him— or heard Buttasingh?

Jonathan made for the back door. With one push, he managed to get through and duck inside. As he stood, trying to catch his breath and still his heart, he looked around.

It was dimly lit, and walls had already been erected. Carefully, he descended a set of steps leading into a central seating area, where a lantern burnt atop a metal trunk. Then he climbed another set of steps that led to a niche where devotional paraphernalia was stored. He hid behind the columns of metal pots, heaps of coconuts, and old furniture.

He heard voices of the dispersing devotees. There's another door to the outside on this wall, he thought. I'm probably in the belly of the temple. This could turn out to be quite catastrophic! What if Buttasingh followed me here?

Seconds later, he heard the door he'd just come through open. From his hiding place, he could make out the figure of a man, slowly descending the stairs. The lantern revealed only his dhoti-swaddled legs as he neared Jonathan. Then, he stopped, turned back, but then changed direction again and headed straight for Jonathan's hideout.

Jonathan held his breath and put a hand over the handle of his knife. He prayed Buttasingh did not have a gun.

Then, without pausing to think it through, Jonathan turned and kicked open the door behind him. Before he darted out, he was able to identify his pursuer. It was not Buttasingh! It was the pujaree who had been giving blessings for cash out front.

On the other side of the door, Jonathan skidded head-on into a mass of foul-smelling discarded fruits. He spat out the repulsive rot, wiped his eyes, and found himself outside again, staring at a pair of dhoti-clad legs and a lantern. And a cloth bag.

"Welcome back, Doc Sahb," Buttasingh said, holding up his lantern. "Here, let me give you a hand."

Jonathan stood up on his own, shaking the garbage from his clothes. His knife was within easy reach. But Buttasingh's guards were beginning to gather and stare like tall, angry vultures.

"Good evening, Councilman," Jonathan said as evenly as possible. "How are you?"

Jonathan never heard Buttasingh's answer. Miraculously, and with commendable timing, a Land Rover blasted through the crowd, squealing to a stop behind Buttasingh. Amid the cloud of dust and confusion, the burly figure of Rasoolmian emerged, a club in one arm, an automatic rifle in the other, and proceeded fearlessly toward Jonathan.

"It's nine o' clock, Doc Sahb," he announced flatly. "We must leave." Then he turned to Buttasingh. "*Jay Ramjiki.*"

"Yes," Jonathan said. "Forgive me, Councilman, but I must go. I'll see you around. Soon, I hope."

chapter twenty-one

Jonathan spent the night at the old Raj hotel in Himpal before ascending the mountain to the Ashram. Originally a boarding house for soldiers and laborers, the hotel had retained its 1920s-style hospitality—a coal burning fireplace, pull-chain toilets, a claw foot bathtub, large enough for two—all well-preserved and functional. A more contemporary amenity was the presence of an armed night guard. Absent the use of a telephone, he was forced to wait until the following day to call Joshi.

After thanking the driver profusely and tipping him, Jonathan began to patch together what he'd learned. He felt as if he'd found a handful of puzzle pieces in a drawer. He had no idea how many pieces were missing or even whether what he had all belonged to the same puzzle. But soon he realized there was a thread. The pujaree at the temple hadn't been Bholanath.

It was then that it hit him. He'd nearly been killed. He was a doctor, volunteering to assist women at the depths of poverty and malicious social distress; victims of a culture and lifestyle with which he had had no previous experience.

Although the thought that he had narrowly escaped a truly dangerous situation scared him, it also somehow invigorated him. There was that strange monk at the discourse, and the way the gang, whoever they were, operated across the border. As charged up as he was, as soon as he lay down, he fell into a deep, restful sleep.

When he awoke, he got up and asked the hotel's night guard about the Ghoom monastery.

The guard told him that the monks from the monastery rose very early in the morning and walked to the Suryapuja hill, where they said their first prayer as the sun rose behind the Kanchanjenga—the third highest Himalayan peak, revered by the Hindus. Jonathan urged the guard to arrange for him to join them—for the sake of the spiritual experience.

The guard shook Jonathan awake at 4 a.m. He quickly got dressed by the fading embers of the coal fire in his room and joined his escort—a Gurkha soldier who apparently spoke neither Hindi nor English—to quietly and distantly follow a row of ten Buddhist monks. The monks' chanting echoed through the tiny streets and the crumbling Victorian buildings.

The dark streets were enlivened by the hum of the chants as the monks swayed ahead of Jonathan, their hands folded, their eyes downcast. He had to admit, it was hypnotically beautiful. Thirty minutes later the monks arrived at an open plateau that faced the mountains. Soon, as though the heavens had heard the monk's wistful words, the mountains released the golden red glow of the rising, majestic sun. The Monks fixed their eyes at the Kanchenjenga and stood without a sound or a movement. The snow-clad summits of the Himalayas began to light up.

The glorious celestial beams lit the pious, calm faces and the saffron robes of the monks. As the sun rose higher, the monks bowed their heads and resumed the chanting. The chant built to a crescendo, then fell silent. After a few moments, the monks turned around and retreated back to the monastery with reverent discipline, folded hands, downcast eyes and an inexorable joy on their faces.

The new, rotund monk Jonathan had seen at the Ashram was not among them. And for some reason the guard politely refused to escort Jonathan to the monastery. Arguing with him was impossible; there was no common language.

At 6:00 a.m. the office was open.

"Good morning," he said in Hindi to the clerk. "Telephone?"

Joshi came abruptly to the point. "I wish you would leave the investigating to the experts. Who do you think you are? James Bond? More like Barney Fife! You could have gotten yourself killed!"

"I don't understand—how did you know . . ."

"Don't you think I have intelligence there? I did not even need to get your message. I knew when I got the report that a Western man had been rescued from a pack of Baramedi wolves by a giant with a club there was no doubt you had decided to become Inspector Clouseau."

Jonathan didn't know whether to laugh or defend himself. "But I have something to tell you—about Buttasingh . . ."

"We know all about Buttasingh," Joshi said.

"You do?" Jonathan was crestfallen.

"Yes, you see, you did not need to jeopardize life and limb. We learned earlier this week that he has opened an account in the governmental bank and set up a trust fund to construct an educational center for young and underprivileged women."

"Well, how philanthropic of the man! How much of the proceeds do you think actually makes it into the fund?"

"My dear boy, if we were to arrest all of our corrupt village officials, the government would likely collapse. The society leaders and the politicians on either side of the border are grateful for Buttasingh's goodwill, and anyway, at least some of the money from the suttee temple will be put to the right task."

"You think I was ever really in any danger there?" Jonathan said.

"When money is at stake, there is always danger. There are many bad things going on in Baramedi. As I said, some of your fellow devotees last night were undercover CBI agents. Please, leave the investigation to them. They are really quite good at it, you know."

"I feel like an idiot."

"As you should."

There was silence for a moment, and then Joshi's hearty laughter burst through the receiver. Jonathan felt relief. "But at least I feel like an appreciated idiot."

"Oh, you're not a fool—not by a long stretch," Joshi said. "But you must allow me to guide your safety. You are a stranger to this country. Even if you were wise to the village ways, as a white man, you stick out like a sore tongue."

Jonathan laughed. "Thumb!" he said. "You can stick out your tongue, or stick out *like* a sore *thumb*—but I understand your meaning."

"No harm done, then."

"No, as long as I haven't screwed things up for you."

"No, I'm sure not. In fact, in some ways it may help to stir things up—bring things more into the open if they feel more pressure."

"Has anyone located the barber, Murli?"

"No, and with the councilman running things at the temple building site, if this character Jalim Singh, or even the pujaree are involved, we may have no way to prove it."

"Yes, we need a break. But I don't think we should go the route of informers again."

"The word you should be using is *you*. Remember? But yes, you are right. We must get a good break—and without anymore bloodshed!"

After he settled his bill, Jonathan retrieved his pony at the post office and began the long journey up the serpentine trail to the Ashram. Birds chirped and flew joyously, and the terror of the night before seemed to fade, like a remnant of a weakening dream.

Then he came upon the trail to the FORBIDDEN ZONE sign. He pulled the pony's reins and stopped.

That meeting he'd witnessed past the sign may just have been a border guard meeting his sweetheart, but with everything else going on around here, could he let a curiosity like that pass? Joshi would have his head if he knew, but Jonathan really hadn't been in any danger the night before. He turned his pony up the trail, tied her to a tree and cautiously stepped over the chains.

The trail wound uphill. Unpicked fruits and waves of flowers adorned the sides of the path. Then he saw fresh horse manure under a deodar tree to his left. While he tried to guess the age of the manure, a baby bird fell out of a nest above and landed at his feet.

Seconds later, the mother bird flapped its wings and hovered around Jonathan, screeching. He pulled his cap from his back pocket and put it on, then put on his sunglasses to protect his eyes.

"Easy, Mama," he said, "I won't harm your baby." He bent down, picked up the chick—

And heard a meaty *thwok* just behind him. He dropped the bird, spun around, then dove into the bush.

A rampuri knife was planted in the trunk at about chest height, its handle still vibrating. If he hadn't bent down . . .

As the bird fluttered over her fallen baby, Jonathan saw someone break from behind a bush up the trail. He tore off his sunglasses, but by then the figure had disappeared into the brush. All he caught was a glimpse of shiny boots.

Jonathan yanked the knife out of the tree and thought about running. But . . . whoever the figure was, he couldn't have another weapon or he would have used it. And he was running away, after all.

Knife in hand, Jonathan set off after him.

Soon he got close enough to see that the big man was limping. He knew he could catch him. Jonathan lengthened his stride.

The man disappeared over the edge of a precipice. When Jonathan arrived at the edge, huffing, he saw it was actually a steep, grassy hillside. A saddled horse was grazing at the bottom, beside a creek.

Someone whistled from the bottom of the hill, and the horse trotted toward the brush. When it was near, the man Jonathan was chasing came into the open, his cap pulled low over his face and guarding his left leg. It was too far to make out who it was. He mounted and disappeared upstream.

Jonathan tucked the knife in his belt and picked his way down the hill. There was no way to catch the rider, but he wanted to see where the man was headed. And who he was.

The trail by the creek seemed fairly well used and eventually led up another hill. Jonathan wasn't entirely sure, but his sense of direction told him he had doubled back and was near the Ashram. Finally he arrived, panting, on top of the plateau. The horse and rider had disappeared. Jonathan bent over his knees to catch his breath.

The trail led around the other side of the hill. By the time he got there, the horseman was out of his sight, but he saw the back of a woman. Curiously, she began running away across the field of wild flowers with an empty panier pressed against her side.

Jonathan rushed to catch up with her. He was pretty winded by then, but her sari held her back, and he soon caught up with her. He grabbed a handful of her sari, flapping in the wind behind her, and she fell.

He stood over her. She lay on the ground, her sari stripped away, her blouse torn, her hands covering her face. She was speaking too fast to be understood, but it sounded like she was begging for her life. Gently, he pulled her hands away from her face.

"Gauri?" he panted. "Why . . . why were you running away from me?"

He realized it was a stupid question as soon as he asked it. A strange man, catching her alone? Of course she ran.

"Babuji!" she yelled, then began to cry.

Jonathan covered her torn blouse with her sari that had spread out across the bed of flowers. "That's okay. Calm down."

Gauri got control and tidied herself up. "Oh, forgive me, Doc Sahb. I did not know it was you. I thought—"

"It's all right," he said. Then he noticed the basket in the flowers nearby. Gathering wildflowers was usually Geeta's job. "Where is Geeta?"

"*Bimaar.*"

"Sick? She wasn't sick yesterday!"

Damn. Mysteries on top of mysteries. He helped Gauri up and started back to the Ashram. They walked quietly, side by side, but Jonathan's thoughts were racing. What was going on here? Who was trying to kill him? And what did Gauri have to do with the deepening mystery?

chapter twenty-two

After a mercifully slow day at the clinic, Jonathan felt inspired to make the short trek to Shantisarover Lake. As he sat down under a lush apple tree, a wave of butterflies fluttered through, reminding him of the quietly flapping wings he'd seen amid the potato blossoms in Allagash, Maine the previous spring.

He sighed contentedly and settled against the smooth trunk of the tree. Time had slipped by like a salamander in the dunes. He watched the butterflies hopping from flower to flower, and the squirrels running up and down the trees. Their spontaneity, their innocence stood in such stark contrast to the deliberate, premeditated fleecing of the villagers he'd witnessed. I shouldn't think of that here, now, he told himself, inhaling deeply.

Suddenly a thought came to mind. Seeta was out there somewhere. The gang clearly wanted her back in the worst way. And Bapuji, her last living relative, would make an excellent hostage. The old man might still be alive somewhere, being held as a bargaining chip.

Jonathan noticed that the sky was growing dark again. First, a few bulbous drops, like a heavenly harbinger, landed randomly around him, leaving splattered imprints on the dusty, dry leaves. Then the downpour began. But there was no lightning. Worms wriggled out of the ground and the birds began to feast. Jonathan, well protected under the tree's generous branches, thought of the parched farmland around Baramedi, hoping the rains would bring better crops and prosperity for the coming season.

Quickly, the downpour passed, leaving the air scrubbed clean. In an unexpected state of peace, he decided to take a short nap.

He had hardly started to drift off when he heard singing along the trail. It sounded like "Hippety, hoppity, hippety, hop." He sat up, feeling confused, and very much like Alice before she fell down the rabbit hole. Before long, he realized that what he had been hearing was the Hindi language, though the song was still recognizably a children's song. It was being sung by a woman.

Then, hair flying unpretentiously, like that of a schoolgirl, Gauri came hopping down the trail, both legs jumping in tandem to the rhythm of the song. Jonathan sat forward, amazed and strangely delighted at the spectacle. The red crystal bangles on her wrists clinked as the white scarf around her neck mixed in with her airborne hair. She wore a wide, beautiful, unspoiled smile on her face. The inner joy he felt at witnessing her simple happiness overwhelmed him.

When she reached the shore, she dropped her sari, and still singing, began to sway side to side. Plainly she had come to the lake to bathe. Jonathan, not wishing to intrude on her privacy, prepared to covertly depart.

But then, Gauri knelt down and began to pick wild flowers, drawing them close to her and inhaling their gentle fragrances. She seemed so at ease, in contrast to the intense and anxious young lady who had arrived such a short time before. Jonathan watched how freely she seemed to almost become the beauty of the nature around her. He was mystified. Enchanted.

Before he could rise to his feet, she had disappeared behind a bush. Then suddenly, she darted out, splashed into the water, and submerged. After a moment, Jonathan panicked. Where was she? But soon she burst up through the water, the sun gleaming over her silky hair, fanning out on the surface of the water around her. There she stood, wearing nothing but her white scarf, which clung to her breasts and her belly. She threw her head back, her hair sending droplets of water in a myriad of directions, and wiped the water from her face.

Jonathan sighed and averted his eyes. He was respectful of her need for privacy, but he longed to indulge himself further in the view of this magnificent woman. Wild thoughts went through his head—standing up with his arms out wide, or even splashing in fully clothed beside her. Then he remembered Joshi's referring to him as Barney Fife and got hold of himself.

The sun was beginning to sink. As Gauri resumed her happy little tune, a flock of birds landed on the tree under which Jonathan sat, and roosted attentively, waiting for dinner. Jonathan slipped quietly away, the vision of Gauri's golden nakedness wrapped tenderly inside his memory.

Yet, he began to struggle as the bright glow faded with the sun. What kind of person am I, he thought. I'm supposed to be helping these women, showing them the respect their own citizens will not. I'm here to set their broken bones, but also to help heal the wounds of the heart. And I sit and spy, like some adolescent or sick voyeur on holiday.

Even as he browbeat himself, he knew his anger was not at his behavior. He hadn't behaved badly—he'd averted his eyes, he'd left before embarrassing himself—and no doubt Gauri, too. Yet, he felt an intense turmoil growing inside that he could not contain. What was antagonizing him so? His heart pounded and he began to sweat so much that he felt afraid. And then it hit him.

He dropped to the ground, awash in guilt. In the shade of a banyan tree, with his heart wrenching apart, he quietly began to cry. And the more he released the pain, the more forcefully it flowed.

"Becky! I'm sorry, Becky. I'm . . ." His heart broke, realizing he hadn't thought of her, of the loss of her, of the pain of losing her, in over two days. Shame and remorse seemed to choke him, rebuking his thoughts and feelings of Gauri. Feelings, he thought. How can I give any thought to feelings—for someone else? She's only been gone two years! What kind of monster am I?

He rested his head against the bark of the tree, trying to catch his breath. When his heart stopped pounding and his breathing slowed, he turned and cautiously looked around. Gauri was gone.

chapter twenty–three

Kate met him at the Ashram. "So where have you been, Your Highness? The local play group is presenting folk dances for the Holi Festivals right after dinner."

Jonathan smiled gently. "Holy? As in holy cow?" His experience had left him drained, but somehow more relaxed.

"Nope, but you'll soon find out. Swamiji will allow us to have some very diluted Bhang."

"Bhang?"

"A drink made of marijuana buds, milk and sugar. When you come, wear only the clothes you always wanted to throw away."

Jonathan grinned. "And will Swamiji be taking part in this bacchanalia?"

"He'll be in his room, resting."

After dinner, Jonathan joined the buzzing audience in the main hall, a freshly cut rose in his lap. Geeta approached him and he motioned her to take a seat next to him. A few moments later, Gauri shyly sat down at his left.

As happy as he was to see Gauri, Jonathan was almost afraid to look at her. Afraid that his shame would show. Afraid that he would either embarrass himself or become overcome again with the emotions that had choked him earlier.

Yet, the warmth of her presence gave him a steadiness, as though he were being gently rocked in a cradle. He looked at her and their gazes locked. Neither spoke.

What is she thinking? he wondered. Did she see me there today? Does she know I saw her? If she were totally disgusted with me, she wouldn't sit next to me, would she? Unless somebody told her to. And what do I care anyway? What is wrong with me? He tried to shake off the awkwardness by attempting a fatherly smile. He offered her the rose.

Gauri smiled, looking, it seemed to Jonathan, as if she were posing for her senior portrait.

Kate scurried around behind the announcer, helping the troupe organize the props.

"My dear madams and sirs," the leader of the group said in Hindi. "Namashkar, good night. Holi Festival is a festival of village folks and farmers celebrating the arrival of the spring and harvesting their crops."

By listening carefully, Jonathan was able to catch the gist of it. His language skills were improving.

"It is a time of joy and welcoming, appreciating and celebrating the bounty from the gods: god of wind, god of rain, goddess of fertility and many, many gods and goddesses.

"First, we will present a folk dance by women. They'll show you how they harvest the crop."

As soon as he had finished his last sentence, the powerful sound of Indian drums, the dholaks, filled the air. Two turbaned and brightly-attired men wearing the barrel-shaped drums over their stomachs appeared from either side. Shrieks and laughter followed the emergence of village women, who were wearing vivid-colored clothes and large nose rings. Each held a sickle in one hand and a wicker basket in the crook of an arm. They hummed and marched in a row at first and then put down their wares and began singing and dancing in a circle, clapping.

"See, Babuji?" Geeta asked Jonathan. "Stick dance."

"Oh, I see." Jonathan craned his neck to see the dancers, and his cheek rubbed against Geeta's. To his surprise, she didn't withdraw.

Quickly, he turned to Gauri. "Did you dance like this in your village, Gauri?"

As he gestured toward the group, his elbow inadvertently brushed against the side of Gauri's breast. To his surprise, she just smiled and said, "One time."

Jonathan decided to watch the rest of the dance sitting straight up, his arms to his sides.

When the first dance ended, Gauri and Geeta both laughed as Jonathan applauded and said in Hindi, "*Accha . . . Accha . . . Bahot . . . Accha.*"

Then the leader of the troupe approached the audience, looking for some volunteers. He selected Jonathan and Gauri. She hesitated at first but was soon guiding Jonathan through the intricate moves. Then the leader grabbed Claus and Geeta by their wrists.

As they got the hang of the thing, the rhythm of the drums picked up. Kate began to dance with the leader, who looked ecstatic. Their adrenaline-pumped bodies swirled and swayed, keeping time with the drums.

Jugs of bhang, colored ocher, marigold petals and pichkaris, the hollowed-out lengths of bamboo were served. One of the troupe took a mouthful of ochre and squirted another through the bamboo. Soon the sky on the maidan turned red with a cloud of ochre and the red glory of the pre-dusk sun. Their hearts beat faster to the pounding drums, and the marigold petals clung to their hair and speckled the floor yellow.

Jonathan enjoyed the bhang, which was sweet and tasted faintly of flowers. Gauri and Geeta had a few sips, too. They all began laughing, giggling and dancing. The tinkle of the cymbals, drumbeats and the ecstasy-filled cries of the piccolos blended with the sound of their stomping and shrieking.

Soon a big bonfire—consisting of bundles of firewood stacked in a circle and adorned by sacred red thread, flowers and coconuts—began crackling, the high flames lighting the prayer ground bright orange. Pairs of women clasped their hands and began swirl-dancing, whirling like an inverted A—their feet close but heads swaying back. Geeta danced with one of the female performers and before long, another female performer paired up with Gauri.

It was a happy sight for Jonathan. After two weeks of dealing with women in the clinic who never smiled and hardly even met his eyes, he couldn't get enough of the beautiful Indian women dancing joyously, their lush bodies exposed as their saris began to furl in the air. Geeta was slightly taller than Gauri, and she wore her hair shorter. It seemed unusual to Jonathan, who had come to expect all Indian women to have long, flowing locks. Geeta seemed more outwardly confident, yet less poised. He guessed that away from him and others, she was the bossier of the two.

Gauri, on the other hand, was not as aggressive in her dancing, yet seemed to be inwardly poised. He did not see the freedom of movement he'd witnessed so recently, but her smile was surely genuine.

They were both good dancers. And with the bhang in their systems, and the music pounding forth, the speed and enthusiasm increased. Before long, Jonathan began to notice that both Geeta and Gauri and their partners were dancing closer to the fire. Jonathan began to work his way through the crowd toward them.

Kate spotted his nervousness. "They'll be okay," she shouted over the din.

He glanced at them again. "You're sure?"

"They've all done this dance by the fire, many times, I'm sure," she yelled. "Don't worry. Enjoy yourself."

"Yeah, but . . . they're awfully relaxed. I . . . I've never seen Gauri so relaxed. I'm afraid they've had too much to drink."

"And I think you bloody well haven't had enough. Just get—"

Just then, Jonathan's fears were realized. Geeta slipped out of her partner's handlock and went hurtling toward the fire, screaming.

Jonathan raced forward toward her.

But it was Gauri who lunged forward and grabbed Geeta by the wrist, yanking her back from certain danger.

By the time Jonathan got there, they were holding each other and crying gratefully. Geeta had her head buried in Gauri's arms, weeping uncontrollably and mumbling something over and over again. The music played on, most of the celebrants oblivious to the near tragedy. Gauri took Geeta's hand and led her to her own room.

"Come on, Claus!" Kate said, taking his arm and dancing. They seemed instantly to have forgotten about the incident, but Jonathan was still agitated. He found himself wanting to comfort Geeta and most of all to praise Gauri's quick thinking. He decided to visit Gauri's room.

He had expected Geeta to have calmed down, but from behind the closed door the two women were clearly arguing vehemently. The Hindi was far too rapid for him to follow, but he listened on to make sure they didn't come to blows. It almost sounded like they might. Soon they fell silent. Hoping all was okay, he turned to go back to the festivities.

Then one of them let out a big cry. He rushed back, fearing the worst, but stopped short again. Just then, they were both laughing!

Feeling very foolish, and not a little confused, Jonathan mumbled, "Forget it! I give up." Dejected, he returned to the Holi Festival.

Kate grabbed him and they began to dance, enjoying the unusual and potent bhang. After a while, Jonathan noticed Gauri standing in the distance, alone, where the bright light of the campfire faded. What was she doing there?

Jonathan squinted. She was still smiling. Then she turned and walked away, but not to the living quarters. She was taking the path to the lake.

"Excuse me, Kate," he said.

Kate seemed too elated to care. She began dancing with Stephan and Guillaume at the same time.

Exhausted, Jonathan returned to his room and threw himself on the bed. He had barely fallen asleep when he spotted someone standing outside his room. Gauri!

She was smiling broadly at him and beckoning him invitingly to join her somewhere.

Reflexively, Jonathan rose and followed Gauri.

Suddenly, he realized he wasn't sleepy anymore. "Gauri, where are you going?"

She turned back and pointed toward the lake, smiling.

Jonathan followed her for quite a distance before finally stopping her. He held her by her arms and turned her around to face him. "Are you feeling okay?"

She didn't reply. Instead she lifted her drowsy head, looked at Jonathan and suddenly hid her head in his chest, wrapping her arms around his body. The moon shone brightly.

He felt her body glide against his. At first she seemed passive, but when he began to kiss her deeply, moving down her neck and her arms, she responded passionately.

He quickly tore the rags off of their bodies and pulled her with him toward the lake. On the shore, they stumbled and fell into each other. Clinging together, they rolled to the water's edge. When they stood, they were partly coated with sand. The rest of their bodies was already covered with colored dyes from the festival. He burst out laughing. They looked like a rainbow of breaded drumsticks. She must have thought so too, because she began to giggle alongside him.

He picked her up and waded into the lake. In the shallow water, splashing away the sand from their bodies, he kissed her mouth and throat. He paused, lifted her chin and looked deep into her beautiful eyes. They were full of love and pleasure.

She wrapped her arms around him tightly as he lowered his head to her bosom. Leaning her head back slightly, she exhaled gently. Then, it was as if a dam had broken loose. He released his hunger for her, and she for him, kissing his mouth hungrily, passionately.

"Gauri," he whispered urgently. "I love you. *Hum aapse... pyar karte hain.*"

When she heard his tender words, she looked up into his eyes. Rapturously, she clung to his body like a tender vine clinging to the trunk of an oak tree. Jonathan felt the grip of her arms; arms that never wanted to let him go.

Against the distant music of cymbals and drums, their two bodies came closer. He swept his hand down from her neck to her long midriff and across her silken belly. His fingers burned into her tingling skin. He touched the skin of her thighs, as they were lying together on a large boulder by the shore. His sweat fell upon her writhing body, like the first raindrops over the thirsty, parched Serengheti. He felt her wanting their union just as much as he, as they fell into a gentle, controlled rhythm. Her head rested back against the edge of the boulder, her long hair swaying, just grazing the surface of the water. His kisses answered her moans.

Instinctively, her body arched toward him. Gently, he lay atop, as she welcomed him. His impatience grew. The passion too rich, the need too strong, he gave in. Her body melted against his and their worlds became filled with each other.

Suddenly, dark clouds veiled the moon. Lightning struck. The horizon thundered and the sky exploded with a downpour. Consumed by her ecstasy, she lost her grip and fell from the rock.

She splashed and gulped the water and cried for help. He dove in, grabbed her hair with his left hand and the edge of the rock with his right, but the lake had an undertow as powerful as any he'd found in the ocean. She became heavier with each raindrop and began sinking, her eyes pleading for help.

He screamed, but he could barely hear himself over the storm. He tried to pull her back, but his arms felt like lead. He could not live if he were to lose another loved one, so he had no option but to sink with her. First the legs, then the chest, then the water rose to his eyes.

No, he would make one more attempt. Diving like a seal, he straddled her body and, with all his might, pulled her toward the world of hope and light.

Then a cloud of vultures descended. Quickly, he blanketed her body with his. The vultures flapped their wings, pecked his back, tearing at his flesh.

"Jonathan!"

"No! Gauri, no," he cried. "I'll never abandon you. Hold onto me tight."

"Jonathan, Jonathan, are you all right?"

Panting and sweating he woke up in his bed. It was morning. Gauri was still alive.

Kate was standing in the doorway.

"Um . . . sure," he said. "I'm fine."

"Whatever you say," she said, and left him mercifully alone.

Jonathan sat up on the edge of the bed. The hangover was unprecedented. After a few seconds, he pounded his fist on his bed. He wanted to go back to the dream. Awake, he felt teased, tired. And cheated.

Then he heard someone knocking on his door.

"Sahb, Sahb," Rasool said. "Please hurry. Somebody brought here. In a stretcher. Very sick . . . I think dying. Please hurry."

chapter twenty-four

When Jonathan rushed out into the lobby he saw a makeshift bamboo stretcher housing a blanket-covered body that thrashed relentlessly, threatening to tear the rickety stretcher apart. Nearby, an old woman held a screaming child. The child reached for the figure on the stretcher, hysterically shrieking, "Maa! Maa!"

Kate arrived at the same time. "Good Lord! What's going on?"

Jonathan pulled back the blanket to reveal a young Himpali woman, foaming and bleeding at her mouth, in violent seizures. Jonathan quickly padded a bamboo chip with a handkerchief and placed it between her teeth and extended her neck to relieve the seizures. When they subsided, he cleaned her tongue and face of blood. She was slightly blue. She was getting little oxygen into her system.

"Let's move her to the clinic," he said to the attendants without looking at them. "Kate, please hurry to the clinic and draw up two ccs of Diazepam into a syringe. Ladies," he said to

Gauri and Geeta, "one of you get me some warm water. Rasool, you hold the stretcher from there, I'll grab the head end."

In the clinic, Jonathan injected the tranquilizer into the patient's jerking shoulder, and began squeezing the rubber ambu-bag over her mouth.

"Okay, Gauri, bring the saline bottle, hold it high in the air and let me start the intravenous line. Kate, see if someone can talk to her relatives and get information—I need her medical history. No, wait, give me a hand with the ambu-bag; I want to listen to her chest. Where's the stethoscope?"

Geeta grabbed the stethoscope from over the dressing cart in the back and placed its earpieces into Jonathan's ears, since his hands were contaminated with the patient's blood. When he grabbed the chest-piece of the stethoscope, it broke off and fell to the cement floor. The rusted metal ring that had held the diaphragm in place had snapped; its parts scattered all over the floor. Jonathan furiously tore the remains of the broken instrument from his ears and flung it against a wall.

He put his left ear under the woman's left breast, where he could feel and smell the unmistakable stench and deterioration of a large abscess. Barely had he been able to catch the sound of her racing heart before the woman began to seize again, thrashing her limbs violently.

"Get some gauze!" Jonathan shouted frantically. "Restrain her wrists and ankles against her body. We can't do a thing for her if she destroys herself first!"

As Kate ran to grab the bandages, Geeta helped Jonathan hold the woman down but her convulsions grew more intense.

"Kate, get me another syringe of . . . of Valium!"

The intravenous line got yanked out in the process. Blood flowed menacingly from her arm. Jonathan, draping his body over the woman's chest to restrain her, put pressure on the bleeding wrist, and with his free hand managed to administer the shot.

Then the restraints that Gauri and Kate had tied broke loose, and the woman tore wildly around on the pallet.

Jonathan jumped on top of her, overcome with her violent energy and his own physical disadvantage. "What did I say!" he demanded furiously. "Did I tell you to wrap a package or to *restrain her!* Get the gauze—do a decent job!"

Geeta froze like a deer in the headlights. Kate, looking abashed, dropped the ambu-bag and began quickly retying the restraints. Gauri followed suit.

Slowly, the seizures subsided and the patient's skin turned pink.

Kate put her hand over Jonathan's.

"I'm sorry . . ." he said softly, looking at Kate and then Geeta.

"No," Kate said. "We should have done a better job. We'll know next time."

Gauri brought a wide bowl of steaming water. Geeta rushed to Gauri and helped her place the bowl on a table. Then, while Gauri began sponging the patient's body Geeta cut a strip of adhesive tape and used it to patch together the chest-piece of the stethoscope. Order was restored and Jonathan felt ashamed of his outburst.

"I need a break," he said. "She looks better, the shot is kicking in. I'll be right outside."

Jonathan paced the lobby, wiping his face. Moments before he'd been in the depths of a fantasy so real that he felt pained that it had not concluded. He'd been unprepared for the sudden change, being flung into a situation so frustratingly destined for failure. It was knocking on the door again, and he could not send it away.

After a few minutes, Kate told him what she had learned from the woman's mother. Apparently, the patient, the mother of the crying two-year-old, had suddenly doubled up with a sharp pain in her back while carrying firewood on her head. And a long-standing lump in the left breast had turned into a pussy abscess. The next day she had turned feverish and started convulsing. Her husband, a Sherpa, had died a year earlier in an avalanche while assisting a mountaineering American team.

It only confirmed what Jonathan had already known. Breast cancer, no doubt, had spread throughout the body. She was going to die, and he wasn't going to be able to stop it.

The woman's painful struggle continued throughout the day. Late in the evening, her relatives, accompanied by some Buddhist monks, arrived. They lit two large candles in the candelabras standing beyond the bed. Her body was calm as the monks meditated with closed eyes. Her mother and sisters sprinkled her body with petunias and white rose petals.

Jonathan watched for a while, furious at his helplessness, furious at the family's calm acceptance of it. Frustrated, he pulled Kate aside. "Tell them all to get out. I can't sit around and wait. I need to start an IV."

Alone with his dying patient, Jonathan set up a saline and morphine IV, and studied the woman's young face. He could do no more. Science had nothing else to offer. He lifted her hand and looked at the fingers. They'd cared for her young daughter, he thought, and before that, the Sherpa. How many meals had she cooked, diapers changed; how many times had she tenderly placed her little one in bed at night? Without any doubt, it would all end in a short while. And he could do nothing to stop it. He could help ease her pain, he thought, but death would win once again.

The grandmother, holding the little girl, appeared in the doorway.

Jonathan motioned them in. He took the baby in his arms and put her little hand on her mother's arm. "See . . . mommy," he said softly. Then he pressed his two hands together against his tilted head. "Sleeping. Mommy . . . sleeping."

The girl said, "Naa . . ." and immediately withdrew her hand. When she began to cry, Jonathan handed her to Gauri. Gauri and Geeta murmured to the little girl, who wiped her swollen eyes with her fist and hid her face in Gauri's shoulder.

Jonathan looked at the calm patient and sighed. "Why don't you all get some rest. I'll keep an eye on her. Do me a favor. Send Rasool here. Tell him to bring me the book that's on my bed."

When the women left, Jonathan parked himself outside on a wicker chair. The grandfather clock in the main hall chimed twelve. He heard the howling of the wild animals. As the night painted the meadow black, a ghastly pack of coyotes had begun to howl in the tall grass of the Portland fields, invisible, but moving closer. The cold air turned their ominous wails fierce and proximal. At times it seemed they were in front of their prey, with erect ears, piercing eyes, bared fangs.

He pulled the two wedding bands from his pocket and looked at them. They glittered in the dim light, reminding him of the glitter of the landing lights that night. They had startled him. He'd been half-sleeping, half-thinking. Becky was fine, he had told himself. He'd told Baggy to keep an eye on her. He tried to feel the humor of that, but he couldn't. Even the cat had seemed to say, "What's the deal? Leaving *again?*" This is important, he told himself. Why would I have been contacted if someone else could do it? Suresh had said to forget about it, someone else would step in. He hadn't listened. A little voice had said, *which is more important?* Yet he had felt he needed to go. And then *bump!* They had touched down and he'd been startled by the ground lights.

He put the rings away.

"Doc Sahb," Rasool said. "Your book."

"Thank you, Rasool."

He had barely opened the book when he heard the charpoi inside shaking violently. He threw down the book and rushed to the seizing patient. "Rasool, call everybody."

Then as Rasool ran toward the living quarters, Jonathan shouted, "Don't bring Swamiji. I don't need him, let him sleep."

In no time, the three women appeared and began assisting Jonathan.

The woman's seizures had returned with a vengeance. Despite two more shots of muscle-relaxant, her convulsions kept coming back—each time more severe and lasting longer. The cancer had reached her brain. She had a day or two at best.

He'd lost again. Someone had tied down his feet and expected him to dance. Then he heard the little girl cry from the room next door. Instantly his eyes welled up, tortured by thoughts of Becky and Sarah. But it had been Becky whose love had gone empty for the child she'd so needed to nurture. Here, the child would suffer the loss of the mother's love. And he could do nothing! He began to pace. Maybe the Buddhist monks had the right idea. Sprinkle her with flower petals and watch her die.

"It's not so bad as all that, you know," a familiar voice said.

Jonathan turned. Swamiji hobbled through the door and approached the bed just as the woman began to thrash about terribly once again. Patiently, Swamiji stood by, behind Jonathan.

After five minutes, Jonathan could stand it no longer. "Dammit!" he yelled, "I've done everything I could. Nothing is working! I don't know what to do!"

Swamiji put his hand on Jonathan's shoulder. Jonathan could feel the tremors in Swamiji's hand. "Beta, do not despair. You have already treated the seizures of the flesh. These are seizures of the soul."

"Seizures of the soul? What kind of crap is that? Show me a miracle! Go ahead!"

Jonathan locked his gaze with Swamiji's, and waited for something enigmatic to emerge from the abyss of his mystical eyes. But Swamiji simply smiled.

"I . . . I'm sorry," Jonathan said. "I guess I—"

"No, no," Swamiji said. "You know how I feel about honesty. I was just waiting until you calmed down enough to listen. Do not doubt your science. It is quite useful and has given renewed life to many. But the soul's entry or exit from this life is beyond the marvels of medicine, and there is no antidote for the soul's seizures. As for miracles, I would not presume, but . . . may I?"

Jonathan sighed and spread his arms. "Go right ahead, please."

Swamiji struggled to get closer to the patient's bed. In doing so, he staggered slightly. Geeta immediately steadied him and

Gauri brought a chair and helped him sit down. Then Geeta and Gauri held each other's hands, smiled at each other and closed their eyes.

Swamiji rested his staff along the bed, scooped up two handfuls of flower petals and began sprinkling them on the patient, beginning at her head and feet and ending over her chest.

"Beta," he said to Kate as the woman's body began to quiver, heralding another wave of seizures, "bring that little child here and lay her beside her mother's body."

Jonathan felt like shouting, *Are you out of your mind?* He gaped at Kate.

She gaped back. "Baba," she said softly, "that poor child has been crying all night. Now she is sound asleep."

"Beta, souls do not sleep. Go ahead, bring the child."

Jonathan shook his head. That poor little girl was going to wake up horrified, seeing her mother seizing, living the rest of her life traumatized. He thought of Judge Joshi at age six, being forced to light the fires under his father's body. What kind of mad culture was this?

Kate brought the child in, draped over her shoulder. She was in deep sleep.

The mother's quivering body began to shake faster and harder. As the bed began to creak, her mouth began to discharge red foam. Then with a violent jolt her body arched up like a bow.

Everyone stood back, their faces wearing shades of terror.

Swamiji gently put his left hand on the woman's head and the right one over her feet. He closed his eyes.

"Oh good soul," he said, "overcome the fears and rejoice in the peace and love of your child. Oh lord! Help this soul to embrace the path of your heavenly tranquility. Have mercy upon her."

The arched body gently relaxed. The seizures gradually subsided.

Swamiji signaled Kate to lay the child beside her mother. Kate reluctantly complied and stood back.

The child instinctively wrapped her arms across the woman's chest, and cooing briefly, "Maa . . ." slipped back into deep sleep, nestled in the crook of her mother's arm.

"Let's all say a prayer," Swamiji said. "Repeat after me."

Swamiji stretched his arms over the mother and began the prayer. After a moment, Jonathan mumbled along.

> "Awaken the quiescent spark of my soul.
> And steady the flickering flames of my faith.
> Give me wings of the angels, and feet of the truth;
> The reach of your rectitude and the celestial stealth.
> And see my soul through the seas of all sorrows,
> With such swiftness, smile and the strength.
> Be proud, O father! Be proud!
> For I shall vanquish the fury of death."

Suddenly Jonathan felt as though he were in the Unitarian Meeting House in Allagash. He envisioned his loved ones in the pews. And he heard the powerful sound of the organ, the pounding joy of Bach's Fugue in G Major. But there was no organ here. Just association; a polymorphic hallucination from lack of sleep. But he didn't care. As the fugue built to its climax, he heard Swamiji's commanding voice.

"Banish the shackles of Maya, oh soul! Listen to the requiem of sins and look up! Let the white-winged angels carry you to the sojourn of serenity. Oh good soul, let those heavenly chariots carry your divine spark to *Untimdham*—the heavenly home of the Holy Father."

Suddenly a cold gust of wind blew open the back window. Jonathan opened his eyes.

On the whistling wind, two white-winged butterflies came to life from the heap of white petals at either end of the patient's body. At first, they looked simply like petals, but then they began flapping their wings and slowly flew over the body. Simultaneously, the large candles in the candelabra overhead blew out, and in the dim light of the porch lantern, the two white-winged butterflies flew across the room and out the window in unison.

Jonathan looked around. Geeta and Gauri looked at each other. They gasped. Then hugged each other warmly. They had seen it, too.

For Jonathan, there was no more shuddering sound of the organ, no squeaking of the charpoi, no crying of the baby. Just the sonorous sounds of Swamiji's voice. His downcast face was faintly illuminated by the dim light of the lantern that squeaked back and forth under the porch with the whistling wind.

And as the grandfather clock struck five times, the first rays of the morning sun cast the shadow of the back window on the wall behind Jonathan.

chapter twenty-five

It was immediately following the woman's death that Jonathan arranged for a meeting with Swamiji. After some sleep, though, doubt was beginning to predominate. Had he really seen what he thought he'd seen? Still, since Swamiji had agreed to meet him at 3:00 p.m. in the library, he would be there. Swamiji was always worth talking to.

Jonathan arrived early. While waiting, he once again looked over the books Swamiji kept. There were about six bookcases, the largest occupied by the books on religion. He reached up for *The Narrow Road to the Deep North* by Japanese Haiku poet and authority on the spirit of Zen Buddhism, Basho. He opened the book but closed it when he heard Swamiji's footsteps.

"You came early, JK." Swamiji slowly hobbled forward with the aid of his staff and closed the door behind him. "In this room, you are in the company of many an enlightened soul."

"Agree," said Jonathan, looking at Swamiji. *Be nice!* he told himself. He was an old man, with a different philosophy on death, and a holy man worth listening to.

Jonathan immediately got on with the questions. "Swamiji, I'd like to know, where do you derive your joy from?"

"Oh, my parents, the poet Rabindranath Tagore, Mahatma Gandhi and my Gurudev. In that order, I'd say."

"I see. Have you met Tagore and the Mahatma?"

"Yes, I was very fortunate in that regard. I met Tagore at Shantiniketan. This is after he published his anthology of poems—*Gitanjali*."

"Isn't that the book that made the German poet, Johann Goethe, put it on his head and dance once he'd read it?"

Swamiji laughed. "Yes, that is true. Tagore does tend to inspire joy. He believed that a nurturing ambiance always helps man release his pure and blissful emotions, because man is nothing but nature's child. He was so close to nature and so erudite that he reminded me of Shakespeare and Henry David Thoreau."

"Was Tagore religious?" Jonathan asked.

"There was not a temple on the entire campus. He believed all religions nurtured man's quest for peace and truth."

"Fascinating," Jonathan said. "My Dad would have loved to visit a place like that. How was your stay there?"

"I blossomed like a flower. Unfortunately, I had to return to my home. My mother had passed on. My father took it very hard. He began fasting. To invoke death."

Jonathan thought he hadn't heard him correctly. He leaned forward. "I'm sorry—to invoke *death?*"

"Yes. He went into seclusion of the puja room and sat there for hours, every day, in front of my mother's photo, reading Bhagvat Gita and reciting *Gitanjali*, as he had for my mother when she'd been alive."

Jonathan swallowed hard. What was this—a suttee, male style?

"All he would take in would be sips of water," Swamiji said. "Within three weeks his bones stuck out. He staggered. He . . . he became disoriented. I beseeched him 'Pitajee, please eat

something. I'm not ready to lose you to death. I'm afraid.'
He said, 'Beta Bikku, do not fear death. Let death fear you. I want to kill the ferocity of death, to invite death on my own terms.'

"When he became unconscious, we called the doctor, who determined his heart had become very slow and feeble. He said my father suffered from spiritual depression. So I held a bedside prayer vigil that night. At about one a.m. he opened his eyes and said: 'Beta, you are a grown man . . . an enlightened soul. My duties are now over. I love you very much. I'm proud of you. I'm looking forward to being with your Matajee. Do not . . . grieve over me.'

"I hugged him and cried. He began stroking my hair and then . . . then I felt his hand go limp and fall on the bed."

Swamiji's eyes teared up. Jonathan sat quietly.

"It was a peaceful death," Swamiji said at last, with a faint smile. "He loved my mother very much and missed her. He was ready for the *untimdham.*"

Jonathan didn't say anything. His thoughts fell to his own frail mother. She loved and missed her husband very much. Jonathan knew she longed to be with him.

A lone crane walked by the doorway, circling and squawking restlessly.

"That is a very sad sight," Swamiji said, looking at the bird. "His mate has died and he is lost. These birds always live and die as pairs."

"That is very sad," Jonathan said softly. Images of Becky joyously running on the beach flashed by.

"After my father's death," Swamiji said, "I joined Mahatma Gandhi in his struggle to liberate India. I went to Wardha, a small town in central India from where the Mahatma attempted to set an example of rural independence, practically sustaining his followers on homemade, homegrown products."

"I envy you," Jonathan said. "I've read his autobiography, *My Experiment With the Truth.* I was baffled by his stark honesty. How did he relate to his family??"

"Not so well, I'm afraid. Of course, he married Kasturbai at 14 and already had a son at 18 when he went to England to become a lawyer. After four sons, both accepted celibacy. It was only in his later years that he recognized her loyalty and endurance. He was surprised how she had put up with his self-accepted poverty and his radical lifestyle. After her death he used to cry like a child."

"His eldest son was a lost soul, from what I've read."

"Yes, he was. His name was Harilal." Swamiji shook his head. "Mahatma was a paradox. He was this great man, yet he utterly neglected his first born. The boy felt unloved and unrecognized, so he began drinking, gambling, visiting prostitutes and he even changed his religion. Eventually he became a street person and diedced unceremoniously at some remote hospital. It was like the darkest spot on the burning candle was right below its bright flame."

"Yes." Jonathan thought about his own childhood and his dad. "I'm sure it was unintentional on the Mahatma's part."

"So Harilal grew up fatherless. That's faulty parenthood. That also explains why we have so many directionless children in our own Ashram."

Jonathan was sure that Swamiji's comments were not directed at him, but he began to think about his own fatherlessness. "Faulty parenthood? Is that a fault of a mother or a father?"

"Mainly a father's. As I see it, a mother instills a sense of nurturing, love, kindness and forgiveness. It's a father's responsibility to teach his children adventure, self-reliance, decisiveness and tolerance. Children without fathers grow up to be insecure, indecisive, intolerant and emotionally fragile. They have no sense of the fine balance between love and lawfulness. Either they are highly emotional or simply hate everything."

Jonathan listened.

"It is easy for a male to impregnate a female. Animals, birds, even worms have been doing it for eons. It is only when a male endeavors to raise his progeny properly that he becomes a man. The rest are just enlarged children—physically grown up but emotionally handicapped. And because they're not raising their own children, their sons grow up the same way. So society becomes a commune of fatherless children, nations of confused and unbalanced siblings, weakened by drugs, crime, apathy, divorce and sexual disorientation."

"Do you think that's why I'm seeing what I see in the clinic?"

"It is possible. There are a lot of lost souls out there. But to resume my story, I left Wardha in 1945. Mahatmaji had heard about this Ashram, which was then run by my Gurudev, God bless his soul. Gandhiji was impressed with the aim of the Ashram—to shelter, rehabilitate and educate abused young women. He learned there was a need for a teacher who spoke several Indian dialects. So Gandhiji said 'Bikku, your destiny is awaiting you in the Himalayas. I told them you are just the right person for the Ashram.'"

"But you were still not a Swami, right?"

"That is true. The person who showed me the ultimate life was my Gurudev."

"How?"

"Oh, Baba! He was my spiritual father, my second father on this earth. After I left Wardha, I spent two years in Benares at a smaller Ashram on the banks of the Ganges. When I felt confident, I left the Benares Ashram in the hands of a young Swami and began my journey here. The trail to the Ashram was unrecognizable, much worse than it is today, especially given that I arrived in a snowstorm. Soon I was lost, and to make matters worse, I slipped and fell into a shallow ditch. My left ankle was swollen from a sprain or fracture—I'd never know which—and I was slowly being buried in the snow. But I was determined to keep my spirits alive. I settled down under a big rock and invoked God. As my body froze and I stilled, I could feel my soul was slowly exiting my body, but that was fine with me. I didn't feel any pain anywhere. Instead, a wave of blissful elation overwhelmed me. I saw smiling and welcoming faces of my parents and my deceased childhood friends.

"Then I felt somebody was shaking me, covering me with a thick blanket and reassuring me that everything was going to be fine. When I opened my eyes, I saw this bearded man with a blessed smile and the kindest eyes and hands. He even had water and food for me. I had no idea how he'd found me or even knew to look for me. After some food and water, I tried standing up. To my surprise there was no swelling or pain in my injured ankle. When I found my balance, I asked the old man, 'Baba, what is your name and where are you from?'

"He smiled at me and said, 'My brother, my name is *Manushya* and I am headed for *Satyadham*. I don't know if these were the real names, because in Sanskrit *Manushya* simply means 'human being' and *Satyadham* means 'abode of truth.' When I gained my strength, he held my hand and showed me the path to this Ashram. The last slope was a steep uphill climb. At his suggestion I remained ahead of him, but he continued talking to me, sharing amusing vignettes with me. I took a deep breath when I put my foot on the Ashram's plateau. 'God bless you, kind Baba,' I said to him. 'Without your timely help, I would have died. Thank you.' But he didn't say anything. The wind was blowing, so I thought perhaps he didn't hear me. I turned and looked back, but he was nowhere to be found."

Swamiji stopped and kept smiling.

"Well," Jonathan asked, "who was he?"

"I still don't know. I asked the same question of Baba. He said it was an angel, and it may have been. But now I suspect it was his bilocution. Baba sent himself to a distant place to save my life and show me the path to my destiny."

Jonathan shifted in his seat and smiled back. Bilocution! Is that, he wondered, what Swamiji did to me on that occasion behind the Taj Mahal, where he offered me his staff to help me on those stairs after I fell?

"I miss my Gurudev," Swamiji said. "This is all I have of him with me that I can see, touch and experience." He retrieved a large multicolored sea conch from a cloth bag hanging on the wall. "He said, 'Beta Bikku, when you reach the point of self-realization and become a Swami, blow this conch from the Gurushikhar. When you blow this conch, I will know you have accepted the Swamihood—the *sanyas*. That will be the happiest sound I'll ever hear.' And it happened. Just the day before he was about to take mahasamadhi, I arrived at that moment of inner conviction."

Jonathan held the conch in his hands and studied it from all sides. "How does it work? May I try?"

Swamiji nodded, his eyes widened with pride and joy.

Jonathan tried to blow the conch, but failed to produce any sound.

"Here, let me show you." Swamiji showed him how to cradle it in his hands, where to place his lips. Then Swamiji pointed at an extra conch resting on the shelf behind him. "You take that one. This is mine. I won't part with it. It is my Gurudev's gift to me, a memory. Practice with my shell whenever you find time."

Jonathan hesitated, then accepted Swamiji's gift. But that was enough of pleasantries. "Swamiji," he said, "there is something I want to talk about, though I don't know where to begin. Take this place, for example. It seems unreal. There is no conflict here. No cheating, lying, beguiling, mugging, murdering—nothing of the sort. Everybody is fair and cooperative. It's all too easy. Do you see what I mean?"

"Your observation is indisputable."

"It's not that I miss all those miseries, but . . . it seems like this place ignores a large part of life."

Swamiji simply listened.

"I mean . . . to take a personal example, how can I find peace when I know how miserably my innocent wife died? Or how on earth did an educated, intelligent father became instrumental in destroying the life of his own little daughter? And the suttee? An innocent 22-year-old woman, who hadn't even seen the world, hadn't even had a chance to bear a child. Is she buried somewhere? Did somebody drown her? Even if she is still alive, her life has been destroyed. No matter how happy we are here, she's still out there somewhere, perhaps still suffering."

"Well, understand that one does not find peace without finding truth. When you find answers to your questions, you will find peace. In the meantime, learn to use the eyes and the ears of your mind. And try not to doubt destiny."

"Frankly, Swamiji, that's it. I have doubts about destiny and God! Who is he? Where is he? Why do I—why does anybody—have to believe in him . . . her . . . whatever? Tell me, why do I need to submit myself to something I don't see, feel or communicate with? Just to conform to the society?"

Swamiji smiled. "Ah, I wish you could see the irony of it. You're fighting to disbelieve in something you have followed all along."

"Pardon me?"

"Do you like what you do for needy people? Poor patients? What Divine inkling from inside you is propelling you to save some innocent souls and bring the culprits to the doors of justice?"

Jonathan thought of the evildoers in Baramedi, the sorrowful loss of the little girl's mother the night before. He shook his head. "I'm just trying to do what I can to prevent more needless deaths. But it's not because I believe in God or that I'm working out my karma or something."

"You would be surprised." Swamiji stroked his beard and looked into the sky. "Jonathan, you and I are talking about the same thing. Goodness. The goodness of your heart. That sense of decency, justice and consideration for others *is* God. You are part of that Godliness, goodness. You are like a child in the womb who doubts the existence of Mother."

Jonathan stood up, impatient and annoyed, and walked toward the door. Then he stopped. He had not yet received what he had come for.

He sat back down. "Swamiji, I'm not trying to insult you. Hear me out, please. I know about this goodness business. But this goodness you're talking about is part of my problem. I'm tired of being good. I'm tired of fighting for life and watching death win, time and time again. Why can't I be just . . . not so good sometime? The whole damn world is being—I'm sorry, I didn't mean to swear."

"Speak your mind; get the rust out of your heart. Divinity awaits you, to assist you in accomplishing your destiny. After all, is it an accident that you have traveled all the way from the land of promise to some desolate little hermitage in a remote part of India?"

Swamiji looked at him with that inscrutable smile.

"I know you know the answers," Jonathan said. "Why won't you share them with me?"

"It is not up to me to know and share. It is up to your soul to learn and endure. That is why you were sent here."

"Sent by whom? To this Ashram?"

"To this life. Your soul chose the respite of this avatar. Your soul wants to go through the Ashram of this life. Let it learn the lessons on its own."

Jonathan stood up and began pacing.

"It's all here," Swamiji said. "Problems are here. So are the solutions. Look for them. You will find them. What else is harming the peace of your mind?"

"Well . . . this is a little . . . embarrassing but . . . Swamiji, I'm having a problem curbing my fantasies. What bothers me most is that I feel like Becky is watching me."

"I believe she is. But how do you know her soul is not smiling? Why shouldn't she be happy to see that your heart is thawing to the nuances of nature?"

Jonathan leaned forward, unable to speak. He hadn't quite expected that.

"Surely you remember the rose petals?" Swamiji asked.

"Rose petals?"

"Four in the morning, at Joshi's house, as you got up to close the squeaking window. In Baramedi, when your heart is grieving, a winged angel—a butterfly—sits on a blossoming rose and transfers the bliss to your face. How did this happen?"

Jonathan buried his head in his hands. He was sure he'd never told anyone about the rose petals. He'd forgotten about them himself. This simply wasn't possible.

"Don't be surprised," Swamiji said gently. "Souls have eyes. My father's soul, your father's soul, Mrs. Joshi's soul, Becky's soul, they are like angels. They watch our peaceful moments as well as our distress."

With effort, Jonathan pulled his mind away from the miracle he'd just experienced. He'd think about it later. "But what do these angelic presences have to do with my sexual fantasies? Are you saying it's normal to have sexual fantasies? And to act on them?"

"Well, in a proper context between two consenting human beings. Make no mistake, I'm not recommending forced sex, extramarital sex or unnatural sex. But I'm also against the unnatural suppression of healthy sex. Would you believe that Shashtras, the Hindu scriptures, regard sex as entertainment for the ancestors' spirits seeking to reincarnate?"

Jonathan said nothing. He had an awful lot occupying his mind. Swamiji appeared to let him work through it, keeping comfortably silent.

Then, to Jonathan's surprise, Swamiji said, "JK, you've got to leave."

"What?"

"You need a change. A challenge. You need to leave this Ashram for a while."

After a moment, Jonathan nodded. "You're right, Swamiji. This place is full of ideas and inspiration. But . . ."

"There is such a thing as too much of a good thing, yes." Swamiji lowered his head and thought. "Do you like the ocean? Do you like mountain climbing?"

Jonathan's face lit up. "Are you kidding? I grew up in Maine. It would be like reliving my childhood."

"Divine!" said Swamiji. "We all need to return to our spawning grounds."

"What do you have in mind?"

"A colleague of mine, Swami Prabhucharan, runs an Ashram in the Andaman-Nicobar Islands. They need a physician to fill-in on weekends. Would you consider giving them a weekend?"

"Sure. I'd love that. They are the islands located in the Bay of Bengal, right?"

"Yes, Beta. They are pristine, unspoiled. They will serve you well. It will be a place for respite, reflection and introspection—a good change. Then, for mountain climbing, I'd recommend an expedition to Lake Mansarover and its progenitor Mount Kailash. It's a bit higher than Maine—20,000 feet—so you need skill and endurance, but you're young and healthy. And, finally, visit the Ganges. You can't leave India without seeing the Ganges."

Jonathan smiled. "It sounds like just what I need."

"Yes. See Gangamaiya. Maa Ganga will unfold the answers like a river of revelation." Then Swamiji leaned forward and put his hand on Jonathan's head. "Time wants to temper and test your soul. Let that goodness, let that small spark inside you—the divinity—be your shepherd. Your destiny is waiting."

While Swamiji uttered the beatific words, Jonathan experienced a strange rush in his head and buzz through the rest of his body. It was like a swirling hot spiral that reverberated through every molecule of his being, dissolving every scintilla of doubt and disquietude. And when Swamiji removed his hand, Jonathan sat up with an unfamiliar confidence. Swamiji smiled at him. He smiled back. Without saying a word he rose, hugged Swamiji and walked toward the door.

When Jonathan touched the doorknob, Swamiji said, "Beta, before you leave. There is one more thing."

Jonathan turned around. "Yes?"

"About you and the souls surrounding you? You need to realign your bonds with them. Something holds you back from Gauri. It is the stagnation of your soul. You have turned incapable of giving, incapable of loving."

Jonathan's good feelings faded. "What do you mean?"

"Love is an innate yearning of all souls. Gauri longs for your love, more than you can know. But it is a love that you are unable to give."

Jonathan stood up. "Swamiji, sometimes I . . . I don't think you understand. Maybe you do, but it certainly doesn't come across that way. How am I supposed to love the world when I'm still grappling with Becky's death?"

"Grappling with what?"

"Becky's death!" Jonathan spun around. "And my father's! Since age eight, I've seen my dead father's body floating in front of my face. Patients! How many times have I stood by and watched patients—relatives, friends—die while holding my hand, looking deep into my eyes, hoping I was going to be their savior."

Jonathan's temples pulsated. He moved in on Swamiji. "And you know what? With all my medical expertise, the goodness and the . . . love, you'd call it, in my heart, it didn't make a damn bit of difference! I saw my own child—Sarah—die in front of me. I watched my wife hold my hand and say 'I love you, Jonathan,' and the next day she was gone. I—"

Jonathan grabbed a chair. He wanted to smash it against the bookshelves and their dead volumes full of meaningless answers. Instead, he waved his fist in the air. "I stood by like a helpless little kid. And believe me, Swamiji, I didn't see anything spiritual or uplifting or inspirational in those deaths. Nothing! It was just plain terror. Death always is."

"It is not Becky's death you are grieving," Swamiji said without looking up.

Jonathan stopped, his breathing labored.

"What you are grieving, Beta, is the circumstances in which Becky died."

"Circumstances?"

"More specifically, your guilt."

"What guilt?"

"That remorse in your heart. You left your sick wife to attend to the need of an ailing patient. You feel you should have been with Becky when she was crying out for your love. Instead, you—"

"Dammit, yes! I flew off to . . . save the world, to . . . to liberate the suffering souls and give them my love. And if I hadn't, Becky would still be alive! And I wouldn't be here, screaming my lungs out." Jonathan's hands began to twist the life out of the chair. "So tell me about the spark of divine in me, the glory of love and death!"

"It was Becky's destiny, Beta."

"Oh, don't give me that shit! I created her destiny. I neglected her and left her alone to die, against the psychiatrist's strict orders. I—"

Jonathan's voice broke. He sank down behind the chair, and began to weep. "I killed her, Swamiji. I . . . I didn't have to argue with that florist. I didn't have to throw a wad of cash in his face . . . and insist on the best bouquet. The one in the glass vase. She . . . she broke the vase and slashed . . . slashed . . ."

"I know, Beta."

In between sobs, Jonathan gasped out, "I had to cremate her . . . it was in her will . . . She . . . she said her birth canal was defiled . . . violated by her own father. And that that's why the baby died. Oh God!"

Jonathan sobbed like a child, like the young boy that had been there, beside his father's stilled body. He tried to say something, he wasn't even sure what, but when it finally came out, it was "How could I? How could I?" His question was punctuated in time with the pounding of his fist on the chair.

Swamiji let him cry. And pound.

He punched through the seat. He yanked out his hand, bleeding and bruised, and grasping the backrest to his face, wept uncontrollably.

He felt Swamiji's hand on his shoulder. Swamiji's eyes were also filled with tears. His Parkinsonian tremor had returned. He drew Jonathan close to him and hugged him. Another wave of uncontrollable emotion took over. The flimsy dam had been washed away. This time he did not fight.

"I'm sorry," he ventured amid sobs. "I can't go on like this anymore . . ."

Swamiji simply stood there, stroking Jonathan's head. After a few moments, when Jonathan had regained his composure, Swamiji said softly: "It is all right, Beta. It is all right."

The Sage's words and his touch were calming. Jonathan withdrew his head from Swamiji's shoulder. "I'm . . . I'm sorry. I guess I got a little . . ."

"No, my son, don't be sorry. Sorry are those who fear being human. Cleanse the rust of pain, sorrow and guilt from your heart, for divinity is waiting for you to begin your mission."

Swamiji obtained a mitten-like glove from a shelf and slipped it over Jonathan's bleeding fist. The glove was a special hand garment used by monks when they prayed the rosary. As Swamiji put it on him, Jonathan noticed for the first time that his fist clutched his and Becky's wedding bands. He must have pulled them out of his pocket during his passion, he thought. At first, the glove hurt his injured hand, but as soon as Swamiji held it between his two, the pain seemed to subside.

Jonathan felt the rings inside his fist heating up and turning over. He didn't know what to think of the strange experience. It might be paresthesia—a false sensation caused by cramped fist muscles.

"Beta," said Swamiji, smiling. "Let go of those barriers. Let the rings bind you with humanity, not separate you from it. That is what Becky and Sarah's souls would want you to do."

Then Swamiji slowly removed the mitten from his hand.

Jonathan could not believe the look and feel of his hand. It wasn't hurt and it wasn't bleeding! He gaped at Swamiji, and then folded his hands at him, one fist still holding the rings.

Still smiling, Swamiji nodded with fatherly pride and kissed Jonathan's hand. Then he enveloped Jonathan's hands into his and said, "Tools of the Almightly. Even God can't hurt them."

Swamiji let go his hands, and picked up the rings. Jonathan gasped.

The two rings were interlocked with one another, both of them chiming and glittering in the sun.

chapter twenty-six

The hospital on the small island at Andoman-Nicobar was even more miserably equipped than the clinic at the Ashram. But the spirit among the nurses, orderlies, and the islanders was high. On his first day, Jonathan had to sew up a fisherman's belly torn apart by an alligator, using plain silk thread for sutures and a locally-brewed rotgut and orderlies sitting on the patient's limbs for anesthesia. Despite the hardships, the patient made it.

Many of the island's inhabitants walked around blind and with half-gangrenous toes. They didn't know they had diabetes or high blood pressure. No X-ray equipment or lab facilities were within a reasonable traveling distance, and Jonathan soon found that the supply of even basic drugs was spotty and irregular. But despite the crushing poverty, the natives looked happy. He saw hardly any sexually transmitted diseases, no violence from rape or incest. Most of his cases were either accidental injuries or malnutrition and hygiene related diseases. And it all felt worthwhile when the grateful villagers kissed his hands and provided free cooking, cleaning and laundry.

His thatched-roof cottage amid the lush foliage turned out to be a good place for introspection. In the evenings, he placed his feet on the railing of his front porch overlooking the Bay of Bengal. Despite the primitive conditions—or perhaps because of them—a successful treatment gave him a tremendous sense of accomplishment. He also learned how much he took the affluence of the United States for granted.

The islanders' philosophy about life and death was different as well. Terminal patients and their relatives found it natural to have the ailing soul take their last breath in their homes.

"Dying is no sad accident," one farmer explained to him. "It is just a part of life. People who go away to big cities in India or foreign countries come back here to die."

He had felt so attached to the island and the natives that he gladly accepted their invitation to a cookout at the chief's ocean-side home. At sunset, when he returned to his solitude, the balmy beach and surf-flinging ocean enticed him to discard all his anxieties. And his clothes.

He stretched out on the beach with his bare soles playing splash-n-leave with the surf. The great big fireball in the sky sank into the ocean, leaving behind red glory. A solemn-slow evening began to roll in. Calm prevailed, light faded and space shrank. Jonathan felt secure amid the growing darkness. As long as light prevailed, everything—the brilliance of the sun, the lightness of the clouds, birdsong, kisses from pets—belonged to man. But as night came on, he felt that ownership expired. Mankind gave up control and settled into a peaceful submission.

The sea gulls settled down. The red began to fade into a hazy gray. All Jonathan could now hear was the hollow booming and soft hissing of the waves. He was so attuned to listening to what the ocean had to say that he could almost hear whispers of the ghosts of fishermen and his father. Voices Swamiji could probably hear clearly, he thought, smiling.

It came back to him then, the miracle he had witnessed before he left the Himalayan Ashram. There was so much about

Swamiji that he couldn't explain. Perhaps didn't want to explain. But whatever the explanation, Swamiji was something more than a frail, well-intentioned old man. From the very beginning, when he had told Jonathan about his mother's health . . .

His thoughts ranged to his frail mother and his sick dog. He thought of Becky sleeping on the hospital bed while he held their dead, beautiful Sarah. Stroking her back, rocking her, kissing her good-bye and trailing his fingers through the fuzz on her head, he had left her in the hands of crying nurses and hurriedly walked away.

He wished he could freeze time.

With a knot in his stomach, he listened to the ocean's murmuring. His gaze spanned the azure sky. Orion rose out of the horizon and clusters of other stars turned the sky lambent. The gentle waves dredged fragments from the burial mounds of the shoals that quietly swallowed up skeletons of man's vessels and giant marine beings that once freely roamed safely and securely, with the ease of a fetus floating in its mother's amniotic sac.

Then, as he lay there on the beach, he realized that compared to all the goodness nature delivered unconditionally, he had no right to complain about his life on this planet. Man's life was nothing but a performance on stage, brief and glorious. It should be lived as intended, with passion and verve, not as a mere ephemeral existence.

He propped his trunk up on his elbows and turned his head toward his humble abode. Then, wearing the cloak of the night, he drifted off, listening to the musical splashes of the ocean waves, feeling the coolness of the big yellow moon.

After his time on the island, he found himself looking forward to a return to the twentieth century. In particular, he wanted to call Joshi before he left the islands for Mount Kailash. He had not spoken with him since the morning after his adventure in Baramedi.

Mount Kailash at 20,000 feet was a far cry from the death-defying 29,028-foot reach of Mt. Everest, but besting it required skill and endurance. As Jonathan prepared for the expedition, he wondered why Swamiji had suggested it. Fortunately, the Ministry of the External Affairs routinely organized expeditions, both for the Hindu faithful making the pilgrimage and for interested outsiders like himself. The expeditions always ran between June and September just after the first melting of the snow and before the dreaded arrival of winter.

A ferry across the Bay of Bengal brought him to Calcutta, from whence he flew to Delhi. In the few minutes before he had to catch a connecting flight to the foothills of the Himalayas in Uttar Pradesh, he found a phone booth. But he had no luck contacting Joshi before his old army turbo prop rolled in.

On his way to Mount Kailash, he stopped at an ashram called Anandadham, meaning *blissville*, at Kate's suggestion. There, an ensemble of entrepreneurs, lawyers, teachers, physicians and artists flocked, looking for peace and happiness. All wore long frilly shirts, beads, bandannas and flowers in their hair. Most of them were Canadian or American. They lived in little communal villas and traded villas as often as they changed mates. Apple wine from the local orchards, locally grown (and potent) cannabis, and sex between consenting partners were all allowed. "It is through joy that one reaches God," their spiritual master preached. "Sing, dance, smoke, drink, make love. Do whatever gives you joy. Because it is this ladder of joy that will help you ascend to God."

Jonathan studied the groggy sycophants who surrounded the preacher. They didn't seem blissful, not like those he had experienced at Swamiji's Ashram. They seemed more like they were lost in a world of eternal fantasy, seeking the perfect charade to mask their pain and find an excuse to let it all hang out. Jonathan was repelled by the extravagance. He left that ashram for Mount Kailash.

On the registration form at Mount Kailash, Jonathan put down Joshi and Swamiji as next of kin to be notified in case of an accident or death. Who better for the job, he thought warmly. The journey began from Tawaghat, a Himalayan foothill town in the Uttar Pradesh, and headed to Lipu Lekh pass to Tibet-China, where Mount Kailash was located. A strong young team of fifteen loaded the cargo on ponies, yaks and porters. Then they began the trek up the same trails that Buddhist monks had used for millennia and quite possibly the trails Babur's army had taken when he invaded, before founding the Mughal Dynasty in India.

First came a valley awash with floral carpets, woven with the vivid colors of red and yellow dahlias, deep blue and snowy white hydrangeas, purple-red fuchsias, and the long pink and red stems of gladioli and canna. Then came a thicket of willow trees and mulberries, great leafy chinars, dark firs and the swaying meadows of the Gulmag. Every turn was bedecked with pansies, gotetias, zinnias, balsams and orchids. It all felt like some quintessentially impossible dream.

Then they left the calcinated terraced fields growing orchids and the Himalayan poppies nurtured by the water gushing through the innumerable springs, trickling down the slopes, from the melting glaciers, higher up.

Slowly the terrain gave way to oaks, then to rhododendrons and finally to snow-draped firs through which the biting wind hissed. And yet, even at that inhospitable altitude, some hardy species of rock flowers smiled through the otherwise impenetrable blocks of boulders: saxifrage, oxalis, fox sorrels, and the fanned-out heads of the cobra-lily on the marshy floors of the forest below.

Jonathan was happily surprised to see a tiny cluster of houses straddled along the spur of craggy hills, the fair-skinned, blue-eyed, blond Hunza tribe—descendants of soldiers from the army of Alexander the Great, as legend had it. They earned livelihoods assisting climbers and growing their own food, near the top of the world.

Then there were the native Sherpas. Jonathan took pictures of the happy faces adorned by high cheekbones, gaping white teeth and eyes flanked by crow's feet. He was amazed and refreshed to see all the villagers unmoved by the bustle and acquisitive hunger of humanity, living their lives in idyllic bliss.

As they resumed their ascent, some trekkers were getting tired and discouraged. Although the guide promised more glories to come, half of the trekkers dropped out from muscle cramps and short windedness. One threw up blood.

But then came the border between India and China. The group had gratefully received the much-needed assistance from the Utter Pradesh Tourism Agency for its meals, beds and medicines all the way to the Chinese border. But there, the ambiance changed. The Chinese demanded heavy entrance fees, and their camps were bereft of any Indian facilities or supplies. Their twenty-five kilogram luggage limit was quickly eaten up with essential items like biscuits, dates, chocolates, batteries, flashlights, bug-repellent, camphor, antiseptics, skin moisturizer, sunscreen, sunglasses, trekking boots, sweaters, gloves, water-bottles and rain gear, leaving no room to spare for purchases. Two more dropped out. The remaining five continued upward under the supervision of a trekking officer who made all the decisions.

The supervisor had hired three new porters from the border camp. To Jonathan, they didn't look very healthy. One was tall and hefty, the second, rotund, and the third was a skinny fellow who appeared to have poor eyesight. They wore hoods, goggles and the trekker's jump suits.

Jonathan's personal luggage consisted only of one small bag, so he had avoided the use of a pony, yak or a porter. Yet, as they approached Kailash Mountain, even he found himself needing assistance. His respiratory rate was up to 20-25 times a minute in the thin air. But with the panache of Hillary or Tenzing, the stubborn five looked at each other, boosted morale, laughed, and stooping forward, lumbered on.

"Keep going," belted out one of the trekkers from Canada. "A dip in lake Mansarovar will end the cycle of the Sansara . . . it will get you to Nirvana . . . Moksha . . . keep going . . . one last hour to Rama."

The expedition turned more treacherous. They tiptoed around a precipitous cliff, then came within sight of sense-stunning Mount Kailash rising in the foreground. A gush of strong wind held them back. The mystical beauty of the sublime loomed so close and yet remained so far. They tried to talk but the wind tore their words away, leaving only the glacial chill. Nevertheless, they advanced. Perhaps the thin air had dulled their awareness that these holy peaks had claimed lives with sickening regularity.

Then, sadly, their leader signaled them to stop. "I am sorry," he yelled over the wind. "Safety forbids our going further. We must turn back."

Jonathan was disappointed, but complied.

The newly hired porters, however, turned out to be inexperienced and began bickering with the guide for advance cash wages. Since the guides didn't have cash with them, the porters spontaneously quit, and the trekkers found themselves having to strip their gear even further.

To make matters worse, on the way back down the mountain, Jonathan and the others began to experience heavy rain. Intending to wait out the storm, the five of them gathered beneath a nearby overhang carved into the hill. The rains fell relentlessly. One trekker, an Icelander named Carl, who had ditched his heavy raincoat when the porters had quit, decided to go back up and retrieve it. The guide refused to allow it unless someone agreed to go with him. Jonathan volunteered.

Jonathan and Carl were successful, yet when they returned to the overhang under which they'd stood, nobody was there. He craned his neck, looking further down the path, figuring that the group had grown impatient and taken off. But the rain had intensified and he could not see anything. The two of them started down the path, hoping to catch up with the rest. But when they turned the next corner, they were confronted with the mass of a landslide, which blocked their way.

Attempting to maneuver around it, Jonathan's knees struck a pair of boots sticking out of the landslide.

"Carl," he yelled. "Here!"

Both began to dig as fast as they could in the rain, and the thin air of 18,000 feet. After a few minutes, Jonathan managed to expose the face that belonged to the boots. It was the guide, and he was still breathing. Jonathan continued on with a new vigor.

Then they heard a roar. Looking up the hill, Carl saw boulders tumbling down in their direction. He screamed at Jonathan to get out of the way, but Jonathan was intent on freeing the guide, who was nearly out. Carl tried to push Jonathan away. But in a twist of irony, it was he who was struck by a boulder.

Carl's body flew through the air and landed on the edge of a ravine of incalculable depth, barely able to hold on.

Immediately, Jonathan whipped a rope around his waist and threw the other end at Carl. Carl grabbed the rope, just as he lost his footing. Jonathan dug his heels into the mud, but the full weight of his companion caused him to slide dangerously toward the edge.

"Leave me. Go!" Carl yelled. "Save yourself."

"Like hell! Hang on!"

Carl's foot caught a rock for a moment and the rope went slack. Jonathan looped the free end around a boulder behind him. Slowly, Carl dragged himself up the rope until Jonathan was able to help him back onto the path. Both were so tired and elated that they began laughing, Carl pounding his right hand in the mud and crying at the same time.

But then as Carl looked gratefully at Jonathan, his eyes suddenly reflected a new terror. Jonathan turned to discover that the boulder with the rope tied to it was rolling toward them. He dove out of the way, missed his landing, and plunged over the edge.

It was cold. It was still. Then, after a moment, Jonathan realized he was alive. It surprised him. But then, was he alive?

He opened his eyes and there, looming close, was the moon, pale and wan in the fading daylight.

Becky used to call him "inconstant, beautiful moon," her nickname for his frequent and unexpected disappearances to attend to patients' emergencies. He remembered the rest of the quote: "O, swear not by the moon, the inconstant moon. That monthly change in her orb: lest that thy love prove variable."

He tried to move and found he couldn't. And he was so cold.

Becky was right, his love had been inconstant. But if only he could show her now how much he had loved her. So much that he couldn't give himself to anybody. No one—not friends, family—anyone.

Then he thought of Gauri. And his developing tender feelings for her. To him, Gauri looked as though she wanted to live . . . but was afraid. And he? He wanted love . . . but could not.

What an odd predicament, he thought, smiling at the irony. I love a woman whom I can no longer love because she's gone—she's dead. And out of attraction for her innocence and beauty, I have wanted to love another, who is alive, but I cannot, because I am dead. Except, I am alive. I think.

He tried to move his foot. It did nothing. He thought of Swamiji, lost in the snow and the angel—or had it been his gurudev's bilocution? He smiled again, this time broader. I'm not going crazy, I'm really not, he thought. It's just funny. It truly is. At the point of my departure—or maybe not, who knows—I finally come around to believing the old fellow. And what had he said, what little thing had he slipped in there? Gauri loves you—more than you know? How did he know? Well, indeed. How did he know anything? He seemed to have a corner on the knowledge market, at least where feelings were concerned.

Yet, Gauri, as gentle, disciplined, alluring, and absolutely beautiful as she was, had no idea how he felt toward her—his departing fit of anger in the clinic probably gave her quite the opposite impression. Maybe not, though. She had such a warmth to her, an almost familiar aura around her.

In his depth of cold, Jonathan giggled. Oh God, yes, I'm dying, he thought. Oh Becky, Becky. He closed his eyes. I know why it's been such a terror-filled road without you. Now I know, my sweet Rebecca. You needed me then, and I failed you. But you needed yourself, too. And you were not there, either. You were lost in the past that you thought you had escaped. The pains of your life that you and I had made better, somehow claimed you again, and I could not help. I'm so sorry, my sad, sweet love.

It wasn't light outside, in fact, it was getting darker. But even with his eyes closed, he felt a strong light outside them shining in on him. It calmed him. Of course, he thought. Of course. I am doing exactly the same. Is that you, Becky? Are you telling me this? As I lie dying, here I am, being born. I have been claimed, too, by the pains of my past. And now I realize that I can be free, just as you could have been, just as I tried to make you. Well, he smiled, I am free; free to die in peace, maybe.

He felt such a deep sense of peace inside. Yet, when he opened his eyes, it was still dark outside. But it was no longer so cold. Yes, he thought, hypothermia. That was right, he'd fallen off the cliff. Something stupendous had hit him in the back, hurtling him into the air. Would anyone come to his rescue, or was he was about to join the ranks of the dead?

What would Swamiji say to all this?

He felt a deep longing to sleep, a longing he couldn't fight any more. Then, when he began to give in and close his eyes for good, his dad appeared.

"Don't worry, J. K.," he said. "You won't be here much longer."

Suddenly, Jonathan felt the urge to laugh, but he didn't have the strength. "You're . . . you're a hallucination, you know."

"Whatever you say, J. K." his father said. "You remember what I used to tell you when you got chilled on our camping trips?"

The poem and the comfort it brought came flooding back to Jonathan. He smiled and began mumbling along with his father's ghost:

> *"Blow, blow, thou winter wind.*
> *Thou art not so unkind as man's ingratitude;*
> *Thy tooth is not so keen because thou art not seen,*
> *Although thy breath be so rude.*
> *Heigh-ho! Sing, heigh-ho!*
> *Unto the green holly:*
> *Most friendship is feigning, most loving mere folly."*

The peaceful sounds from his childhood in Allagash, Maine, began suffusing his entire being. Waking up in the morning to the splitting sounds of grains cracking under the grind-stone of a quern, the clang of hammer and anvil from the farmer's smithy, and sounds of wind running through screens of birches where sunlight played peek-a-boo to the grating sounds of wind-swayed stems of corn plants and bulbous rain drops hitting the stacks of parched maple leaves. And the sounds of birds fluttering their wings—shaking off sloth—at sunrise, and the sound of galloping cavalry kicking off clouds of dust with their hooves, and ultimately at the end of the day, all sounds culminating into the quietude of still space, enriched by emptiness of all voices.

Maybe Swamiji was right; maybe this dying thing wasn't as hard as it seemed. Jonathan closed his eyes and slipped into the deepest sleep he had ever experienced.

chapter twenty–seven

The next thing he was conscious of was the scent of freshly-starched sheets, and the sight of pristine, white walls. Then he saw a woman in a nurse's outfit. He was in the base-camp hospital.

He'd lived.

Painfully, he turned his head and saw Carl in the bed across the room. Carl's leg was in a cast and suspended to a metal frame over his bed.

Jonathan smiled. "Hi. How . . . how are you feeling?"

Carl smiled back. "Alive! And how do you feel?"

Jonathan raised his heavily-bandaged hands in the air. "Got my gloves on."

Both laughed, less at the feeble joke and more at the simple fact that they were both still able to.

Suddenly Carl sobered. "Dr. Kingsley, thank you so much for saving my life."

"Please, Carl, call me Jonathan. And don't thank me, thank God."

Jonathan was startled, realizing the words he'd spoken sounded more like Swamiji's than his own. Then he began to remember. "Carl, what happened? How are the rest?"

"The guide is in the intensive care for broken ribs and exposure. The rest..."

"I see."

"The authorities told me earlier that they keep an eye on the weather. Not long after you went over the edge, a rescue helicopter appeared overhead."

Over the edge? Suddenly all the details came back to Jonathan: the battle with the rope, the boulder bearing down, the sickening drop. He looked at his bandaged hands, and took stock of the rest of his body. It didn't seem that anything was broken, yet shouldn't something have been—after that plunge? Then he had an image of himself floating gently to the bottom of the ravine. Was it one of Swamiji's miracles?

"Um... Carl, how did I—"

"There was a rock ledge maybe two meters below the path. The rescue workers spotted you there. Even though they moved quickly, you were close to death because of exposure by the time they got you here."

A rock ledge? Well, you might call it a miracle of a sort. He remembered his father, the poem. Hallucinations? Did it matter?

"Uh..." Carl said, "there was one other thing. I am not sure if it really happened or if it was a dream but... you remember the three porters?"

Details of the trip were beginning to fill themselves in. "The ones who went on strike at the top of the world?"

"Ja, them. They were there."

"Helping the rescue crew? Well, that's a surprise after—"

A nurse stuck her head in. "Excuse me, Dr. Kingsley. You have a visitor. I tried to tell him you needed rest, but—"

Judge Joshi pushed past her and rushed to Jonathan's bedside. "Jonathan, thank God you're all right. I got here as soon as I could."

"Judge Sahb," Jonathan said. "Why . . . I hardly expected you. Thank you for coming."

A doctor followed Joshi into the room.

"I think I'm all right," Jonathan said with a glance at the doctor. "Am I?"

"Severe salt and water depletion, compounded by mild brain concussion and a severe case of rhabdomyolysis."

"Oh dear," Joshi said. "This is not fatal, is it?"

Jonathan grinned. "Rhabdomyolysis is a breakdown of muscular tissue due to prolonged and strenuous use. In other words, I've got stiff muscles. I'd have them even if I hadn't fallen off a cliff."

"There are also some abrasions on the hands," the doctor said. "A few days of rest, and you will be fully fit again."

Jonathan tried stretching his limbs. He felt like a block of cement, but he could tell he'd be all right in time.

Joshi asked the doctor for some privacy and then leaned forward. "Tell me my friend, what do you remember?"

Jonathan almost smiled. Joshi seemed so earnest. "Remember? I fell off a cliff. But apparently I'll be all right."

"Yes, but what else?"

It only occurred to him then that it was odd that Joshi would have traveled all that way just to see him. At least so quickly. "Judge Joshi, what's going on here?"

"I was about to tell him," Carl said. "I did not get the chance."

Jonathan looked back and forth between Joshi and Carl.

"My friend," Joshi said, "I would have come to visit you from friendship alone, but I'm afraid my presence here also has a professional dimension. You see, you did not fall from the cliff. You were pushed."

"Pushed?" Jonathan remembered the boulder bearing down on him, the leap into the abyss. "No, Judge Sahb, it was an accident. That boulder—"

"That boulder was rolled toward you," Carl said. "When you were gone, I could see the men who did it, clearly."

"But why would they—"

"Can you not guess, my friend?" Joshi said. "Your friend here was able to give us a description of them, and I have no doubts. The three porters were not Chinese, they were our old friends from Baramedi: Jalim Singh, Bholanath and Murli."

"That gang? But why—"

"They said something," Carl said. "My Hindi is not as good as my English, but I think it was that they had finished with the doctor and now were going to get the girl."

"The girl?" Jonathan said. "Dear God!"

"Yes," Joshi said, "that is the only bit of good news in all of this. They have not found her yet. She is still alive."

"Forgive me, Judge," Carl said. "Since we talked, I remember more details. It was a name, I think. Sakkar, or something."

"Sarkar?" Joshi said.

"Yes, that may be it."

"The boss," Joshi said. "Was this name used amongst them or referring to someone else?"

"I . . . I can not . . ."

"Of course not. So you see Jonathan, it seems you are still their target. I have guards posted discretely here at the hospital, but I would suggest that you cut the rest of your trip short. Return to the Ashram."

"I . . . will certainly consider it, Judge Sahb."

Joshi and he visited for some time, trading gossip about Mohan and his family. Mohan's new daughter was apparently the delight of the household. They also shared news of the Ashram. Finally, Jonathan began to grow weary and Joshi left him to his rest.

Morning sun broke through the window on Carl's side. Jonathan felt rejuvenated. He craved a hardy breakfast: home fries, crispy bacon, orange juice, piping hot coffee, and two eggs, sunny-side up. Instead the nurse brought craggy-edged Undabread made with toasted onions and black pepper, scrambled eggs, Himpal tea and lychee juice. Still it was delicious enough that he had two helpings.

Jonathan chuckled, thinking about Swamiji's teaching on life and death. It seemed that, just as he was beginning to accept death, death slapped him in the face. Was he supposed to face death and survive like this? Was this a test envisioned by Swamiji? A test arranged by destiny? And if this happened on his way to Lake Mansarovar, what would happen if he visited the Holy Ganges?

"Maa Ganga," Swamiji had said, "the river of revelations. Ganges . . . where the answers will unfold."

Well, I could use some answers, he figured.

"Okay" he mumbled, "Mother Ganges, be ready with your book of answers. Show me what you've got. I'm coming."

PART THREE

chapter twenty-eight

As he eased his still-stiff body from the rickshaw, Jonathan experienced an eerie feeling inside his stomach. Before him lay Benares, the holiest place in India, and . . . it looked a little bizarre. Colorful crowds milled around the narrow streets and courtyards, laughing, chattering, singing, chanting. Hawkers selling food and various relics shouted out their wares. Beggars accosted people on the street, showing off their deformities and holding out their bowls. Occasional raucous funeral processions elbowed their way through the mob, presumably trying to find Mother Ganges, who was nowhere in sight. A blend of sandalwood smoke and unwashed bodies hung heavily in the air.

And he was supposed to find the answers here?

"Ah, holy Varanasi. What do you think, doctor?"

Behind Jonathan, H. K. Pandey, a retired Hindu mythology professor hand-picked by Joshi as Jonathan's experienced guide, also stepped from the rickshaw. Pandey was a short, squat, bald man in his fifties, wearing a white kurta, dhoti, and well-worn black leather shoes without socks. When he tried to make a point with carefully-enunciated words, his vermilion splattered forehead—hedged in front, by thick and unruly eyebrows—tensed, his nose twitched and his loose-fitting upper denture whistled.

"Well," Jonathan said, "it is very . . . energetic. But where is the—"

"Oh no, please, dear God." The professor froze and held back Jonathan with his outstretched arms.

"What happened, Professor?"

Pandey's eyes were glued to a funeral procession that had just crossed their path and headed down toward the river. Four pallbearers carried the body, which was tied tightly onto a makeshift wooden platform. The jute strings over the white cloth clearly picked out the feet, knees, trunk and head of the deceased. The unrestrained head bobbed from side to side.

"This is very ominous for us Hindus," Pandey said. "Never come across a dead body. Not first thing in the morning."

"I see. What are they chanting?"

"*Ram Bolo Bhai Ram.* That means, 'Praise the Lord.' Lord Rama, in this case."

Jonathan's hand reached for the camera inside his shoulder bag, then he decided against taking the picture of the mourners. "Why is that ominous? I thought Hindus were at home with death."

"With death, yes, but dead bodies are still traditionally considered unclean. But—I mean, I can nullify the negative power of such an inauspicious happening. I am a devout Hindu—Lord Shiva's ardent disciple. See this temple? That's Lord Shiva's temple. I'll go inside and say a quick prayer. That will rectify everything. It will take only five minutes. Fine?"

"Sure, Professor. Go ahead."

As the professor entered the temple, he smiled and waved.

Jonathan sat down on a stone bench, and amid the waves of humanity and freely roaming plump cows, listened to the clang of the temple bells and the rising and falling chants of the devout. The modality was strange to his western ears and didn't make him feel any closer to the divine. But then, listening carefully, he could hear the roar of a river in the distance. Maybe things would be different when he got to Mother Ganges herself.

Presently Professor Pandey returned to Jonathan and looked at his watch. "Four minutes, that's all it took. We are in fine shape now." Just then a cow crossed in front of them. "It is already paying off. See, Gaumata, mother cow, has already affirmed it."

"That's great," Jonathan said. He'd have to remember that. Bodies, bad. Cows, good.

As they descended the steps, the Ganges opened before them, wide, fast-flowing, and . . . brown. There was a dazzling panorama of colors—red, green, yellow, blue, white and dirty white, lots of dirty white—in the clothes and marks adorning all creeds and castes descending to the Ganges, all the way from Shrinagar to Sri Lanka. Flags flapped over white-domed mandirs and the crumbling cupolas of the castles that time seemed to have forgotten. There were conches blowing and bells pealing, mantras and the blessings of the professionally holy rising unfailingly, competing with the fluttering and the screeching of the ravens and the crows claiming their picking rights for the rice grains strewn over the expansive banks. After the peace of the Ashram and the mountains, it was almost enough to make Jonathan ill.

And the smell didn't help. Sandalwood smoke drifted from the crackling pyres, as pious fragrances of burning incense were waved by overweight pujarees at the devotees seeking to modify their karmas. Sweltering humanity reigned—some naked, some half-naked, and some looking naked with their meager saris and dhotis sticking to their bodies after the cleansing dip meant to wash off the sins of their avatars. But there was something deeper, darker in the scent. Rotting flesh. Burning flesh.

Amid the soiree of senses, he saw clusters of men holding their hollowed, stubbly, dark faces and sitting around the smoldering pyres, looking stoic. Either they were unfazed by the wrath of death or their hearts were far too numbed by the pains and the shortcomings of life.

"Good Lord!" exclaimed Jonathan, looking at the professor and then at the pyres. "There is so . . . much!"

"Yes, these are cremation ghats," the professor said. "They burn the dead bodies and sprinkle the ashes into the holy river, but there are so many people coming here to die that there is literally a traffic jam. India has a saying: 'If you want to die, go to Kashi, meaning Benares. If you want to dine, go to Surat.' That's an East Coast city north of Bombay, famous for its spicily splendid meals."

"Yes. I certainly don't have much of an appetite here."

"The snow in the mountains was particularly heavy this year, and with the spring floods, many animals were washed away and downstream. And to tell you the truth, there is such a demand on the cremation ghats that some operators do not wait until the bodies are fully burned before moving on to the next one."

So they simply dumped half-burned bodies into the river. That would explain the smell. "And as I understand it, when one takes a dip into these holy waters, all your sins are washed away. Is that correct?'

"Absolutely. Just like the ultimate resting-place for a dead body, I mean the ashes, is in the holy waters. Have you heard of the Kumbhmela?"

"No. What is it?"

"Please come with me, I'll explain. First let me take a quick dip into Gangamaiya." Pandey tossed his shirt ashore and walked into the shallow water. "You may do the same. All are welcome at Maa Ganga."

"Aaaah . . . how about if you take a dip and I . . . wade. Is that okay?"

"Whatever suits you, sir."

The stench horrified Jonathan. It was like immersing himself in death itself. But he didn't want to offend Pandey, who was devout, so he slung his shoes over his shoulder, rolled up his pants and waded in, trusting in his inoculations. Jonathan cringed when Pandey held his nose and went under the turbid waters.

When Jonathan was up to his knees, something caught on his leg. It felt like a tree branch. He reached into the muddy water, pulled the thing loose by feel, then lifted it to the surface.

It was a half-burnt human arm—its clawed hand having encircled Jonathan's ankle. The next thing he realized, Jonathan was on the shore, breathing deeply and trying to erase the vision of what he had just seen. He had no idea how he'd gotten there. Probably, he reasoned, in a single leap.

Pandey came up from under the surface, apparently unaware of Jonathan's headlong flight from the holy waters. He calmly waded out of the river.

"It is marvelous, isn't it?" Pandey asked, as he put on his long white shirt over his wet dhoti. "During the Mahakumbh Mela, the pulse of the holy city reaches a fever pitch."

Jonathan was still breathing deeply and thinking about the shower back at the hotel. But maybe he could keep Pandey talking until he calmed down. "Mahakumbh Mela?"

"A special festival of the full moon that comes only once every twelve years. Hopeful devotees from all walks of life, from all over India, pour in and nestle on the bank of the great Ganges. Ascetics with knotted manes and ash-covered bodies descend from their quiet caves in the mountains. As the full moon glows over the river, euphoric crowds of milling devotees surge forward in a frenzy for the ritual cleansing dip."

Jonathan's breathing was slowing. "Why is that?"

"The legend dates back to the creation of the universe. To settle their differences, the deities and the devils churned the ocean floor so they could retrieve the Kumbha—the pot of immortality—and share it equally. When they retrieved the pot, the top layer contained a dark poisonous substance capable of destroying the entire world."

"The world?"

"Yes, the entire world. It was Lord Shiva who came to their

rescue and promptly swallowed the poison and held it in his throat. His throat turned dark blue, giving him the title of 'Neel-Kanth,' or 'God with the Blue Throat.' When the two parties fought for this immortality potion at the bottom of the pot, they accidentally spilled the precious elixir over four places in India. These are Prayag or Allahabad, Nasik, Ujjain, and Haridwar. Do you like astronomy, Doctor?"

"Like it? Yes. Know much about it? No."

"Well, ever since then, when Jupiter enters Aquarius and the sun is in the Aries, the waters of the Ganges running through these four holy cities turns into nectar, and a dip in this nectar cleanses the soul and the body." He laughed. "Allegedly."

Jonathan had calmed down some, but he still didn't feel exactly clean. He reached into his pants pocket for his handkerchief to wipe his hands. Maybe he could get some disinfectant soap on their way back to the hotel. When he pulled the handkerchief from his pocket, the intertwined wedding bands fell out and clanged onto the rocks at his feet. He scooped them up and knotted them into his handkerchief so he wouldn't risk losing them again.

"Oh, turn your back," Pandey said, turning to face toward the river.

Jonathan did so. "Another part of the ritual?"

"No, simply preparation for the wind." Even as Pandey spoke, a brisk wind hit them in the back, peppering them with dust and small debris. "Part of the end of the monsoon season," Pandey said, speaking over the breeze. "Yesterday, a little twister destroyed some huts on the bank. Corrugated metal sheets flew through the air like razor blades."

"Really? Good Lord," Jonathan said as some pilgrim's drying clothing hit him in the back.

"Thanks to the good Lord, no one was hurt. And this little breeze will pass quickly."

Jonathan squeezed his eyes closed and waited. Sand grains

hit his neck and ears like little darts, and he covered them with his hands. Then he felt his handkerchief taking flight from his shirt pocket, the rings hitting his chin on their way out. As soon as the twister moved past them, Jonathan opened his eyes and saw the handkerchief swirling around with other debris, gathering force, moving forward.

"Excuse me professor," said Jonathan, "I've got to get that." Jonathan had to run quite a bit, for the handkerchief settled down on the ground a few times, only to be airborne again as he lunged forward to catch it. Finally, near a clutch of mourners having their heads shaved, the twister dropped the handkerchief on the bank and moved across the waters of the Ganges. Jonathan swiftly picked it up, and re-pocketed it securely, deep into his pants pocket.

Feeling happy and relieved at the retrieval of Becky's memento, he turned around and smiled at the mourners. The barber, busy shaving heads, looked engrossed in his work. The mourners smiled back at him. Jonathan stood there, observing the barber's work and waiting for the professor to catch up with him.

"I am so . . . so sorry, doctor," Pandey lamented as he approached Jonathan, his arms wide open, his face bearing a guarded silly grin. "I only wish Lord had granted me a mindful fortitude of the nuisance storm. I certainly hope no harm has reached you, subsequent to my negligence."

Jonathan heard Pandey's apology, but his eyes were glued to the archaic way in which the barber shaved the mourners' heads. Pandey, recognizing Jonathan's fascination, stood quietly behind him and watched the head shaving ceremony for a couple of minutes. When they moved on, Pandey resumed his chatter about the storm. Jonathan listened passively, his mind distracted, a strange sense of familiarity drawing him backward.

Jonathan stopped and said, "Excuse me, Professor." He returned to the group being shaved. Pandey, confused but compliant, followed. Jonathan looked at the barber very carefully. There was something painfully familiar about him—was it the way he shaved? Was it his clothes, or the way he looked? Jonathan felt that he had seen the barber somewhere before, but the barber's shaved head didn't quite fit into the picture. Jonathan made his way closer to the group.

"*Abey make laudey, kya ghoor ghoor ke dekhta hai? Safed chutiya nahin dekha pehle? Chal chal, jaldi kar. Aur meri gardan mat katna.*" The villagers laughed as Jonathan heard the client speak to the barber, who stared at Jonathan through his thick glasses that reflected the sun.

Thick glasses, Jonathan thought. This guy looks familiar. Jonathan understood only a few words of Hindi, so he wanted to know the meaning of what the villager had said to the barber. He grabbed the professor's arm firmly and asked, "Professor, what did he say to the barber? Why are they all laughing?"

"I am sorry, Doctor. It's nothing. He is just a smart-ass. He has no *tameez*. Mannerless country-bumpkin."

"No, professor." Jonathan firmed his grip on Pandey's arm. "You don't understand. I must know what the customer said to the barber. I must."

"Fine with me, sir. A word of caution, though. It is a little embarrassing. I don't think you'll find the translation very flattering."

"Tell me. I don't care. What did he say?"

"Well, if you insist. The client said to the barber, 'What the hell are you gawking at, you dumb jerks? Haven't you ever seen a white asshole before? C'mon, hurry up. And don't cut my neck.'"

Jonathan watched the man continuing to sharpen his long razor blade against the leather strap hanging over his leg. Carefully, he shaved his client's beard and neck, his razor making a very gritty sound. Then he piled up the dirty, stubble-filled foam on his left forearm, which he also used to steady the customer's head. Jonathan noticed that the barber's razor-bearing arm was shaking, and his eyes, magnified behind the Coke-bottle glasses, were helplessly roaming from side-to-side.

That was it! Jonathan knew who he was.

"Professor, wait a minute!" Jonathan said quickly.

His heart pounding, Jonathan casually advanced a couple of steps toward him. The villagers, under the wrong impression that it was the archaic shaving process that fascinated him, thawed to him, feeling complimented. The barber forced a smile, but one side of his face clearly twitched. Jonathan pulled out his camera from his shoulder bag. The barber's tremor worsened. Jonathan came closer, deliberately focusing his camera on the barber's face, which by then was drenched with sweat. He waited until the barber was wiping the used foam onto his arm.

"Smile, Murli," Jonathan said, and clicked the shutter.

At the sound of the shutter, the barber's hand jerked, slicing his forearm. Blood spilled out onto the customer's neck. The frightened villager, believing he'd been cut, stood up screaming, pressed his neck with his hand and began to kick and curse the barber.

Jonathan spun around. "Dr. Pandey, could you—" But Pandey was as pale as a ghost, traumatized by the sight of blood. Jonathan dropped his plan of asking Pandey to go for a policeman while he stayed with Murli. "Professor," he yelled over the uproar. "Um . . . please help these men. They're both bleeding. I'm running up the steps to the bazaar to fetch some medicine and some bandages. Okay, Professor? Stay with them. Don't let them leave. Tell the villagers not to let anyone leave. Doctor's orders. They could both die if they leave."

Jonathan leaped like a cheetah, taking two, three steps at a time. When he arrived at the plateau, he looked around for a policeman, but there were none in sight. Great, he thought, so now what? In his frenzy, he forgot every word of Hindi he had learned. That was when he spotted the phone booth. Just as he picked up the receiver, he slammed it back down, realizing he didn't have any change. He ran to the nearest coconut shop, and in broken, frenzied Hindi, explained to the shopkeeper his urgency to make a phone call. The proprietor gave him a couple of coins and he ran back to the phone booth. Scared he would forget Joshi's phone number, he picked up the receiver, closed his eyes, took a deep breath and dialed slowly. When he looked up, he found that the curious shopkeeper had followed him and stood outside the booth watching.

Joshi's line was busy.

"Dammit!" He hung up, waited a moment, then dialed again. Still busy. 'Please, God, let me be trying the right number.'

On the sixth try, he connected.

"Yes?"

"Judge Sahb? Judge Sahb, is that you? Oh, thank God!"

"Jonathan? How pleasant to hear from you. I hope nothing—"

"Forgive me, Judge, but this is an emergency. I'm calling from the Ganges." He looked toward the river. "From one of the ghats. I need your help . . . I . . . I . . ."

"My dear man, calm down, calm down. Take a deep breath, first. I can hardly understand you."

"Right. I'm sorry. Listen. I don't have time. I need your help. I found the barber shaving heads . . . on the ghat."

"Well, that is what they do, after all."

"No, no, no. THE barber. From Baramedi. Murli. You know, the one with the Coke-bottle glasses."

"Are you sure?"

"Absolutely. Hundred percent. When he knew I recognized him, he got nervous and cut his own arm."

"Good Lord! All right, Jonathan, stay where you are. I'm notifying the police sub-inspector in Benares right away. All you have to do is . . . Wait a minute. Where are you? What part of the Ganges?"

Jonathan looked around to spot a distinctive landmark. "OK, I'm at a ghat with the big banyan tree."

"Banyan tree?" asked Joshi. "There are so many of them. Is there any other peculiarity in the area?"

"Uh . . . Yes, a temple of Lord Shiva. Tall, white—"

"Jonathan," Joshi said, "you are in a holy city. There are temples on every street corner."

"Wait a minute, Judge Sahb." Jonathan dropped the receiver, opened the booth and grabbed the curious shopkeeper. He shoved the receiver into the shopkeeper's hand and shouted as he headed back to the barber, "This man will give you the exact location. I've got to run. I don't want the crook to escape. Bye!"

He dashed back through the crowd and down the steps to the banyan tree. He was relieved to see the crowd was still there. In fact, it had gotten bigger. And he could hear screams. He ran along the shore.

When he forced his way through the thick knot of people under the tree, he saw Murli lying on the ground, wailing and begging for mercy, his arm wrapped in his towel, now soaked in blood. His clothes were torn, glasses broken and his tools strewn all over. The villager he'd bled on was in a corner looking disgusted, his neck wrapped in a blood-spotted bandana. When the villagers saw Jonathan they began beating and kicking the barber again.

"Stop. Gentlemen." Jonathan waded in and began pulling them off. "Please stop beating him. Your friend isn't badly hurt, and I can help him. I'm a doctor."

Professor Pandey stepped in and began speaking rapid, authoritative Hindi. Jonathan caught something about the doctor from America keeping their friend from bleeding to death. Slowly the crowd fell back.

"Professor, have them boil some water."

Jonathan went to the villager, wiped the blood from his neck and pronounced him cured, then turned to Murli.

"So brother, how's your pain now?" It was a phrase he used often, and it brought his Hindi back to him.

Murli said nothing.

He unwrapped the towel. It looked as if the razor had missed the artery, but it was a pretty deep cut, good for five or six stitches at least. Jonathan pulled out his handkerchief from his pocket and tied it above the wound, which slowly stopped bleeding. Jonathan looked at the rings at the end of the handkerchief, swinging in the air, shining brightly.

Thanks, honey, he thought warmly.

Jonathan glanced back toward the Ganges. "So this is the river of truth—I guess I understand why now, Swamiji," he said to himself.

He heard police whistles clearing the traffic, getting closer to the crowd. Jonathan put his hand on the barber's shoulder. "Murli, hang in there. The worst is over for you. No more running scared. Now all you have to do is tell the truth."

"Excuse me, Doctor," Padney said, "but what is going on? Who is this man?"

"It's a long story, Professor," Jonathan said. "But I can tell you this. You say great prayers."

chapter twenty-nine

When Joshi, Jonathan and Kate arrived, there was not even standing room left in the court. Politicians, reporters, pro-female groups and the simply curious jammed the old Victorian building. It had quickly become national news that one of India's most notorious criminals had been caught. And when Murli was faced with the evidence of the bones and witnesses, he had agreed to testify against his accomplices in order to earn immunity.

Joshi had hated cutting a deal of that sort, and stipulated that the judge could determine the degree of immunity Murli received, based on the accuracy of his testimony. The sensationalism of the exploits of Baramedi's evil citizen had also nearly made Murli a folk hero. The whole capital was eager to hear his confession.

Jonathan and Kate made their way through the crowd to the seats Joshi had reserved for them in the front. Joshi sat and went through a multitude of notes and reports that lay strewn on the prosecutor's table. Because of his official involvement in the case since the beginning, the government had asked that Joshi serve as government counsel—prosecutor, in American terms—a request he had readily granted.

Gauri, Mohan, and Geeta would also be in attendance. Gauri had never seen Delhi, so at Swamiji's suggestion, she and Geeta had gone along. Mohan acted once again as tour guide before delivering them to the courtroom. They had some seats reserved further back.

Behind Jonathan someone said, "I read in the paper that a villager named Gopal told the CBI how the barber used to brag about a big salon his brother owned in Gorakhpur and how he could make ten times more money there."

"So they must have caught him scalping money from the city-slickers, eh?"

"No! He's not that stupid. He was in disguise. He shaved his head, grew a beard and wore Tilak on his forehead. But no matter how you paint a crow, you can't turn him into a peacock."

"I heard some foreign tourist caught him at a cremation ghat on the river Ganges, shaving mourners' heads."

Kate leaned toward him. "Hear that, mate? You're famous."

"I'll always remember the little people," he said.

"Thanks. So tell me, given all the crimes this lot has committed over the years, why are they prosecuting the bugger for a failed murder?"

"It's the one they've got evidence against. You've seen how the women victims don't want to talk, and what happens to those that do."

"What about you? You'll talk. Didn't they take a shot at your life?"

"Yes. In Himpal. Beyond Joshi's jurisdiction." Jonathan thought a moment. "Besides, if he were to pay for one crime, I'd like it to be the suttee. It seems fitting."

"All rise," a court bailiff sang out. "His Eminence, Judge Trivedi presiding."

Kate translated as the bailiff announced that out of respect for the international press, the proceedings would be in English. She raised her eyebrows. "This thing is big," she said.

Everyone in the court stood up. The judge, dressed in flowing black robes and a white wig, took his seat and struck the wooden gavel on the bench. The crowd sat down. As he did, Jonathan glanced toward the back of the room. Mohan, Gauri and Geeta had arrived for the show.

Joshi, who was to interrogate the barber, stood and smiled at Jonathan and Kate.

When the handcuffed barber was led in, a murmur arose from the crowd and heads bobbed this way and that. The barber nervously glanced at the court through his Coke-bottle spectacles, his face sweaty and pale, his gray beard scraggly. The court aide deposited him in the dock and removed his handcuffs.

Joshi and Murli went through the initial formalities; the reading of the plea arrangement for the record, the swearing in, a series of technical motions by the state-appointed defense attorney that Jonathan didn't follow. Then, when the stage was finally set, Joshi fired his first question at the barber. "State your full name, age, occupation, and your past and present addresses."

Murli slid his glasses back up his nose. "My name is Murli Manohar Nai. I'm fifty-five years old. I lived in Baramedi. Lately, I live with my brother in Benares. I'm a barber by occupation."

Joshi stood obliquely in front of the witness box. "Mr. Nai, as the only barber in Baramedi, I hear you were quite busy. Tell us, what class of customers did you serve?"

"All classes, Maalik. Farmers, laborers, traders, even pujarees and police officers. Business was good—by God's grace."

"All these police officers and pujarees, they talked to you freely, didn't they?" Joshi's voice was calm, deceptively conversational.

"Always, Maalik. They sat in that chair and—" The barber snapped his fingers. "—they were hypnotized."

Jonathan shook his head. The bastard was enjoying his notoriety.

"Murli, as I'm sure you know, a large number of murders, rapes and robberies have been reported in recent years from Baramedi. Who do you think was responsible for these heinous crimes?"

"Gangs, Maalik, gangs. They did all that. Fearlessly... openly."

Joshi turned around and squarely faced the barber. "Do you personally know any of the gang members that operated out of Baramedi?"

"Well... um... Maalik... all kinds of people came and went. They said lots of things. Some just brag. You just don't know who is noble and who is thief, so how do I—"

"Nonsense!" Joshi thundered. "Listen to me, you weasel. You have agreed to work with us to stop these crimes, like an honorable man. You have sworn with your hand on the Bhagvat Gita that you will tell the truth. So the only reason you can have to cover up these crimes now is that you support the criminals. Is this true?"

Murli looked stunned. He blinked and looked down, his fingers clasping the railing of the witness box. With tremulous hands, he pushed up his glasses. "I... I'm sorry, Maalik. Very sorry. Please forgive me."

"It is up to the court to forgive you or not. Now tell us, who were the members of the gang in Baramedi?"

The barber began breathing heavily. "Um, there were... several... um, people that—"

"Names!"

Murli held his temples with shaking hands and bit his lip.

"I am waiting, Mr. Nai."

"Maalik," wailed the barber with outstretched hands. "I'm scared. I am afraid for my life. I know, if I... they'll kill me."

"Murli!" Joshi said. "You are in the protective custody of the law. Law's arms are long and powerful. Now give us the names of the gang members."

The barber looked up, wiped his eyes with his fists, and swallowed. "Pujaree Bholanath..."

THE ASHRAM

"And?"

"I . . . I was too, Maalik. But no longer. I gave all that up. I'm so sorry . . ."

Murli broke down and began crying. Jonathan shook his head. Kate whispered, "If it's an act, it's a good one."

When Murli regained his composure, he said, "God will strike us dead. The gang did so many terrible things. Many innocent women and children died. But Sahb, I just passed on information from one member to another, that's all."

"That fat holy man couldn't do all this alone. Who else was part of your gang?"

"A congressman, Maalik. From New Delhi. The Honorable—"

The defense council leapt to his feet. "Objection, your honor. This is outside the scope of our—"

"Objection overruled."

"Still," Joshi said quietly, "you need not name the member of the legislative assembly. Not yet. But Murli, listen and listen to me carefully. I'm about to ask you a plain and simple question. And I want a plain and simple answer. Understand?"

The barber nodded.

"Good. Who is your gang leader?"

The barber froze. His lips quivered.

"I'm waiting for your answer, Mr. Nai."

"Ssssrarrk—" the barber stammered.

Joshi clasped the guardrail of the witness box with two hands. "I did not hear you. Please repeat the answer."

It felt like the entire court was leaning forward and holding its breath.

"Mr. Nai?" Joshi said.

"Sarkar. He is the leader, Sahb—Sarkar."

"And who is Sarkar? I would like to hear his first name, his last name. Not his titles."

The audience murmured their guesses to each other.

"Now, Mr. Nai!"

The barber looked around and stuttered meekly, "Juh-juh-juh-Jalim Singh."
"Louder!" Joshi shouted.
"Jalim Singh!"
"The chief of police?" Joshi said.
A hubbub broke out in the crowd and kept building despite the judge's gaveling for silence. Murli seemed to be trying to look in all directions at once. Trails of sweat ran down his face, his repaired glasses fell to the floor. He picked them up and quickly began cleaning them with his checkered prison outfit.
Jonathan took a deep breath and shook his head at Kate. Then he attempted to look back at Gauri, but his view was blocked. Some well-nourished women had risen to their feet, holding up banners. They began to shout slogans. Quickly, the police ushered them out.
Joshi turned to the bailiff and handed him a note. It read: *Dispatch officers immediately to Baramedi to pick up Jalim Singh for questioning.*
When the crowd finally quieted down, the judge motioned Joshi to resume the interrogations.
"So you personally know Bholanath, the priest, and Jalim Singh, the police chief, both from Baramedi?"
"I used to."
"I see. You used to." Joshi faced the barber squarely. "In what capacity?"
"As you yourself just described. Bholanath was our village priest, Jalim Singh was a—"
"Nonsense!" Joshi wagged his finger at Murli. "Listen to me. We already know far more than you think we do. If you refuse to tell the truth, your lies will find you out. Now tell us, in what capacity did you know Jalim Singh?"
The barber's fingers clasped the railing of the witness box more tightly. He trembled. "I beg for your forgiveness, Maalik. Jalim Singh . . . it was he who plotted Seeta's murder."

"Ah, now we are making progress. What led to plotting Seeta's murder?"

"It was actually Seeta's father-in-law, Bapuji. He first called Jalim Singh."

Jonathan leaned over to Kate. "I'll never believe that."

"Bapuji begged Jalim Singh for help," Murli said. "He said, 'Jalim Sahb, I'm afraid to lose my credit in the village. My daughter-in-law is pregnant. I don't know how this happened because my son is dying of TB and is too weak to impregnate her. Please help me.'"

"What did Jalim Singh say?"

"He said: 'Look, old man. You have three options here: We can have the barber do the coat-hanger abortion, drown her in the river or sell her to a brothel in New Delhi.'"

There was a murmur from some of the women packed in the courtroom. Someone behind Jonathan whispered, "It is always the way."

"I see," Joshi said. "Did Bapuji agree to any of these options?"

"No, Maalik, he didn't." The barber's face glistened with sweat. "So Jalim Singh got together with the pujaree and myself."

"And?"

"And we gave him the idea. Um . . . actually it was Jalim Singh who came up with the idea, and the priest supported it. Even Bapuji liked the new idea."

Joshi looked down his nose at Murli. "And you were opposed to it, I suppose."

"I . . . I am a weak man, Maalik. I feared for—"

"Never mind. Go on."

"Well, we said if and when the sick son dies—and we knew he was ready to kick the bucket any time—then we could cremate him in the town square with his wife."

"And Seeta was to be alive for this, yes?"

Jonathan's stomach gave a lurch. He had to remind himself that she had not been on the pyre.

"Um, yes, Your Honor. The idea was to erase the blemish from Bapuji's family—God only knows who knocked her up.

So this way, not only does his son get a proper cremation, but it also brings the prestige and respect back to Bapuji's family and the whole village."

"Did the old man agree to this new idea?"

"In the beginning he was very reluctant, but when he thought about the boost he'd receive to his honor and the income—"

"Income from where, Mr. Nai?"

"Jalim Singh said lots of people would visit—devotees, villagers, even reporters. He told us foreign reporters are crazy for sensational stories. They will pay anything for such a rare and stomach-sickening story like this."

The crowd murmured. Jonathan saw a couple of reporters down the aisle from him shake their heads.

"I see," Joshi said. "You wanted to force this young girl to a fiery death so you could line your pockets. And how much was your share, Murli?"

"Nothing, Maalik. The priest and I both told Jalim Singh, 'We don't want the blood money. Take our share and instead build the temple at the suttee site so we—'"

"Could make even more money from the devotees at the temple, yes?" Joshi took a sip of water, allowing Murli to swing in the wind a moment. When he resumed, his manner was almost avuncular. "So how did you convince Seeta to sit on the pyre? She didn't exactly volunteer, did she?"

The barber wiped sweat off his face with his forearm. "Yes, Your Honor . . . I mean no, Your Honor. She did in the beginning; hungry for glory, I'm sure. But as the night progressed, she became shaky. We knew she'd cause problems so we drugged her and locked her up in Jalim Singh's barn."

"I'm listening."

"When we were busy bathing her husband's corpse and gathering ornaments and a bridal gown for her, we thought she was sound asleep. But when we came to get her at about one-thirty or two, she was gone. Now everybody was scared. We'd already made the proclamation informing the villagers that the suttee ceremony would start at sunrise."

"A difficult problem."

"Indeed, Maalik. We had to find Seeta's replacement. So I came up with an idea."

"You did. Interesting."

"Well, I mean . . . I thought—"

"Carry on, Murli."

"Well . . . a laborer had accidentally fallen from a tall building and died the previous day. His family was very poor. They couldn't even afford enough logs and ghee to burn him. I had to shave his mourners' heads for free."

"Very generous of you."

"I, well I . . . thank you, Maalik. Anyway, his half-burnt body was still smoldering at the cremation ghat, so we stole the body."

"Ah. So your generosity was repaid? A shave for a body?"

"Well, no, Your Honor. I mean, the man would want to be cremated properly, wouldn't he? We were just helping—"

"Of course."

"Well, we gathered his bones and made an effigy of them, looking like some woman's body. We dressed it in a red and gold embroidered sari, garlands and the gold ornaments and—"

"Gold ornaments?"

The barber scratched his stubble. "Well, fake gold ornaments, Your Honor."

"And no one noticed the dummy on the pyre?"

"They could have. But Bholanath made a second proclamation—that the suttee wished to leave this ugly world earlier, well before the sun showed her again how sinful this world is."

"I certainly agree," Joshi said, his eyes riveting Murli. "It is a sinful world. Is that it?"

"And we had lots of flowers and hired laborers to scream incantations and beat drums. Plus we had the fire blazing on the periphery, but lots of smoke in the center."

"So no one could see who was burning in the center of the pyre. I see."

The barber timidly nodded.

"Very clever. How did that bridge collapse?"

The barber squinted. "Bridge?"

"When we were in Baramedi, we were told that a truck loaded with villagers—"

"Oh, oh, I know, the bridge over Vasundhara. That was the police chief's idea. He had his men weaken the pillars and set up the accident."

"Why?"

"We were afraid, Your Honor. Jalim Singh said, 'That son of a bitch American doctor is no good. The guards told me he visited the pyre. He had figured out our game.'"

Kate leaned toward Jonathan. "You never told me you played Sherlock Holmes."

"You never asked," he whispered back.

Joshi proudly glanced at Jonathan, giving him an ambiguous smile, then looked back at the barber. "So?"

"So he wanted to detain you all and have someone kill the doctor. So that it would seem like an accident."

"Ah, but the rest of us were to go free, I suppose?"

"Well, no, Maalik. I think you were to have been killed as well."

Joshi looked up at a scowling Judge Trivedi. "A Judge in the Indian legal system, eliminated as an inconvenience?"

"Maalik, I'm sorry. I didn't know what he was planning. I thought he just wanted to detain—"

"Of course, Murli, we all know you are a good and honorable man. Who accosted the doctor and my driver in the bush that night when they slipped out to inspect the pyre?"

"The police chief and some of his men. He had his Rampuri knife with him, but something went wrong and he lost the knife in the bush."

Kate leaned toward him again. "You were a busy boy, weren't you?"

Jonathan shrugged.

"And who placed the boulders on the road near Gopal's farm?" Joshi said.

"Jalim Singh's men. He said that was his last chance to hold you people back. The police chief followed your car in the jeep."

"What happened to Bapuji?"

"He was kidnapped—by Jalim Singh's men."

"Where is he currently, Bapuji?"

"I don't know, Sahb. He was taken to Jalim Singh's headquarters in Himpal, but by now—"

"Where in Himpal?"

"Maalik, I do not know," Murli wailed. "We were never told about that. He didn't always tell us everything, and I was such a small man—"

"Yes, you were," Joshi said. "Tell us whose idea was it to wipe the site clean and dump the bones in the river?"

"Bholanath's."

"What happened?"

"Maalik, that was supposed to be my job. In the dark, the night after you left, I had the sack of bones and was walking to the river. I think I spotted Gopal from a distance and a lot of headlights, so I got scared. I left the whole bag in his barn under the hay bales and ran away."

"Was Bapuji pressured to tell us lies?"

"Yes, he was. Jalim Singh had threatened him. If he didn't go along, not only would he lose his share of the money, but his life as well."

"Bapuji did tell us some lies. Didn't he?"

"He did, Your Honor, but Jalim Singh didn't like his performance. Bapuji was too reluctant. Besides, Jalim Singh was afraid he'd squeal on all of us later."

"So he was kidnapped. Tell me Murli, why wasn't he killed? Killing seems to come easy to your gang."

"It . . . it was felt we could use him to get to the damned woman, Seeta."

"Ah, yes, the fish that got away. Where is she now?"

"Maalik, I wish I knew. She simply disappeared off the face of the earth. Probably found and killed by some other gang or wild animals. And, forgive me, Maalik, but Bapuji has probably been done in by now as well."

"What was your last assignment?"

"Kailash mountain. To eliminate the doctor. Jalim Singh was determined to do it, and we were forced to go along. He assured us it was a far away place, and it would look like an accident."

"And at this too, you failed. And since then?"

"Then we three split up our shares and went separate ways. After that I never heard from Sarkar again."

"Where in Himpal is he located?"

"Himpal? I did not know that, Maalik, I swear."

Joshi smiled, clasped his hand behind his back and walked to the barber. "Murli, you seem to be a good fellow—"

"Thank you, Your Honor. Your mercy means everything to me."

"Tell us honestly and fearlessly. Why did Jalim Singh kill all of these women? For money, or for joy?"

"Eh . . . both, Maalik. Mostly for joy. He was the happiest when he killed a beautiful woman. He said to me one day, 'Murli, I could walk in a field of women's skulls and hear them crack under my iron-bottomed boots. Oh, that would satisfy the burning fire inside my body.'"

Joshi swallowed and momentarily closed his eyes. Audible sighs emerged from the court.

"That right bastard," Kate murmured.

Joshi looked up. "Why, Murli? Why did he hate women so much?"

"I don't know, Maalik. He settled in Baramedi, after the Pakistani war, some twenty-five years ago. One day I was shaving the pujaree's head and he told me Sarkar had a painful, black past."

Joshi stared at the barber. "What do you mean?"

"I don't know, Huzoor, how much is truth, and how much is not, but the pujaree said that Sarkar never knew his father.

He was born to a prostitute in Lukhnow. Poor guy grew up seeing all day . . . men coming and going, seeing his mother . . . doing . . . you know—"

"Yes, I know."

"So he—when he was a little boy—ran away. He roamed from place to place like a stray dog. Today this orphanage, tomorrow that orphanage. He ate whatever bits he could find, from garbage along the footpath. Slept in boxes . . . in the cold rain. Then he joined the army, first as an orderly, then as Jawan at the frontier."

"Did he ever marry?"

"Yes, Maalik. But his wife died."

"Died?"

"Well, I am not going to lie. Bholanath said he was badly wounded in the war. A grenade exploded near him, I don't know . . . something. But his *Biwi* never visited him in the hospital at the frontier. So he got very angry. He cried a lot, waited and waited. But she never came. So one day, when they discharged him early, because of his injuries, he came home. In the middle of the night—unannounced."

"What happened?"

"He found his wife in bed with another man. Right there, he shot both of them—point-blank in the bed."

"What else did the pujaree say?"

"He and Sarkar drank together. Lots of times. One day Bholanath asked Sarkar, when they were a little drunk. He said, 'Why do you hate women so much? They are God's gift to us men. If they are happy, they can make our day—and night. *Yaar*, leave them alone. Just use them for pleasure. Don't kill them.' Sarkar said, 'No! I don't want them to please me at their will. I want them to spread their thighs for me at my command. At gun point. I want to kiss them or bite them as I please. And if they say no, I want to chew them between my teeth like a struggling little fish.'"

Joshi poured himself a glass of water, the picture of calm reassurance, while another wave of disgust ran through the crowd. "What is Sarkar doing at present?" he asked quietly.

"Flesh trade. He asked me to join him as a manager. He said there is a lot of demand for young virgins. They are paying lots of money in New Delhi, Bombay, Calcutta and Goa. Lots of GoraSahb pay lots of American dollars for children. I said no."

"When was the last time you heard from him?"

"Never. I didn't."

"And you never called him?"

"No. I wouldn't know where. He said he could shift back and forth between Himpal, Sikkim, and Bhutan where Indian laws couldn't reach him."

"Thank you, Murli. You have been very helpful."

"Your mercy means a lot to this poor man, Your Honor."

Murli stood up to leave the dock, but Joshi held up one hand, with a glance at Jonathan.

"Murli," he said, "before you step down, tell us about Seeta. Tell us about her character."

"Oh, nobody liked her, Maalik. They said she was too smart for her own britches."

"What did you think of her?"

"Me? I thought she was nice-looking but loose-charactered."

"What do you mean?"

"You know, Maalik, her husband was a very sickly man. Ever since he married her, he couldn't . . . do anything. And this woman was very healthy. So she started screwing farmers, policemen—anybody who could satisfy her and give her money. She was a whore, pardon the expression."

"Lies! All lies!"

Jonathan swiveled around to see, but the voice had come from the back of the hall, and half the audience were on their feet. There had been plenty of protest over Sarkar's abuse of women, but who would object to an attack on Seeta's reputation? Who knew her well enough and cared enough to stand up? What was going on?

Listening to Murli, Jonathan felt angrier by the moment, at the hypocrisy and greed behind the lionizing of a woman's death. Perhaps, he thought, Seeta was forced by irresistible social pressure to give up her life for people like Murli. How could a woman lose herself so thoroughly to believe that death was better than life? How had Becky done it? Why had Becky done it? How did one live in the face of injustice, the horror, the sheer inexplicability of women, who embrace death rather than life and love?

Judge Trivedi was pounding his gavel and shouting for order. Uniformed figures were wading through the crowd toward the back.

"What he says is not true, Your Honor," the person shouted over the hubbub. It was a woman's voice, raised loud but not shrill. "Seeta is not a whore—she never has been. With the court's permission, I am willing to disclose what really happened."

"Silence," Judge Travedi roared. "Silence now, or I'll order this courtroom cleared."

Slowly the crowd settled back into their seats until there were just two figures standing alone at the back of the room. Mohan and—

Gauri?

She seemed to be leaning on Mohan for support, her eyes on the floor, trying to shrink back into herself and disappear. God, she was shy enough when Jonathan tried to talk to her alone. Now, he thought, she must be terrified!

Jonathan glanced at Kate, who was also staring at Gauri with slack-jawed amazement. He glanced back to the dock.

Murli had gone white.

"Who are you, young lady?" Judge Travedi said. "Why are you harassing my court with your emotionalism? Either you sit down or I'll have you thrown—"

"No!" Jonathan yelled. "Forgive me, your honor, but I think—"

"Dr. Kingsley, sit down. I'm also perfectly willing to throw distinguished foreigners out of my—"

"Judge Sahb," Jonathan said, "please, she's not hysterical. Listen to her, please."

Jonathan sank back to the edge of his seat as Joshi turned to Judge Trivedi and spread his arms wide. "My Lord, it can do no harm to at least find out who she is."

Judge Trivedi scowled at Gauri, who nearly wilted under his gaze, then at Joshi, who smiled. But it was when he glanced at Murli, capturing his obvious terror, that he made his decision.

"Very well," he said. "Young lady, come forward and tell us who you are."

Mohan made a movement as if he would help Gauri to the front, but she shook her head and walked forward. She was visibly unsteady, but she made her own way.

"Forgive me for interrupting," she said when she reached the front. There was a tremor in her voice that made her hard to hear. "Honorable Judge Sahb, forgive me for not coming forward to help you in your investigation. I . . . I was frightened."

"Of course you were, child," Joshi said gently. "These men are quite dangerous. And you are very brave to come forward now. Have no fear, I will see that you are protected."

"I thank you. I hoped I would not have to, but now I must speak out if justice is to be done."

"Dear lady," Judge Trivedi said, "on what basis do you demand justice? Would you care to tell me who you are?"

"Her name is Gauri," Joshi said. "She is, I believe, a resident at the Ashram in the hills above Baramedi. Is that where you heard what you have to tell us, child?"

"No, sir." A shudder ran through Gauri's frame. "It was earlier. Before I was given the name Gauri."

"Oh? And what was your name before?"

Slowly she raised her head until her eyes met Joshi's. "Seeta."

chapter thirty

Seeta stood still, clutching her hands tightly together under the folds of her sari as the crowds erupted around her. There was a trembling deep inside her, a trembling that threatened to take over her body and shake her apart if she did not keep a strangling grip on it.

Never meet a man's eyes, her mother had told her. Never put yourself where they will notice you, for if they do, they will hurt and kill you. All through her youth, this advice had kept her alive until she had met her blessed Moti, her protector. But now this judge was screaming for order and glaring down at her, the Honorable Joshi was glaring at her, the eyes of countless men in the audience were also staring at her, flashbulbs were going off. And from the dock behind her, she could feel the eyes of the monster Murli, that lying reptile squirming to escape his deserved punishment, his eyes boring into her, telegraphing their hatred and fear.

What was she doing? She was standing up to Sarkar! The man who had murdered Savita. The man who had raped and kidnapped and killed women for miles around Baramedi. How could she, alone, hope to bring down a man who terrorized an entire county?

Instinctively, she glanced back at the good doctor. He met her eyes as he had so often tried to do at the Ashram. His liquid blue eyes that stared back with astonishment, joy, and compassion. The trembling inside subsided a little. Maybe she wasn't entirely alone.

As the noise slowly died down, the Honorable Joshi cleared his throat. "My Lord, I think you would agree that perhaps this woman has some valuable information."

"She lies," Murli screamed. "I know her, she is a lying whore from—"

"Silence!" The Honorable Joshi and Judge Trivedi yelled at the same time.

"Counselor," Judge Trivedi said, "I was uncertain as to whether to allow her testimony until that outburst. Please have her sworn and let us hear what she has to say."

The Honorable Joshi brought a copy of the Bhagvat Gita. Gauri placed a trembling hand on it and, repeating his words, swore to tell the truth. Then she sank back into a chair.

"My Lord?"

Seeta's eyes swiveled around. The attorney defending the monster Murli was on his feet.

"Since this young woman's testimony directly affects my client's welfare," he said smoothly, "I would ask that I be the one to examine her."

"With respect to my esteemed colleague," Joshi said, "I don't think the young woman could be considered a hostile witness."

"And yet," the other man said, "the lenience my client will receive depends on the court's assessment of his testimony. Her counter testimony could directly affect his welfare."

"He has a point, Counselor," Judge Travedi said.

The Honorable Joshi gave a small bow and sat down.

The other man stalked toward her in his flowing black robes, his wig mildly askew, and glared down at her in her chair. His gaze was cold and malevolent, like so many she'd seen. She wished she could fade into the floor.

"State your full name and address," he said.

"My name . . . my name is Seetabai Shivram Chaudhary. I'm from Baramedi, Bihar."

"But now you call yourself Gauri, isn't that correct?"

"The Ashram's Baba has named me . . . Gauri."

"State your occupation."

"I was a primary school teacher before—"

"I asked for your current occupation, not the past. I don't care what you did—"

"My Lord!" Joshi was on his feet. "Look at this poor girl. She's been terrorized by men all of her life, men who would kill her and chew her like a piece of raw liver. How can we condone terrorizing her further?"

"My client—"

"The truth!" the Honorable Joshi yelled. "It has doubtless taken all of her courage simply to be here. If we push her beyond her courage, we may never discover the truth that is the point of these proceedings." He glared at Murli in the dock. "Which would doubtless suit *some* very well."

The judge shifted his gaze between the three men. Then he brought his gavel down. "You're right Counselor. Objection sustained."

"But my client—"

"When deciding on your client's punishment," Judge Travedi said, "I will take this irregularity into account. Now sit down and let your colleague continue."

With a stiff bow, the other lawyer sat down. Murli gave a small groan. Seeta realized that she had been holding her breath and let it out with a hiss.

"Now, my child," Joshi said. "I'm not even going to ask you any questions. Simply tell us your full story in your own words."

Seeta opened her mouth, but nothing came out.

"Miss Chaudhary," the judge said softly, "please proceed with what you have to say. You have nothing to fear."

Seeta looked to Jonathan and Kate. Both were smiling and nodding.

"Your Honor . . .," Seeta looked at the floor. "I'm not a whore. Sarkar and his men did unsuccessfully attempt to gang rape me. I have never slept with anyone but my deceased husband. I . . . I . . ."

Seeta could not finish. How could she talk about such private matters in front of all these people?

There was a soft murmur from the audience. Honorable Joshi pretended to write something down. Murli looked as if he might be sick. And with what she had to tell . . .

He would be stopped, Gauri thought. Sarkar would be stopped. Savita would be avenged at last, and the women of her village would grow up safe.

Joshi was in front of her with a glass of water. She took a sip, then held the edge of her seat until her knuckles were white.

"I was the eldest of nine children," Gauri said. "We were very poor. Although my child-marriage took place at age six, I remained with my parents and helped my mother with the house chores. My mother was a maid to a local schoolteacher, who taught me how to read and write. But education is a taboo to my caste. At my mother's request, I pretended to be illiterate.

"I went to live with my husband when I was fifteen years old. My husband's family did not get very much in the way of a dowry, so some of the men in town, including Murli the barber, encouraged him to kill me or have me killed and then remarry. But he loved me so . . . and then . . . the sickness . . ."

There was a warm hand resting on hers. She looked up into the eyes of Honorable Joshi. He smiled and gave her hand a fatherly pat.

She took a deep breath. "One day, as I sat beside my husband's deathbed, I heard a familiar voice from outside yelling at my father-in-law. It was Sarkar. I listened to everything quietly and observed everything from inside very carefully. Sarkar started talking to Bapuji about my being pregnant by some farmhand, which I wasn't, and started devising ways to rid my father-in-law of me and this supposed problem. He started talking about abortion, sending me to another state, selling me to a brothel house in Old Delhi or pushing me down a well. When he left, he promised my father-in-law he'd 'take care of it.' I got scared. I started to cry."

"Forgive me," Judge Joshi said, "but how did Bapuji feel about these plans?"

"He hated them and would never agree. But he was frightened of Sarkar. We all were."

"Of course. Please continue."

"That same night, my husband died. Immediately, Sarkar showed up smiling. He had plotted a clever scheme that he said, 'would not only nix the thorn, but the dying thorn would prick open a secret to a big fortune.' He would force me to be a suttee."

Once again, a murmur erupted from the crowd and the judge gaveled them back to silence.

"Bapuji didn't want to do it?" Joshi said.

"Bapuji objected, even when Sarkar threatened him. But Sarkar and his men were stronger. After midnight, the police chief, the priest and the barber ganged up on my father-in-law and threatened to make him disappear forever. The police chief had that knife. They said they had already spread the word that I had vowed to God that I wanted to hold my husband's head in my lap and burn with him. I heard them say the money was to be divided equally among all and a temple was to be constructed at the suttee site. Bapuji was ordered to stay in the background and mourn and wail as expected by the society.

"So they started on their plan. The priest's wife invited me to her home while the women prepared my husband's body. She offered me a glass of warm milk. So that I wouldn't suspect anything, she also poured herself a glass of plain milk. I had a feeling that the milk may be laced with something, so I asked her to kindly fetch me some sugar, and when she left for the kitchen, I switched the glasses and faked grogginess."

"Very smart," Honorable Joshi said.

"I felt someone was watching over me, Maalik. Soon I was moved to Sarkar's barn and temporarily locked up there. When they were bathing my husband's corpse, Bapuji started to cry and wail. The gang ordered him to go outside and lie down on the jute-cot, which he did. But when nobody was looking, he came running to the barn and released me."

"Very brave."

"Oh, indeed, he was a good man. I was sorry . . ." Murli interjected.

Honorable Joshi glared at Murli for a moment, then turned back to her. "Please."

"Bapuji gave me a packet of puffed rice and some water, and then he showed me the path. He said to me, 'Beta, keep running in the direction of the wind—that will be east. And protect yourself from wild animals with this.' He gave me a small flashlight and a small knife. I touched his feet and headed for the woods. Bapuji, I think, returned to the cot and kept up the crying, so I could run far away.

"It was a dark night. I fell several times . . . my knees bled. I was afraid of wild animals, but I kept running. I don't know how many miles I ran, but before daybreak, when I was crossing a stream, I saw some lights on the hillock on the other side of the bank. Quickly, I ran up the hill. Then I heard some noise. It sounded like a couple of men talking. I got scared and ran into the bushes. That was a mistake because my foot fell into an animal trap. I screamed with pain and passed out.

"When I awoke, I saw two men sprinkling water on my face and gawking at me. Their beards were covered with cloths and one had a rifle on his shoulder. I screamed and tried to run but fell back because my foot was still locked in the trap. I thought they were robbers and feared that they would finish what Sarkar had started.

"But they were honorable men; hunters, I think. They undid the trap, then asked me who I was. I didn't answer them. One of the men then asked me if I was running away from some women's shelter. I heard the word 'shelter' and nodded. Quickly the man supported me on his shoulder, walked me to a small building and left.

"The building looked like a school. I tried to stand up but felt dizzy. My legs were soaked with blood. I think I passed out in the school compound. I was very lucky because the place was a rehabilitation center for young runaways, widows and ex-prostitutes. An ex-victim named Paro ran the shelter. When I told her everything she quickly sized up the situation. She bathed me, rested me, fed me and kept me in isolation. When it turned dark, Paro hired an expensive motorcar and took me to the Northeastern Express. She brought me to Gorakhpur. From there we took a bus to the border town of Sunali, and from there we snuck into Himpal on foot. Paro's uncle, Birendra, owned a small restaurant in Himpal, where I was given a temporary shelter. Paro asked me to keep quiet about my past and start a new life.

"But my leg was not healing properly. They said there was an Ashram nearby. Its Baba was a kind sage who protected abused, poor women. Paro's uncle said he had heard they had a doctor newly arrived from America who might help me. So they took me there in a palanquin."

"My dear," Joshi said, "you said your name was Seeta, and yet now you are known as Gauri. How did that come about? Tell us, just so that we can be sure you are who you say you are."

"Swamiji gave me this name. When I met him, I touched his feet and stared at the floor. The meeting was like destiny. Swamiji talked to me for a long time, but never asked me about my past. It was like he knew I needed to be alone with my grief for a time. Swamiji put his divine hand over my head and said, 'Beta, don't be afraid. You have come to your new home. Here you are not a widow. Here you will remain married to the goodness of God.' He rubbed vermilion on my forehead and said, 'As a token of divine fertility, you'll always wear this mark. Today you are reborn and will bear the name of Lord Shiva's sacred cow—Gauri.' He then blessed me. I never forgot that moment. I really felt reborn. Ever since, I wear this Om Shanti talisman around my neck." She paused and raised it for him to see. "To remind me that God saved me."

As she pulled the talisman from around her neck, Seeta realized that she was no longer trembling, inside or out. Swamiji was right. She had nothing to fear.

"And the doctor did heal you?"

"Oh, yes, of my outside wounds. But I still carried great fear around inside of me. Baba Swamiji has been healing me of that, but slowly."

"So you are an honest and honorable woman who was saved by God's grace from becoming a sacrifice to the greed of men." He gestured to Murli. "Including that one. Thank you for your information. It has been a—"

"But Honorable Sir, there is more."

"I'm sure you could tell us about many other horrors these beasts have inflicted on yourself and the women of your village. But there is no need—"

"No, it is the largest lie. I must correct it."

The Honorable Joshi raised his eyebrows. "And what is that, dear lady?"

"Sarkar. All, which that man," she dared to look Murli in the eye, "said of him is true. His cruelty, his hatred of women, his ways of abusing them. But not his identity. He is not Jalim Singh, the police chief. He is our councilman—Buttasingh."

The courtroom sat stunned for a moment. Slowly rose the murmur that quickly turned into shouting and cursing. In the midst of confusion, Jonathan spotted Mohan struggling to stop a woman from exiting the court. Geeta?

Seeta was able to make out little in the confusion that followed. She was vaguely aware that Murli was screaming that she was a dead woman before the court guards wrestled him to the ground. More flashbulbs were popping all around her, the judge was shouting for order, the Honorable Joshi was yelling commands to Mohan about relaying an order to arrest the councilman. And in the middle of it was little Seeta, who in all of her short life had never imagined that so much excitement, so much to-do, would erupt around her.

Jonathan looked at Gauri and sighed deeply. Gauri was standing, smiling at him, clicking her nails. Her chest was heaving with all her love for him. There she was! The woman he was looking for all along was standing right before him. Alive and full of love. All along she wanted to love but could not, because she was running scared for her life. And he? He couldn't care for his life; he just couldn't love anyone . . . anymore. And how brave she was! She risked her life and gathered enough audacity to rise and speak up. She could have been shot right in that witness box; she must have known that. But she transcended her fears and won! Now he had to do the same. Conquer his fears. And begin to love!

He rose slowly. His eyes teared up. He was incapable of subduing his visible breathing and the tornado of emotions that was swirling inside his chest.

Then the doctor was in front of her, his blue eyes full of tears. And then, as she had dreamed so often since she'd first seen him, his arms were around her and he was holding her close. The angel her dear Moti had promised.

No, she was no longer alone.

chapter thirty-one

Jonathan and Gauri, under tight security ordered by Judge Joshi, began the last leg of their journey, from Shivner to the Ashram. Jonathan had been of the opinion that the guards were unnecessary since Buttasingh wouldn't dare to attack under the circumstances. Surely, Jonathan pointed out, Buttasingh had nothing to gain. But Joshi had said that Jonathan underestimated the drive for revenge in a mind such as Buttasingh's.

So as they began the slow uphill ride of five kilometers to the hermitage, two armed guards, directed by Rasoolmian, rode stout horses in front, while two others rode in the back. Kate, having elected to follow later, would arrive that night.

Jonathan glanced at Gauri—Seeta—no, Gauri. That was the name Swamiji had given her, and Jonathan would respect it. She seemed to glow from inside; a rich, full beauty that flowed from her spirit through her body. It was so strange, so improbable—so miraculous—that he should have found her right under his nose. He thought back to their very first embrace hours before in the courtroom. It had been so natural, with no hesitation at all. Yet, without all of the wild experiences—the near-death in the mountains, particularly—he would never have been guided to make such a gesture. Guided. He knew he was growing again. And it felt good.

Gauri glanced at him and their eyes met. She smiled a slight, delicate smile, more an intensification of her inner glow than anything overt, and Jonathan felt tears come to his eyes. "This is so, so unreal and yet so . . ." he started.

". . . very real," she finished.

"Yes. It's like a miracle."

"It *is* a miracle," she said softly.

"You're right, it actually is a miracle, and I don't even believe in those." He stopped. "Well, I didn't used to, anyway."

"I guess that's another miracle," she said with a lilt in her voice he'd never heard before.

He smiled broadly. And she had a sense of humor too, this beautiful woman! "You could say that," he agreed.

Her eyes grew gentle, more serious. "Thank you," she said. "I know there must be a stronger way to say what I feel, but 'thank you' is the only way I know."

"I think I know," he said, "And I don't have the right words, either, Gauri." They were quiet for a few minutes. "This has been such a long journey," he continued, "and yet it's only been a few short weeks. I never knew—I just never believed, I guess, that I could find such a rich world of happiness again."

"Nor did I," Gauri said in a small, childlike voice. "But my husband, Moti, told me before he died that you would come."

"That *I* would?" Jonathan was incredulous.

"He said, 'an angel' would protect me. And when I met you, I knew—I mean, I hoped and I believed—that it was you." She lowered her eyes, shy again. "It is my heaven that this wish has come true. If . . . if it has . . ."

"It was mine too," Jonathan said, reaching for her small, gentle hand. "If that comes true, it is a dream come true, a wish granted for us both."

She exhaled gently, as if not wanting to spoil the perfect moment. The air smelled of roses and herbs, as their ponies crunched along the well-worn trail. Jonathan sensed that she felt protected again, but in a different way. Her testimony had freed her of something she was yet to understand. It had strengthened her and given her an inner ability to cope against threats in the future. But most of all, it had broken the wall of deceit between Jonathan and her. Just as truth had been her freedom, as she had testified, with Murli wrestled to the ground and Sarkar's arrest ordered, truth had also been freedom to Jonathan, who needed to know who she was. She rested her face against the strong warm hand that had taken hers.

Jonathan felt a thrill of energy racing his heart. He loved her, loved her as deeply as he had loved Becky. He hadn't dreamed it was possible that he could be so blessed twice in one lifetime, and yet here she was. Beautiful, intelligent, compassionate, brave. Everything he had ever longed for.

Geeta's disappearance was the only cloud in the blue skies of the day. Once the confusion in the courtroom had sorted itself out, Geeta was nowhere to be found. Mohan had tried to keep her from mixing into the hubbub, but she had her own opinion on the matter. Judge Joshi had set his men looking for her, but so far there had been no news.

Jonathan steered his pony closer to Gauri's. He patted her pony's neck. Gauri's smile enraptured him. Her rich, dark hair blew like wings in the wind. Jonathan sensed that she too, had become lighter, freer. The burden of fear and secrecy that she had carried for all the time he had known her, had lifted, and she was blossoming like a flower.

He leaned close, wanting to share a kiss, but the toe of his boot accidentally dug into her pony's ribs. The animal lurched forward, and he nearly fell off while reaching for her. The spectacle made Gauri laugh so hard that she nearly fell off her own pony, which made them both laugh all the harder.

Then they heard the roaring Durga gorge. Stopping their ponies successfully, Jonathan took his lovely new life in his arms for a brief but passionate kiss. "I love you, Gauri," he barely breathed.

She drew back slightly, smiling. Her face was so red it could burst.

Jonathan heard the slow hooves approaching them. Supposing the rear guards were catching up, he leaned back, turning his pony. "I guess we should go on," he said gently.

Suddenly Gauri's expression changed radically. "No!" she exclaimed almost silently.

Jonathan spun around to see the vision of a nightmare. A black turbaned rider, awash in a black outfit, shiny tall boots and the gun belt across his chest, sat brazenly upon what appeared to be an enormous black horse. Not his usual uniform, but Jonathan recognized him anyway.

Jalim Singh.

"Well, this is sweet," he said.

Jonathan tried to maneuver in front, blocking Gauri. "What do you want? It's no use. They know who you are; they're on their way right now. You're done for. There's nothing for you here. You're better off escaping."

Jalim Singh pulled out a knife, as large and deadly as the one Jonathan had encountered before. "I'm not a coward, Dr. Kingsley. I'm here on a mission, and I intend to be successful this time." He bore his eyes into Gauri. "Sarkar would like a word with you."

"No!" Gauri shouted. Her voice held terror, but there was also a streak of defiance, new and strange. She secretly slipped her feet out of the stirrups.

At the sound of her voice, several other armed horsemen stepped out of well-concealed places, dismounted, and surrounded the two.

"We have guards," Jonathan began. "It's only a matter of time—"

"We've seen your so called guards," Jalim Singh sneered, spitting at the ground. "Those two could not guard a vegetable garden."

The others laughed.

Jonathan looked around, frantic, seeking some sort of weapon. Finding nothing, he flung a stick, striking a tree far ahead, and bellowed at the top of his lungs. "Rasool! Back here!"

The large horses, fearing the unfamiliar sound and voice, began to turn and whinny like little colts. Taken by the surprise, the desperate rogues rushed to retrieve their mounts. Then Rasoolmian and the other forward guards pounded toward the confusion, securely armed and ready for battle.

In the mayhem that followed, nobody noticed the object of the ambush taking things into her own hands. And when they did, Gauri was too fast for them. She rose and leapt from her pony to one of the unoccupied horses, an enormous mare, and coaxed her out of the knot of chaos, then quickly shot away, breaking apart from the villains, and destroying their strategy.

"Get her—get her before she gets away!" Jalim Singh screamed. Then he yanked his own horse around, and took chase himself.

"Rasool!" Jonathan yelled. "Help her!"

Rasoolmian's two companions rode faster horses, and pursued as best they could. Jonathan did his best to keep up, but felt a sickening impotence reclaiming him as the larger animals rapidly outdistanced him. In the fading light, he could no longer see Gauri, the guards, Jalim Singh's hoods, or Jalim Singh himself.

Rasoolmian turned back and met up with him. "I told them to track them and let us know where they go," he said. "But I cannot risk your being attacked as well. Come, we must go back to Baramedi quickly and alert the authorities."

Jonathan's heart was laid bare. It was as if he could feel the hooves of wild horses trouncing it to nothingness. But he knew Rasool was right. He would need every ounce of what remained of him to get Gauri back before it was too late. And he would prevail. Of that, he had no doubt.

chapter thirty-two

Several helicopters thundered over the mountains and around Joshi's impromptu command post at the hotel in Aakash Mahal, located in Shivner, the capital of Himpal, at the foot of Ashram Hill. Rasoolmian stood in one corner, his arms folded. They had told him he wouldn't be needed, but after the abduction of Gauri, he refused to let Jonathan out of his sight. Joshi, chomping on an unlit cigar, paced. Brigadier General Tewari—a tall, mustachioed man, wearing a crisp, willow-green uniform—focused his binoculars at the sputter of gunfire and a trail of smoke emerging from the distant dale.

Jonathan sat thinking, trying to conjure up a plan once the CBI located Gauri. Kate had joined them as well. Filled with guilt for having stayed late in New Delhi and not having been there with them during their horrifying experience, she'd come to the hotel to be supportive in whatever way she could. She stood at the hotel's small stove, heating water for tea.

Jonathan glanced at the ever-unflappable Joshi, now looking more agitated than Jonathan had ever seen him. Yet there they were, in less than an hour, already in radio contact with the guards, who had tracked Gauri as far as the base of the mountain. She'd tried to lose her pursuers and in the process, she'd lost Joshi's men. Their unfortunate tale suggested that maybe she had been less successful in throwing Jalim Singh's men off her track.

"Judge Sahb, there is a copter approaching the hotel compound," Tewari said.

"It better be good news; it better," Joshi said softly. "This is embarrassing as hell; despite the juggernaut of two governments, that two-bit thug is still at large."

But Jonathan knew it went far deeper than simply an embarrassment to his friend.

Tewari locked his gaze with Joshi and held his hands behind his back. "I understand your position. Twenty-four hours. That's all I need to catch this crook—alive or dead. Twenty-four hours."

Joshi took the binoculars from Tewari and focused them at the smoke rising from the valley and the approaching helicopter. "What is happening out there?"

Tewari began to drone on about a well-fortified safe house his men were trying to crack. He talked about emplacements, maneuvers, firepower, but Jonathan hardly heard a word. All he could think about was Gauri, somewhere out there in the hands of that monster. And he in a comfortable hotel, doing nothing.

There was a knock at the door.

For a moment, no one moved. The entire hotel had been reserved by the government. Tewari had put the word out that no one was to disturb them—no one was, in fact, to even know their location.

Cautiously, Rasoolmian stepped behind the door, ready to spring. Tewari with his right hand on the gun holster walked to the door and opened it.

A uniformed man, looking much like a Tewari clone, stiffly saluted him. "Sir!"

Tewari nonchalantly returned the salute. "What is it, Captain?"

"I'm sorry for the interruption, sir. A woman was just flown in from the valley. She claims to have important information. 'Time is short,' she insists."

Joshi looked at Jonathan. He shrugged, but . . . who could it be?

"What is her name?" Joshi asked the captain.

"Chameli, your honor."

"Chameli?"

"Send her in," Tewari said. "And make sure she is unarmed. No room for stupid mistakes."

"Yes, sir." The captain threw a crisp salute, made a neat about-face, and marched away, his boots squeaking on the marble floor.

Within five minutes, the captain returned. Two soldiers behind him held a woman by the arms. When the captain ushered the woman in, Kate put her hand over her mouth and shrieked. "Geeta!"

At first, Jonathan froze. Some part of him had guessed it would be she. Who else but this traitor could have been meeting with gang members near the Ashram? Who else could have told Jalim Singh where to find him and Gauri? But it made no sense. Geeta and Gauri had become friends. Geeta and he were friends—he thought.

"Chameli?" Joshi said. "Geeta? What the bloody hell is going on here?"

Geeta stood in front of the door silently. She first looked at Jonathan, blinked her eyes and immediately looked down. It was then he realized that she was injured. Her face, partially covered, was bleeding and she held her side, obviously in pain. Her face looked worn. Her hair was wild and unkempt. The Ashram sari had been replaced by a multi-pocketed hunter's jacket, a belt, and a pair of dirty khaki pants tucked inside of scarred and muddy boots.

"What is going on, Geeta?" Jonathan said quietly. "Where is Gauri?"

And suddenly Geeta threw herself at Jonathan's feet, crying and babbling. "Please, Doc Sahb, forgive me, I'm . . . I'm sorry. I never meant to do this to you. Please . . ."

Without moving, Jonathan looked down at her. "You've been wounded," he said.

"They beat me," she said, trying to catch her breath. "When they saw me at the court, they knew I had not poisoned Gauri. While she was speaking to the judge, I tried to escape, but they found me. They told me I would die if I did not tell them where you were! I am so sorry." She began to wail again, still at his feet, barely able to breathe in her emotional agony.

"Come on Geeta," Jonathan said as gently as possible, leaning toward her. "Get up."

But Joshi was less sympathetic. "You are the cause of a possible death, and my guess is that you are also the reason for the attacks on Jonathan at Mt. Kailash. You will have to provide more in the way of reparation than a teary apology."

"Shall I take her into custody now?" Tewari asked.

"No, no," Jonathan insisted. "Geeta." He looked intensely at her. "What is your story? Quickly."

"I was to report to Jalim Singh if there were any new girls brought to the Ashram," she said. "He had heard that a good woman had helped Seeta to escape, but he did not know who it was. It made him crazy. So I was told to work at the Ashram and report back to him any new arrivals. When Gauri came, I told him about it. He told me that she was an evil woman who had brought harm to our city and would bring shame on us all and that she had to die. But he did not want to raise suspicion in such a small place. By then, I had watched Doctor Babu serving my poor brothers and sisters without money and . . . away from his own country and family. How he fought for their lives, cared deeply about them. And the men at the Ashram treated me with kindness, with respect, for the first time in my life. And then Gauri saved my life." Her face dropped as she struggled to keep her emotions under control. "She pulled me from the fire at the Holi Festival. I have always had an absurd fear of fire and water. I never learned to swim, and I could only dance at Holi Festival near the fire because of the bhang. Anyway, Swamiji was . . . so . . . with his talk about the soul and love. When I thought of doing evil . . . I couldn't.

"So when Doc Sahb arranged to go away, I told Jalim Singh that Gauri would accompany him. They were sure that was true, but when it turned out to be not only false, but also an unsuccessful murder attempt, Jalim Singh was furious with me. It was then I was ordered to poison her. I told him that I had done it, but that she would die slowly, to avert suspicion. In the courtroom, Jalim Singh had some friends. They knew he was looking for me, and they took me to his house and beat me. But I escaped when the man watching me received a call on his radio. Buttasingh did not know that I was there and he told the man where he was and that he was waiting for Gauri to be delivered to him. It was awful. I ran from the back of his hut and that is when I contacted the pilot and came here. The pilot's radio is . . . not working right at the moment," she finished with a small but ironic smile.

Kate stood stiffly for a moment, then put her arms around Geeta and held her close. "Well, at least you did something right," she said, trying to make light of the moment.

Jonathan sighed and looked at Joshi, who motioned him to sit down on the couch with him. Tewari ordered his men away, then took his position at the door, motionless and emotionless. Rasoolmian simply glared.

"You came by helicopter?" Joshi asked flatly.

"Yes."

He stared at her for a moment. "Ms. Chameli, or Geeta, a relationship such as this—a female spy as it were—is highly irregular. On top of that, I must honestly say that I know of no Indian woman other than perhaps Indira Gandhi herself who goes about India by way of helicopter." He paused, letting it sink in. "Perhaps you can fill in the details to make your story at least the slightest bit convincing."

Tewari shook his head, indicating it sounded to him like a set-up.

"Please!" Geeta began. "Please believe me!"

"Why!" Joshi demanded. "So that we can walk into another trap! I don't think so. I'm not sure what your game is yet, but I have heard nothing to convince me."

"Because!" screamed Geeta, in a sudden desperate change of tone, "I was trusted by Jalim Singh and I have come in a helicopter yes, from only miles away. Because it was important to me—and because I *could*." She interrupted herself with deeply-felt, heartbreaking emotion, sobbing from the depths of her soul. She looked up at Jonathan, her eyes full of pain, begging him for forgiveness.

But he thought of Gauri off somewhere in the clutches of that maniac, and he couldn't find any forgiveness within him. Perhaps Swamiji could forgive her. He could not.

Kate put her arms around Geeta's shoulders. "Come on Jonathan, she is trying to help. She's made mistakes, we all have, but she's trying her best to make things right."

Jonathan was about to say that his mistakes had never gotten anybody killed, but he remembered Becky and bitterly held back his response.

Still, Gauri was out there, in the hands of a madman who liked to kill women—and to torture them. And Geeta had made it all possible.

"Why?" he asked. "Geeta, I need to know why. Why would you work with such a monster?"

"Maalik," she said softly. "I was badly misled all of my life. Now I am finding—"

"But how *could* you? After you had seen evidence—seen what he did to women, how could you?"

Slowly Geeta raised her eyes until they met Jonathan's. "I had no choice. You see, Sarkar is my father."

chapter thirty-three

The room became deadly silent. Only the rotors of the helicopter, slowly idling on the hotel parking lot, made any sound.

"Buttasingh's daughter?" Joshi asked, haltingly. "Why have I not known of your existence? I napped at that monster's house, ate his food! Where were you?"

"I was at the Ashram, Judge Sahb," Geeta said. "I knew nothing of your visit until much later. I knew nothing of his plot to kill you and . . . and Doctor Kingsley," she finished breathlessly.

Jonathan stepped close to her, pulling Kate away. "Where is Gauri?" he said, his eyes never leaving hers.

"They are probably there in his hideout," she said. "We are so near, that is why I came. He thinks I do not know, but as I said, I heard them talking. It is not far from here. That is why I brought my father's helicopter. We could get there quickly and—"

"I don't think you'll be going anywhere," Tewari said harshly.

"I'm afraid she may come in handy," Joshi countered. "But for the moment, if you'll be so kind as to instruct us to their whereabouts, we'll coordinate this."

Geeta nodded. Tewari spoke to an orderly at the door, and a few moments later unfolded a map of the area. Geeta pinpointed the location of the hideout.

"He is known as Sheru there. He's shaved his head and grown a mustache. There are also several outposts along the borders of Himpal, Sikkim, Bhutan, and Nepal. This way he easily dodges the local law and keeps his own workforce confused."

General Tewari and Joshi studied the map for a moment. "We would have to seek permission from the Himpali government to go in after him. Probably as a joint operation between their troops and—"

"You cannot," Geeta said. "He has many informants in the Himpali military. If you reveal your plans to them, he will hear of them and be gone by the time you get there."

Jonathan was beyond worrying about the niceties. "Go get him anyway."

"And cause an international incident?" Joshi said mildly.

"It's easier to apologize than ask permission. A woman could be dying as we sit around deciding how to ask permission of a country who would just as soon allow him to do it!" Jonathan screamed.

"No, no, Jonathan," Kate tried to soothe him. "He is acting on his own, surely. But still," she raised her eyes to Joshi, "going through channels at this point does seem illogical. It isn't as if there's any time for that sort of thing."

Tewari shrugged and Joshi raised his hands in resignation. As Geeta instructed Tewari and Joshi on Buttasingh's location, Jonathan sat down next to Kate.

"Rasool, Mohan," Joshi said officiously. "You two stay with Jonathan and Kate." He turned to Tewari. "I'm sure Geeta can assist us. Besides, we could much better use all your men with us. Let's go!"

"Wait a minute . . . Judge Sahb," Jonathan said. "I'm going with you."

"No you are most certainly not. Jonathan, have you lost your mind? Do you know how dangerous this is?"

"I'm not going to sit back and be helpless," Jonathan said resolutely. "I've done enough of that in my life."

"Yes, you are!" Joshi waved his hands violently. "If you were to get killed under my care in an illegal operation in a foreign country—"

"Are you prepared to arrest me?"

"I might be. Jonathan, this is madness—"

"I love her, Judge Sahb," Jonathan said softly.

Joshi glared at Jonathan a moment, then threw his hands in the air and stalked to the window. "Bah! Would someone around here care to tell me why everyone wants to die here?"

"Listen Doctor, here is the situation," said Tewari sternly. "Judge Sahb . . . we need him for his negotiating skills. You are a healer by profession. You may well have to kill in this operation. Could you do that?"

Jonathan smiled a grim smile. "Try me."

"My dear boy!" Joshi shouted. "This is not the time for love and emotions; it's time for action. The answer is a non-negotiable 'No!' You are staying here. Period . . . I'm sorry, Jonathan." Joshi slammed the door.

Jonathan stared at the closed door incredulously. He turned around and began kicking the couch.

"Jonathan—" Kate began.

"I feel like I'm on pins and needles, Kate," Jonathan said. "I know they don't want me there, but I just feel I could do something, contribute in some way."

Kate patted his hand. "Joshi Sahb knows best," she said. "He wants to rescue her just as much as you do, although for slightly different reasons."

"It's no use, Kate," he said. "I am incapable of relaxing."

"I know. It isn't that. It's just, perhaps I could have a word with you?"

Jonathan turned. What could it be? "Of course."

They moved to other side of the room, where Kate took a seat and began to clear her throat and rearrange the pleats of her skirt.

"What's on your mind?" Jonathan asked, becoming curious. He sat down and stared at Kate blankly.

"Well, it's hard to say this. I guess maybe I should just come out with it and be done with it."

"I'd say that's a good idea," Jonathan said, "under the circumstances."

Kate's face relaxed. "I guess you probably know, or maybe have sensed, that I was, have been, had been sort of attracted to, well . . . you."

Jonathan raised his eyebrows, uncomprehending at first. Now he was more confused than angry.

"Or maybe not!" Kate went on, becoming almost amused. "The fact is, it's been a lonely life in some respects for me, and when a man comes into my life, which isn't often by the way, who meets certain criteria, and who offers—well, solace and humor and a certain degree of promise—of course the good looks don't hurt either . . ."

"Me?"

"You. Hard as it is to believe," she giggled. "But then, well, when it became fairly clear that your feelings were not reciprocal, I guess it's fair to say I had my little anger—jealousy fit, really. It's so hard to lose, and particularly when it seems so logical that, well, that being of the same sort of culture, you would have . . ."

"Been attracted to you."

"Yes."

Jonathan was quiet a moment. "I can't say I'm not attracted to you, Kate. It would be hard not to be! You're bright and charming, witty—almost as witty as me, I think." He chuckled. "And you're absolutely gorgeous. But it's just a chemistry thing, maybe. The quality I was seeking, although I had no idea I was seeking it, and could not have known, was . . . elsewhere."

"In Gauri."

"Yes. Yes." He sighed. "I hope you understand?"

"Oh I understand. I'm telling you all this in hopes that you, well, that you'll forgive me."

"Oh Kate!" he exclaimed, embracing her. "For heaven's sakes! There's nothing to forgive! Please, I hope, say we'll go on being friends."

"Yes, of course."

Jonathan sighed heavily. They returned to the kitchen area of the room and had cups of tea. Before long, he rose and began to pace again. "Where did you say they were?" he asked Kate.

"I know where it is," Rasoolmian spoke out. "I saw the map."

"As did I, Doc Sahb," said Mohan.

Both wore eager faces, worthy of trust and a great degree of enthusiasm.

"I can drive good," Rasoolmian said.

Jonathan laughed in spite of his state of mind. "That's a fact!" He remembered Rasool's timely arrival at the construction site of the temple.

"You guys are wonderful," said a smiling Jonathan, putting his arms round Mohan and Rasool.

When Kate—who had momentarily slipped into the kitchen to fetch more tea—returned, she cringed at Mohan and asked, "Mohan, where is Jonathan? Where is Rasool?"

"Mm—mam Sahb," stammered pale-faced Mohan. "I . . . I . . . they . . . they." He could not finish. His hand still pointed at the closed door.

chapter thirty-four

Jalim Singh flung open the door and slammed Gauri forward with his knee.

"A gift for you, Maalik," he said.

Buttasingh stood tall and powerful, darkly robed and demonic, in all Satanic majesty—Sarkar. He wore a red turban.

Gauri felt the blood in her body begin to turn to jelly; her hands wouldn't respond to her orders; her legs felt limp to her shoes. Her throat had became as parched as the leather on her sandals. Breath escaped somehow from her as new breath entered, but she did not know how or have any control of it.

Buttasingh smiled. "You are a worthy comrade, Jalim Singh. One day, I hope to reward you with such a gift. This one, as you know, is a long-awaited prize that I plan to peel one layer at a time."

He stepped toward her. "I will unwrap you whore, as if you were a precious fruit bestowed on me by a king. I will suck the life out of each of your layers, enjoying the taste on my tongue, and the texture between my teeth." He reached for her frozen face. "And all of the juices I will rub into my body, and lay wide open your flesh with mine."

Gauri fell back against the wall as he took a step closer. His breath was hideous, a combination of old tobacco and stale blood. Involuntarily, she steadied herself, when to her surprise, she felt the sheath of the small knife given to her by Bapuji still tucked into the fabric of her trousers, in a pocket just above the knee. She could make her body do nothing just then, but her mind began to work. She commanded her face to continue to show fear, and to reveal nothing of her small, newborn hope.

Buttasingh turned to Jalim Singh. "I think I will be all right guarding this young woman," he said. "Perhaps it would be best if you and the others took a rest after your long, hard day of work. You have done well. You deserve it. And yes, please close the door. We may wish to have some private . . . discourse," he finished, his smile so deeply ugly that even the narrow slits of his eyes did not show.

When the door closed, he unleashed a deep, slowly released, hideous groan, obviously withheld for some time, and meant to intimidate his small victim out of her mind.

Its power was not lost on Gauri, whose knees gave way and pounded hard to the ground below her. Her mind fought between reality and the deathly fear that she was in hell.

In seconds, Buttasingh was upon her, his powerful hands grasping her two arms high above her head, and looking her over, as if she were a fruit at the market.

"You have nice breasts, it looks like from here," he said conversationally. "Of course, it is so hard to tell through these layers." With his other hand, he deftly cut away the clothing at her middle and crept his hairy hand up underneath. He looked her fully in the face, as he did so, hoping to see more fear, but she kept her eyes downcast. Only her breath and the insistent rapid trembling of her body gave her away.

"Look at me," he said gently, as though to a child.

When she did not, his demeanor exploded. Continuing to grab her hands with one hand, he pulled off her top with the other, and jammed his knees on top of her thighs. He breathed hard and lustfully.

"Oh, this looks delicious," he said, speaking to her bared breasts. "But what does it feel like?" He bent close and grabbed at one breast hard with his hand, the other with his teeth.

Gauri screamed, cursing herself, knowing it would only empower him.

"You liked that?" he said. "I was so hoping you would! They always do."

Gauri knew he had planned out every step of his assault, down to its deadly end. The only thing she could rely on was his loss of control—and she could make that happen, she was certain. But she would have to endure first. *For you, Savita,* she thought. The dedication gave her strength.

"Didn't I ask you nicely the first time to look at me?" Buttasingh said.

Gauri looked at him.

"Yes, that's right. Very good." His hands traveled to her middle. "Keep looking at me." He picked up his knife. "This is where I like to cut away the extra rind," he said. "It doesn't taste good."

Gauri looked away.

"Look!" he screamed.

She looked back.

His knife tore away savagely at her clothing, nicking her belly just above the pubic line. She froze.

Buttasingh, now certain that his victim was psychologically disabled, released her hands to use both of his to disrobe. He turned his back to her, and in the seconds that followed, Gauri saw with horror the hairy back that had stood still in her mind all those years as he raped and mutilated her young friend. *It won't happen to me, too,* she decided. *It will not.*

Not far from Buttasingh's secret den, down the hill, at the gorge crossing, Tewari stopped all vehicles. He ordered Geeta to stay with some of his soldiers. Joshi, Tewari and a few select commandos began climbing the hill as per Geeta's directions. After half an hour of toiling up a stiff slope, Joshi spotted a low two-story ranch-like flat dwelling, built right against the hillside. Its walls, festooned with moss and vines, were barely discernible.

As they walked toward it, Joshi spotted a gardener in front of the building, trimming the deadwood out of the ivy. The man was old and emaciated, his body barely covered in rags, with welts from beatings on his back and bloody hands. Joshi fought every instinct he had to reach out and offer what comfort he could when the man turned toward him.

Bapuji!

"Shh . . ." Joshi motioned the old man to continue gardening.

Tewari gestured for his men to surround the place from all directions.

Just then, a scuffling could be heard outside the room. Voices raged, some in surprise, some in fury. Instinctively, Gauri pulled her clothing toward her and backed away. The knife fell from its pocket and onto the floor. Instantly, Gauri covered it with her hand.

Unnoticing, the naked Buttasingh raced to the door, locked and barricaded it.

It was then that Gauri saw the revolting monster in another light—an ill-prepared, malicious fool, a coward afraid to face the wrath of genuine power. Her fear, as strong as it had been only seconds before, was converted to rage. It took all of her self-control to keep her hand from shaking where it lay concealing her weapon.

"I see we have some company," Buttasingh said, trying in vain to sound suave. "Don't expect to be lucky. I'll kill you with my bare hands before you are freed."

A shot rang through the door. "Give her up, Councilman." Tewari's voice rang through. "You have no way out. You might as well make it easier on yourself."

"One more step and I will kill her," Buttasingh said, his voice rising. "I'll kill her!"

"No, you don't want to do that," Joshi said evenly. "It would only make things worse for you. Release her to us and we will do the best for you that we can. You are under stress. Surely the authorities will understand."

"Shut up! I am no fool," Buttasingh screamed. He reached for his clothing, his mind on too many things to concern himself with Gauri, who had covered herself, feigning modesty while actually concealing her knife into an accessible position. "I'll kill her! Get your men away from the back!" His voice had grown eerily high, like that of a small child.

"Back?" Joshi asked Tewari, startled.

"Judge Sahb," hollered Buttasingh. "Law is supposed to be blind, not the law man—especially one like you. I see that white ass and the traitor Pathan climbing from the back of the hill."

Joshi mumbled under his breath, "Stupid . . . suicidal . . ." Then he looked at Tewari and said, "What now General?"

Before the proud general could say anything Buttasingh shouted, "It's a trick!" Grabbing Gauri, he frantically forced her toward the window. Crouching behind her, he studied the area to the rear of the building. "They're hiding out there!" he claimed.

Gauri could feel his hands, so recently full of power and confidence, shaking with fear and confusion.

His breath was labored and uneven. "I'll kill you," he chanted, scaring no one. "I want to speak to that coward American doctor. Unless I speak to him, I won't let her go."

Joshi motioned the CBI men to bring forward Jonathan and Rasool from the back. When Joshi saw Jonathan, he gave him a dirty look, sighed and shook his head in disbelief.

"Don't try to lie to me," ranted Buttasingh. "I heard his spineless voice out there. Sissy bastard!"

Then suddenly, he was focused on Gauri again. "You are not worth all this trouble," he said flatly, and knocked her to the floor with a single blow of his fist.

Gauri screamed, taken by surprise and pain. Jonathan heard her cry. "I'll do it!" he yelled. Everyone was silent for a split second.

Joshi ground his teeth and told Jonathan softly, his breathing audible, "Surely he'll kill you, my friend. He has no intention of keeping his word."

"Judge Sahb, I love her. I must do this. I would rather die than live without her."

Joshi put his hand on Jonathan's shoulder and stared at him, his sweaty face twitching in fear.

Tewari banged on the solid door. "Councilman! Dr. Kingsley is coming in. We'll leave this door open so we can monitor your behavior."

"Fine, fine," Buttasingh called through the door.

Jonathan entered, eager just to be in the same room with Gauri. Walking resolutely through the door, he spotted her. His anger rose as he saw her there, her clothing ripped. "I'm here, Sarkar," he spat out. He walked past the man, approaching Gauri. "What is your deal?"

There was a boom from behind Jonathan. He glanced to one side. He spun around to see Buttasingh standing by the door—the closed and latched door—with an evil grin on his face.

Someone began pounding on the door from the other side. It was Rasoolmian, screaming "Doc Sahb! Doc Sahb!"

"Yes," Buttasingh said, drawing his gun and aiming it at Jonathan's midriff. "Doc Sahb. Welcome to my humble home."

"Babuji!" Gauri screamed and flung her arms around his neck.

He swept her behind him, putting himself between her and the gun. If he could distract Buttasingh for a moment, he might be able to draw his own pistol.

Buttasingh regarded her with disgust. "You will die before him, I assure you. But in the meantime . . ." He gestured with the gun toward another wall hanging. "Over there. Doc Sahb ke bacchey!"

"No," Jonathan said.

Buttasingh shrugged. "Suit yourself. But if you do not, I will have to shoot your precious Seeta. Not to kill, of course. Perhaps in the elbow, perhaps the knee. As long as she can still spread her legs, I don't care."

The pounding on the door increased in volume. The men had evidently found something to use as a battering ram.

"It's a very well made door," Buttasingh said. "Now move. Alone."

Trembling with rage, Jonathan walked to the wall hanging, leaving Gauri nearly undressed in the middle of the room. It was the hardest thing he'd ever done.

Buttasingh stepped back to keep them both in range. "Pull back the curtain."

Jonathan drew the hanging back. Behind it, pinned to the wall, was a pair of iron shackles.

"Put them on," Buttasingh said. "I want to hear them click."

"You're mad!" Jonathan said. "You'll never—"

Buttasingh fired a shot that struck chips from the floor between Gauri's feet. She flinched and began crying. Outside the door, Rasoolmian yelled, "Doc Sahb!"

Jonathan placed the shackles around his wrists, pressed them together until they snapped shut. Help was coming, he kept telling himself, help was coming. General Tewari's troops would get in. Buttasingh did not know how many were out there. Jonathan just had to keep the madman busy a little longer.

Buttasingh holstered his gun. "Ah, that's better. Now we can all relax and enjoy ourselves. And now for the blushing bride."

He advanced toward Gauri. She backed away. Jonathan yanked at the shackles until his wrists throbbed, but they wouldn't budge.

Buttasingh grabbed at her, but she ducked and slipped away, keeping him constantly in front of her, her eyes searching. Jonathan found he was straining at the shackles, his breathing heavy. His wrists were beginning to bleed.

Think, he had to think!

Meanwhile Gauri seemed to have a plan. She carefully twisted the knife into position and raised it over her head.

At the last split second, Buttasingh saw the flash of metal. He tried to move to the side, but there was no chance to do so. The knife met the flesh of his lower belly, knocking the breath from him and enraging him like a jungle lion. He pressed his belly from where the blood poured on the floor. He opened his mouth wide and looking aghast collapsed, face down, his hands still splinting the wound. His gun fell and spun toward his feet. His turban came undone.

Gauri stumbled to her feet, then ran to Jonathan and buried her head in his chest and wept uncontrollably.

Jonathan let her cry for a while, then glanced around. There was a set of keys hanging on a peg a few feet away. "Gauri, honey, the keys. Get me down."

She pulled the keys down, dropped them, then managed to unlatch the shackles. He let his arms drop around her, holding her tight and massaging his wrists. He had her now. He would never let her go.

"Oh, Maalik," she said, trembling, "I was . . . I was so . . ."

"It's okay," he whispered. "You did fine. You saved us both."

He threw off his robe and wrapped it around her, then squeezed her tight. Slowly her trembling subsided.

Jonathan tightly held Gauri in his arms. He let her cry for a while, her words drowned out in her sobs.

"It's all right . . . it's all right," said Jonathan, stroking Gauri's back tenderly. She clung onto him tightly, like a vein around the trunk of an oak tree. He could feel her flesh with his body, but she didn't withdraw, as though she wanted him to cover her naked self with his entire strong and protective body.

He helped her get dressed. Gauri, seeming embarrassed and cold, over-dressed herself with whatever was in the room.

When she calmed down, Jonathan whispered in her ear. "I love you . . . very much."

Then he lifted her head up from her chin and looking into her big black eyes, said "Close your eyes."

She looked at him, perplexed, still crying and shaking.

"Close your eyes," he commanded lovingly. When she did, he held her head between his hands and planted a long kiss on her lips. In his palms he could feel her whole face pulsating. She whispered something tender into his ear and then readily buried her head between his pectorals.

Shyly, she whispered again into his chest. Jonathan thought he heard her saying, *Babuji, Mein Aapse Bahot Pyar Karti Hun. Muje Kabhi Akeli Mat Chhodna*: "My loving sir, I love you very much. Please never abandon me."

Jonathan's eyes filled up. He held her head away from his chest, and looking right into her dark eyes, he said, "I love you too. I'll never leave you alone."

Wide-eyed, she looked at him, smiling but still crying. "Really?"

"Really, Gauri." He began kissing her—a kiss that lasted interminably. "Nobody will ever take me away from you, I'll return. That's a promise—I'll return."

And then he did something. He grabbed the knife, spliced the tip of his thumb and rubbed his blood on her forehead, forming a teardrop shaped tilak—a symbol of the Hindu matrimonial ceremony where a man rubs vermilion onto his bride's forehead and proclaims solemnly: "Hereby, I accept you as my wife, my other half. And I will remain yours until death does us apart."

chapter thirty-five

With Gauri's arms wrapped around his torso, Jonathan turned his head and looked at Buttasingh's body, lying flat on the floor, his bloodied hands curling up to his side, his mouth gasping for air. Was he dead? Carefully, Jonathan picked up the gun lying beside Buttasingh's body and rolled him over with the help of his foot. That was some task!

The maneuver appeared to foster life into Buttasingh, for soon he began grunting and attempted sitting up, in vain; his propped hands slipped into his own blood. All he could do was lift his head. And seeing Jonathan witnessing his helplessness, he screamed.

"What are you looking at? Go ahead, shoot me!"

Jonathan merely grinned at him and felt Gauri tightening her arms around his waist. Would Buttasingh now know what suffering is? Would he now realize the pain he had inflicted upon countless innocent women and children?

"I know you can't shoot," taunted Buttasingh. "You are a coward. You are afraid of death."

Jonathan nodded and smiled at the wailing monster. Then slowly releasing Gauri from her embrace, he raised his gun at Buttasingh. Jonathan could hear Gauri whining behind him.

"C'mon, you gutless bastard! Shoot me, kill me . . . end my misery . . . please." Buttasingh cried out and let his head fall back on the floor, his chest heaving like giant bellows.

Witnessing Buttasingh's unforeseen vulnerability, Jonathan experienced a quandary: should he kill this rogue once and for all, or should he let him suffer through a slow painful death. He glanced at Gauri watching the drama.

Gauri, now fully composed, looked back at him, confidently and unblinkingly.

Jonathan resolutely turned to Buttasingh and stood astride his massive belly, pointing the gun squarely at his heart.

"Buttasingh, I'm not going to torture you like you tortured so many helpless people. Here you go," said Jonathan, as he proceeded to pull the trigger. But the gun didn't fire; the trigger seemed to be jammed. That was strange! This was the very gun that Buttasingh had fired just moments earlier!

He raised the gun to his eye level and looked at it. The gun looked fine. Again, he took point blank aim at Buttasingh's head and attempted to pull the trigger. Again the trigger jammed. Then he heard Buttasingh take a long shuddering breath and saw his arms sprung out, his bellows turning still.

Strangely, on the wall, right behind Buttasingh's head, Jonathan saw a peculiar illumination developing. The spot of light began to grow wider and brighter. Soon he found himself standing there dazzled by the intensity of the light and completely frozen. He saw nobody, and heard nothing in the room. Just the light. Then from the center of the illumination, a low-pitched, vibrating voice emerged. It said:

> "Let not death win over you. Each death strengthens
> the wrath of the next death. Be not instrumental to

another death. Shame that curse with the rectitude of life, for life is the only antidote to death's anathema. Win over death."

The voice silenced, the illumination began to fade. When it completely disappeared, Jonathan's hand, holding the gun up high like a dead weight, jerkily dropped to his front. He wiggled his fingers for a reality check. They moved. He looked back and saw Gauri smiling at him, her arms wide open to receive him in her embrace.

A wave of anger surged into Jonathan's head. He picked up Buttasingh by his collar and struck his head hard with the butt of his gun. Buttasingh's head hit the floor with a thud and rolled over. Jonathan backed off and angrily threw the gun against the wall with as much force as he could. The gun struck the wall with a thud and then spun around on the floor, landing beside Buttasingh's blood-coated, motionless hand.

Jonathan sighed and embraced Gauri. "Don't worry, he hasn't got long to go." For a few seconds, both remained clung to each other, Jonathan comforting Gauri by gently stroking her back, which she savored with closed eyes.

When Gauri—her head resting over Jonathan's shoulder—opened her eyes, she soon realized Jonathan's mistake. She saw the touch of the death weapon, irrigating life juice into Satan's stilled hand. Buttasingh's fingers flickered, his eyes opened. Gauri pointed in his direction and screamed, "No!"

By the time Jonathan turned around to assess the situation, Buttasingh's hand, like a piece of iron darting to a magnet, had already united with the gun.

Holding the gun in his right hand, he dragged his body and propped himself up against the corner of the room. And still gasping for short breaths and his face smeared with blood, he pointed the gun at Jonathan and Gauri.

Gauri, still clinging to Jonathan, began whining frightfully.

Jonathan tried to leap forward and knock the gun out of Buttasingh's shaky hand, but Gauri forbade that and held him back.

"You . . . you white fool," ventured short-winded Buttasingh, and spit a blood clot at Jonathan. "You . . . thought I was . . . dead! To this day . . ." Buttasingh's voice strengthened, a taunting smile painted his face. "To this day, one . . . one who can kill me is unborn. And you! You bitch. Couldn't even . . . wield the knife right."

Buttasingh got hold of his turban and wrapped it around his waist, splinting the wound. That seemed to stabilize him.

Jonathan became aware of the deafening silence in the room. Rasoolmian had given up on the door. Perhaps to go for help? If he could just stall a bit . . .

Gauri had started easing toward the door.

"That would be a mistake, *Chhokari*," Buttasingh said. "You move an inch . . . just one inch, and I'll blow off your *yaar's* head. Now step over here."

"Go ahead," Jonathan whispered. "Slowly." Buttasingh was very close to shock and still losing blood. Just a few more minutes.

Gauri, shivering, wrapped Jonathan's robe tightly around herself and slowly walked over to him. Buttasingh grabbed her by the wrist and jerked her onto his lap. She screamed, and Jonathan instinctively moved forward.

"Come with me, you whore," he said, steadying himself. He grabbed her by the hair, and dragged her to the corner of the room. He lifted an area rug and tugged on a string hook. That opened a door to a chute-like, dimly-lit passage. Buttasingh forced Gauri to enter the opening, and followed right behind her. They seemed to be going down steps. Buttasingh quickly closed the trap door over his head.

Within seconds, Jonathan heard a rumble of a car engine underneath the building. When he looked out the window, he saw—from the valley of the hill-top—a willow-green Land Rover dart out, blasting through a thick cover of vegetation.

The entrance harboring the vehicle had to be camouflaged with greenery, for Jonathan did not recall noticing a garage or a vehicle. There had to be a tunnel under the building.

Quickly, Jonathan opened up the massive entrance doors. When Joshi, Tewari and his men rushed in, he showed them the Land Rover heading down the hill.

"General, can a chopper see Buttasingh's vehicle from above?" Joshi demanded.

"Yes and no, sir. Lot of thick brush covers the road like a canopy."

"How many roads are there?"

"That's the good news," said Tewari, smiling. "All small roads lead to only one main road. That crook has to pass through the gorge crossing where my men are stationed."

"Great!" Jonathan said. "Let's chase him, track him down. And tell your men to hold their fire."

"Hold the fire?" said annoyed Tewari, looking at Jonathan and then at Joshi.

"You got it, pal. That bastard has my lady with him, you understand? No fire."

Tewari sighed and nodded.

As they were exiting, an old man came running to Jonathan. His toothless mouth wore a big smile, his hands folded.

"Namaste, Doc Sahb!"

"Bapuji!" Jonathan took the sweaty old man in his embrace.

Bapuji looked up and urged, "Doc Sahb, let's hurry and catch that heartless *Badmaash. Meri beti zinda hai!*"

chapter thirty-six

Buttasingh had to deal with Gauri, who put up a fight in the vehicle. The struggle swayed the car dangerously. In the struggle, Gauri bit Buttasingh's hand. Screaming with pain and anger, Buttasingh hit Gauri with the butt of his gun. Instantaneously, she passed out on her seat.

Buttasingh saw and heard the chopper overhead. He drove faster, recklessly. He had a destination in mind—a place where nobody could reach him, not even the best of Indian armed forces:Tibet, a Chinese territory. He stepped on the gas pedal.

"Who the hell is this?" mumbled Buttasingh as he saw a dark green vehicle approaching him head-on. He immediately halted his car and carefully studied the oncoming vehicle. It was a convertible Land Rover. He veered the car sideways and hid it behind the bush. He turned the ignition off and waited. It was a CBI vehicle but there were no CBI men inside. A woman drove the vehicle! "Hmm," Buttasingh grunted.

"Let the bitch come closer."

The oncoming Land Rover stopped a few yards away. A woman stood up on the driver's seat, holding a military rifle on the edge of the windshield.

Buttasingh started his Land Rover. Instead of coming forward, he sped backward. The woman charged on. Despite his skillful driving, Buttasingh's car almost fell off the narrow dirt road into the valley. He finally found a detour, halted the car and put it in forward. The CBI Land Rover followed. Buttasingh sped the car recklessly until he arrived at a dead end. The road ended on a cliff overlooking a vast gorge.

Buttasingh heard the sound of the waterfall and smiled. Water from the river on the side of the cliff fell from a ten-story height and formed a rainbow. Right at the cliff, he turned the car around, parked it and awaited the CBI vehicle.

Amid a dusty cloud, the CBI vehicle came to a screeching halt. A woman bearing a rifle in her hand exited. Buttasingh looked at her. She wore sunglasses, a hunter's jacket, a wide belt, pants and tall shiny boots. She looked mysteriously fearless. The safari hat concealed her face.

"Who are you, woman?" hollered Buttasingh. "What the hell do you want?"

The woman didn't say anything. He exited the car and studied her.

Then suddenly he recognized the rifle-bearing woman. Geeta!

"Beta, Chameli! My sweet child! I'm so glad to see it's you. For a moment I . . . I thought it was our enemy. Come, help me take care of this piece of—"

"No!"

"No? Did you say, 'no?' I . . . I don't think you heard me. Come, help me. I'm wounded . . . my child."

"I'm not your child. Not anymore."

"You're not? Whose are you then? That crazy old man at the Ashram?"

"That's right."

That stunned Buttasingh. He stared at Geeta and said, "Who ... who says you ... you ... I mean I ... I—are you all right, Beta?"

Geeta, resting the butt of the rifle on the ground, fiddled with the barrel. "What do you think?"

"Chameli, my little princess," Buttasingh said softly and walked up a step, his wide arms inviting the rebellious child into a father's embrace. "What is the matter with you? Look at me... Beta. I am your Bapu, your papa. And you ... you are my little daughter."

Geeta didn't answer. She swallowed and stared at Buttasingh, her chest beginning to heave. She firmed her grip around the rifle.

Suddenly, Buttasingh's countenance changed. His confounding face turned joyous. Confidently, he rested his arms on his waist and laughed. "Oh, you are playing that stubborn little girl of mine, aren't you? I remember when you were small. Unless I turned into a four-legged donkey and circled around you, you wouldn't eat your meal. You remember that?"

"I remember fire," said Geeta sternly. "I remember the robberies, the burning huts, villagers screaming and running for their lives. I remember little infants wailing in the cradle ... seeing the flames ... hearing the cries of their parents. I—"

"Stop!" Buttasingh screamed. He then paused and stared at Geeta elegiacally, his eyes welling up. In a soft voice he said, "Don't you care that it was I who raised you? I was your father and I was your ... mother. All those toys, servants, jewelry, I gave you everything I ever had. Everything I wanted to give to anyone. You are all I have. Look at me. Look at your old Bapu. I have nobody but you. I ... I love you, my child ..." Tears rolled down Buttasingh's bloodied face.

Geeta bit her lips. Tears flooded her eyes too. "I'm sorry ... father. The food and toys you gave to me from the toiling poor villagers; I hear their hungry children's cries. The jewelry you showered at my feet was stolen; I hear the sighs of the barren brides. The happiness you brought to my childhood was dirty; I see the stains of so many helpless children's blood. You stole me from my own parents."

Buttasingh looked down for a moment. Then he looked up and wiped off his tears. He stared at Geeta, stone-faced, his nostrils flaring, his blinded eye roving.

"I know," he said sighing. "I know what has happened. My little daughter has turned into a . . . woman. And I have known all along, every woman is a whore! My mother was a whore, my wife was a whore, and now you! You have turned into a whore too—you have sold out." Buttasingh pulled out his gun and pointed it at Geeta. Then he said coldly, "Leave. Now."

"Let her go, Father," Geeta begged, crying. "Please let Gauri go."

The sound of the approaching helicopter could be heard.

Buttasingh sidled away from Geeta and clutching semiconscious Gauri in the crook of his arm, labored towards the edge of the chasm. He looked back at Geeta and shouted, "I cannot let her go!"

Just then, the helicopter's loudspeaker began to call out, "Give her up, Buttasingh. Back away—"

Suddenly shots from Buttasingh's gun rang out, missing the helicopter's occupants, but starting an onslaught of a volley in response.

"Bapu . . ." Cried out Geeta. She threw away the rifle, and with her arms wide open, ran towards Buttasingh, attempting to block her father's body from harm.

"My child . . ." said Buttasingh, and as he desperately reached out for her, he fell, knocking both women and himself into the deadly gorge below.

Suddenly all was silent. The only sound was the rotors of the helicopter carrying the horrified Jonathan Kingsley.

chapter thirty-seven

The sun sank in the Shantsarovar, painting the sky crimson and turning the mourning faces surrounding Jonathan into silhouettes. Before him, the flames of Gauri and Geeta's ceremonial prayer vigil were echoed in the lake. Kate began singing "What Child is This," the carol Gauri and Geeta had liked so much that they had learned to sing it. Kate began, and soon everybody joined in:

> *What child is this who laid to rest on Mary's lap is sleeping?*
> *Whom angels greet with anthems sweet, while shepherds watch are keeping.*

Jonathan, too numb to cry, attempted to comfort those sobbing and suffering around him. Geeta was dead. Gauri was dead. Death had won. Again. Why wasn't he ranting, or crying? Was he accepting it? Death? Such an irony, he thought, deeply saddened. 'As I lay on that mountain, finally realizing that Gauri was life, finally understanding that Becky is precious, but Becky is gone, I had no idea how soon my hopes and dreams would crash again. Maybe it hasn't hit me yet,' he mused, looking at the others in such a state of grief. 'Maybe I've been through too much and I just don't feel anything anymore.' But deep down, he knew he didn't believe that.

Then he spotted Bapuji wailing on the other side of the pyre, and Kate trying to comfort him. When Jonathan put his hand on Bapuji's shoulder, Bapuji pointed skyward and said, "Doc Sahb, Meri Beti Zinda hai . . . Swargame."

Jonathan sat down and hugged the old man: "Yes, Bapuji. Gauri zinda hai up there in the heaven. Yes she is."

When it turned dark, Jonathan calmly urged everybody to go ahead and join the prayer that was about to begin in the main hall. He stayed behind. When everyone had gone, he rose and walked around the pyre.

The moon shone. Stars twinkled. The blazing pyre crumbled into a heap of ash blending with the earth beneath. Jonathan plucked some wildflowers and rested them beside the ashes. He was inspired to say a prayer, although he had not done so for as long as he could remember. What he could remember, though, was Geeta's departing expression. As she and Gauri had left, he saw relief on her face. There was no doubt in his mind that the relief came from knowing that he had forgiven her. Maybe, in some small way, his making that choice to forgive her during such a challenging time, had provided him his current degree of calm. Maybe there was such a thing as karma, he thought ruefully.

Jonathan arranged the wildflowers, their faint scent growing stronger from the heat. He didn't want to leave her. He rested his arms and head on a boulder that faced the pyre and closed his weary eyes.

A few hours later he felt somebody tapping on his shoulder and calling his name. Kate, Claus and Stephen had come looking for him. He let them lead him back to the Ashram.

His appetite was gone. His direction was gone. His whole life was gone. He sat in the library. So many things, so many spots, so many memories reminded him. They'd been a team of sorts. Geeta and Gauri. Still exhausted, as soon as he rested his head on the table, he fell asleep.

Numerous strokes from the grandfather clock awakened him but his head did not move. Then he heard somebody's footsteps. He lifted his head. Joshi came closer, rubbed his shoulder and muttered, "I'm so sorry."

Jonathan nodded.

Joshi pulled out a cigar but didn't light it. He moved it around his mouth, scratched his gray stubble and paced in the main hall. Then he stopped and looked at his watch.

"It's almost bloody midnight. Mohan should be back soon."

"Where did you send him?"

"To CBI headquarters at the Aakash Mahal."

Jonathan said nothing.

"My dear doctor," Joshi said. "He will find her body. We will have an official cremation. It will help."

"Nothing will help."

The copters had spotted the jeep. Then, after many hours of hellish suspense, Jonathan had gotten word that Gauri's body had been fished from the stream several miles down on the River Durga. By then, the Himpali government had noticed the troops working over their border, and the political situation had become complicated. Mohan had been sent in to try to bring some humanity to the situation.

"Maalik . . ."

Jonathan turned to see Mohan standing at the entrance.

"Here you are." Joshi said. "What took you so long?"

Jonathan approached Mohan, patted his back, walking into the room with him. "That's okay, catch your breath."

"Huzoor." Mohan looked at Joshi and said, "I am very, very sorry. I looked for the villagers who had found Gauridevi's body for a long time. Up and down. They kept—"

"For heaven's sake!" shouted Joshi. Then looking at Swamiji's sanctum, he said more softly, "For heaven's sake, would you stop rambling and tell us once and for all? Did you find her body?"

"No, Maalik, I'm sorry." Mohan's eyes brimmed with tears. "The villagers who found Gauridevi's body, they've cremated her already on the banks of the Durga. Along with the others."

Jonathan patted Mohan's shoulder. "That's all right, Mohan. I really didn't expect—"

"Wait," Joshi said. "What do you mean, 'the others?'"

"They found many other people. All drowned. They cremated all of them."

Hope started to rise in Jonathan's heart. As far as they knew, only Geeta and Buttasingh had fallen with Gauri, so maybe . . .

Joshi was already there. "How do you know, or how did they know, that it was Gauri's body?"

"Well, the body was . . . forgive me, Maalik . . . they said it was bruised and bloated. But they described a young village woman. Long black hair and . . ." Mohan fumbled and pulled something out of his pants pocket. He held it in his open palm and presented it to Joshi. "And this Maalik. Her *Om Shanti* talisman."

Joshi held the talisman in the air and studied it. Round. Metallic. With "Om Shanti" engraved on it. He wore one just like it under his shirt.

Jonathan sighed deeply and slumped down in the chair, whispering almost inaudibly. "Yes. It was Gauri."

A door opened behind them and Swamiji hobbled in. He made his way quietly across the room and sat down.

"How are you doing, J.K.?" he said.

Jonathan held up the talisman. "She's gone, Swamiji."

"I was asking about you."

"I don't . . . numb, I think. Shock." Jonathan smiled a grim smile. "The anger and hatred of death will come later."

Swamiji seriously studied his face. "I don't think so. Not this time."

"Take these, Swamiji. Let them help the poor. I've been . . . holding onto them too long." Jonathan's spontaneous gesture surprised him as much as anyone else. He withdrew from his pocket the interlocked wedding rings and offered them to Swamiji.

Swamiji accepted the rings solemnly. "J.K., I'd like you to join me for a session of Kriya Yoga in the morning. Will you?"

Jonathan had heard the term before, describing a sort of spiritual communication session. "Sure," Jonathan said softly. What did he have to lose?

chapter thirty-eight

Jonathan left Joshi and Mohan with Swamiji and lay somberly in his bed. All were dead. His only loved one remaining alive was his mother. And she was probably dying too, back home in Allagash. Yet he was not angry about Gauri's death. He missed Gauri terribly, just the way he had missed his wife—still did. But he didn't feel resentful. Something inside seemed to have given way to accepting nature's inevitable cycle of birth and death. Instead of ranting, he closed his eyelids and said a prayer.

It was then that he heard his mother saying something to him from her bed in their home in Allagash, Maine. She seemed to be urging him to respect something . . . ominous.

"Jonathan, I'm dying," she said, her smile faint. She put her frail hand on his head as if she were about to say good-bye. "Let me go."

He closed her drapes, turned off the flickering fluorescent light over her head and watched her weak bellows rise and shrink in the yellow of a small bedside lamp. When he sat down on a stool near the head of her bed, he heard a brief and incomprehensible mumble from her.

The wrinkles on her face appeared beguiling; her sixty-five-year-old face had turned into the dull and senescent face of someone in her nineties. The sweet face that had breast-fed him, rocked him in her protecting arms, fed his tiny mouth with a porcelain spoon, and at night told him Bible stories and sung lullabies was withering away.

After a while she opened her eyes. "Jonathan, honey," she said, smiling feebly. "You know, last night I dreamt of Dad." Her eyes teared up.

Jonathan looked at her face, so full of happiness.

"He came rushing into the house with his pipe in his mouth and Chauncey following, yelping behind him. He said, 'Darling, where is my boy—JK?' He then . . . greeted me with a kiss and said, 'Darling, are you sure that little rascal still remembers the names of all the Maine flowers?'"

Maine flowers!

The farmhouse there, his birthplace, came to his mind. Surrounded by acres of snow-laden frigid land for miles and miles, the only other living creatures that lurked around the sparse neighborhood were bears, moose, gray wolves or an occasional hunter looking for directions, food or shelter. He grew up listening to the tales of subzero temperatures, moose antlers, tall pine trees and little birds called chickadees.

He saw little Jonathan running amid potato fields, arms waving in the air, eyes closed, gleefully screaming and chasing multicolored butterflies that hopped from flower to flower. At times he'd fall down but get up swiftly and dust off his bruised knees. He'd then run again among the white potato blossoms of the summer and the reddening sheets of autumnal barley and maple blossoms. And ah! Those memories of Allagash wilderness and waterways of the Allagash River, which his ancestors paddled through in canoes to settle into Aroostook County.

"*Bright and luminous,* that's what the word Aroostook means. You remember that now," the teacher had explained to Jonathan during a school fieldtrip.

Jonathan loved listening to his mother's tales of when, "you were this little" and "that much tall" because they were stories with happy endings—stories about simple folks with substance. But mostly they were stories about his favorite folks: Grammy, Aunt Edna, Mom and Dad.

Dad. Tall, confident, one hell of a handsome man and a legendary forest ranger. A hero. Jonathan wished he could have spent more time with him.

Instantaneously, a few scenes scampered by his eyes: a photo of Dad proudly holding him, seated on the hood of his 1930 Austin-Healy . . . his legs dangling on his father's shoulders . . . Jonathan trying to figure out how Dad held his legs and managed to keep the pipe in his mouth. But, yes . . . Dad can do anything . . . Dad taking him to Madawaska's Tante Blanche museum and pointing at the Voyager's statue and drinking Moxie with Dad.

"Ooo-yuk." Jonathan promptly spit out the drink, his face distorting with the distaste.

Dad laughed heartily and said, "Sip slowly, slowly, my boy. It'll grow on you." And Dad guzzled down a whole bottle just like that.

And the way he used to pronounce Madawaska: "Mavavakka!"

Dad had accepted his version. "Now remember son. Mavavakka means the land of the porcupine."

"Porcupine! Watch out, Dad. I'm a big, bad porcupine." Flinging saliva, he hissed and crowned his head with fanned-out fingers,—making everybody double up with his acting prowess.

Dad drew Jonathan into a tight embrace. Ouch! That tickly sensation of his long sideburns and toothbrush-like mustache handles left a smarting patch of redness on his cheek. Ooo-yuk!

He remembered how all the relatives coaxed him to make those wilderness calls of the animals—bear, wolf, moose and all—that Dad had taught him. Jonathan grinned at his silliness.

When he caught the largest salmon from the mother of all funs, the eighty-mile-long Fish River, he so proudly held the fish high in the air at Dad.

"Dad... Dad... hurry... look what I caught."

And when Dad weighed the fish, which had surpassed any of *his* previous catches, he had given him a bear hug and lifted him in the air, proudly pronouncing to the fellow anglers that his boy had turned into a skillful fisherman.

Frederick Allistair Kingsley was a six-foot-two-inch, blue-eyed rugged forest ranger with long sideburns and lush handles of mustache that rode over his ever-present black mahogany pipe. In his outfit of a hat, multi-pocketed hunter's jacket, binoculars around his neck and the boots, he looked fearsome, but he had never used his double barrel rifle to hurt a soul.

He had rescued so many lost men and weakened animals that he had become a local legend. The word of his bravery and benevolence had spread all the way to the stuffy offices of *The Portland Gazette*.

One day, little Jonathan was perplexed to see a mob of photographers at his house. He was unable to figure out the reason for the commotion.

"That's because your dad is a brave man, and he is very kind to weak animals and poor human beings." His mom stroked his back. "And when you grow up honey, you'll be as kind and brave as your dad. They will put your name and your picture in the newspaper too."

One morning Jonathan demanded to join Dad in the wilderness. At the breakfast table, early in the morning, while Dad packed in the precious calories to last through the long and cold day, Jonathan fussed and held vigilance, begging his dad to take him along. But Dad wouldn't budge. Jonathan cried, sobbed and badgered, but to no avail.

"Okay, honey... listen to me." Mom intervened to break the deadlock. "If you can recite the entire list of our state flowers, maybe Dad will reconsider... right Dad?" She had looked at Dad with that furtive, pleading look.

Dad smiled, still chewing the bacon, winked at her and said, "Maybe. But only if JK can name the flowers—alphabetically."

"See, honey. Now, don't rush. Think nice and slow, and only when you are sure, begin."

"OK," Jonathan began. "Anemone... Aster... Bittersweet... Blackeyed Susan... Buttercup... Goldenrod..."

Jonathan stopped to take a break of mock-cough, a ploy to jog his memory.

"What's next, honey? After Goldenrod?"

"Goldenrod... Harebell... Hepatica... Indian-pipe... Hawkweed... White Oxeye daisy... and..."

"One more, honey. One more." Mom prompted encouragingly.

"And... and..." Jonathan scratched his head. "Wild Bergamot."

"Wonderful, honey. Good job." She looked at Dad for his reward.

"You did it, my boy! Good job. Now pack your bag." Proud papa took him in an embrace, winked and smiled at Mom.

The next day at school, Jonathan was a star. The teacher had heard about his rendezvous in the wilderness with his famous father and asked him to come up and share with his little classmates the wonderful experience of his bivouac.

He was so nervous at first, but when he described to his cheering classmates a 1200-pound, five-foot-tall moose that he had spotted standing in the middle of a pond drinking water, they all asked him, "Were you scared, Jonathan? Were you scared?"

"Oh no!" Jonathan replied confidently. "Why would I be scared? I was with my dad and he is even taller than the bull." He vertically stretched his arm-span to give the kids an idea about his dad's supreme height. "And he carries a double-barrel gun, a big one." He nodded his head and said, "Yeah..."

"Then what happened?" one of the kids asked.

"When he looked at me and my dad, he stretched his big fat neck and bugled at us." Jonathan imitated the sound. "And then . . . then he sprayed water through his nose. He was mad. Yeah."

"Were you scared *now*?" There was a raucous stir among the kids.

"Who? Me? No. But my dad told me to shush and to lie down on the grass quietly. And when we did that, the bull drank his water and walked away into the woods." Puffing his cheeks he said, "Boy, he was h*uuumungus*!"

Beside the visions of trips to the woods with his father, different kinds of sights and sounds—all very soothing—occupied Jonathan's imagination.

He recalled sounds of wild animals. Moose, bobcats, black bears and gray wolves changing their pitch and timber with various acts of predation, playfulness and mating—sounds of their bodies brushing against the outside of his bedroom walls, the decibels enhanced and their breath made visible by the moon of the cold nights.

And then, that fateful Christmas Eve when the school bell rang, little Jonathan darted home to be picked up by his big brave daddy, to be held in his arms and tickled to death by his enormous mustache. But when he arrived, a big crowd had gathered in the doorway. He took them as photographers or reporters, probably recording Dad's newest act of heroism. He made his way through the legs of the grown-ups and spotted Dad's still body on the stretcher in the living room and his mother crying and embracing his father's body with both arms. Stunned and bewildered, he stood there looking at them. Later, he learned from Aunt Edna that Dad, while trying to help a wounded fawn, was accidentally shot in the chest by a stray bullet from a hunter.

Thinking about the bittersweet memories of his childhood, Jonathan was unaware at what time he had fallen asleep. When he awoke, in the midst of pre-dawn hue, he spotted a robin at his window. The bird dropped a dark-blue round fruit on the windowsill and flew away. He looked closely. It was a blueberry. A blueberry, he thought. There are no blueberries here!

chapter thirty-nine

Jonathan had slept very poorly. He felt his entire existence was being ratcheted through a series of crises, and he had no idea what any of them meant, if anything. And tomorrow . . . well, he had ceased believing that Swamiji was a crazy old man, but he still couldn't believe in the kind of healing he offered for . . . everything. In fact, he had no idea what to expect in the hours that followed.

He rose lackadaisically just before four o'clock and cleansed his body with a long shower. When he arrived in the main hall, Swamiji's doors were open. When he knocked, Swamiji motioned him in. Reciting some mantra, Swamiji took a large candle, lit it, and set it on top of a small box covered with a clean, white cloth. He had gathered some flowers too. Then he closed the big round window in the back wall and the two rectangular ones on the side walls. The fragrance of burning incense filled the room.

At Swamiji's request, Jonathan fetched two glasses of water, closed the doors behind him and sat down under the round window facing Swamiji, with the candle and the flowers between them. Swamiji looked at the wall-clock, which showed 4:00 a.m.

"Are you ready?" Swamiji asked.

"As ready as I'll ever be," Jonathan said.

"Good. Close your eyes and pray; open when I say to," he whispered to Jonathan.

Both sat motionless in the lotus position for about ten to fifteen minutes, then Jonathan heard Swamiji say softly, "Dear Lord . . . I'm at your feet. Help us to be worthy of your mercy . . . your divine light. Take me to those good souls . . . we await their inspiring presence."

Jonathan suddenly felt a chill over his neck, and he could not understand why the curtains of the closed round window brushed back and forth against the wall.

"Always start your meditation with the Sanatan Stuti," Swamiji said softly, referring to the universal prayer, a synthesis of flagship mantras honoring the world's four major religions cited in sequence of their seniority. Quietly, they recited them together, starting with the Hebrew Shema. "*Shema Yisrael Adonoi Eloheanou Adonoi Echod,*" followed by Hinduism's Gayatri: "*Ohm, bhur burvah swaha, om tat . . .,*" then Christianity's Lord's prayer: "*Our Father, who art in heaven, hallowed be thy name . . .*" And finally Islam's Darood Sharif: "*Allahumma salley ala, saiyadena, mohammadiu va ala ale saiyadena . . .*"

After a few more moments of silence, Swamiji said, "Ah, he is back. I have been seeing this strong man in my vision every morning for the last three days."

"Uh-huh . . ."

"I could sense that the spirit of a good soul was trying to come through. So this morning, I cooperated and I welcomed him."

"I see . . ."

"A tall man with blue eyes, long sideburns, wearing a coat with many pockets and buttons, and holding a rifle in his hand." Swamiji stared into space, covered the left side of his chest with his right hand and said, "He stumbled and grabbed his chest with his left hand. He seemed to be bleeding."

Jonathan listened without moving, spellbound.

"I asked, 'What is your name, good soul?'

"He replied, 'My name is Fredrick Allistair Kingsley. I'm Jonathan's father.' I welcomed him and urged him to proceed with his message."

"That's . . . that's how Dad died," Jonathan said. "A hunting accident. He came between a hunter and a doe."

"I see. I thought he was a good soul. He said, 'Please tell my son I'm not hurting. I had shot innocent people in the war and felt very sorry for them and their families. I swore to God since that day that I'd protect all living souls. The bullet that killed me saved that doe, and I'm all right with that. Please convey this to my son.'"

Jonathan sucked in his trembling lips and looked away.

"I asked your father's soul if there was anything else he wanted me to convey. 'Yes', he said 'tell my boy I'm very proud of him and I love him very much!' Then he thanked me profusely for listening to him and my custodianship of you here at the Ashram."

"Thank you."

"Om Shanti," Swamiji said. "Now I see an elderly woman, spry and laughing. What is your name please? Dorothy? Dorothy says she is your grandmother."

Jonathan nodded at Swamiji, whose eyes appeared to be focused on the sheers above Jonathan's head.

"She is showing me a photo. A photo of a child, held by a mustachioed man, sitting atop an old car. Is that your father, J.K.?"

"Yes, that's my dad. That's his Austin-Healey."

"Now I see two shaggy dogs. One is bigger, and licking the head of a puppy. Do you know them?"

Jonathan laughed, despite himself. "Yes, Shasha and Gruffy."

"Dorothy gives you her love. She says it's heavenly where she is and that you're a good boy. God bless you, she says."

"Thank you, Granny."

"Now I see a young beautiful woman. She is waving at somebody on the beach. Sarah . . . Sarah? She says she is with Sarah. And she is sorry—very sorry that she left the earth unnaturally. Left you alone."

Jonathan felt such a catch in his throat he could hardly speak. "Becky. Oh, Becky."

"But she is now very happy. She has a flower . . . a rose . . . in her hand. She says she is very lucky to have spent time with you on the earth, and thanks you."

Jonathan said nothing. Then he struggled to say something, unsuccessfully. Two tears fell in his lap. Finally, he managed, "I love you Becky. I miss you."

"'I love you too,' she says, 'and I am very proud of your current mission. Don't hold back because of what happened to me. Don't feel guilty about any of that. I want you to be free to give real, genuine love to everybody around you, even if to a woman.'

"Now I see a little baby . . . a girl . . . waddling toward her. She has picked her up and says that this is Sarah."

"My daughter . . . she died just after birth."

"'Thank you, Daddy,' the little one says, 'thank you for holding me when I was so cold, and for touching my hair and giving me all those kisses.' She wishes she had been able to live with you; to spend more of her life with you."

"God!" Jonathan broke down. After a moment, when he had regained his composure, he asked, "Why did you leave us, Sarah?"

"The child's spirit is trying to convey to me that she willingly chose the avatar of being your daughter, but when she opened her eyes and ears, she saw too much guile and greed on this earth. As an infant she was still closer to the blissfully beautiful world of God. So she chose to return to the Divine father." Swamiji paused. Then he said, "I see another dog . . . he is barking . . . running . . . fetching a stick. Now he is standing on a suitcase. What a playful animal!"

Jonathan wiped his eyes. "That's Chauncey. He hated when I had to leave after a visit to Allagash."

"There is a young man dressed in a tuxedo. Do you know him?"

"Tuxedo?"

"Yes, he says he wore this when he got married. There is a butterfly-like tie under his tiny collars. He says you know him."

"I do?"

"Yes, he says if you don't name all the flowers of your state . . . alphabetically . . . he says he won't take you to the forest."

Jonathan welcomed his sudden urge to laugh. "That's my dad. How are you, Dad?"

"He says he has been feeling very good, but now he feels even better."

"I'm glad, Dad."

"He says, 'So what happened to the flowers? Recite the flowers.'"

Jonathan laughed. "He made me do that once before he let me come on a camping trip. Let me see . . ." Jonathan cleared his mind, and soon the old-remembered list surfaced and began to roll off of his tongue, from Anemone and Aster all the way down to Wild Bergamot.

"Your father says he is very proud of you and he loves you."

Jonathan's voice again crackled. "I love you too, Dad. I love you very much. Dad, thank you for my childhood memories. I often think of the things we did together. It makes me very happy."

"Your dad says he feels privileged to have been your father. He says he misses the fishing trips with you. Trips to . . . to . . . oh, my, and westerners say Hindi is unpronounceable."

"Passamaquady. I remember them too, Dad."

"Now I see a young woman approaching your father. She looks very happy."

"Becky?" Jonathan asked.

"She is wearing a bridal gown. She hugs and kisses your father."

"My father? A young woman?"

"Your father is showing me a photo hanging on a wall

somewhere. He says it's above the fireplace at your home in Allagash."

Jonathan looked up. "God . . . please . . . no. Mom?"

"Now I see a still view of their faces and upper bodies, smiling just like in that photo on the wall. It's your father and your mother in their youth, when they got married."

Jonathan began to cry anew. His mother too, was gone.

Swamiji kept mum. A little later he offered Jonathan a glass of water. "You know, accepting death doesn't mean you shouldn't grieve. You loved them all very much."

Swamiji returned to the lotus position and closed his eyes. "They are now holding hands and leaving. Your mother says she loves you very much and always has been very proud of you. She says, 'You'll never have to worry about me because finally I'm back with my soul mate.'"

"Mom . . . I love you, Mom. I'm sorry I left you alone. I wish you could have waited for me." He tried, but failed, to control himself. The tears flowed freely, from a place deep within, unvisited in years. After a few minutes, he sat up and got hold of himself. "Mom, I'm glad you're with Dad again. I love you both. Mom, thank you. Thank you for everything."

"Beta, she passed away peacefully. That robin who brought you the loving offering of blueberries earlier was her soul. She is at peace. Her soul blessed you on your final journey and reunited with your father's soul. And there is one more here to see you. Yes, welcome, my child."

Jonathan's voice was a whisper. "Gauri?"

"Geeta. She wishes to ask your forgiveness for all the pain she has caused you, has caused all of us. But Beta, it is nothing to the pain you have caused yourself."

"Geeta!"

"She did her best to make things right. She has worked through her karma and will have a much better life in her next avatar."

Swamiji sat silently for some moments. "That is all for this morning, I think."

Both sat quietly and somberly for a few moments with their eyes closed.

Jonathan thought about the surreal session, communicating with the souls of his loved ones. It was all true. Swamiji simply had no other way of knowing the details he had seen in his vision. Jonathan had even forgotten about his father's Austin-Healy. But one thing confused him. It left him wondering.

"Baba, what about—"

"Beta, I think it's time for you to go. I've done all I can for you, and you've come a long way."

"Baba?"

"Go back to Maine, bury your mother, mourn. Reacquaint yourself with the sights and sounds of your childhood. Heal." Swamiji smiled his smile. "You can do it, now."

"But Baba, what about Gauri? Where is her soul? All my loved ones came through, why not Gauri?"

Swamiji looked up with that inscrutable smile. "Yes. That is curious, isn't it?"

Jonathan felt angry and frustrated. The joy of communicating with his lost loved ones was muted by Gauri's silence. Where was she? Why didn't she have something to say? How could he ever find true peace and satisfaction without knowing that dear Gauri's gentle soul was also at rest?

chapter forty

On that morning, the rainy season decided not to leave the Himalayan hills without one last ferocious farewell. The lightning and the thunder began rattling the Ashram. The stormy winds howled menacingly and brought thick screens of torrential rains, pounding the walls and roof relentlessly. Jonathan returned to his room and lit the kerosene lantern.

He pondered the messages he had received from Becky and little Sarah, and those from his dad, which brought him some peace. But the message of his mother's passing on—especially in his absence—created a mixture of guilt and lament that nearly broke his heart all over again. Yet, he knew she was happy. And that was what he had wanted all those fatherless years. And then his thoughts fell again to Gauri. Where was her soul? Swamiji had merely responded with that inexplicable smile. What did that mean?

The flickering flame of the lantern illuminated the pictures set on his bureau: a wedding picture of his youthful parents, Becky on the beach with her ebullient stride and the flowing sheers, elegiac faces of Joshi and Mohan bidding Jonathan goodbye at the railway station, and the ever-naughty Kate and Geeta spraying him and Gauri with dyed water on the Holi Festival, all parked in front of a large, black and white photograph of Swamiji, bearing the immutable, blissful smile.

Jonathan sighed deeply and sat down on the edge of his bed. He touched all the photographs, one by one. Then he rose and walked toward his door where he thought he heard a repetitive knocking sound coming from Gauri's room.

He entered Gauri's room with the lantern, closed the door and looked around. Her room was simple and immaculate. Her bed looked as if nobody had slept there in ages. He saw a mat and a pillow on the floor; the mat was hardly wide enough to accommodate one person. He held the candle to the mat and found a hair-pin and a long black hair on the dented pillow. He picked them up and held them against his heart.

All of a sudden, a bolt of lightning flashed through the room. He closed the window that knocked in the wind, and raised the flame of his lantern. It was then that he noticed his stethoscope lying atop the bureau.

He stared at it. There was something new, something wholesome about it. But what? He picked it up to examine it. It was the metal rim! There was a new golden rim that snugly held the membrane against the chest piece. How had Swamiji managed to mend the broken stethoscope? Then he remembered submitting the wedding bands to Swamiji. Were the two wedding bands somehow melded to form a stethoscope rim? Of course! He remembered Swamiji's exhortation: "Let these rings link you to humanity, not separate you from it. Use them to nurture and sustain life."

Nurture and sustain life! And what was it Becky had said to him? She was proud of his current misson? Yes, Becky would have wanted him to do exactly this for others. Nurture and sustain life. He kissed the chest piece, roped the stethoscope around his neck, and smiled.

There was a miniature wooden temple, perched along the back wall. He opened its small doors, and saw his own picture, bearing rice and vermilion on the forehead, ashes of half-burnt incense still emitting the familiar flowery scent that had always surrounded Gauri. He touched the dark wick firmly held by softly frozen ghee, contained in a boat-shaped small brass diya with an hourglass stem. He touched the diya around its edges and lit it. Also inside the temple was a photo of the newlywed couple: wide-eyed Seeta, beaming with a captivating smile, and the turbaned groom's face covered by a veil of flowers. Suddenly, Jonathan recalled seeing a similar photo—but one covered by dust and glaring under the sun—placed in the proximity of the pyre in Baramedi. And he realized why all along, Gauri's face had looked vaguely familiar.

He noticed the Bhagvat Gita lying in front of his photo. A bookmark consisting of a dried rose stem parted the middle of the holy book. He recognized the rose; one he had given to her at the Holi Festival. Its white petals, browned and shriveled, still emitted the fragrance. Printed on the top left side was the familiar Sanskrit verse that each morning Gauri sang at the prayer, and which Swamiji translated aloud. The English translation underneath the Sanskrit vernacular he knew almost by heart.

He kneeled in front of the temple and began reciting the verse:

> *Na jayate mriyate va kadachin, Nayam bhutva bhavita, va na bhuyah ajo nityah sasvato yam purano, na hanyate hanyamane sarire.* "For the soul there is never birth nor death. Nor having once been, does he ever cease to be. He is unborn, eternal ever-existing, undying and primeval. He is not slain when the body is slain."

He recited it again and again, until his recitation grew fainter as he slipped into a trance. A few minutes later, his peace was disrupted by a loud clap of thunder. He rose with a smile and exited Gauri's room without any concern for the tempestuous sky. When he entered his own room, he calmly began gathering all the memorabilia in front of Swamiji's large photo. Then he looked at the conch—Swamiji's gift—and placed it in a bag.

When all his mementos were parked on the bureau, he closed his eyes and silently stood in the center of his room, still experiencing the sounds and the sights of the storm, through the cracks in the old door.

Suddenly a strong gust of wind blew open the hackney door. Across the oblique screen of rain, he looked out. A thunderclap and lightning showed him the path away from his protected sanctuary.

Alas! It was all over. He had nobody to call his own. No bond of relationship held him back. And death? Death was no longer an anathema. Death had done all the damage it could. For the first time, he was fearless of death. Come on, you silly scourge!

Another bolt of lightning lit up the Gurushikhar where Swamiji's Gurudev had embraced Mahasamadhi, embraced death. On his own terms. At his own volition. How ironic, he thought, as he courageously began his journey into the raging storm.

Ensuring the conch's presence in the bag, he roped it around his shoulder, and with the rain splashing on his smiling face, he walked into the storm.

chapter forty-one

"Take me ashore, take me ashore;
O' Sailor Supreme, take my little boat ashore.
Rein on the floods, lock up the winds in your fist;
Shine the sun ever bright, and burn up the mist.
Take me ashore, take me ashore;
O' Sailor Supreme, take my little boat ashore."

That morning, Gomti's raspy voice had more closely resembled a man's than a woman's, but that never precluded her from singing the folk songs. Some passengers laughed at the boatwoman's odd-voiced audacity; some just joined her and sang along. And as she sang, columns of sturdy metal bracelets over her wrists clanked, and a large ring in her nose loomed over her strong white teeth. The villagers loved the kind-hearted woman who often ferried them across the flooded Durga.

Gomti made her passengers aware that the raging river calmed down as it entered the plains of the lower Himalayan hamlets. But there was still some drag to its waters, which shimmered with golden ripples of the sunset.

"Take me ashore, take . . . me . . . ash—"

Suddenly the boatwoman's song came to a halt. Her studied eye had caught something floating upstream, approaching the boat. And it looked like a body. But then, she thought, was it floating?

"Look!" she burst out, summoning her male assistant. "Over there!" She pointed in the direction of a red sari-clad woman who was thrashing wildly, but mostly, it seemed certain, drowning.

But the assistant protested, reluctant to jump in the water to rescue the stranger.

"You stay in the boat!" Gomti hollered at the man. "I'm jumping in the water. Throw that rope at me, *okay*? Huh, men!"

Gomti jumped into the river and grabbed the woman around the waist. Her assistant threw the rope and both were pulled up into the boat.

Once they were safely on board, Gomti and the man raised the drowning woman's body upside down to drain the water from her airways and upper gut. Then they wrapped her in two blankets. When she stopped shivering and gained her orientation with the surroundings, she began to look around and cry.

"How did you manage to swallow so much water, *Chhokari*?" asked the boatwoman with a motherly reproach. "All village girls know how to swim. Tell me who did this to you."

The rescued woman again fearfully looked around and said nothing.

"Where are you from, honey? And what is your name?"

"My name?" asked the rescuee, her eyes blinking.

"Yes, your name. What is your name?"

"I think she is confused," the man said. "Let the poor girl rest."

"Confused?" Gomti turned around and snarled at the man. "She is not confused, you are! Look at her clothes. You are blind, too."

"My name is . . ." the rescued woman ventured.

Gomti bent down with her palm at her ear. "What! Speak up girl."

"My name is—I don't know." Her crying resumed.

"Oh, Lord Buddha!" Gomti turned upright and shook her head at the man. "What have I gotten myself into? For the first time, you are right. She is confused!"

The rescued woman stared at the boatwoman, dazed and bewildered. Her hands clasped the end of her sari, her pale knuckles covering her chattering teeth.

The man said, "I think she is tired. Let her rest."

"No! I am fine. Please . . . take me back to . . ." the stranger insisted, pointing to the mountains.

The boatwoman looked up in exasperation and said, "This is crazy. Where do we take her? We don't even know her name!"

Quickly Gomti docked the ferry. She fetched some wild leaves and bandaged the rescued woman's lacerations. Then Gomti and the man walked her down the dock and waited for the transportation. A few minutes later, Gomti spotted a familiar pony cart approaching.

"Stop! O' Cartwalla," yelled out Gomti.

Bhondup was a local errand-man who did odd jobs, including transporting people in his pony cart or via palanquin where the pony cart did not travel. Gomti had taken advantage of Bhondup's help before in getting people where they wanted to go. Bhondup stopped the cart.

"Listen, Bhondup," she said. "This poor girl is sick. I saved her from drowning. Now you escort her to . . . wherever she is from, okay? I'll take care of your money when you return."

"C'mon, Gomtibahen, it is the end of my day. My wife and children are expecting me home. How can I?"

"Yes, you can. Here. Take this money," snarled Gomti. "Shame on you. You are a man! This is my entire day's earning. Take it. I just don't want another young girl to be the victim of some butcher." Gomti quickly thought of the tall, patch-eyed predator who had kidnapped her only daughter—the daughter she had never seen or heard from again.

"What butcher?"

"Never mind. Help me get her aboard. And Bhondup, keep your mouth shut. Okay? Don't talk to any strangers unless you have to. That flesh-trader's disguised men posses are everywhere. You understand?"

Bhondup nodded.

"Wait. One more thing." Gomti looked at the young woman and said, "Look at you, silly girl! This locket around your neck . . . give me that . . . and put my cobra locket around your neck . . ." Gomti switched lockets. "That way nobody will recognize you.

"And Bhondup, remember, no matter who asks you about this girl, you tell them her name is Gomti—Gomti the cobra-tribe girl. Understand?"

"Understand."

Gomti hugged the rescued girl and returned to the river to make up for her lost earnings. It was getting dark.

Bhondup had made an overnight stop at his village to get some food, shawls, a palanquin and a man to help him. His wife had dispensed willow extract in an attempt to heal the feverish young woman who refused to eat. Bhondup ate a good supper and then slept. Early in the morning, Bhondup's wife fed the ponies and located, from the neighborhood, an assistant for her husband's task.

"*Chalo Bhaiya.*" Bhondup signaled his helper to stoop under the back bars of the palanquin and lift it. Bhondup took the front bars.

"*Chalo.*"

"*Jay Ramjiki.*" Both uttered the auspicious words simultaneously, and raised the palanquin. Carefully, they settled it into the back of the pony cart and got themselves situated in the front. Bhondup's wife suggested a place she had heard of in which the sick woman could be looked after.

"We had better say a prayer," the driver said, as the cart began moving.

"Why prayer?" his companion asked.

"Look at the sky. Last night, it was a big clear moon. Now it's all dark clouds."

When the driver whipped the ponies, a bolt of lightning, followed by thunder, startled the ponies. They sprang up on their hind legs, neighed fiercely and pulled the squeaking cargo forward. "The storm is coming," he said. "We've got to get moving quickly."

"Moving where?" the assistant complained. "Where are we taking her? We don't know her destination, her name—nothing. I hate that big fat Gomti and her—"

"Shut up!" Bhondup yelled out at his help. "God will never forgive you, that big fat woman, Gomti, is dead."

"Dead! What do you . . . how . . . just yesterday—"

"Yeah, yesterday evening. At her last trip. Ferry was overloaded. She just couldn't say no to poor, crying villagers. A tree trunk hit the boat in the middle of the river. Sunk in no time. No survivors but one young guy. Only he lived to tell what happened. Rest washed away."

"How do you know all this?"

"Somebody from the village told my wife early this morning when she was feeding the ponies. All the bodies are being cremated, down the plain."

The woman from inside the cart stirred and whimpered.

The men stopped the cart. "I think she is feeling better now. That willow extract is working. Sister, what is your name, and where is your place?" Bhondhup asked.

The woman replied with feeble voice, crying, "Brother, take me . . . take me to . . . Baba's Ashram. My name is Seeta." She began breathing heavily. "No! I'm not . . . Seeta. My name is . . . Gauri."

chapter forty-two

As the cart resumed its rocky ride, feverish Gauri slipped back and forth into the awareness of the men talking, the thunder and the lightning, and the rain hitting the canvas of the canopy.

She thought about her miraculous survival. Although Geeta had free-fallen into the rapid water, Gauri, wrapped in long flowing clothes, remained entangled, snared by the heavy undergrowth of vegetation. Plunging into the startlingly cold rapids had alarmed her. She knew she had to escape the belly of the gorge, where strong current spun eddies, drowning anything in its mouth or spitting it out into the flooded Durga river.

Without proper orientation, she had swum in the wrong direction, catching herself on jutting rocks, and grabbing hold of anything to conserve her strength. It had been with her very last ounce of energy that she made the frantic endeavor for Gomti's boat.

"*Arrey Bhaiya*, which way is the Ashram?" Gauri heard the pony-cart driver asking someone on the road.

"Ashram?" The man from the outside responded.
Gauri dreamed the voice was that of her angel's, her Babu. She struggled to hear the familiar tones of Jonathan's voice. Then she dreamed of rain, buckets of rain. It was not soft, but angry as it struck her meager protection. Thunder rolled across the rain like giant boulders, marching through her oasis, the sound of Jonathan's voice. "Come back," she said so softly as to be inaudible. "Don't let the thunder turn you away."

Just outside the cart, Jonathan stood, weary from his journey through the storm, and fatigued from his heart's journey as well. He looked into the cart and saw someone lying in an open palanquin. It was hard to discern whether the person was alive or dead; man or woman. Then a flash of lightning revealed more detail; long dark hair and a thick black yarn around the neck. A shawl covered the rest of the body. Jonathan looked at the driver with heightened curiosity.

"Sir," the driver repeated, "do you know where I might find the Ashram?"

"Yes," Jonathan said absently. "The Ashram is that way." Then he looked at the driver and said, "This person. This passenger in the back. Who—"

"A woman is sick. Pneumonia," explained the cart driver. "She is delirious with fever."

"Pneumonia?" Jonathan came closer to the body. "Is she breathing?"

"I don't know. She said she won't quit her breath until she reaches the Ashram. Probably wants to die at a holy place, okay?"

"Wait a minute. Who is she? Did you ask her name?" Jonathan looked at the driver pleadingly. "Let me look at her."

Gauri turned her head, still in the dream. Oh yes, Jonathan. Look at me. Let's sit peacefully in fields of wildflowers, counting the butterflies and watching the sun set.

"Gomti. That's her name," the driver replied emphatically.
"Gomti? No, No. How do you know?"
"I know, that's it, okay? Now, I've got to get going!"
"Wait. Where did you find her?"

"River Durga's bank."

"What part of the River Durga?"

"What part of Durga? Why? Does it matter?"

"It does to me," Jonathan mumbled. He made a move to examine the woman, but the driver promptly held up his hand. "*Nahin, nahin.* I can't let you do that. A stranger can't touch an unconscious woman's body. Law of the land. Okay! Now, back off."

Gauri, hearing a rifle bolt click, was released from her dreamlike state. Uncomprehending, she felt something clutching at her heart. She tried to cry out, but she couldn't.

Jonathan raised his hand in submission, but then quickly thought better of it, catching sight of the black yarn around the woman's neck.

"Listen . . ." Jonathan said very politely. "I'm really sorry, Bhaiya. I really am. But this locket. Did you see this locket around her neck? That could identi—."

"Now, what do you think? You think we didn't look at it?" The other man spoke up. "Here." He held his rifle erect with one hand while with the other he tugged at the thread. "See this? Talisman. What does it show? Cobra." The silvery round metal shone in the lightning and highlighted an engraved head of the king cobra. "She is from a cobra-tribe. Satisfied? Listen, we've got to go now, or this poor—"

"I know, I know *Bhaiya*, but—"

"But what? Who are you, anyway?"

"I am . . . I am . . . a doctor at—" Jonathan's answer got lost in the thunder. The driver whipped the pony. As the lightning lit up the crisscross paths, Jonathan hopelessly stared as the cart began to pull away.

chapter forty-three

"Crazy westerners. Why the hell do they come all the way over here to bother us?"

As the pony cart began to move again, every bit of Gauri's being cried out for her Babu. But the cart kept moving, squeaking its way up the trail. How could it be that even the *Om Shanti* talisman, blessed by Baba, had not helped her? She felt for the beloved figure around her neck. Instead, she found the cobra. It was then she remembered the switch. It belonged to the woman who had helped her out of the river.

Strengthened by the thought of a stranger's coming selflessly to her aid, she began to raise herself up. The Ashram was up the hill, yes. But be that as it may, she was headed in the wrong direction! She lifted her head, trying to call out to the driver, "Please, stop this cart!" But the hissing wind swallowed up her feeble effort.

Nevertheless, the cart did stop. But why? Gauri shuddered. Oh, Bhagwan, please. Not those thugs *again!* Baba . . . Babuji . . . somebody, be by my side. Please!

"A tree has crashed in our path," said the driver's helper as he dismounted the cart.

He tried to move the tree, but couldn't. Bhondup got off the cart.

Gauri lay back, relieved at not being in danger, and tried to regain her strength.

The two men worked at lifting the tree, newly fallen in the storm, but it barely budged.

As the men struggled and cursed at the tree, they heard another voice. "I think you fellas could use some help."

"Who the hell are you?" Bhondup's helper strained through the rain to identify the stranger.

"I'm Jonathan Kingsley. Let me—"

"Just a minute."

It was her Babuji. He'd heard her. He'd come back!

"Look stranger," the cart man said, "I don't care if you are white, you don't get to do whatever you want. I protect my passengers."

"But I'm telling you, I want to help her. To make sure she is all right."

"She'll get help soon enough."

"Come on, brother. Women have been raped and murdered around here for years and you're telling me—" Jonathan began.

"What, you think that because a couple of monsters have been causing trouble that all of us are like that? Some of us are honorable, and I am one." The rifle made its ominous noise again. "Now, *move on!*"

"Are you willing to shoot me?" her Babu said softly.

Remember your strength, Gauri told herself. Remember how you held on before—you can do it now. You are strong inside. Make your body take commands!

"Oh, hell." Gauri heard the cart-man put down the rifle. "Come on then, if you're that determined."

But before they reached the back of the cart, a small figure rose, emerging from the blanket. "Babuji! My everything!"

"Gauri!" Jonathan rushed to her and pulled her from the cart.

At that moment, the world stopped turning, and seconds stopped ticking. They even stopped breathing.

"Hey!" The driver was hitting Babu on the back. "What's going on?"

"It's all right," Gauri whispered through her joy. "Everything is all right now!"

She closed her eyes and buried her head in his chest. Her angel had returned.

chapter forty-four

The rain had finally subsided to a drizzle. The Ashram was slowly awakening into the late silver of pre-dawn hue. Shehnai and sitar music began fostering life in the main hall and the library.

Joshi, Mohan, Claus, Stephan, Guillaume and the others gathered into the main hall and awaited Swamiji's emergence.

When Swamiji appeared in the doorway, he was hunched up, bearing the staff in one hand and blessing the assemblage with the other. "*Om Shanti,*" he whispered.

"*Om Shanti,* Baba." Joshi approached the frail sage with folded hands and assisted him. Mohan rushed to hold Swamiji from the other side.

Swamiji stopped and gratefully stroked Joshi and Mohan's heads. Then he looked at the others, who had remained standing.

"The chair." Joshi looked at Mohan and pointed at a wheelchair.

"Nahin, Bete. I would like to walk; it's a beautiful morning."

Unsupported but holding the staff, Swamiji slowly walked to the prayer maiden.

They helped him settle into a padded chair. Beside him, an enlarged photo of festive Jonathan, Kate and Gauri was set up on a wooden easel. Flowers, garlands, ribbons and handwritten messages bedecked every inch of the frame and the photo. Incense sticks emitted pious redolence from the perforated brass-holders perched on small tables at either side of the photo.

Swamiji waved the standing group to sit down. Joshi sat at Swamiji's right foot and Mohan, proudly holding Swamiji's staff in his lap, sat to his left.

Swamiji closed his eyes, clasped his hands in his lap and began the predawn meditation. Everyone followed, all keenly aware of Jonathan's absence. People kept turning their heads and looking at each other. Soon murmurs began that grew into louder, confused conversation.

Even more noticeable than Jonathan's absence was Swamiji's silence. He sat in the chair, looking down as if he were still meditating or attentively viewing something. The sage's silence, no matter how purposefully pregnant, generated renewed questions, comments and innuendoes from the Ashramites.

Then Swamiji lifted his head and smiled at everyone, and things seemed all right again.

He touched his staff in Mohan's lap. Mohan helped him stand up. He held the head of the staff with both hands and smiled broadly as if he had just received news of some monumentally auspicious event.

"My children, *Om Shanti!*"

"*Om Shanti*," they echoed.

"This is a divine moment. Sadness at such a moment?" He wagged his finger. "No, no. Sorrow does not suit this special morning. A sun of great enlightenment is about to rise. You, my flowers, at such a divine occasion, have no choice but to blossom, to smile. Look at these flowers." He pointed at the flower bushes on either side of the group. "Look at the flowers, for dispassion fears flowers."

Then a large black hornet flew in, hovered around the crowd and entered a bulbous flower nearby. The hornet became trapped and his effort to exit the flower shook the branch. Finally he emerged from the sweet smelling petals and took off.

"Did you see that insect? He persevered. He severed his prison and flew away. What was life to that little creature? The sensual trap of the flower or the boundless freedom of the air in this vast sky?"

Then Swamiji sat down and spread his arms. "Let us all hold hands and invoke God."

Joshi and Mohan held Swamiji's hands and they connected with the rest, forming a circle. Some looked at Swamiji, others remained distracted. Their ears anticipated Jonathan's footsteps and the familiar voice bidding them, "*Om Shanti.*" Nothing of the sort happened. People looked at each other with curiosity and disappointment.

"Let us pray to the Almighty," Swamiji resumed, "for the souls and well being of those beloved ones who are not among us." He held his hands skyward. "Dear Father, nothing is secret from you. You know all about our ailments and insecurities. You know what is in our hearts and on our minds. Yes, we have our fears and pains, but we are your children." He paused for a breath. "We implore you, dear God, to grant the eternal bliss and peace of your heavens to those souls who have accomplished their missions and left us to come to you." He paused again. "And grant your divine protection and custody to those who are alive and searching for your shelter. Amen!"

"Amen!" the crowd murmured.

Swamiji picked up his conch shell, but he made no attempt to blow it. An ambiance of mystery, confusion and somberness prevailed. Any minute the sun would burst through the cloud. A gold rim began to form in the sky. Yesterday he had been barely able to make a sound with the conch, and today?

Swamiji himself turned, facing the rising sun. With the sunrays growing bolder and the birds chirping, all sang the prayer. Swamiji signaled the bell ringer to keep ringing. He sang the prayer, for some reason, more loudly than usual.

When the prayer ended, he turned to the group, and with the bells still pealing, he chanted, "*Om Shanti.*"

Everyone echoed, "*Om Shanti.*"

He said it again, louder this time. The rest responded with similar vigor and intensity. Now there was an intuitive harmony of bell ringing, followed by the chants of '*Om Shanti*'. The growing light bathed their faces. In the middle of the chants, he motioned Stephan and Claus to come close to him, and when they did so, he let his staff fall to the ground and rested his arms over their shoulders. And then suddenly, as if his eyes and ears were drawn somewhere else, he beckoned the bells and the chants to stop.

Swamiji turned around with a big smile and looked at the edge of the Ashram, from whence emerged a couple. Everyone looked at each other incredulously. Mohan was the first person to recognize Jonathan, escorting Gauri.

"Maalik! Doc Sahb!"

Joshi ran toward them. "Jonathan! Gauri!" Mohan first looked around, then followed Joshi. As Mohan and Joshi assisted a weary Jonathan and Gauri to the prayer grounds, people cheered and jumped in exhilaration.

Swamiji turned to the arriving couple and watched them, his face wearing a beatific smile. Jonathan and Gauri touched Swamiji's feet and stood in front of him with folded hands. Swamiji let Stephan and Claus go and wrapped his arms around Jonathan and Gauri. Gauri cried on Swamiji's chest. Jonathan contentedly looked at Swamiji comforting crying Gauri like a father, and smiled. His smile echoed Swamiji's perfectly.

With tears in his eyes and a childlike smile on his face, Swamiji gazed at Jonathan and kissed him on his head. Then he faced the Himalayas and said: "O Blessed Father, thank you for your love, thank you for you mercy, thank you for this wonderful journey."

Jonathan and Gauri experienced the weight of Swamiji's arms around their shoulders.

Swamiji continued louder, his voice breaking. "Dear God, we are at your doorstep; look at these souls." Swamiji looked to his either side, then at Gauri and finally at Jonathan. "Now they are in your hands. Help them! Protect them! Love them! Empower them!"

Joshi, Claus, Stephan, Guillaume and Rasoolmian came to the assistance of Gauri and Jonathan, who reeled somewhat from the increasing weight on their shoulders. Swamiji's body seemed to be collapsing, its full weight bearing upon them.

Before he slumped to the ground, a final cry of joy emerged from his frail body. "And now, dear Father, I am ready to come home!"

Jonathan continued to hold Swamiji's body. He sat down, gently resting the sage's head in his lap. He put his fingers on Swamiji's neck to palpate his carotids. No pulse. He had moved on. May God bless him.

Before he could share the outcome with the rest, Guillaume, looking tense and restless screamed out, "What are you checking? The poor man is dying. Aren't you going to do something? You're a doctor!"

Claus put a comforting hand on Guillaume's shoulder. "Guillaume... please. Swamiji is already dead."

Gauri pressed her head against Swamiji's chest and wailed, "No! No, God, No!"

Jonathan looked unperturbed. He glanced up at the hovering Ashramites. With the parting of bodies, the light fell onto Swamiji, and the sun bathed his peaceful face, which bore a faint, but distinct smile.

Jonathan stroked his grieving Gauri's back and said softly, "It's okay... it's okay. This is not the death of Swamiji; it is only the death of his body; his soul is still with us." And then he began reciting the Sanskrit verse from Bhagvat Gita that Gauri sang at every morning prayer: "*Na jayate-mriyate va, nayam bhutva bhavita... hanyamane sarire.*"

Wiping her tears, Gauri sat up and looked at Jonathan. The sunshine lit up his calm and steady face. She held onto his arm and began humming the translation. Soon everybody joined in:

"For the soul there is never birth nor death. Nor having once been, does he ever cease to be. He is unborn, undying, primeval. He is not slain when the body is slain."

Jonathan picked up Swamiji's great sea-conch and sounded it at the rising sun. And amid reverberations of the ancient sound and the intense rings of sunlight forming around the Gurushikhar, he saw something shapeless smiling at him. Gathering Kate and Bapuji to him, he held Gauri's hand and smiled back at the radiant energy.

The End

AUTHOR'S BIO

(THE ASHRAM BY SATTAR MEMON)

Born in a small village in India, when I arrived here, America's riches dazzled me. Then the real life began, when I started practicing cancer medicine. There were some successes. What I remember most are those sleepless nights, when all I could do was pray. Each death intensified the quest for IT! Teaching at Brown University as Clinical Professor of Medicine became a respite. What really helped was singing and writing. Writing about my beautiful childhood and adolescence, replete with memories of rivers flowing from bank to bank, fatherly lush mountains looming over the horizon, and pre-dawn sounds of that distant train that never came to my remote village. Memories of poor, industrious villagers, carrying wood, hay or rocks on their heads—and innocent smiles on their faces. I have tried to share these vivid and precious memories with you in *The Ashram*.

LITERARY PUBLICATIONS

1) *Manohar*—Short story about the oppressed life of a poor gardener in India. Magazine Section—Providence Journal, May, 1988.

2) *Valji The Vegetable Wallah*—A short story of an altruistic vegetable farmer ruined by monsoon floods, published in Advocate, 1989.

3) *Indomitable Hope*—Saga of a struggling young breast cancer patient, who conquers her disease. Providence Journal, 1992.

4) *The Lesson a Patient Taught Me*—Confessions of a doctor. Medical Economics, October, 1992.

5) *Doctors, the Infallible Species*—Medical Economics, April, 1996.

6) *Send Me An Angel*: Spirituality and Medicine. A WWII veteran fights against his imminent death—until a miracle helps him embrace the inevitable peacefully. Lifestyle Magazine, Providence Journal, December 16th, 2001.

7) *The Ashram* (novel): An underprivileged Indian woman's emancipation from her oppressive culture and fear of men; an American physician's overcoming of his inability to cope with death and learn to love again. An inspiring tale of two souls' journey halfway around the world toward spiritual enlightenment. Submitted for publication by a print publish house. Xlibris/Random House Print-on-Demand Subsidiary, 2004.

Made in the USA